"Vivid."
—*Publishers Weekly* on
Good Night, Sweet Angel

"Is there any . . . ?"

Grace's words ended in a gasp when she looked into a face that was so like her own that this woman could be Grace's twin.

"Oh . . ." Grace whispered, and could say no more.

The woman stood frozen for a moment, staring. It gave Grace a chance to see that the woman was older than she, her lackluster hair was too wavy, her lips too thin. But there was no denying the deep blue eyes, small nose and high cheekbones. Grace felt her heart quicken. After years of hope, had she finally, miraculously, run into a relative?

"What's your name?" she asked softly.

A look of terror suddenly came over the woman's face. She hunched her shoulders and fussed with her hands like a scared little mouse, her eyes darting all around.

"Please, who are you?" Grace asked again.

"I . . . I only thought . . ." the woman stammered. "When I saw you, I thought . . .

Her eyes seemed to drop down at the corners, and her mouth twisted as if she was going to burst into tears.

"I'm sorry! she cried. "Forget you saw me!"

With that, she turned and disappeared through the crowd of shoppers strolling along the mall. Grace tried to call out to her, but she was already gone. For a moment, Grace hesitated. She'd look silly running through the mall, wouldn't she?

She ran after her, nearly knocking down a clerk with a basket of perfume samples.

"Please?" she asked, "I just want to know who you are. I'm an orphan, and you look so much like me! I wondered if we might be family. I mean . . ."

Before she could finish, the woman, wild-eyed, hissed, "My God! Get away from me!"

Later Grace was so bewildered that she wished she could go straight home. She opted for a phone call. When the answering machine picked up, she remembered that Craig had promised to take the kids out to the video arcade. Feeling a little down, and very lonely, she had room service bring up a late dinner. Soon after she finished eating, she went to bed. As she drifted off to sleep, she wondered if she would ever understand what really happened that day.

Tor Books by Clare McNally

Clare McNally

► BLOOD ◄ RELATIONS

TOR®

A TOM DOHERTY ASSOCIATES BOOK
NEW YORK

This is a work of fiction. All the characters and events portrayed in this book are either products of the author's imagination or are used fictitiously.

BLOOD RELATIONS

Cover art by Eric Peterson

A Tor Book
Published by Tom Doherty Associates, Inc.
175 Fifth Avenue
New York, NY 10010

Tor® is a registered trademark of Tom Doherty Associates, Inc.

ISBN: 0-812-55104-4

First edition: June 1996

Printed in the United States of America

0 9 8 7 6 5 4 3 2 1

ONE

▼

Grace Matheson's worst nightmare began one spring Saturday in a crowded shopping mall just outside Indianapolis, Indiana. She was working a crafts fair, hoping some of the shoppers hurrying from store to store would stop and buy the beautiful porcelain dolls she had created. She was happy, confident, and totally unaware that her life was about to change forever.

She didn't stand much taller than the highest shelf of her display, only five-foot-four. She arranged her dolls with such care that it seemed she was a doll herself, animated by her own enthusiasm. When a potential customer sighed in awe over one of her creations, the smile on her full lips spread all over her face. A new customer took home not only a doll, but the joy Grace had put into it. If she were lucky, many people would share that joy today, and her long trip from Tulip Tree, her hometown in the northwestern corner of the state, would be a success.

It had been a good show so far, with six dolls sold. She'd enjoyed the company of familiar faces, other crafters who made these rounds like she did. Judy Althoff was selling Victorian bric-a-brac in the stall next to hers. The two women, who'd known each other for several years, often watched each other's booths if one had to leave for a moment. This kind of company made Grace feel almost as secure as when she was with her family.

As she straightened up her business cards, Grace smiled to think of Craig, her husband, playing basketball with ten-year-old Trevor. The twins, six-year-old Seth and Sarah, might be roller-skating with friends. Or maybe the four of them had gone swimming at the lake . . .

Grace longed for the day when she could create dolls for the pleasure of art alone. It didn't matter that this was only a two-day excursion. She really missed Craig and the kids. But she had to travel to these shows for one very basic reason: they needed the money. Some of her profit would help pay bills, but most of it would go into a special account she and Craig had opened. Someday, there might be enough for a down payment on a pretty Colonial she'd seen in a better part of Tulip Tree.

Grace picked up Little Jack Horner. She'd used Trevor as a model, and the doll had the same dark blue eyes. They were the color of lapis lazuli, shining and almost liquid in the mall lights. She recalled that a man had once said she had "lapis eyes." She'd gone to the library first chance to find out what lapis was and had been delighted to learn it was a treasured stone of ancient Egypt. Who had said that? A mailman? A teacher? No matter, the compliment had made her feel very pretty. There hadn't been much opportunity to feel pretty growing up. She'd been overweight, pale, and nervous. Moving from foster home to foster home did little to bolster her ego.

Grace put the doll down and adjusted the skirt on Little Bopeep. Craig had once said he marveled at the beauty she could put in her work after such a dreary, loveless childhood. Grace had replied that she did it out of necessity, creating loveliness where little existed. Her very first doll, fashioned from a pillowcase when she was only ten, had an exquisitely drawn face that smiled even when Grace couldn't. She'd created many fantasies around that doll, fantasies of a mother who loved her more than anything.

Grace always dreamed that one day she would find the woman who had given her up at birth. Surely she had loved her as much as Grace herself loved that pillowcase doll. Surely she'd been forced to leave her baby. Grace loved Craig and the children with all her heart, but there was still that empty space within her that she hoped might someday be filled with maternal love.

Sighing, but refusing to let herself be dragged down into the melancholy of lost years, she was glad for the distraction of another customer. A few minutes later, a baby doll in a christening gown went home with a new owner. Grace moved the other dolls to fill the space the baby had taken up.

Her eyes were drawn to the large, sparkling marquise diamond on a slender hand that was reaching across the table. She quickly let her eyes skim over the designer-logo buttons on a raincoat and was already greeting the customer before she saw her face.

"Is there any . . . ?"

Grace's words ended in a gasp when she looked into a face that was so like her own that this woman could be Grace's twin.

"Oh," Grace whispered, and could say no more.

The woman stood frozen for a moment, staring. It gave Grace a chance to see that the woman was older than she; her lackluster hair was too wavy, her lips too thin. But there was no denying the deep blue eyes, small nose, and high cheekbones. Grace felt her heart quicken. After years of hope, had she finally, miraculously, run into a relative?

"What's your name?" she asked softly.

A look of terror suddenly came over the woman's face. She hunched her shoulders and fussed with her hands like a scared little mouse, her eyes darting all around.

"Please, who are you?" Grace asked again.

"I . . . I only thought . . ." the woman stammered. "When I saw you, I thought . . ."

Her eyes seemed to droop at the corners, and her mouth twisted as if she were going to burst into tears.

"I'm sorry!" she cried. "Forget you saw me!"

With that, she turned and disappeared through the crowd of shoppers strolling along the mall. Grace tried to call out to her, but she was already gone. For a moment, Grace hesitated. She'd look silly running through the mall, wouldn't she?

But that was a voice from the past talking to her, a voice admonishing her to be quiet and ladylike. Grace pushed it aside and waved to get Judy's attention. After ensuring her neighbor would watch her booth, she hurried after the woman. It was easy to spot her bright pink raincoat through the throng of shoppers. Grace saw her disappear into Tweedy's Department Store. She ran after her, nearly knocking down a clerk with a basket of perfume samples. The woman turned left at the juniors' department, Grace in pursuit.

Halfway up an escalator, Grace reached out to touch the woman's arm.

"Please?" she asked. "I just want to know who you are. I'm an orphan, and you look so much like me! I wondered if we might be family. I mean . . ."

Before she could finish, the woman, wild-eyed, hissed, "My God! Get away from me!"

She pushed Grace with all her might. With no chance to catch her balance, Grace tumbled down the length of the escalator steps. She landed on the stone floor, cut and dazed. As she watched, too stunned to move, the woman stopped at the top of the escalator and looked down at her for a moment. Then she ran away.

Shoppers came to Grace's aid from all directions. Seeing her cuts, a security guard called for an ambulance over his walkie-talkie.

"My . . . my dolls," Grace mumbled.

One of the other crafters, a man who carved wood, recognized Grace and explained she was one of the people working the show. The security guard took information and promised her things would be taken care of. Grace, completely disoriented, tried to stand up to pursue the strange woman. She was so dizzy she staggered, and a woman grabbed her arm to steady her.

"Take it easy, dear," she said kindly.

The ambulance came a few minutes later, and she was taken to the hospital. In the emergency room, a young doctor treated her wounds and examined her to make certain she hadn't hit her head too hard. He asked her questions, shone a light into her eyes, made her wiggle her fingers and toes. He instructed her to rest for a while and assured Grace her wounds were probably superficial.

"You haven't broken anything," he said, "and you're awake and alert now. I think you probably had the wind knocked out of you, is all. You're lucky. For now, Mrs. Matheson, just relax. I want to keep an eye on you for a few hours."

Lying there on the gurney, Grace had time to consider what had happened. Why had she been so stupid? Why had she chased after that woman, scaring her? If she'd stopped to think, she might have been able to approach her in a more quiet, gentle manner. Then she might have been able to find out who she was. Now perhaps she'd never see her again.

After half an hour, she became restless and got up to walk around. After an hour, she complained of hunger and was offered juice and cookies. As she was eating them, someone from the mall came to speak to her, to make certain she was uninjured. Tweedy's offered to pay her hospital bill and asked her to sign an accident report. Grace, who just wanted this whole thing to be over with, agreed.

Judy showed up just as the young doctor released Grace, offering to drive her back to her hotel. She explained that her things had already been packed up and returned. As they drove, Judy told her that everyone was very worried. She could not, however, reveal the name of the woman who had attacked Grace.

Later, alone in her room, Grace was so bewildered that she wished she could go straight home. She opted for a phone call. When the answering machine picked up, she remembered that Craig had promised to take the kids out to the video arcade. Feeling a little down, and very lonely, she had room service bring up a late dinner. Soon after she finished eating, she went to bed. As she drifted off to sleep, she wondered if she would ever understand what had really happened that day.

TWO

▼

Dull pain from her cuts and bruises woke Grace the next morning, a half-hour before her travel alarm was set to go off. She got up, showered, and dressed, then checked to be sure she'd packed everything for her early-morning flight. She had a bellhop come to bring down her doll trunk but carried her own suitcase and overnight bag. After squaring things at the front desk, she headed toward the front door. She couldn't think of anything but seeing her family again.

"Mrs. Matheson?"

A woman with shoulder-length salt-and-pepper hair and light brown skin stepped in front of her. Her expression was serious, businesslike, in a face that Grace would describe as handsome. Grace quickly took in her cream linen suit and pearl earrings and guessed she might be the mall's lawyer. Perhaps they wanted to be certain she didn't plan to sue.

"Yes?"

The woman held out a hand. Her chocolate-colored eyes seemed to be soaking in every aspect of Grace's face.

"My name is Ivy Haberman," she said, long, cool fingers

gripping Grace's firmly. "I represent the Chadman family."

She saw the confused look on Grace's face and added, "Veronica Chadman's daughter, Amanda, is the woman who attacked you."

Well, Grace thought, the lawyer part had been right. Veronica Chadman, whoever she was, had wasted no time in getting counsel for her daughter.

"They don't need a lawyer, really," Grace insisted. "I don't plan to sue. The doctor says I'm going to be all right, and I'm just very sorry I frightened the woman the way I did."

Ivy gave her head a slight nod. "Amanda has . . . problems. Of course, we'll make this up to you in any way we can. Your medical bills will be covered."

"Tweedy's took care of that," Grace said, starting to walk again. "I wish I could ask about Amanda. I couldn't help noticing the resemblance to me. But, unfortunately, I'm in a hurry to get to the airport. Maybe I could take your card and call you tonight?"

In truth, right now the need to be with her family overshadowed her curiosity. This whole thing was almost surreal, and she wanted Craig's support before she dealt with it further.

"Let me drive you," Ivy said, "I'd like to ask you a few questions on Mrs. Chadman's behalf. And I could fill you in."

Grace agreed to the ride.

"I'll bring my car around," Ivy said, and left.

A moment later, she pulled up in a dark green Cadillac. A bellhop helped fit the doll chest in the trunk of the car and hoisted Grace's suitcase and overnight bag into the backseat. Grace took in a deep breath as she settled into the passenger seat. She loved the smell of new cars. The Caddie was very comfortable, much nicer than any car Grace had ever driven. She wondered what kind of clients Ms. Haberman represented in order to afford a luxury car. Grace thought she'd never see a car like this in a thousand years of selling dolls.

"So, you don't know the Chadmans?" Ivy asked as she pulled away from the hotel.

"Sorry," Grace replied. "I'm not from Indianapolis. I live just outside Tulip Tree. It's about an hour south of Gary."

"You're a long way from home," Ivy said. "Everyone around here knows of Veronica Chadman. Her family owns Windsborough Botanicals."

"Oh, I've heard of them," Grace replied. "They've got a boutique in our local mall."

"There are several thousand franchises worldwide," Ivy said.

Craig's mother had given Grace a basket of toiletries from the shop a few years back. Grace herself would never have been able to afford the pricey items.

"So, tell me," Ivy said, "what brings you down to Indianapolis?"

Grace told her about the crafts fair.

"That's where I saw Amanda," she said. "Who is she, exactly?"

"I'll answer your questions as best as I can," Ivy offered. "But I must begin with my own."

"Go ahead," Grace said.

Grace watched her as she drove, realizing now that the woman hadn't smiled once. Businesslike wasn't enough to describe her, Grace thought. She was friendly enough, but there was something dark and brooding about her. But Grace pushed the thoughts aside. Ivy's personality was no concern of hers.

They were out of the parking lot and on the highway before she spoke again.

"Let me begin with my most important question," she said. "Mrs. Matheson, were you adopted?"

Grace caught her breath. A thousand thoughts sprang into her mind in just a few seconds. She was right—Amanda was her relative. Veronica must be too. Was Chadman her real name? Would she soon meet her mother?

"Mrs. Matheson?"

"Oh! Oh, yes," Grace said at last. "Yes, I was adopted."

"You're twenty-nine years old?" Ivy went on. "You'll be thirty in October?"

"Yes," her voice was barely a whisper.

"Do you have a heart-shaped birthmark on the back of your left ankle?"

Grace brought her hands to her mouth, blocking the urge to cry out. No one but a relative would know about that, would they?

"I'm sorry, I didn't hear you," Ivy prompted.

"I do," Grace said. "Ms. Haberman, what does this mean?"

"It's 'Missus,' " said Ivy. "My husband passed away, but I was always proud to bear his name."

She turned a corner before finally answering Grace's question. "I'm not completely certain yet. But by a strange coincidence, I believe you might have been attacked by your own half-sister."

"Half-sister!" Grace exclaimed. "Then . . . Veronica Chadman is my mother?"

"We don't know that yet," Ivy warned. "But she'd like to talk with you. I'd like to arrange a meeting as soon as you can return to Indianapolis."

Grace thought a moment. She wanted to talk to the woman but was disappointed to realize it couldn't be soon. The twins were in a school play this week, Trevor had a basketball championship game, and she was doing a talk on her dolls at the library.

She took a deep breath. Although it made her heart ache to know the truth would be delayed, she said, "I can't see her for at least two weeks."

"All right, then," Ivy said. "I'll explain the situation."

Grace appreciated the way Ivy accepted her answer without argument or questions.

"I wish I could do it right now," Grace said regretfully. She shook her head. "All my life, I dreamed of meeting my mother."

Ivy stopped at a red light and said, "Mrs. Chadman is very excited that she might have found her long-lost daughter."

"Believe me," Grace said, "no one's as excited as I am."

It wasn't until she was on the airplane that Grace admitted to herself that she was as frightened as she was thrilled. She'd dreamed of this miracle for so long that now she was unsure that her mother would be the woman she had created in her imagination. Who could ever match that perfect dream-mother? Worse, what if Veronica didn't like her?

Lulled by the hum of the engines, breathing the plane's recirculated air, she dozed off and dreamed she was six years old again.

"Stand up straight," someone was telling her. She was aware of hands fluttering about her, straightening the bow in her hair, tugging her skirt. "Mrs. Billingsly thinks you might be the baby she was forced to give up for adoption. You want to impress her, don't you? You want to go home with her?"

"Oh, yes," the little girl had said. "Oh yes, so very much!"

She almost skipped as she walked down the hall to meet the woman. Her real mother at last! No more foster homes, no more mean people who either hit her too much or paid no attention to her at all. No more . . .

They entered the room. The woman stood up slowly, staring at her.

"Are you my mommy?"

The woman's red lips pressed into a frown so tight that, more than twenty years later, Grace shivered in her airplane seat at the memory.

"No," she said. "Someone like you could not possibly be my daughter."

With no further ado, Grace was led from the room. She caught sight of herself in a mirror and knew why the woman hated her. She wasn't blonde and delicate. She was fat, her hair was always messy, her nose runny . . .

Grace's head snapped up at the sound of a warning bell. The passengers were being told to fasten their seatbelts for landing. Grace shook away the vestiges of the memory. That chubby, awkward little girl was long gone.

And yet, she felt as uneasy about this whole situation as if she were six again.

Craig and the children were waiting for her when she got off the plane. When she saw her precious family, all her worries flew from her mind. She hurried down the ramp to them, smiling. They looked so cute together: her handsome husband with his hazel eyes and big smile, Seth and Sarah miniature copies of him from their straight noses to their auburn hair. The only hint of Grace in them was their dark blue eyes, wide now with anticipation. She wondered how much they looked like the Chadman family. Trevor, standing back a little from the group as if his stocky frame was anchored to the tiled floor, looked so much like Grace that she was certain he'd probably find many new relatives he resembled.

She hurried up to them with open arms. Sarah pointed at the bruise on her forehead and frowned.

"Oh, Mommy," she said in a worried tone.

"Grace!" Craig said. "What is that? Gracie, what happened?"

"It's a long story," Grace said. "I'll tell you about it in the car."

"But, Grace . . ."

She smiled to reassure him, knowing he would worry until she explained everything. But she wanted to greet her children first, so it would have to wait. She smiled at Trevor. He was studying her head with a frown on his face and a glint of anger in his eyes. Grace smiled to think how like Craig he was—very protective of his family. She could tell he wanted to know who had dared to hurt her.

"How about a hug?" Grace asked. "Didn't you miss me?"

Trevor nodded, then came forward. His hug was brief, but coming from him it was enough for Grace. He had recently decided that kissing his mother in public was a silly thing for a ten-year-old to do. But as they walked to the baggage claim area, Trevor took her overnight bag. Although he struggled with it, Grace knew it was his way of showing his love for her.

When Craig came back from the baggage carousel with her trunk, they headed out to the parking lot. In the car, he pursued the matter of her injury.

"How did you do it, honey?" he asked. "Are you going to be okay?"

"Did a mugger get you?" Seth asked, his eyes bright with excitement.

"Not a mugger," Grace said. "Someone far more interesting. Buckle up and I'll tell you everything."

They had arrived home by the time she finished her story.

"Cool!" Seth said.

Sarah chimed in, "A long-lost sister! Maybe I've got one too! Then I wouldn't be the only girl!"

Her parents laughed at that. Sarah often begged them for a little sister.

"I have another aunt?" Trevor asked, raking his fingers through his thick chestnut hair as he shook his head in wonder.

"Maybe," Grace said. "I'm not sure. Veronica Chadman is supposed to get in touch with me."

"Gee . . ."

Craig patted his son's shoulder as they walked into the apartment building.

"Don't worry, Trev," he said, "I'm a little overwhelmed myself."

No one said another word as they ascended the stairs to the fourth floor. Inside the apartment, Grace kicked off her shoes and plunked down onto the couch. She closed her eyes and moaned loudly.

"I am *so* glad to be home!"

The twins cuddled up to either side of her, while Trevor carried her bag into her room.

"You say that every time," Seth said.

"So how come you keep going?" Sarah asked.

Grace opened one eye.

"We need the money," she said, honestly.

Now she opened her other eye and looked up at Craig, who had come out of the kitchen to offer her a tall glass of iced tea.

"Six dolls this trip," she said. "Not my best ever, but at least we can put a few bucks in the bank."

Craig sat in a rust-colored armchair. "Walcheck called me yesterday with a few ads to write. It isn't much, but it'll help."

Craig was an advertising copywriter, currently working freelance. He hoped to get a steady job at a small ad agency in Gary, but for now there just wasn't enough work to employ him on a full-time basis. They really needed every penny Grace brought home.

"So, this Veronica Chadman owns a chain of stores?" he asked.

"Windsborough Botanicals," Grace said. "You know, those fancy bath things your mom gave me a few years back."

Craig was thoughtful for a few moments. Then he asked the twins to leave the room.

"Why?" Seth whined.

"Seth . . ."

The warning tone in his father's voice pushed the six-year-olds from the couch at once. They went into Trevor's room to bug him while he worked on a new spaceship model he was building. His wails of protest came moments later, but for now his parents ignored him.

Craig sat beside his wife and said, "Gracie, I can see how excited you are about all this."

"You bet I'm excited," Grace said. "I might have a chance to be reunited with my real mother! Oh, Craig, if you could have seen . . ."

She stopped talking, her full lips parted slightly. Seeing how Craig's brows knit together, she realized he didn't fully believe what had happened. She remained silent for now, not wanting to start an argument and ruin a wonderful situation. Instead, she shifted and tucked one small foot underneath her, gazing into Craig's eyes.

Craig seemed to recognize her defensive look, because he said quickly, "Gracie, it's all happening so fast. I'm afraid to see you get hurt. The chances of finding your mother aren't so minute. People do it all the time. But to imagine she might be very, very wealthy . . ."

He looked around the simple living room, taking in the sagging furniture, the badly scratched coffee table, the old TV. Grace knew he thought she might be getting her hopes up, thinking she might be related to a rich woman. A poor little girl dreaming she's really a princess.

"I can't help it!" Grace said, standing. "This isn't just one of my fantasies, Craig, one of my dreams of the perfect mother. And I won't give up hoping! Not until Veronica Chadman decides we're not related, after all!''

With that, she stormed into the kitchen. Craig sat alone for a moment, absorbing what she'd said. Was it so far-fetched that her dreams could come true? It was something she'd talked about from the day he'd met her. She was barely eighteen, selling dolls at an outdoor flea market. He was shopping for cheap furniture to fill a bachelor's apartment, when a sudden downpour sent people scurrying. Grace was frantically trying to rescue her dolls, the look of dismay in her incredibly beautiful eyes making him wonder if it was rain or tears on her cheeks. He'd stopped to help her, covering the dolls with sheets of plastic. Grace had been thankful enough to offer him a cup of coffee, but he'd ended up buying her dinner. She'd told him she had no family, that she'd been a ward of the state until only recently.

"But my mother is out there, somewhere," she'd said. "I know she is, and I know that, someday, I'll find her."

Craig had heard that line so many times in the past twelve years that it had become like the man who keeps using the same Lotto numbers because "someday these numbers are bound to come up." So, now that she seemed about to hit a jackpot, it was hard for him to accept it. Still, he had to trust her common sense, her ability to seek out the truth. Maybe he'd spoken too hastily, treating her as if she were still a naive little kid. He got up and went into the kitchen.

There was a small work area set up under the window, a makeshift studio where Grace did all her work. She had taken out a blob of clay and slapped it on the table. Craig knew it was only a tool to vent her frustrations, more pliable, she was probably thinking, than her narrow-minded husband.

Craig came up behind her and began to massage her shoulders.

"I'm sorry, Grace," he said. "I know you'll find out the truth behind this."

"I plan to," Grace insisted, pulling away bits of clay. Her small hands worked quickly, transferring her frustration to the clump in her hands. She began to smooth the shape into a round ball, deciding this one was going to be a baby. A baby that would be loved more than she had been, even if it was only a doll. "Veronica Chadman wanted to see me in a few days. She was even going to pay for my plane ticket. But I told her lawyer that I had other things to do. I—I couldn't miss Trevor's basketball championship, of course. And the twins' play . . ."

"I should have known you wouldn't jump into this," Craig said.

"Yes, you should have," Grace said calmly, looking up to stare out the window. "I thought you would be happy for me, Craig. Just because you're almost ten years older than me, doesn't mean I'll always be a little girl to you."

"I don't think of you as a little girl, Grace," Craig insisted. He buried his face in her soft hair, kissing her. Then he whispered just behind her ear, "When Mrs. Chadman calls, tell her you don't need a ticket. I'll drive you there myself."

Grace put down the clay and turned to hug him. Standing six feet tall, his arms strong and loving, he was Grace's rock, the one thing in life she knew would always be there for her. Why had she doubted him? He wasn't like the unfeeling, no-nonsense people who raised her! He wanted her to be happy.

She reached up to run her fingers through his thick hair, loving the feel of it. Then she laughed.

"Oops! I got clay in your hair."

"You'll just have to help me wash it out," he said.

With that, he led her to the bathroom, for a shower and whatever else the warmth and closeness might lead to.

THREE

▼

The next weeks were such a bustle of family activity that Grace hardly had time to dwell on her upcoming visit with Veronica Chadman. She and Craig attended the twins' play— there was one advantage to working freelance, at least—and applauded proudly. Grace was certain Seth spoke his lines more eloquently than any other first-grader, and Craig whispered that Sarah had to be the cutest mermaid he'd ever seen. The twins joined them for Trevor's basketball championship, screeching with more exuberance than their parents when Trevor made a difficult basket. His team won, earning a huge trophy for the junior high school. Craig treated everyone to dinner at a Chinese restaurant afterwards.

"Craig, can we do this?" Grace whispered over a plate of dim sum.

Craig grinned. "When else does a kid win the divisional basketball championship?"

"Well, the whole team did great," Grace said, deciding the frivolous dinner was worth it. "You guys should be really proud of yourselves, Trevor. Trevor?"

She saw now that her son was listlessly stirring his bowl of wonton soup.

"What's wrong, Trev?" Craig asked.

"You're going to see that woman tomorrow, aren't you?"

Grace and Craig exchanged glances. How many times had they discussed this with their children?

"Well, yes," Grace said. "You know that. Trevor, are you still worried?"

Trevor shrugged.

"Oh, it'll be so wonderful to have a new grandmother," Grace offered.

"I don't want a new one," Trevor insisted. "I liked Grandma Matheson good enough. What if this lady is mean? What if she doesn't like us?"

Craig poured a new cup of tea for his son and handed him the three packs of sugar he'd use for it.

"We've talked about this," he said. "You don't have to worry. Any woman who has a daughter as sweet as your mother must be nice herself."

Trevor's eyes seemed to grow darker. "She gave her away, didn't she?"

Grace sighed, realizing there was no point in discussing this right now. She'd already been through it with Trevor. Why couldn't he accept her good fortune as the twins had? What was he afraid of?

The next morning, outside the home of Grace's good friend, Paula Bishop, Trevor stood there frowning. Paula had offered to take the kids while Grace and Craig drove down to Careyton, Veronica Chadman's hometown.

"Say good-bye to your folks, now, kids," Paula said.

"Bye, Mom," Seth said. "Bring me home a cousin!"

"A girl cousin!" Sarah put in.

Grace looked at her older son. Trevor ran his fingers through his hair, shifting from one foot to the other.

"Aren't you going to wish me luck, Trev?"

"You're gonna come back, aren't you?"

Grace put her hands on his arms. Even though he was a muscular child, he seemed small and fragile right now.

"Of course I will," she promised. "We talked about this already. There's nothing I can find there that would ever tear me away from you kids. Daddy and I will only be gone until tomorrow night."

The poor little guy. She realized now that he was afraid she might like her new-found mother more than her own family! Still, he'd have to get used to the idea. And for now, there was enough for her to think about during the long car ride ahead without stewing over Trevor's moodiness. Given time to consider everything, she had begun to take Craig's skeptic view a little more seriously. The doubts that had plagued her during the airplane ride came back again. What if she were setting herself up for a big disappointment? What if Veronica Chadman were a horrible person, or maybe not even her mother at all? She heard Craig's deep laugh and felt his hand pat hers.

"Easy!" he said. "We haven't gone a block from home and you're already looking scared as a kid about to get a licking!"

"This might be as hard to take," Grace said.

"Everything will work out just fine," Craig reassured her.

Now it was Grace's turn to laugh. "That's supposed to be my line! You're the cynic here, remember?"

But his support made her feel much better. Over the next four hours, they talked, listened to music, and took turns driving along Route 65. Miles of factories and farms seemed to go by with aching slowness, until Grace thought if she saw one more field of soy beans or another hog she'd scream. But when they finally arrived in Indianapolis in the late afternoon, Grace realized the time had flown by. This was too fast! She wasn't ready for this!

And yet she'd had twenty-nine years to get ready.

They drove for another twenty minutes to the outskirts of the city, until they reached the suburb of Careyton. It was a pretty town, its streets lined with large Georgian, Federal, and Greek Revival homes, all with perfectly mowed lawns and manicured gardens.

"What's that address again?" Craig asked.

Grace read it to him. Craig drove a little, peered at a number on a fieldstone column, then asked for the address once more. Grace repeated it patiently.

"You gotta be kidding," Craig said, his eyes wide.

Grace was speechless herself. This was her *mother*'s house? She gazed in wonder through a wrought-iron fence decorated with scrolls and fleurs-de-lis. At a distance that seemed miles away, there stood a huge, red brick building that seemed more like a hotel than a house. Five pedimented dormers of white wood jutted from the gambrel roof. Below, Grace counted nine shuttered windows on the next floor. The white door, topped with a Palladian window, was set off by Ionic-style piers.

"That's Late Georgian," Grace said.

"How do you know?"

"From that art history class I was taking when we first met," Grace said.

Suddenly, the gates opened as if by magic.

"I guess they know we're here," Craig said. "Must have surveillance camera somewhere. Big Mama is watching you."

"Craig, that's terrible," Grace scolded. "I'm sure she isn't like that."

He turned the car onto the driveway, rolling slowly towards the mansion. Ancient trees, sycamores and red maples, stood majestically to either side like an honor guard welcoming them. Along the very edge of the road, red and yellow hollyhocks alternated in perfect patterns with jagged stones. Grace could see acres of land beyond the trees: there was emerald-green grass rolling on one side of the driveway and a variety of plants covering the other as far as she could see. Several workers tending to their cultivation stopped and stared as the Matheson's modest Reliant drove by, freezing as stiff as the marble statues that decorated the vast lawn.

Grace opened her window to let in some fresh air. She breathed in deeply, detecting roses, mint, and, strangely, something like vinegar. It was as if the wind was bringing a different scent to her each time it shifted.

"Do you smell that?" she asked.

Craig sniffed the air. "Mint. It must be growing nearby; and a lot of it, if it smells that strong. No, wait—roses."

He made a face. "And vinegar. What kind of plant smells like vinegar?"

"Maybe Windsborough uses unusual herbs in some of its products," Grace suggested.

Craig parked the car in the circular driveway that curved in front of the house. No one but a pair of copper griffins, long-since turned green, was there to greet them as they approached the stairs. Grace heard rustling in the rhododendron bushes; when she turned, she saw a shadow slip around a corner. A chill washed over her, a sense of being watched.

"Are you coming, Gracie?" Craig asked. He was already at the door, holding out a hand as if to offer his support. Grace hurried up, deciding not to mention the "spy."

"Ready as I'll ever be, I guess," she said.

She took a deep breath.

"Well, here we go," she said. When they got to the door, Grace reached for the lion's head knocker. In her nervous state, she half-expected it to change into Marley's ghost and sneer at her.

Then, a moment later, Marley really was standing there. Grace sucked in a loud breath.

"Mr. and Mrs. Matheson?" the ghost asked in a deep voice.

"That's us," Craig said.

Now Grace realized it wasn't a ghost at all, but a man so pale and gaunt he might as well have been one. His shock of white hair fluffed about his head like an aura, his eyes were such a pale blue they seemed nearly invisible. The dark suit he wore gave him an overall moribund appearance, not helped a bit by his dour expression. He backed into the house.

"Mrs. Chadman is expecting you," he said. "Follow me."

Grace looked at her husband. Craig took her small hand in his big one and held it firmly as they entered a foyer bigger than their own bedroom. Grace's sandals clicked as she walked across the parquetry floor, and she followed the echo up to the ceiling to see intricately carved moldings around a glimmering crystal chandelier. The cream-colored walls were painted with a mural of trees. As they followed the servant, Grace tried to look into rooms with opened doors. The quickest glance was all she needed to see how luxurious the interior of this house was.

The servant led them into what Grace supposed would be calling a drawing room. It was a mix of pastels and gold filigree, sweet and opulent at the same time. The focal point was a pale yellow damask couch, tossed over with embroidered charmeuse pillows of pink and powder blue.

"Mrs. Chadman, your guests have arrived."

"Thank you, Andros."

Until the woman spoke, neither Grace nor Craig knew she was in the room. Her yellow silk dress was like camouflage against the yellow walls. When she turned, her peaches-and-cream skin and platinum-blonde hair made her seem as delicate as the gossamer swags that topped in the tall windows. But it was her eyes that made Grace's heart skip a beat: deep blue, lapis lazuli eyes.

"Oh, can it really be you?" Veronica Chadman whispered hopefully. "Can it really be my baby, after all these years?"

Without waiting for Grace's response, she hurried to the younger woman with open arms and took her into a warm embrace. Grace was overwhelmed by floral scent, and couldn't help wondering if it was Veronica's perfume, or the virtually hundreds of flowers scattered in antique vases around the room.

"Let me look at you," Veronica said, pulling back but keeping her hands on Grace's shoulders.

Grace immediately felt uncomfortable about her appearance. She'd put on one of her nicest outfits, a pair of beige three-quarter-length pants, a brown-and-white striped T-shirt and a long, straight vest of beige linen. Many people had complimented her on it when she wore it before, but today it seemed very middle-class, even tacky, when compared to Veronica's gorgeous yellow silk. And four hours in the car must have taken its toll.

She bit her lip and told herself to stop. This was her real mother, not someone who was considering adopting her! It wasn't twenty years ago, and she didn't need to feel so self-conscious!

"I always dreamed you'd be beautiful," Veronica said, and eased Grace's mind at once. Now Veronica looked concerned, staring at Grace as if she could still detect the bruises from her fall. "Are you all right? When I heard what Amanda did, I was so upset. But to think she might have found her half-sister!"

Grace couldn't help a nervous laugh. "I'm just fine, really. Oh! I'd like you to meet my husband, Craig."

Veronica gave Craig a quick glance and a smile, but immediately returned her gaze to her new-found daughter.

"Now, where are my manners?" Veronica asked. "Me, chattering away with questions when you must be tired after such a long ride. I do wish you would have let me send you airfare. Please, sit down and make yourselves comfortable. I had the cook prepare some sandwiches and tea."

Grace and Craig sat on a pink Chippendale settee. Grace couldn't help noticing how Craig pulled himself in, as if he felt awkward on the delicate-looking piece of furniture. There was a glass-topped table in front of them, held up by an intricately carved gold sculpture. Veronica leaned forward and filled two Delft china plates. She handed one to Grace, one to Craig. He took it as carefully and as nervously as he might a fine museum piece.

"I'm so sorry you didn't bring the children," Veronica said.

"I thought it would be best if we had some time alone, first," Grace said. "But they're all very excited to meet you."

She saw no reason to mention that only the twins were enthusiastic.

"You tell them we'll get together as soon as possible," Veronica promised.

Grace took a bite of her sandwich because she was hungry after the long ride, but she hardly tasted it.

"Please, tell me your story," Grace urged.

"I've gone over my words a thousand times since Ivy spoke to you," Veronica told them, "and maybe a million times over the past twenty-nine years. And yet I feel I don't really know where to begin."

"Maybe when you were pregnant?" Craig suggested.

"Yes, of course," Veronica agreed, offering him only a moment's glance. She seemed to have eyes for only Grace. "I was sixteen years old at the time, in love with a college boy. When he learned of my condition, he went off to his junior year at a British university and left me. I was terrified, alone."

"Wasn't anyone there to help you?" Grace asked. "Your mother?"

Veronica shook her head sadly, staring down at her small hands as if still ashamed of what had happened so long ago. She played with an emerald ring as big as Craig's thumbnail.

"You must place yourself back in that era," she said. "The sixties were no time for an unmarried mother."

"I always thought love was pretty free in the sixties," Craig said.

"Not here in the Midwest," Veronica told him, "and certainly not in a family with the prestige and history of the Winstons. That was my maiden name. I was sent off to live with my aunt, so the family could hide its shame."

"A baby seems like a silly thing to be ashamed of," Grace said.

"Attitudes have changed," Veronica said, reaching for her glass of iced tea. "But back then, my father told everyone I had gone to Rome to study Italian."

She took a long sip of tea, staring at the medallion of flowers on the rug as if remembering that bitter time. Finally, she looked up.

"Grace is such a pretty name," she went on. "I was going to name you Deborah Mary. Deborah for my mother and Mary for my favorite aunt."

Grace suddenly felt as if her heart had been struck with an invisible hammer. Gazing at Veronica with huge eyes, she began to turn pale. Craig put a comforting hand on her arm. Grace turned and saw that he was taken aback, too. He knew why the name meant something to her.

"What's wrong, dear?" Veronica asked with great worry in her voice.

"I . . . I can't believe this," Grace said, her voice barely a whisper.

"Neither can I," Craig agreed.

Grace blinked a few times.

"My real name is Deborah Maria," she said in a voice that was half-choked with awe. "That's what it says on the foster care records. I changed it to Grace Clarissa when I was eighteen. It was my way of starting a new life."

Craig shook his head in wonder.

"This is unbelievable."

"It's one more piece to the puzzle," Veronica said. "Grace, dear, may I ask you one more question? I think it might completely verify this."

Grace nodded her head slowly.

"Do you know much about your early medical history?"

"A little," Grace said. "Why? What do you know?"

"My baby had a small hole in her heart when she was born," Veronica reported.

If Grace's heart had been hit with an invisible hammer a moment ago, now it seemed ready to burst. A disbelieving smile spread across her face.

"I had a hole in my heart too," she said. "It closed up by the time I was four. But I remember always being told to be a little lady because everyone was afraid it would open up again."

Now Veronica was smiling.

"It's a miracle," she whispered.

"Whoa!" Craig cried out, holding up both hands. "Anyone could have found out information like that."

Veronica stared hard at him and said, "My baby was taken away in secret. I overheard the nurses talking in the hospital, and this is how I know of her early condition. I'd have no access to her medical records."

"Well," Craig countered, "I'm sure a hole in the heart isn't a rare condition. I don't suppose you have the birth certificate?"

Grace practically jumped on him. "Why should she? She isn't under investigation, Craig!"

Veronica held up a hand, her rings glistening. "Oh, but I have tried to get it. I thought you'd want to see it, Grace.

However, since you were born under such secret conditions, it's been hard to find it. I think my family may have registered your birth in another county to be certain no one could trace you to the Winstons.''

"It must have been terribly lonely for you," Grace said.

Veronica's smile was warm. "I kept going by imagining you were in a happy home," she said. She stood up now. "Well, this is all too much to take at once. We have so many things to catch up on, so many questions to ask each other and to answer. Maybe it's best that we do it a little at a time."

"I'm all for that," Craig said.

Grace felt like kicking him, and the thought surprised her. She resented the way he had suddenly butted in, taking charge. This was her mother. Couldn't he see that?

There was no time to fight with him. Veronica was holding out her hand to Grace. She took it and stood herself, and the two women walked hand-in-hand towards the arched entrance-way.

"I'll have Mrs. Treetorn show you to your room," Veronica said. "I'm sure you'd like some time to relax and freshen up. It's so terribly humid today, isn't it? And this is only May!"

Grace ran her fingers through her hair, her eyes wide with wonder.

"I hadn't noticed the heat," she said. "I'm still trying to absorb all this."

Veronica squeezed her hand. "Dinner is at seven. You'll have time to think things over."

A dark movement in the sitting room caught the corner of Grace's eye. She looked through the archway, but of course there was no one else in there. She decided it was probably a sudden wind stirring the trees outside the French doors, a trick of the light making it seem like a person in the room.

Now a small, pumpkin-shaped woman, no taller than Grace's chin, appeared. Veronica gave her instructions, and she took them upstairs.

"Oh, ma'am," Mrs. Treetorn said, her voice shaking as if she was on the verge of bursting out laughing. "We're all so excited! I want you to know that I'm here to help you settle in, so you just ring and I'll be there.''

Her green eyes were bright and wide, as round as her pink cheeks.

"That's nice of you," Grace said.

The housekeeper led them to a bedroom as richly furnished as the rest of the house. Craig whistled.

"Y'know something, Toto?" he asked an invisible dog, "I don't think we're on Hollyhock Street any more."

"This certainly isn't our apartment," Grace agreed.

The room was done up in various shades of beige and white, from the cream-colored rug to the yards and yards of white batiste draped over the windows. At its center stood a four-poster bed so large that Grace thought she, Craig, and their three kids could all sleep in it and still have room to stretch. There was a white vanity on one side laden with crystal perfume bottles and pastel-colored toiletries wrapped in gold ribbons. Its mirror reflected its masculine partner across the room: a mahogany dressing table set up for a man. Craig went to it and picked up a gold-and-silver bottle. He opened it and sniffed.

"Nice stuff," he said.

"It ought to be," Grace replied. "That cologne runs about two hundred dollars an ounce.''

Craig put the bottle down quickly. Laughing, Grace sat down and began to brush her hair.

"You look just right sitting there," Craig said, "like a princess."

"Having Veronica for my mother would make me *feel* like a princess," Grace said. The surroundings were so luxurious that she decided to forgive Craig's indiscretion. He'd asked about the birth certificate out of concern for her, not because he wanted to be in control of the situation.

She put the brush down and picked up a bottle of hand lotion. It was marked with the Windsborough Botanicals logo. When she opened it, the smell of mint and roses, with a slight hint of vinegar, wafted up to her nose.

"Well, here's one place they use that odd-smelling plant,"

she said, and rubbed some on her hands. She sniffed and found it left only a minty smell behind. "Mmm . . . it's a treat to use stuff like this. It makes me feel luxurious."

"It's a nice life," Craig commented.

Grace watched his reflection as he sat on the edge of the bed and kicked off his shoes. He rolled onto the huge bed, stretching comfortably over the white chenille spread.

"Well, I for one am going to take Mrs. Chadman's advice," he said, yawning noisily. "A rest sounds like a good idea to me."

Grace took off her own shoes and padded across a rug so thick it seemed she was walking on pillows. She climbed in beside him, resting her head on his chest. She listened to the sound of Craig's heartbeat, his chest rising and falling in sync with her own breathing.

"So, what do you think?" she asked. "Are you happy for me?"

Craig paused so long that she pulled herself up on an elbow. "Craig?"

He opened his eyes and sighed deeply. "I wish I could be sure about this, Gracie. I mean, how hard could it be to get a birth certificate?"

"I was never able to find it," Grace said. "All my ID is based on foster care records. Veronica is probably right—her parents registered my birth in another county. But she knew things about me that no one could know. Did I tell you that her lawyer, Ivy Haberman, mentioned that birthmark on the back of my ankle? And how did Veronica know I had a hole in my heart when I was a baby?"

"People can get all kinds of information," Craig replied. "Especially someone who has money, and, probably, power."

Grace sat up. "Craig Matheson, I think you're jealous! You're worse than Trevor!"

"What's that supposed to mean?"

"Don't think I didn't see the way Veronica practically ignored you," Grace said. "Did it hurt your ego? Do you think that anyone could ever take the place of you and the kids?"

"Grace, I don't think that," Craig said. "But you're right,

I did think she was ignoring me. I also think that's to be expected, at least for now."

"So what do you think?"

Craig sighed. "I think that you should proceed with caution. What if you find out you aren't related? Don't you think Veronica's going to expect some kind of test to prove the relation? And if she doesn't, what about other family members? How do you think they're going to feel knowing there's another heir to the Windsborough fortune?"

"Oh, Craig," Grace said, her voice breathy. "I hadn't thought of that. Money is the furthest thing from my mind right now."

"That may not be what others think," Craig pointed out. "A poor girl with an unemployed husband, someone a few mean-spirited people might call white trash, shows up claiming to be a rich woman's daughter. I just don't want to see you hurt, Grace, is all."

He took her into his strong arms, and she knew at once why he couldn't be happy for her. Because he was afraid. His own father had deserted his family when Craig was ten, and he'd vowed he'd always be there for his family. It was hard for him to trust anyone when it came to Grace and the children. She turned to hug him back.

"I'll be all right," Grace insisted, her voice barely louder than the hum of the crickets outside. "I knew Veronica was my mother the moment I laid eyes on her. She looks exactly like me, except for her white hair. Her eyes and nose and mouth are mine. And no other family member could deny it to see us together!"

Craig always knew from the tone of Grace's voice when there was no point in arguing with her. He decided all he could do was support her.

"All right, then," he said. "You've got me at your side the whole time, okay?"

Grace kissed him.

"Okay. Love you."

"I love you, Gracie."

He held her tightly as they fell asleep together. They woke

up about two hours later, and the catnap had done them both good. Craig was still skeptical, and Grace was still hopeful, but they felt refreshed enough to face the next step of this situation. After changing clothes—Grace had decided her suit was too wrinkled from the car ride and the nap—they went downstairs. Andros was standing in the foyer. He bowed a little, then walked away without a word. Grace and Craig exchanged glances, shrugged, and followed him. The tall, morose servant took them into a dining room. Veronica sat at the head of a vast mahogany table, laid out with white china and silver that appeared to be antique. Her chair was so big she looked like a child sitting in it. She was wearing a dress of raw peach silk with a dark green jade necklace and matching earrings. With a smile, she indicated the seats next to her.

"Did you rest well?" Veronica inquired politely.

"Very well," Grace said, taking her seat. She smoothed her full, floral-print cotton skirt. "That was the most comfortable bed I've ever slept in."

"I'm glad you like it," Veronica said. "When you decide to move in here, that will be your room."

Craig's eyebrows went up.

"Move in?"

"We'll discuss it later," Veronica said. "Felix, our cook, has prepared a remarkable dinner just for this wonderful occasion. Smoked shrimp in orange marmalade, broccoli with hollandaise—"

Craig cut her off. "Wait a minute. What's this about us moving in?"

"I thought I'd bring it up during dinner," Veronica said. "I know this is all very much to take, but don't you agree we could know each other better if we had more time together?"

"Yes, but—"

"So I thought, with vacation coming, you might spend part of the summer here with me."

Grace glanced over a low arrangement of peonies and roses and gave her husband a surprised look.

"Oh, now, you don't really want to spend the whole summer cooped up in that hot little apartment of yours, do you?

And I'm sure Craig can write copy here as easily as he can up in Gary. He might even do a few things for Windsborough."

Now Craig returned Grace's look of surprise with an "I told you so" expression. So Veronica had been spying on them! How else would she know about the apartment or that Craig freelanced for an ad agency in Gary?

"Did it seem I was spying?" Veronica asked with chilling astuteness. "It's just that, when I thought I'd found you, I couldn't wait two weeks to learn about you. I had a private detective learn a few things about you."

"Like the hole in her heart?" Craig asked with sarcasm.

Grace felt a chill rush over her to think someone had been watching them these past two weeks.

Veronica patted her hand. "I didn't mean to upset you. Forgive me for being so enthusiastic. My heart was so full I just had to do something!"

Grace didn't know what to say. When two maids brought in the food, it provided a segue for her. She took a taste of the shrimp—it was absolutely delicious. The delighted moan that Craig gave told her he agreed with her.

"Wow," Craig said. "This is great stuff."

"Thank you," Veronica replied.

Grace took a sip of wine. She caught the way Craig was staring at her and with her eyes begged him not to judge Veronica too harshly. His shoulders went up and down with his inaudible sigh, and she knew he wouldn't argue about the detective. Still, it was too unnerving to Grace, and she decided to change the subject.

"I wanted to ask you about Amanda," she said.

Veronica bowed her head a little and shook it sadly.

"Poor Amanda," she said. "I love her dearly, but she has been so much trouble for me. She's not well, you know."

That had been obvious to Grace from the moment she spoke to the woman in the mall. With her forkful of shrimp halfway to her mouth, she nodded.

"She has problems," Veronica said. "She's been diagnosed

as paranoid/schizophrenic. We've tried to help her in many ways, but it's an ongoing struggle."

"Do you think it was wise to let someone like that walk around a shopping mall by herself?" Craig demanded. His tone indicated he blamed Veronica completely for the attack on his wife.

"She was with a nurse," Veronica replied. "Somehow, Amanda got away from her. I've since fired the woman. She should have been much more careful. If she had been, this might never have happened."

Grace smiled. "Then again, if she had been, perhaps we would never have met each other."

Veronica returned her smile, and Craig saw that they both had a small dimple just to the left corner of their lips. The resemblance was uncanny, and yet he still couldn't be certain.

"It's a miracle," Veronica said.

Grace reached over and touched Veronica's wrinkled hand. Something about the gesture bothered Craig, but whatever it was remained stuck somewhere in the back of his mind, giving off only a very, very vague sense that something was *wrong* here.

"I believe you are my mother," Grace said. "But if it will prove this beyond a shadow of a doubt, I'll submit to whatever tests are necessary. Blood, DNA . . ."

"No need," Veronica replied. "I'm convinced myself. You, my dear Grace Clarissa, Deborah Maria, Deborah Mary, are a Chadman."

"What does Mr. Chadman think?" Craig asked.

Both women's heads turned so abruptly it seemed they were attached to the same switch. Grace frowned, and Veronica looked annoyed at the interruption.

"Mr. Chadman is dead," Veronica said.

"Oh, I'm so sorry," Grace replied. "I was hoping . . ."

Veronica smiled at her. "Yes, it is regretful. Although, of course, he's not your real father, he would have liked you. Cole was a good man. My own father was fond enough of him to make him CEO of Windsborough Botanicals. The company prospered under his care. I myself see to things in my own small way, but I have no head for business. I leave most of that to my CEO.''

They spent the rest of dinner talking about the company, about Grace, about the children. Never once, Craig noticed, did Veronica mention another member of the family.

Later, as he embraced his wife in the darkness of their room, Craig had to express his doubts.

"I'm still not convinced," he said. "Why didn't she tell you about your other relatives?"

"How much do you want her to tell me in one evening?" Grace inquired. "Craig, stop looking for trouble, okay?"

Craig paused for a moment. He suddenly realized they were about to engage in the second argument they'd had that day. And all because he was being paranoid. Maybe he was crazy to think something was wrong. Maybe Grace was right—there was just too much to find out in such a short time.

"I'm . . . I'm sorry, Gracie," he said, moving closer to her. He tucked himself against her small body in spoon fashion. "I just want you to be careful."

"Stop being overprotective of me," Grace snarled. "Growing up in foster care made me pretty tough, you know."

What Craig knew, actually, was that the neglect of foster care had made Grace more kind-hearted and vulnerable than anyone he knew. But he kept this belief to himself.

"I'll try," he promised.

He waited for a reply.

"Gracie?"

Her steady breathing told him that she'd slipped into the first stage of sleep. He himself couldn't even begin to grow tired. Nagging worries gnawed at him, eating away any bits of lethargy. Very few things brought out Grace's hidden temper. Was he wrong to push the matter? Was Grace right, accusing him of being overprotective? He realized he might be treating her like a stupid child. He vowed he'd try harder to trust her instincts.

As he held Grace in his arms, various bits of the day's conversations came back to him:

I was sixteen years old at the time.
A baby is a silly thing to be ashamed of.
I mean, the way I'll look in twenty-nine years.
. . . sixteen years old at the time.
. . . the way I'll look in twenty-nine years.
. . . sixteen.

"Sixteen plus twenty-nine makes forty-five," Craig whispered.

Grace stirred in her sleep but didn't waken.

Craig figured that Veronica Chadman should be about forty-five years old.

Why, then, did she look like a woman approaching sixty?

Someone was touching Grace, someone with cold fingers. Startled awake, Grace clutched at the thick down comforter on her bed and stared in wonder at a girl who seemed no older than sixteen. Her hair was parted down the middle, hanging loosely over the shoulders of her white nightgown. Grace could barely make out her pale face, almost luminescent in the darkness.

"Who are you?" Grace whispered, pushing the covers away. Beside her, Craig snored softly in deep sleep.

"Go away and don't come back here!" the teenager whispered. "She wants your children! Get away before she kills you!"

Like stardust sucked into a black hole, the girl stepped back into the shadows and vanished. Grace moved forward to catch her, only to find herself touching the blank wall.

"Hello?" she whispered.

No one answered her. She went to Craig and tried to shake him awake.

And then he was shaking her, propped up on one elbow beside her in the bed.

"You were moaning in your sleep," he said. "Having a nightmare?"

Grace was back in bed again, the covers pulled up to her chin. Confused, she nodded slowly. She let Craig hug her, clinging to him as her heart slowed its pace, wondering when she'd ever had a dream that was so *real*.

FOUR

▼

Sometimes, when Craig woke up before Grace, he liked to lie gazing at her, taking in the porcelain-skinned face and delicate features he thought were so beautiful. This morning, lost in the huge four-poster bed with its mounds of covers and pillows, Grace seemed smaller than usual. He wanted to gather her into his arms and keep her safe forever.

In spite of his vow to trust Grace's instincts, he couldn't fight a growing sense of dread. He didn't like the way Veronica had sent a private detective to snoop after Grace. And while she was warm and loving to her new-found daughter, she seemed cold towards him, maybe even annoyed by his presence.

He sighed, wondering if Grace was right, that there might be a little bit of jealousy at work here. A quick look around the room, at the paintings on the walls and the antique vases and the fine furnishings reminded him of the rich things he could never provide for his family, even if he were writing ads full-time in a big city like New York or even Indianapolis.

How many years had they been saving for that modest little Colonial house?

No matter what happened, though, he'd be with Grace. He would never desert her or the kids. Not the way his father had deserted his family.

Grace grimaced in her sleep, and he recalled the cry of pain that had awakened him last night. She'd had a nightmare then, he guessed. Was she dreaming of her own childhood now, he wondered. Was she thinking of the cold rooms where she'd slept or the awful food she'd had to eat? Was she dreaming of the emptiness? Or perhaps of the terrible day when the "system," for whatever reasons, tore her away from the one family that had treated her kindly. He knew that was why she so desperately wanted to believe Veronica Chadman was her mother. Finding her biological family would fill in so many gaps in her life . . .

As if aware of his gaze, Grace opened her eyes suddenly and smiled dreamily.

"Hello," she said.

"Hi," Craig replied.

Grace gave him a quick kiss.

"Is that all I get?" Craig asked.

"I have a disgusting taste in my mouth," Grace said, pulling herself out of the bed. "Must have been that garlic bread we ate last night."

She padded off to the adjacent bathroom, hanging her tongue like a hound dog. Craig laughed.

"You don't seem any worse for last night," he said, turning to sit on the edge of the bed. "It must have been some dream."

He heard the *ch-ch-ch* sound of a toothbrush. Water splashed, and a moment later Grace opened the bathroom door.

"It was almost real," she said. "A teenaged girl appeared and told me to leave and never return. I got up, but she vanished. Next thing I knew, you were waking me up."

"Well, I don't know about dreams," Craig said, "but I like the idea of leaving. I just don't feel comfortable in this big old place. I thought we'd leave after breakfast."

Sitting in the gilt chair at dinner last night, he'd worried for a moment it would crash beneath him. But mostly it was his fear that things were happening too fast.

"You'll be okay," Grace said, coming to sit beside him. She rubbed his back lazily. "It isn't like we're going to live here."

"Not the way Veronica talks," Craig said. "I like the way she plans our summer for us."

"She's just eager, like me," Grace pointed out.

She turned and fingered the soft sheets.

"But it sure would be nice," she said, "living in a place like this. Like all my dreams have come true."

"Wanna know what I think would be nice?" Craig asked.

"What?"

He put his arms around her and gently lowered her back onto the bed.

"Trying out this bed just one more time before we meet with Veronica again."

With that, he leaned forward and kissed her.

As it happened, they didn't get to see Veronica again that day. Andros appeared while they were eating breakfast, staring over their heads and out the French doors as he spoke.

"Mrs. Chadman has been called away," he said in a deep voice. "She regrets having to leave you and will contact you as soon as she can."

He turned and left.

"That's strange," Grace said.

"Yeah, I know," Craig replied. "I think that guy takes lessons from Lurch."

"Not Andros!" Grace cried. "My mother! Why would my mother leave when she's only just met me?"

"Lurch—I mean Andros—said she was called away," Craig said. "Sounds like a business kind of thing. Probably something going on at Windsborough."

"Or maybe with my sister," Grace said.

She finished the last of her omelet. Loaded with cheese and vegetables, it was as delicious as any she'd had in a restaurant.

"I wonder if they eat like this all the time."

"They?"

"My mother and . . ."

She stopped. Who else lived here, she wondered. It had only been the three of them at dinner the night before. Except for a brief explanation of Amanda's whereabouts, Veronica hadn't mentioned any other family members. Did those two women live in this huge house alone except for servants?

Grace put her napkin on the table and stood up.

"My mother and Amanda," she said at last. "I never had the chance to ask about other family members."

"Funny how Veronica never gave you the chance," Craig said. "Maybe we ought to hire a private detective of our own."

Grace's eyes flashed. "Craig, you know she meant no harm by that. It was just her enthusiasm! And what is there to find out about us? We aren't hiding any secrets."

"She didn't know that," Craig said. "And maybe she wants to be certain about you before she welcomes you into her millions."

"I couldn't blame her for that, Craig," Grace said softly. "She has no way of knowing I'm not some kind of golddigger."

"But you didn't come looking for her," Craig pointed out.

Grace finished the last of her orange juice and stood up.

"Please," she said, "don't twist this around with your practicality. I'm not stupid, but I don't see what's wrong with accepting Veronica and not being suspicious."

Craig resisted the urge to tell her again to be careful.

When they returned to their room, they found the bed had been made up and the curtains had been tied back to show off a view of the gardens below. Servants were busy sweeping leaves from the basketball and tennis courts, trimming bushes, leading the horses out to graze. Grace went to a round table where a vase of yellow roses had been set out. She closed her eyes and breathed in their beautiful scent. When she opened them again, she found a note. She read it out loud.

" 'My darling Grace: You can't imagine what joy I feel inside to have you back again. You are more beautiful and kind than I could ever have hoped. I'm sorry that duty calls me away so abruptly, but I promise I will be in touch. Do you mind if I sign this note . . . Mother? P.S. Bring the vase home with you.' ''

Grace looked over at Craig, who had placed the suitcase on the bed and was packing.

"See that?" she said. "No mystery at all. I just hope it doesn't take too long to hear from her."

"I don't know," Craig said with a frown. "Why didn't she mention this last night? Or why didn't she at least knock at our door this morning to say good-bye? She had time to write a note and get the flowers."

"Craig," Grace sighed. "Can't you stop being suspicious? I mean, the woman is more than generous to us, and she hardly knows us! Look at this vase . . ." She held it up, reading the imprint on the bottom. "It's Limoges, for heaven's sake. Awfully nice to just give away."

"Well, I . . ."

"Oh, just stop!" Grace snapped. "Not another fight, okay?"

Craig fell silent, but Grace grumbled under her breath as she packed. When they were ready, they carried their bags downstairs. A maid was on her hands and knees scrubbing the parquetry floor, but there was no one else in sight. They tried to find Andros, to let him know they were leaving and to convey a message to Veronica. But the man was nowhere to be found.

"Nice good-bye," Craig said sarcastically. "Makes us feel really important."

Grace did not respond. The four-hour drive home was filled with silence, punctuated by shallow snippets of conversation. Grace was fuming inside, angry that Craig misunderstood everything. His protective attitude towards her was beginning to wear thin. The roses seemed to reflect her frustration, fading with each passing hour. Their petals had already begun to fall off when Craig pulled into Paula Bishop's driveway.

"Grace, let's not upset the kids," Craig said finally. "I just need time to adjust to this, that's all. You know I'll support you no matter what you do. And I'm sorry if I upset you."

"It took you four hours to say so?"

"Now who's being sarcastic?" Craig asked.

The sight of their children pushed their argument to the background. Sarah was the first to come bounding down the steps to greet them, her auburn braids flying. Seth was only steps behind. By the time they got out of the car, Trevor and Paula had come out too.

"Mom! Dad!" Seth called. "What happened?"

"Is she your mother, Mommy?" Sarah asked.

The twins bound around their parents like puppies. Craig laughed and grabbed Seth for a bear hug. But Grace's eyes were drawn to Trevor, who stood running his fingers through his hair and squinting his eyes in his usual scrutinizing manner. She could tell he was worried and tried to appease him.

"It's okay, Trevor," she said. "I've brought back good news."

Paula brought her freckled hands to her mouth and grinned with anticipation. Grace told them at once how certain she was that she'd found her mother.

"All right!" Seth said. "I've got a new grandma!"

"Is she nice?" Sarah asked. "Did she like you, Mom?"

Grace touched her soft cheek and smiled.

"She's very nice," she said. "I liked her a lot, and I know she liked me."

Paula beckoned them towards the door.

"Come in and relax after your long ride," she said. "I've got lunch ready."

In the house, they settled around the table. Seth and Sarah devoured their sandwiches, but Trevor ate slowly. His attentions were turned more towards the conversation at the table than to his lunch. He wished he could stop this weird feeling inside, a feeling that something was wrong here. Even Dad had said they should be careful, just in case. But just in case of what? His mother seemed so *happy*. Why couldn't he be happy for her? Why did he feel so *scared?* That lady named Veronica had taken so many years to find his mother, and he didn't trust her. She couldn't really be a nice person if she gave up her own baby, could she?

"Looks like you've got some questions, Trev," Craig said, snapping the boy from his reverie.

Trevor had a million of them, a million worries he wanted eradicated. Somehow, he felt this wasn't the time. His mother just looked too happy to be bothered. He shook his head.

"No, Dad."

"I have a question," Seth said. "When are we going to meet her?"

"I don't know," Grace admitted. "She left a message that she'd call us."

And every time the phone rang over the next few days, Grace expected it to be her mother. She heard from friends, from the director of the library where she planned to talk about her dolls, from various solicitors. It seemed strange to her that her mother didn't contact her almost at once. Wasn't she as eager to hear from Grace as vice versa? Grace considered calling first, but she didn't want to be too forward. Living in a house like that, Veronica was probably used to the finest people with the best manners. She didn't want her mother to think she'd found a pushy, obnoxious daughter. At last, she simply resigned herself to the fact that Veronica must be very busy with her company.

Four days after leaving her mother's house, she finally heard Veronica's name over the phone.

"Is this Grace Matheson?" the voice, tremulous and soft as a small child's, asked. "Do you know of Veronica Chadman?"

"Yes and yes," Grace answered both questions. "Who is this?"

Now the childlike voice rose to the pitch of frenzy.

"Why didn't you listen to me?" it demanded. "Why did you let her find you? She'll kill you all! She'll take the blood of your children like she took mine and she'll kill you all!"

The screamed words were so piercing that Grace was forced to hold the phone away from her ear. At once, she realized who it must be on the phone.

"Amanda?" she asked.

"She'll kill you all! It's blood she wants!"

Grace took a deep breath to steady herself. She was glad the children were in school, unable to witness this strange incident. Amanda's cries were so loud they could be heard across the room.

"Amanda, it's okay," Grace said in a soothing tone. "Veronica isn't going to hurt me. I'm her daughter, your sister. She loves us both, I'm sure!"

"She's not your mother," Amanda hissed. Grace could almost imagine her curled-up lips. "And I'm not your sister."

Just then, Grace heard new voices and the shuffling of feet. There was a struggle taking place on the other end, punctuated by Amanda's screams of protest. Moments later, a calm, male voice came on:

"Hello? Who is this?"

"My name is Grace Matheson," Grace said. "Was that my sister, Amanda Chadman?"

The man affirmed this. "I'm sorry, Mrs. Matheson. Somehow, she got at the desk phone. Did she upset you?"

Is the Pope Catholic? Grace wanted to retort. What kind of place was that, where her sister could escape from a nurse in a mall to attack her and later harass her by telephone?

Instead, she spoke calmly: "I'm all right. Do you want to tell my mother of this incident or should I?"

"I'll take care of it," the man said.

They exchanged perfunctory good-byes, and Grace hung up. She was surprised to see her hand was shaking a little bit. She went to her worktable and picked up a sketch pad and pencil. The action served to calm her down. She began to design an outfit for her newest baby doll, and her thoughts grew steadily calm.

Poor Amanda. What kind of dreams haunted her that she thought her own mother was after her blood? Grace realized that finding her mother meant finding an entire family, with all its joys and curses. Now she was more determined than ever to be with her mother, to help her through the hard times with Amanda.

When Craig came home that evening, she told him of Amanda's strange call.

"Did she threaten you?" Craig asked, worriedly.

"It was more like a warning," Grace said. "She insisted Veronica isn't my mother and she's not my sister."

"Oh?"

"I wouldn't give much thought to talk from a disturbed woman," Grace said evenly.

"Well, if it happens again you should tell Veronica," Craig said. He could tell Grace didn't want to pursue the matter and changed the subject. "I have some news, Grace. Do you remember that ad I did for that new supermarket just east of here?"

"The place that's so big you could practically live there?" Grace replied. "Sure, it was one of your best."

Craig smiled. "Well, Carson's thought so too. They've asked me to come for an interview, to join their publicity department. They're planning on opening a series of those stores throughout the Midwest, and they want to launch a big campaign."

"Oh, Craig!" Grace cried, throwing her arms around him.

It was wonderful news. Craig had been working freelance for over a year now, and it had become harder and harder to make ends meet on their unsteady incomes. A company as big as Carson's could keep Craig employed for years, maybe even to retirement. When she thought about how they'd struggled ever since they first married, the thought of Craig having a steady, secure job was exhilarating.

"It's surely a month for dreams to happen, isn't it?"

"It hasn't come true yet, Gracie," Craig reminded her. "My interview is set up for next week, at the main offices in Bryce City."

Grace's dark blue eyes rounded. "Bryce City? Craig, that's fifty miles from here. You'd be working there?"

"I know," Craig said, "it would mean leaving Tulip Tree and starting a new life. But Bryce City is an upper-middle-class community. It would be a change for the better."

"I'm not sure the kids will be happy about leaving their friends," Grace said worriedly.

"Let's talk to them," Craig said. "Where are they?"

"Trevor's down the block playing basketball with Nicky, and the twins are at the park," Grace said.

"I'll go out and get them," Craig said. He lifted his head a little and sniffed. "Is that cinnamon I smell?"

"Apple cobbler," Grace said. "We're having it for dessert, so you might mention that to Trevor. You know it's his favorite."

As they sat together at the dinner table a half-hour later, enjoying pot roast so tender it cut with a fork and buttery fried potato skins, the children listened with great interest to their father's news. Trevor, always the skeptic, was a little wary about any possible change in his life. It was bad enough Mom had a new mother and a scary sister. Why did Dad have to get a job so far away?

"It hasn't happened yet, Trevor," Craig said, reading his son's mind. "But you'll do fine if it does. Grace, I was thinking I'd spend a few days there. A few of my old schoolmates moved to Bryce City, and I'd like to look them up."

Grace nodded, then said, "The kids are out of school the end of this week, and my next show isn't scheduled until the first week of August. What if we all go up together?"

"I had another idea," Craig said. "Why don't you call your mother and arrange to bring the kids to meet her? I'll rent a car, and you can take the Reliant."

"Yay!" Seth cried. "We're gonna meet our new grandma!"

"Be quiet, Seth," Trevor growled around a mouthful of salad.

No one paid attention to him. Grace had gotten up and went to put her arms around her husband.

"That's a great idea," she said, kissing him again and again.

She wasn't just happy about going to see her mother again.

She was happy that it was Craig who'd suggested it. Maybe he was finally coming around to accepting Veronica Chadman. But as she went back to her place, she saw the brooding look in Trevor's eyes. If only she could convince her son!

FIVE

▼

Veronica was thrilled to hear that Grace wanted to visit with the children, and plans were made. When the day came, they drove Craig to the airport and continued on their way to Careyton. The twins played travel games in the backseat, while Trevor rode shotgun and read a Bruce Coville novel. But as the miles passed, he found it harder and harder to concentrate. Thoughts of the many discussions his parents had had about his new-found grandmother kept crowding out the words of the stories. He'd noted how worried his father was, how he had warned his mother not to get her hopes up too high. And he'd heard the anger in his mother's voice, saying Dad should be happy for her and not be so cynical. Trevor didn't know what "cynical" meant, but he supposed it was something bad.

Seth's shrill whine cut into his thoughts. "MO-OM! Sarah says she saw that New York license plate first, and it was me! She's cheating!"

"I did see it," Sarah insisted. "I know the colors, so I saw it from far away."

"Cheater!"

Grace managed to avert the squabble by redirecting the twins' attention.

"There's a rest stop," she said. "Let's get out and stretch our legs."

After his mother angled the car into a parking space, Trevor got out and headed for the men's room.

"Take Seth," Grace ordered.

"I don't hafta go," Seth said.

"Yes, you do," Grace said firmly. "I don't want to stop again until Careyton, and that's two hours from here."

"Come on," Trevor growled at his brother.

Seth hurried up beside him as Trevor entered the brick building. "Trevor, how come you look so grumpy today? Are you carsick? Are you gonna puke?"

Trevor wrinkled his nose. "No, I'm not carsick. I just don't wanna meet this new grandma, that's all."

"I do," Seth said. They entered the men's room. "Mommy says she's rich. Maybe she'll buy us lots of toys."

"Who cares about that?" Trevor said. "She sent Mom away when she was a baby. Toys don't make up for that."

"I like toys," Seth said, pushing into a stall.

Trevor rolled his eyes. Seth missed the whole point, but what use was it to talk to a dumb six-year-old?

When they finished, they went outside. Sarah and Seth played tag on the grass and Trevor plunked quarters into a vending machine. He sat down on a bench with his mother and shared his root beer.

"Are you excited, Trevor?" Grace asked.

Trevor shrugged.

"You don't have to be so worried," Grace said. "We've talked about this before. No matter how many new relatives I meet, no one will ever take the place of you kids and your father."

"I know," Trevor said. He didn't want to talk about this. He couldn't explain his uneasy feelings to himself, let alone make a grownup understand. Sometimes, grownups were thicker than dumb six-year-old brothers.

He stood up. "Can we go now?"

"All right," his mother replied. She called to the twins.

Trevor traded the front seat with Seth, who bombarded his mother with almost non-stop questions for the rest of the trip. Sarah fell asleep, her head pressed against the side of Trevor's thigh. He wiggled to get comfortable, then tried to lose himself in a video game. The second half of the trip seemed to pass more quickly than the first, and just as he beat the fourth level of his game, his mother announced they'd arrived.

Sarah sat up, rubbing her eyes. Sleep fell completely away from her as she took in the vast grounds of her new grandmother's estate.

"Horses!" she cried. "Mommy, they have horses! Look, Seth; look, Trevor!"

But the other children were too caught up in their own amazement to reply. Trevor gazed up at the majestic trees that flanked the road, across the field of plants, then straight ahead to the big house. His new grandmother lived in a place like *this*?

"Mommy, is that a hotel?" Seth asked.

"That's not a hotel, dummy," Trevor said. "It's a mansion. Wow, Mom. She's loaded, isn't she?"

"She's very wealthy, Trevor," Grace said. "Now listen, you guys. Best behavior, okay?"

The children didn't seem to hear her.

"Okay?" Grace repeated.

"Okay!" the kids cried in unison.

Grace parked her car in front of the house. When Trevor got out, he noticed a strange smell in the air and made a face.

"How come it smells like salad dressing?" he asked.

"Like vinegar," his mother corrected. "And do you smell mint and roses too? And other plants?"

"I smell mint," Sarah said. "Grandma grows mints?"

"Mint leaves of some kind," Grace said. "But Daddy and I couldn't figure out what smells like vinegar. Some strange herb."

Seth, who cared nothing about strange herbs, had already run up to the front door and was reaching for the knocker. Grace came up behind him and tapped it a few times. When the door opened, the three children stared in wonder at the tall, grim-faced servant who answered.

"Hello, Andros," Grace said. "Is my mother here?"

"She's waiting for you in the dining room," Andros replied. "Lunch is ready for you."

He stared down at the children, his expression showing neither distaste or approval. Trevor shivered a little, thinking the man looked half-dead. What a creep! If his grandmother had a butler like this, what was she like?

He was hardly prepared for the beautiful, chestnut-haired woman who suddenly came towards them with open arms and a big smile. A fluffy-skirted pink dress floated around her, and the diamond bracelet around her wrist glistened in the sunlight that poured through the opened front door.

"Grace, dear!" she cried.

Trevor watched his mother embrace the woman. He guessed she had to be his grandmother, because she looked so much like his mother. But why wasn't her hair gray? Grandma Matheson's hair was gray when she died. He frowned as his mother stepped back and fingered the new grandmother's hair.

"Mom, you look great," she said.

Veronica smiled, touching the waves that fell over her shoulders. "I had it colored this past week. I thought the white hair made me look too old. And now that I'm a new mother again, I want to look young!"

Grace laughed, then turned to the children. "Mom, I want you to meet your grandchildren. This is Sarah . . ."

Veronica knelt down to the little girl's level and gazed into her eyes. "You're so beautiful, Sarah dear. Did your mommy do those lovely braids?"

Sarah nodded, smiling shyly.

"And this is her twin, Seth," Grace went on.

"Twins! Oh, Grace, I never imagined . . ."

Veronica seemed about to cry when she looked at Seth. He started giggling, then moved closer to his mother. Trevor rolled his eyes. Now Veronica stood up and smiled at him.

"You must be Trevor," she said. "I hear your team won the basketball championship."

"Yeah," Trevor said, simply.

"We have a basketball court right here on the property," Veronica said. "After lunch, you can try it out."

Now Trevor's whole demeanor changed. A basketball court, right here? Maybe his grandmother did a bad thing years ago when she gave up his mother, but if she had a basketball court, she couldn't be too mean, could she? Especially since she'd let him use it. He felt himself relaxing. They'd only be here a few days, after all, and he could pass the time shooting baskets. He supposed he'd get through this okay.

He saw his little brother tugging his mother's sleeve. Grace leaned down and listened, then laughed a little.

"Seth wants to know what to call you, Mom," she said as she straightened. "They still think of Craig's mother as grandma. They could call you that, too, but . . ."

Grace seemed at a loss for words. Trevor didn't want to call this new woman "grandma," a title of honor he thought belonged only to Grandma Matheson, even if she had died a few years ago.

"I suppose it's too early to use that name," Veronica said. "You haven't had time to get to know me. Would 'Nana' do?"

The twins nodded. Trevor shrugged and ran his fingers through his hair. "Nana" sounded like babytalk, but he supposed it would do.

"I'm hungry," Seth said now.

"Of course you are, Seth dear," Veronica said. "After such a long ride! Come out on the deck. Our cook, Felix, made a special lunch just for your arrival."

She led them through the parlor, and out through the French doors onto a huge redwood deck. There was a round, white wrought-iron table at one end, shaded by a brightly colored umbrella. Five place settings had been laid out, each one a different color. A pitcher of pink lemonade sat in the middle, ice cubes shimmering in the sunlight. The twins ran to take their places, each picking a favorite color.

"It's like a party!" Sarah cried.

As she took her seat, Veronica replied, "this is Fiestaware.

My parents collected it years ago. Trevor, would you like to take the yellow set?''

"Fine," Trevor said, sitting down. "But my favorite color is red."

"You won't find that color in the original design," Veronica told him. "Years ago, red Fiestaware was made from an element later found to be radioactive. Women broke up the dishes and buried them out of fear of contamination."

Trevor, who loved science stories, sat up with interest. Radioactive dishes? Weird!

"An old red Fiestaware plate would be worth a fortune now," Veronica went on. "If you could even find it."

"Who'd want to eat from it?" Grace pondered.

"Who cares?" Seth put in. "When do we eat?"

"Seth!" Grace cried.

But a maid was already bringing out a big plate of sandwiches. The twins squealed with delight to see they'd been cut in shapes, stars, hearts, moons. Another maid brought out a bowl of fruit, and still another set a tray of sliced tomatoes, cucumbers, and carrots in front of them. The children filled their plates, and for the next half-hour they enjoyed lunch together. Trevor realized he wasn't as nervous as he'd been before. His grandmother seemed nice enough, but he decided he'd wait and see before he accepted her completely.

The afternoon passed quickly. Trevor spent most of his time on the basketball court, even engaging one of the field hands in a one-on-one game. The twins could hardly be dragged from the swimming pool, and Grace accompanied her mother on a tour of the grounds. By late afternoon, she was filled with more wonderment than the first time she'd been here. She realized she was tired too, and excused herself to take a nap. The long car ride, combined with the heat of the day, had taken its toll.

Stretched out on the same four-poster bed she had shared with Craig a few weeks earlier, she closed her eyes and let the hum of the air conditioner lull her. Instead of sleep, though, memories flooded into her mind. She became eight years old again, another time of happiness in her life. That had been the year she was taken in by the Lynch family, an older couple with a daughter who'd just gone away to college. She'd been given Susan Lynch's room, with a complete set of pink-and-white gingham bedding purchased just for her. The Lynches had been the kindest family she'd ever lived with, treating her just like a daughter. There were no lonely times in that house, no strict rules. For two years, Grace (known by her childhood name of Debbie at the time) was happier than she'd ever been.

And then, for reasons she never knew, she was removed from the Lynches' home. She thought it had to do with Mr. Lynch, who had suddenly become very sick. But she hadn't cared about that. She'd loved those people and wanted to stay with them.

A tear escaped the corner of Grace's eye as she recalled the day Social Services took her back to the orphanage.

"Don't let anyone take this from me now," she whispered. "Don't let this all be a big mistake."

She fell asleep praying.

The sound of knocking woke her up. When she answered, Mrs. Treetorn, the housekeeper, poked her round head into the room and announced dinner.

"The little ones are hungry," she said. "They are a cute bunch, aren't they?"

Grace smiled at her. "Thanks. Tell my mother I'll be down in a few minutes. Oh! And could you be certain the children wash up?"

"I'll do that," Mrs. Treetorn promised.

Seth and Sarah came running up to Grace when she left her room.

"Mommy, we have our own bathroom!" Sarah cried. "Mrs. Treetorn showed us our rooms. Seth and me are right next to Trevor."

"There's a door between the rooms, like a hotel," Seth said. "It's neat!"

Now Trevor met them. Grace was pleased to see he'd changed into a fresh pair of jeans and a clean blue shirt.

"Just what I need," he said, "a door so you pests can bother me all night."

Grace laughed. "Let's go see what Felix made for dinner."

If lunch was like a party, dinner was like eating in a restaurant. Fine china was laid out over the long dining room table, the place settings perfectly ordered. As soon as the children sat, creamy soup was ladled into bowls rimmed with gold. As they enjoyed dinner, Veronica asked them how they liked the place. Even Trevor had to agree it was fun. Grace felt better than she had when she went in for her nap. She wasn't a little girl now, and no one was going to take this from her! If even Trevor could accept their good fortune, she had nothing to worry about.

After dinner, Mrs. Treetorn set the children up with a video and a snack. Veronica took out a deck of cards, and Grace joined her on the deck for a game of gin. They shared a pleasant conversation as they played.

"The children seem happy here," Veronica said.

"It must be like Disneyland to them," Grace said. She frowned. "I mean, what they'd imagine Disneyland to be. We've never gone there."

She didn't add that she and Craig could never afford it, but Veronica seemed to understand.

"We'll have to make it a point to go," she said. "Perhaps in August?"

"Well, I have a doll show in California the first week," Grace said. "It's my biggest one of the year."

"Then we'll do it later in the month," Veronica offered.

"You're so generous," Grace said with a smile. "In all my dreams, I could never have imagined a mother like you."

"Nor I such a beautiful daughter," Veronica said. She laid down her cards. "Gin!"

Grace tallied the score. She thought of her sister Amanda, and wondered what her life had been like. Was she too disturbed to even realize what kind of home she had?

"Would it be possible to visit Amanda while I'm here?"

"I don't know," Veronica said. "I'll have to ask her doctor."

She dealt the cards, and the game continued. Grace didn't bring up Amanda again. She thought the subject seemed painful to her mother and decided it would be better to let Veronica initiate any more talk of her.

It was late before the children were wound down enough to go to bed. As Grace tucked Sarah into her bed, Trevor stood in the doorway between the two rooms buttoning the top of his pajamas. Grace tucked a lock of auburn hair behind Sarah's ear, smiling.

"How do you like your new grandma?" she asked.

Sarah grinned and replied, "Nana's the best."

Seth, cuddled under his own blanket, added, "Can we stay here for a long time?"

"No way," Trevor insisted.

Grace turned to him. "I thought you seemed happy today, Trevor."

"It's a neat place," Trevor said, "but I don't wanna stay too long. When are we gonna see Dad again, anyway?"

"In three days," Grace said. "Think you can put up with good food, room to run, and a basketball court for that long?"

"I'll force myself," Trevor said.

His impish grin lightened Grace's heart, because it told her that he might finally be coming around. She had thought he would, once he met Veronica. How could he not like a woman who was so kind, so generous?

She bent to kiss Sarah good night.

"See you in the morning," she said, then got up to kiss Seth good night. He gave her such a big hug she grunted. "What a big old bear you are!"

"Thanks for finding me a new grandma, Mommy," Seth said.

Grace smiled, kissed him again, then followed Trevor into his room.

"I'm glad you've changed your mind, Trevor," she said. "You'll really enjoy yourself here, you'll see."

"I guess," Trevor said noncommittally. "Good night, Mom."

Grace said good night and left the room. As she walked down the hall, she could hear the sound of a broom swishing over a wooden floor, of furniture being moved. The servants were finishing up their daily chores.

She had to stop in the middle of the hall to absorb that idea. Servants finishing chores! It seemed impossible that she could be living in a home where she wasn't expected to run herself ragged keeping up with her family, her apartment, her art.

"I am not going to wake up from this dream," she whispered with determination.

In her room, she found her suitcase had been set up on a bench at the foot of the bed. She hadn't had time to unpack it earlier. Now she opened it and began to fill the drawers of a tall cherrywood dresser. She had brought along her few pieces of good jewelry, and as she set these on the Battenburg dresser, her eyes were drawn to the reflection of the man's dresser across the room. She laughed to think how nervous Craig had felt the first day they were here.

"Don't laugh," someone said.

Grace saw a pale face staring at her from the mirror across the room. She gasped, swinging around.

The mirror over the other dresser only reflected her own frightened expression. For a moment, she stood there staring at it.

Then the air conditioner's thermostat clicked on, making her jump.

She rubbed her hands over her face.

"Too much time in the sun," she told herself firmly.

That, and nothing more. She wasn't hearing things or seeing things!

She turned back to her suitcase to concentrate on her unpacking. There, she found the baby doll she'd been working on these past weeks. Complete to its blonde, curly wig, the doll awaited only Grace's final touch—an exquisite costume. This one would depict the nursery rhyme "Rock-A-Bye Baby." Grace had already sewn a mob cap and bunting for it, and would hand-embroider the details during her stay here. Cradling the doll like a real baby, she carried it to the red-

and-gold damask wingback chair next to her bed. She laid it down carefully, then got undressed for bed.

Before she fell asleep, she couldn't resist one last prayer begging that this was all real.

Sometime in the night, she awoke to the feeling of little hands pushing her back and forth. She snapped awake and looked up at Seth. The little boy's eyes were glazed over, his auburn hair looking as if he'd combed it with an electric mixer.

"What's wrong, Seth?" she asked softly.

"Too noisy," Seth mumbled, his head tilting to one side. "They keep making too much noise."

Grace listened a moment, but the house was quiet.

"Who?"

"The people behind the walls," Seth whined. "They're keeping me awake."

"You must have been dreaming," Grace said, getting up. "Come on, I'll walk you back to your room."

She squinted hard when she turned on her room light, and had to wait until her eyes adjusted to the brightness. Leaving her door open so the light from her room would illuminate the way, she walked Seth back to his room. He fell asleep as soon as she tucked him into bed. Grace arranged his covers. She was worried; Seth had never walked in his sleep before. Why now?

Out in the hall, she caught the silhouette of someone standing outside a door. But when she called to them, the figure stepped inside the room and the door slammed shut.

It suddenly occurred to her that, other than Mrs. Treetorn and Andros, none of the servants had spoken to her that day. Were they instructed to behave that way, or were they wary of her? She laughed to imagine being treated like a snob by servants who were "supposed to know their place." Tomorrow, she would rectify that, and let them know she wasn't like that at all.

She fell asleep feeling a mix of worry and content, but in the end exhaustion took over and she slept so deeply she did not dream.

A clap of thunder awoke her the next morning. She fumbled for the clock beside her bed. It was nearly nine o'clock, much later than she or the children had ever slept before. Maybe the previous day's excitement had made them all very tired, or maybe it was just this wonderfully comfortable bed. Grace stretched luxuriously, feeling like a princess on a cloud, and snuggled back into the pillows. She'd sleep a little longer . . .

The weather had other ideas, and another clap of thunder made her sit up straight.

"All right!" she said. "I guess I do want to see what Felix has for breakfast."

She got up and put on her robe and slippers, then went to the window to pull back the curtains. The sky was dark gray, and sheets of rain turned the grounds below into a drab, cold landscape. Grace sighed, hoping the kids could find enough to do in this big house to allay any boredom.

The air conditioner kicked on again. Grace started for it to turn it off; it wouldn't be needed during the storm. But as she passed the wingbacked chair where she'd laid down her doll last night, she stopped short with a gasp.

The doll was lying on its back now, its head dangling over the edge of a chair. There was an IV needle stuck to its forehead with a big X of masking tape. With a groan of disgust, Grace picked up the note that had been left on the chair and read:

THIS IS HOW THEY GET BLOOD FROM BABYS.

It was written in shaky letters, as if the person who had done this was afraid. Grace's jaw began to stiffen. She snatched up the doll and the note and turned to leave her room.

"They should be afraid!" she growled. "How dare they do this to me?"

She asked one of the maids where to find her mother, and was directed to a room. Without knocking, Grace burst inside. She held out the doll, its heavy porcelain arms and head flopping away from its soft body, the IV needle jiggling crazily. Veronica, sitting behind a large desk spread over with paperwork, gasped.

"Grace, what is that?"

"I was hoping you could tell me," Grace said, laying the offensive toy down on the desktop. "I found it in my room this morning. Who would do a thing like this? Mom, is there someone here who's a danger to my children?"

Veronica brought her hands to her face, sighing. When she drew them away, Grace was surprised to see her blue irises shimmered with nascent tears.

"I haven't been completely honest with you," Veronica admitted. "I think your sister did that. That's the way she spells 'babies.'"

"Amanda?" Grace said with surprise. "She's here?"

Veronica nodded. "I had hoped to reunite you two in a careful way that wouldn't upset her, but Amanda was very angry about your presence here. She became uncontrollable. We planned to take her back to the hospital in the night, but she must have found your room and . . ."

She indicated the doll.

"But why?" Grace asked. "What does this mean?"

"It's a product of her twisted mind," Veronica said. A tear slid down her pale cheek. "She lost a baby years ago, to a strange blood disease. The tragedy exacerbated problems she already had, and sometimes she fantasizes the baby is alive."

"How awful," Grace said with a shudder. What other family secrets would she learn? "I would like to talk to her, when she's ready."

Veronica smiled wearily. "Maybe someday."

Another clap of thunder sounded just then, almost as if to contradict Veronica's words.

SIX

The children were disappointed to see the heavy rain draw a damp curtain over their outdoor play.

"No pool today," Seth moaned, gazing out his window.

"And no basketball," Trevor added. "What else is there to do here?"

"Maybe we can watch TV," Sarah suggested.

The boys turned to her. She was sitting in the middle of the rug with a doll, buttoning and unbuttoning its crisp white pinafore.

"There's nothing on now," Trevor said, "except dumb talk shows and stuff like that."

"And we've seen everything on Nickelodeon about a million times," Seth put in.

Sarah shrugged and reached for a brush to style the doll's hair. The door opened, and Mrs. Treetorn came in with a stack of towels. She surveyed the unhappy faces and laughed.

"I think it's time for a surprise," she said. "Your Nana had a special room set up for you children."

Sarah got to her feet, and Seth hurried to the woman's side.

"What kind of room?" he asked.

"Let me put these towels away, honey, and I'll show you."

A few minutes later, she was leading them into a downstairs room that was nothing short of a child's paradise. It was well stocked with toys and games, set out among comfortable-looking chairs and a long, low table.

"Wow!" Seth cried. "It's like a toy store!"

Sarah went straight for a little white table, set up with a pretty china tea set. Two bears and a large rag doll waited for her. Seth found an army set and took over an area of the floor to create a mock battle. Trevor took his time to peruse the games and books that stacked the floor-to-ceiling shelves. It seemed there was every new game here, and all the old ones he liked. There were even models of spaceships to build, one of his favorite hobbies. He moved on to a closed cabinet. When he opened it, he gasped in wonder.

"Look at these video games!" he cried. "There must be a hundred here!"

He scanned the spines of the brightly-colored boxes, then pulled one out.

"Nitro-Death 2000!" he said. "I can't believe it! I read about this, but it isn't supposed to come out until next year."

He looked down at Seth, who was lining up soldiers.

"You suppose Nana went and got this stuff just for us?"

"Yeah, maybe she did," Seth agreed. "This is great!"

"Nana's the best," Sarah put in, pouring invisible tea for a teddy bear. "I could stay here forever."

Trevor kept his eyes on his video game as he inquired, "What do you want to stay here forever for? Wouldn't you miss your friends?"

"Maybe they could come visit," Sarah suggested.

"Yeah, dream on," Trevor said. "Like anyone's gonna drive four hours just to play with you."

He turned his attention back to his game and played for the next hour. By now, the twins were involved in a board game, one that was too young for Trevor to enjoy. He decided he wasn't in the mood to play, but wondered what else there was to do in this big house. The idea to go exploring struck him, and he set off without telling the twins. He didn't want them tagging along.

The house was dimly lit, sunshine casting angled shadows over the fancy floors, cutting corners on tables and chairs. He could hear the distant sound of a lawnmower, the steady ticking of a clock somewhere, footsteps moving over the floors upstairs. Trevor's fascination grew with each room he entered. There was a library that he was certain had more books than the little library in Tulip Tree. Closer inspection found dozens of classic novels, as well as medical and scientific journals. Trevor counted at least eight volumes on human blood, and wondered how so much could be written on one subject.

"Who'd want to read about blood, anyway?"

"She would," came a voice.

Trevor turned around, but the room was empty. Shoving the book back in place, he went out to the hall. Seth and Sarah were just walking up to him.

"Did you say that?" Trevor asked.

"What?" Seth asked.

The twins looked innocent enough. Trevor shrugged off the voice as his imagination. It was obvious he'd been alone.

"How come you guys are here?" he asked, annoyed.

"We want to play with you," Sarah said. "What're you doing, Trevor?"

"Exploring," Trevor said. "Alone."

Seth, taking no hint from his brother's tone of voice, beckoned them to follow him down the hall.

"Let's check the basement! I'll betcha there's a ton of neat junk down there!"

Trevor raced after him down a hall illuminated with antique brass sconces. He resigned himself to the fact that the twins wouldn't leave him alone. "But where is it? How do we find it?"

"I think I saw stairs leading down from the kitchen," Seth called back.

"You guys wait for me!" Sarah cried.

They turned a corner, and saw their mother come out of a room.

"Hey, Mom!" Seth cried. "We're gonna . . ."

But she disappeared into another room without a word.

"Why didn't Mommy answer?" Sarah asked.

"Maybe she didn't hear us," Trevor said.

He had thought there was something funny about the way his mother looked, the way she held her head down and wrapped her arms around herself as if afraid of something.

"Can't we talk to her later?" Seth whined. "I wanna check out the basement."

Trevor hesitated a moment, then decided his mother was probably busy thinking about something.

"Okay," he said. "Seth, where did you see those stairs?"

"Right around here," Seth said, leading his brother and sister to the basement door.

It was situated just before a small bend in the hall that led to the kitchen. Seth pushed it open to reveal a chasm of darkness. Sarah made a face.

"Looks creepy," she said.

"Looks cool," Seth countered.

He felt inside the doorway until he found a switch, then flipped it on. It barely illuminated the stairs, but that didn't stop Seth. He bounded down them without a thought that they might be dangerous. Sarah, although afraid of the dark below, didn't want to be left behind and hurried after her twin. Trevor was much more cautious, hearing every creak and feeling every sway of the wood. By the time he reached the bottom, his heart was thumping.

"I can't see anything much," he said.

They moved forward slowly, until Trevor found a button on the wall and pressed it to light up the rest of the basement. All three children gasped at once. They'd never seen a room so big that the farthest corners were still hidden in shadow. There were boxes stacked neatly in the center, but for the most part it was wide-open and empty.

"We could ride our bikes in here!" Seth cried.

They started walking, gazing at the boxes in the hopes of seeing something interesting, like souvenirs from some war or old toys. To their disappointment, however, there seemed to be nothing much else here but crates and boxes containing old dishes, clothes, and paperwork. They had nearly made a full circle when Trevor noticed a tall dresser. It was the only piece of furniture in the whole basement.

"I think there's a door behind it," Trevor said. "Look! Can you see that crack in the wall?"

The break ran along one side of the dresser, almost to the top, then disappeared. The piece was so large they couldn't see the top, but when Trevor pressed his face to the cool cement wall he could just barely make out a doorknob.

"What do you suppose is back there?" he asked.

"Maybe it's a secret hiding place," Sarah imagined.

"Well, whatever it is, I wish we could move this big old thing and see," Seth said.

At that moment, a strong hand fell on each boy's back, so unexpected that they screamed in unison as they swung around. Andros was frowning at them, his thin face ghoulish in the cellar shadows. Sarah backed up, pressing herself against her older brother. Trevor put an arm around her.

"What are you doing?" the butler demanded.

They shook their heads, mouths hanging open. Sarah started blubbering, her sobs quickly turning to wails of terror. Seth kicked Andros, hard enough to make even that towering figure wince.

"You made my sister cry, you jerk!" Seth yelled.

Andros's face darkened, and it seemed he would strike the small boy. But, a moment later, he seemed to calm down and let the children go.

"There is no need to be afraid," he said in his deep, cold voice. "But this is no place for children."

"We were exploring," Trevor said. He cocked his thumb at the dresser. "What's behind there?"

"Nothing, of course," Andros said.

"Yes, there is," Seth insisted. "There's a door."

"It's an old room we no longer need," Andros offered. "But it's forbidden. Go on upstairs now. This is no place for you."

He started to walk away. The children bounded after him.

"Why is the room forbidden?" Seth asked. "What's in there?"

Andros didn't answer.

"Is it something illegal?" Seth pressed. "Something you don't want the police to see?"

"Oooh, I hope it isn't drugs!" Sarah cried.

"Certainly not," Andros said, stopping abruptly. The children came to a halt and took a step back from him. "It's the electrical center for the entire house. It's dangerous."

"Okay," Seth accepted. "We don't mess with electricity. We aren't stupid, y'know."

The twins started to follow the butler up the stairs, but Trevor held his ground.

"If that's all it is," he demanded, his eyes thinning, "then how come you don't just lock the door?"

Andros paused on the fourth step, his head bowed as if considering the question. Then, without turning, he said, "Respecting the privacy of others is the sign of a gentleman."

"What's so private about electricity?" Trevor asked, coming up the stairs now. "And how do you get at the place with that big dresser in front of the door?" He was growing more and more suspicious.

"Just stay away from that room," Andros said now. "There are far more interesting things in this house."

"Yeah, this is a cool place," Seth agreed.

Andros didn't say another word as he led them up the staircase. Then, in the hall, he walked away without another word. The children looked at each other.

"Weird," Seth said.

"He's scary," Sarah put in.

"You know what?" Trevor said. "I'm going to find out what's behind that dresser first chance I get. You want to help me?"

"I don't want to go back down there," Sarah said. "It's cold and creepy."

"I'll go," Seth offered. "I want to see what . . ." He paused. "What's that smell?"

Seth sniffed at the air as a delicious scent suddenly wafted into the hall from the kitchen. He smiled at his twin.

"Something sweet!" he said.

They went to investigate, the strange doorway forgotten for the moment.

As the children were enjoying strawberry shortcake in the kitchen, Grace was taking a call from Craig in her room upstairs. She sat comfortably in the wingbacked chair, her feet propped up on a velvet ottoman. The doll bunting sat to one side of her, a needle poking out from an unfinished stitch.

"Hi, Craig," she greeted him warmly. "Is it as wet there as it is here?"

"The sun's shining in Bryce City," Craig said.

"We've got a storm," Grace replied. "So, how did the interview go?"

"I got the job," Craig said brightly.

Grace could almost imagine his triumphant grin, his green eyes lighting up with pride.

"Oh, Craig!" she said, sitting up straighter. "That's wonderful! They really liked you?"

"They were impressed by my work," Craig said. "I start next week. Listen, there's going to be some big changes for us."

Grace nodded, even though he couldn't see her. "I know. We talked about the possibility before. What do you want to do next?"

"Well, I thought I'd just poke around the real estate here," Craig said. "While you stay down in Careyton with the kids. Just to get a feel for it, you know?"

"That sounds fine," Grace said. She knew Craig would never make a major decision, like renting a new apartment, without talking to her. And she trusted his good judgement. "I can come up and look at anything you find. How long do you suppose it'll take?"

"If we're lucky," Craig said, "I might find something for us in a week. Bryce City isn't a very big town. But we also have to move out of Tulip Tree. I'll head back there tomorrow to make those arrangements. In the meantime, you don't think your mother would mind having you a little longer, do you?''

Grace laughed. ''Are you kidding? She'd lock the door and keep us forever if she could. And the twins would be happy to stay here.''

''What about Trevor?''

''He seems to be coming around,'' Grace said. ''I think the basketball court swayed him a little. But I can still see doubt in his eyes.'' She sighed. ''Maybe it would be good to stay a little longer, to give him a chance to get used to the idea of a new grandmother.''

''You know Trevor,'' Craig said. ''He's always been a little leery of strangers.''

''That's partly our fault,'' Grace said. ''I hate living in a society where children have to be taught to mistrust anyone they don't know.''

She took a deep breath and changed the subject.

''Anyway,'' she went on, ''I think I'll call Paula Bishop and ask her to have our mail forwarded for us. I had ordered my tickets to California a while back, and I don't want them sitting in the mailbox.''

''Good idea,'' Craig said. ''Your show is only a few weeks away, isn't it?''

''Yes, and I've been so preoccupied with Mom that I haven't really prepared for it,'' Grace said.

''You'll do fine,'' Craig said. ''You always pull things together at the last minute.''

They chatted for a few more minutes, then exchanged affectionate good-byes. Grace hung up the phone, then put her embroidery aside and got up to find the children. They were heading to the game room when she met up with them and told them the news. As she anticipated, their feelings were mixed.

''A new job?'' Trevor asked. ''What about my friends? What about the basketball team? Coach said we had a good chance of winning next year too.''

''Then you can lead a new team to victory,'' Grace said.

''I won't see Martha or Annie any more,'' Sarah said

thoughtfully. Then she brightened. "But I'll make new friends, right?"

"Right," Grace replied. "How about you, Seth? What do you think?"

"I think a new home'll be cool," he said. Once he'd left his crowd behind on the last day of school, they were all but forgotten. There weren't many boys his age in their neighborhood.

"It sure will be," Grace said. "A new beginning for all of us. But we have the whole summer to think about that. What are you guys up to now?"

"We're going to the game room," Trevor said.

Grace looked down the hall. "I saw it. You kids must think you died and went to heaven."

Seth was tugging her arm now. She looked down at him.

"Mommy? How come you didn't talk to us when you were near the cellar before? In the hall?"

Seth explained how he'd seen her, but she'd passed into a room without speaking.

"That wasn't me, Seth," Grace said.

"It looked just like you, Mommy," Sarah said.

"Well, I've been upstairs the whole time," Grace replied. "What were you doing near the cellar?"

The children told her how they'd gone exploring. Seth took hold of her hand and pulled her along, eager to show her the hidden room. But when they reached the cellar door, the children were surprised to see someone had put a padlock on it!

"This wasn't here before," Trevor said, holding the heavy lock. "I bet Andros put it there since we were downstairs."

"I thought I heard hammering when we were eating ice cream," Seth agreed.

"Well," Grace said, "if Andros put a lock on the cellar, he must know it isn't safe for you."

"I bet he's got something bad hidden down there," Seth said.

"Something creepy," Sarah agreed.

Grace only laughed at their imaginations. But Trevor stared at the lock. Something was hidden down there, in that secret room. He was sure of it. And as soon as he could, he'd find a way inside.

After lunch, Grace decided to sit down and write a letter to Craig's sister. Kitty lived with her husband and two children on a farm in Ohio, and it had been a long time since they'd had contact with her. Grace was certain she'd be glad to hear of Craig's good news. There was a writing desk in her bedroom, set between the two tall windows. When she sat down and opened it, she was pleased to see that her mother had left some stationary and envelopes. She shook her head in wonder at the woman's graciousness, then took out a pink sheet and began to write. The light coming in through the windows changed from gray, to misty blue, to white as the weather changed and the sun broke through the clouds. Grace was addressing the envelope when the twins came barging in the room.

"Can we go swimming?" Seth asked. "The sun's out!"

"And we've been stuck inside all day," Sarah put in.

Grace stood up. "I have to walk down to the road to mail this, but you can go in when I come back."

She left the room, the twins tagging close behind her.

"Oh, that'll take forever!" Seth protested. "It's a million miles to the street."

Mrs. Treetorn, who was carrying a basket of laundry towards the bedrooms, stopped and offered, "Is there anything I can do?"

"We want to go swimming," Sarah said.

The rotund little woman smiled at her. "Do you, now? Well, what a wonderful idea in this sunny weather!"

"I told them I'd watch them when I get back from mailing a letter," Grace said.

"Oh, I can take care of it, Mrs. Matheson," the housekeeper said, setting her basket on the floor. "The clothes can wait until later. And I'd love to have a chance to put up my feet at the poolside."

"Well . . ."

Mrs. Treetorn's putty face became hard now, her eyes very serious.

"I'm a good swimmer, Mrs. Matheson," she said. "I wouldn't take my eyes off them for a minute."

"Please, Mom! Please?" Seth tugged at her arm.

Sarah looked up hopefully. Finally, Grace sighed and relented.

"All right, but no rough stuff, you two," she said. "And where's Trevor?"

"In the game room," Sarah reported, "building a model."

"Come on, Sarah!" Seth urged. "Let's get our bathing suits!"

They scampered off to change, leaving their mother and Mrs. Treetorn almost breathless from their energy. Mrs. Treetorn sighed.

"My goodness, what a pair! I'll bet they bring you a lot of joy."

"Oh, they do," Grace agreed.

"Mrs. Chadman is so very happy to have them here," Mrs. Treetorn went on, gazing down the hall. She paused as if thinking of something, then turned to Grace and added, "And the older boy too, of course."

"Of course," Grace agreed with a nod. Why had Mrs. Treetorn mentioned Trevor as if he were only an afterthought? Well, maybe it was because he wasn't standing right here. She let herself relax and held up the letter. "I'll be right back."

"No hurry," Mrs. Treetorn said.

The rainstorm had done little to lower the temperature, and Grace found herself sweating almost as soon as she stepped out of the house. She was grateful for the trees that shaded the driveway. Under their cooling branches, she breathed in the beautiful smells of the plants and flowers around her. She didn't detect that strange mix of roses, mint, and vinegar, but guessed it was probably downwind from her. Beneath her feet, gravel crunched softly. When she saw a rabbit sitting near one of the stones that lined the driveway, she paused to watch it quietly. It took one look at her, turned, and bolted.

This was such a beautiful place, she thought as she went on

her way. Horses running across fields, colorful flowers, majestic trees. What a wonderful time the children would have on their next visits here, with all this nature around them! Tulip Tree was a nice little town, but there was nothing like this there. She thought about Craig in Bryce City. Would she be able to live there after this place?

"Anyplace I'm with my family is fine," she told herself firmly. "Better not get too used to the good life!"

She reached the road and walked down to the mailbox to post her letter. As she was turning away from it, movement in the woods caught her attention. She looked around and spotted a young girl, half-hidden behind a tree. She paused and cocked her head to one side, smiling slightly in greeting. Shyly, the girl, who seemed no older than fourteen, stepped out into view. Grace was immediately struck by the resemblance the girl held to the family: chestnut hair, lapis eyes. Her face was drawn and pale.

The sight of someone dressed in a nightgown on a sunny July afternoon was so incongruous that at first it didn't register with Grace. When she realized the girl was wearing bedclothes, and that the front was stained with bright red blood, Grace moved swiftly towards the girl.

"Are you hurt?" she asked. "What happened to you?"

The girl took a step back, as if afraid of her.

"It's okay," Grace said in a soothing tone. She wondered if the poor kid had been attacked and dragged into these woods. "My name is Grace. I'll help you . . ."

The girl smiled slightly, looking like someone in a daze. She reached a hand towards Grace, as if to offer her something.

"It's okay . . ." Grace said, carefully.

The teenager opened her mouth to speak, then clamped it shut again. A look of terror came over her face as she looked beyond Grace's shoulder. Grace turned to follow her gaze, and nearly lost her breath.

Andros was standing right behind her.

"Andros!" she cried. "What are you doing there?"

"Mrs. Chadman is looking for you," he replied. "She would like you to join her for tea."

"Fine," Grace said. "Tell her I'll be back in a little while, but I've got to help this poor girl, first."

Andros frowned at her. "What girl?"

Grace turned around. Somehow, she wasn't surprised the girl was gone.

"You've scared her off," she snapped at Andros. "You shouldn't sneak up on people like that!"

"I saw no one," Andros said.

Raising her eyes to heaven, Grace heaved a sigh and turned to walk back to the house. There, she found her mother sitting in the parlor, a silver tea service set up in front of her.

"Grace, dear," she said. "I was just cutting you a piece of blackout cake."

Grace sat down next to her and took the offered dessert. As she wedged her fork into the thick, dark chocolate, she told Veronica about the girl.

"She was wearing a nightgown?" Veronica repeated after hearing the story. "How strange! She sounds like someone strung out on drugs. It's unfortunate a main road passes in front of the estate. Once in a while, we do get a vagrant dropped off after hitchhiking."

Shaking her head, Grace took a bite of cake before continuing.

"She didn't seem that type," she said. "She looked scared, and that blood was fresh. And there was something else too. She bore a resemblance to our family."

"Coincidence," Veronica insisted. "You're the only family around here, now that Amanda's back in the hospital."

"Relative or not, she was hurt," Grace said. "I think I'd better call the police about it."

Veronica, angling her teacup to her mouth, paused to say, "That's a good idea, but why don't you let me take care of it? I know the sheriff rather well."

"All right," Grace agreed. "As long as she gets help."

She ate half her cake before speaking again. "Andros didn't see her. I wonder how that could be?"

"Maybe she truly was a vagrant," Veronica said. "Someone like that would move quickly to avoid detection."

Grace nodded at the possibility, but she wasn't so sure. Deep inside, feelings were beginning to stir that told her the girl wasn't what she seemed at all.

SEVEN

▼

After dinner that night, the twins went outside to catch fire-flies as their mother and grandmother sat drinking coffee on the deck. Trevor, piqued with curiosity after finding the hidden room in the cellar, decided to stay inside to do some further exploring. He had been intrigued earlier to find a back stair-case leading away from the kitchen. Felix had told him it was a way for servants to get upstairs and down without disturbing members of the household. It seemed silly to Trevor, who had little notion of the caste system in old, rich families like his grandmother's that insisted servants use a separate staircase.

He decided to check out the stairs now. The servants work-ing in the kitchen paid no attention to him as he entered the stairwell. With the sounds of running water and clanking plates behind him, Trevor ascended.

It was different from the big front staircase, barely wide enough for a big man to fit through. The steps were not car-peted, and the walls were plain. Trevor was surprised to find a door at the top. He opened it to enter a dark, unfamiliar hallway, lit only by the last remains of sunlight that came in through a window at its end. Paintings hung on the wall, rectangular silhouettes that held no interest for him. He guessed he'd found another wing of the house, and as he poked his head in the doorways of empty room after empty room, he realized it hadn't been used in years.

"A house with two staircases," he said, running his thick fingers through his chestnut mop of hair, "and so many rooms they don't use some of 'em! Wow!"

Something scurried from one dark corner to another, making him jump back with a gasp. Well, maybe people weren't using this part of the house, but mice certainly were. He thought about the silly way Seth kept insisting people were walking behind the walls in his bedroom. He was probably hearing mice.

He was about to give up investigating the rooms when he finally came upon one that was still furnished. If you could call an empty bedframe and a dresser covered with a white sheet "furnished," he amended. In the dim light that shone through the filmy window, the dresser looked like a fat little ghost, and Trevor had to suppress a shudder.

"Just a dumb old dresser," he told himself, moving farther into the room.

The floor creaked softly beneath his feet as he crossed over to the window. He rubbed years of dust away and looked out. From this high up, he could see that the gardens were laid out in an intricate pattern of interlocking circles. Colorful Japanese lanterns strung from one rose trellis to another told him he was over the deck. He tilted his head and could just make out the table where his mother and grandmother sat drinking coffee.

A flash of movement made him turn his head. Seth was leaping for a firefly. Trevor watched as he caught it and put it in a jar, then turned away from the window. He noticed the pattern on the wallpaper now. It was covered with drums, trumpets, and soldiers in Revolutionary-style costume. This must have belonged to a young boy, long ago. Trevor wondered what had happened to him.

The floor creaked again, loud enough this time for Trevor

to glance down. He saw that his foot had loosened a board, sticking up now like a seesaw. He knelt down and pulled it up, surprised at how easily it came off in his hand. He was even more surprised to find an old cigar box hidden beneath the floor.

"Cool!" he said, taking it out.

Inside, he was dismayed to find a collection of religious items: rosary beads, holy cards, a small statue of a saint he didn't recognize. What kind of kid collected stuff like this, he wondered. And why did he keep it hidden under the floor? Then he pulled out a yellowed piece of newspaper. He could tell the picture was of a man and a woman by the way they were dressed, but there were no faces to see. Someone had scratched them out with black crayon. Trevor carried the picture to the window and held it up, squinting in the remaining light. The picture was dated 1935, but there were no other words.

"Weird," he said, folding it up again.

This house was full of mystery, and he was beginning to have doubts. If Nana was as nice as she seemed to be, why was there a hidden room in the basement? Why had someone put a padlock on the door? And why did a boy think he had to hide dumb old religious junk? Where was this boy?

"Here I am," came a voice.

Trevor whirled around, the picture in his hands. A boy who seemed a few years younger than him, but older than Seth, stood in the doorway. He was wearing a dark suit and a tie, and his brown hair was slicked back from his pale, thin face. He was so sad looking that Trevor was reminded, for just a moment, of Andros.

"Hi," he said.

"Hi," the boy came back. "Read the letter."

"What letter?" Trevor asked. "Who are you?"

The boy looked around nervously, as if to make certain they were alone, then pointed at the box, left on the floor. Trevor picked it up and found a letter taped inside its cover. He tore it away and began to open it.

Just then, he heard his mother calling his name from down

the hall. Something made him want to keep the box he'd found a secret, so he put it back into its hiding place. Then he looked up at the new boy, who shook his head and backed away, the darkness of the hall consuming him. When Trevor went out to find him, he saw only his mother and grandmother. His mother had a flashlight. Quickly, Trevor shoved the letter into the pocket of his jeans. He had a feeling he didn't want the grownups to know about it, although he could never have explained why.

"Trevor, what are you doing up here?" Grace asked.

"Just exploring," Trevor said. He looked back over his shoulder. "I met another kid, but he took off."

"Another kid?" Veronica echoed. "You must be mistaken, Trevor dear. There are no other children in this house."

"But I saw . . ."

He cut himself off. Even in the pale beam offered by the flashlight, he could make out the doubtful smile on his grandmother's face.

"It's dark up here," Veronica said, "and full of shadows. You must have imagined seeing someone."

Trevor was about to say he'd heard him speak too, but changed his mind. Like the letter, he thought it was best not to reveal too much to the adults. At least, not until he knew what was going on. Maybe the boy was hiding up here. He *did* seem like he was scared. Trevor wouldn't want to rat on him and get him in trouble.

"I guess so," he said at last.

"Well, come on," Grace said. "This is no place for you. There's nothing to do or see in here, is there?"

"Not much," Trevor agreed.

"We've had this wing cut off for years," Veronica told them as they walked down the hall. "Long ago, there were a lot more people living here, and my parents often had guests. But Cole and I never had the time for social engagements. The company kept us too busy."

She pushed open a door and they entered a brighter hallway, the one leading to the children's bedrooms.

"I'll say good night now," Veronica said. "If you need

me, Grace, I'll be in my office. We have an idea for a new preteen bath line, and I want to go over the reports.''

"Good night, Mom," Grace said, and kissed her on the cheek.

Veronica turned to Trevor, but he backed away. No way was he going to kiss Nana, with her wrinkly skin and those funny lines that ran from her nose to the corner of her lips. Dad and Mom had said she looked just like his mother, but he couldn't see the resemblance at all. Mom was pretty, but Nana was . . . old.

Veronica, taking his gesture as shyness, laughed a little. "Good night, Trevor."

He nodded at her and hurried to his room.

The twins were sitting on the rug in Sarah's room, holding jars with holes poked into the top. Snippets of green-yellow light flashed within. Seth held up his jar and proudly announced, "I caught twelve lightening bugs!"

"I got ten," Sarah put in. "But one of mine is bigger so it's almost as much as Seth."

"You'll be letting them go now," Grace told them.

The twins moaned.

"We talked about this, guys," Grace said. "You don't want to be cruel to the little bugs, do you?"

Sarah's eyes widened. "Oh no, Mommy."

They got up and carried the jars to the window. Grace opened it and put the jars out on the ledge. Then she unscrewed each top and closed the window again. As the twins stood watching, the fireflies took to the sky one by one. They waved good-bye to them.

"See you again tomorrow," Seth promised.

Trevor shook his head. He had taken off his T-shirt and stood barechested in the doorway between the two rooms.

"Like you'd find the exact same lightening bugs again," he said.

"Maybe," Seth insisted.

Grace turned down Sarah's bed. She looked back over her shoulder and said, "Never mind the bugs now. Give your clothes to me and I'll throw them into the laundery chute.''

Sarah gave her a pair of pink shorts and a matching flowered top, then pulled a nightgown over her head.

"Do you think it'll rain again tomorrow?" she asked as she climbed into bed.

Grace covered her and replied, "I hope not. Nana says we can all have a riding lesson tomorrow, if we'd like."

Sarah's eyes went completely round, their lapis blue reflecting the light from her bedlamp.

"Horses! We're gonna ride horses?"

"Yep," Grace said with a smile and a nod.

"Oh boy," Seth said, delighted.

Grace gave Sarah a kiss and got up. She ruffled Seth's hair. "So get into bed, okay? You've got a big day coming up!"

One by one, the children said good night to her. As she walked from their rooms, a bundle of laundry in her arms, Trevor called to her. He thought about again mentioning the boy he'd seen. Maybe, without Nana there, he could convince his mother and ask her advice.

"Yes, Trevor?" Grace asked, turning.

"Uhm . . ."

But then again, she spent so much time talking to her new mother that she'd probably tell her what Trevor had found. And then the boy would be discovered, and it would be Trevor's fault.

"Uh, nothing," Trevor said. "I just wanted to say . . . it's pretty cool here, after all."

Grace gazed at him strangely for a moment, as if she knew he was keeping something back. Then she smiled and said, "I'm glad you're happy. Sleep tight."

"Don't let the bedbugs bite!" Seth called from his bed.

Trevor fell asleep to the sounds of his little brother giggling.

In her own room, Grace was having trouble concentrating on the novel she'd been trying to finish for the past three weeks. Between end-of-the-school-year activities and the excitement of finding her mother, Grace had hardly had time to pick it up. Tonight, although the house was quiet and this was one of her favorite authors, she found herself unable to absorb the words. Her mind kept turning back to Trevor. Twice tonight, he'd seemed ready to tell her something. He'd seemed so happy these past two days, playing basketball and enjoying the game room. Was he holding something inside? Were his smiles of delight only a show?

When she'd been sitting outside with her mother, the woman had suddenly looked up towards the windows on the left side of the house. Grace had followed her gaze, but the panes were dark and unrevealing. For the first time, she wondered how her mother could have known Trevor was up there. The boy didn't have a flashlight, so she couldn't have seen the beam through the windows.

"Maybe he came right up to one of them, and it caught her eye," she reasoned, putting the book on her nightstand.

She got up, and finding herself tired, headed to her private bathroom to get ready for bed. As she was washing her face, using the luxurious liquid cleanser her mother had given her, she recalled something else. When they were walking down the hall, she thought she'd seen Trevor shove something into his back pocket. What was he keeping hidden from her? She trusted him—he was a good boy, in spite of his shy ways— but she was curious. Had he found something interesting in that bedroom?

She dried her face and stood brushing her hair. Without her makeup, she looked younger than her twenty-nine years. Wearing the right clothes on her petite frame, she might have passed for a teenager.

What had happened to that teenager she saw on the road earlier today? She hoped the poor kid had found her way home again. Her mother was probably right, she was probably a vagrant strung out on drugs. But that didn't make Grace any less sympathetic. The bloodstain on her gown worried Grace, but since she wasn't doubled over in pain and was able to move fast enough to run when Andros appeared, she had to assume it wasn't as mortal a wound as it seemed. Maybe it wasn't even her blood.

"Now that's a comfortable thought," Grace whispered sarcastically, heading for her bed.

Grace was a day person, sometimes going to bed as early as nine P.M. Craig, his mind full of thoughts that didn't fade with the setting sun, would stay up in the living room and watch television until nearly midnight. Once in a while, though, he'd sneak into the bedroom and cuddle up next to her. Grace would sigh, half-asleep, until he kissed her into wakefulness and draw her closer to him in love.

Alone in the huge bed, Grace reached out instinctively, only to feel the cool sheets. She sighed, wishing Craig were there. Maybe, between the two of them, they could figure out what was going on with Trevor. Grace decided she'd have to handle the situation on her own, at least for the next few days. She'd keep a closer watch on her son, and if the opportunity arose to speak to him, she'd grab it.

Even though she'd shut off the air conditioner, the room was chilly tonight. She pulled the comforter up around her shoulders and burrowed deeper into her pillows.

A shuffling noise across the room made her open her eyes and listen. When it sounded again, she realized it was coming from inside the walls, near the closet. Seth had come in last night complaining about people walking behind the walls. Now Grace heard it for what it probably was—mice.

"Or rats," she said with a shudder.

She noticed the closet door was open, a gaping, dark cavern that could easily allow passage into her room. She got up and sped across the room to close it. Rats! It was a hideous thought. When she got back into bed, she pulled the covers tighter around herself, as if they were a protective barrier. As she did so, something fell to the floor with a thump.

At first, Grace thought it was the book. But then she clearly remembered putting it on the night table. Curious, she sat up and turned on the light. Then she crawled to the other side of the bed and looked down at the floor.

And began to scream in horror.

Within seconds, Veronica, Andros, and several other servants had run into the room. Grace, kneeling up on the bed, pointed to the floor. A look of complete disgust twisted her face into a hideous mask.

"Oh, Andros!" Veronica cried, gazing down at the floor.

Andros crouched down and poked a long finger at the desiccated remains of a rat. One of the maids ran from the room, retching.

"It was in my bed!" Grace wailed. "Someone put it in my bed!"

She realized she'd been thinking of rats just moments before finding the horrid thing.

"It looks as if it's been dead for weeks," Andros said. He looked over his shoulder, at the young man who stood behind him. "William, get me a shovel."

William nodded, his eyes wide and his nose wrinkled. He ran from the room.

"I—I don't want to sleep in here," Grace stammered.

"Of course not," Veronica said. "Come on, I'll have Mrs. Treetorn set up another room for you."

She put her arms around her daughter and led her from the room. Grace was shaking all over, her stomach doing flip-flops.

"It was in my bed," she said again, her voice full of sickened awe.

"I don't know how that happened," Veronica said. "I'm so sorry, Grace. Perhaps it was tangled up in the bedding when it was brought up from the cellar. Somehow, the maid didn't see it."

Grace nodded, too horrified to accept any other answer. Later, when she at last settled into her new bedroom, it was a long time before she could manage to fall asleep.

Late into the night, Trevor felt someone shaking him. He threw out his hand and moaned, "Seth, go away," but the shaking persisted until he sat up and rubbed sleep from his eyes. The boy he had seen in the old bedroom was standing there.

"Hi," Trevor whispered. "What're you doing?"

"Read the letter," the boy said.

"Huh?" Trevor asked, confused. "What letter. Tell me who you are, kid, will you?"

"Read the letter," was all the boy would say.

And then he vanished. Trevor stared for a few moments at the spot where he'd been standing. He hadn't walked away, hadn't ducked into a dark corner of the room. He'd just . . . *disappeared.*

"Wow," Trevor whispered, pushing his covers aside. He got up and walked around the room, still expecting to find the boy. If that was a dream, it was his most real one ever! And what did that kid mean, "Read the letter"?

He remembered the envelope he'd found in the cigar box and winced to realize it was in the jeans his mother had thrown down the laundery chute. Well, if the letter could explain things, he wanted to read it right away. Kids didn't disappear right before your eyes, unless they were . . .

"Ghosts," Trevor whispered.

His heart began to beat with excitement. Was the kid a ghost? Was this house haunted? If it was, this might turn out to be the most exciting summer he'd ever had! He wasn't afraid of the spirit, who wasn't even as big or as old as he was. If the kid wanted to hurt him, he could have done it already. Instead, he seemed to think it was very important that Trevor read some letter.

Trevor pulled on a robe and left the room, moving quietly through the darkened house. By this hour, everyone was sound asleep, and no one saw his passage down the stairs and through the hall leading to the cellar. He stood there for a few moments, gazing at the padlock. How was he going to get down there? How was he going to get the letter?

If there was a second staircase going upstairs, was there a second one leading down? Trevor thought the servants would find it a big pain to have to unlock the door every time they wanted to do a load of laundry. He started towards the kitchen, hoping to find an entrance to the cellar from there.

Someone screamed, a sound so full of terror that Trevor felt a chill wrap around his arms. It seemed to be coming from downstairs. He went back to the door and listened, and heard a woman cry out. Was someone trapped down there? Trevor knocked on the door, but no one answered. The screams stopped abruptly.

"Hey!" Trevor called, knocking again.

He reached up in a futile attempt to pull at the lock.

And a large hand clamped around his wrist. Trevor cried out, swinging around to press his back against the door. He found himself looking up at Andros.

"What are you doing here?" the old man demanded.

"I . . . I heard someone yelling downstairs," he said. "I think someone's locked in."

Andros looked at the door. Trevor had a creepy feeling he could see right through it, like one of the aliens in the sci-fi books he liked to read. But of course, that was ridiculous.

"Perhaps one of the maids locked herself in," Andros suggested. He let go of the boy. "Go back to bed now. I'll take care of it."

Not wanting to be near the creepy old servant any longer than necessary, Trevor bolted. By the time he crawled under the covers, he was shaking all over. He didn't know which was scarier: Andros, the screaming woman, or the boy who had vanished before his eyes.

EIGHT

▼

Knowing her neighbor would be on her way to work by 8:30, Grace called her first thing the next morning.

"Grace!" Paula cried. "I'm surprised to hear from you. How are things going down there?"

"It's been . . . interesting," Grace said, stopping short of the word "strange."

"Interesting? I'll bet," Paula said. "I can't imagine anything more exciting than finding my long-lost mother, and having it turn out she's a millionaire. So, what are you doing?"

"Catching up, mostly," Grace said. "There's a lot of history here for me to learn, and I think it's going to take forever."

She heard Paula laugh on the other end. "With your sense of curiosity, Grace, I'm surprised you haven't gone off to the library to look up old magazine and newspaper articles."

"Newspaper articles?" Grace echoed.

"Well, wouldn't you think someone who's the CEO of a

big company like Windsborough would have things written about her?''

"I guess you're right," she said. "It would be interesting to trace the company's history. And maybe I'll learn a little about my family too. So far, I've only met my mother and sister. I've wondered who else there might be."

"Veronica didn't mention anyone?"

"Not yet," Grace said, "but then, I've only been here a few days."

A few days in which you found a rat in your bed and saw a girl who vanished into thin air . . .

She saw no reason to mention these strange occurrences to Paula.

"Oh, before I forget," Grace said, deftly changing the subject. "Could you have my mail forwarded to this address?"

"It sounds like you plan to be there awhile," Paula replied.

"Paula, we're probably not coming back to Tulip Tree," Grace said. "Craig has a new job in Bryce City!"

"Oh, Grace, that's wonderful!" Paula cried. "I knew he'd get it—he's so talented."

There was a pause.

"We'll all miss you here, you know," Paula added, her tone a little more somber.

"Indiana isn't a big state," Grace said. "We can meet at some halfway point."

"That's a promise," Paula said.

The two women chatted until Paula announced her carpool was honking outside, and with promises to call soon, they hung up. Grace kept her hand on the receiver for a few moments, sighing. She really would miss her friends. But, she decided, right now there were other things to consider.

Grace dressed in khaki shorts and a matching sleeveless top. After cinching a brown belt around her waist, she headed down for breakfast. Although her thoughts were for Trevor as she approached the dining room, her concerns were immediately pushed aside when she saw her daughter. Sarah sat with one flushed cheek pressed into the heel of her palm, her elbow up on the pale peach tablecloth. Her full lips were curled in a pout, and her eyes had a glazed-over, sleepy quality. Grace went to kneel beside her and put a hand on her forehead. It felt cool.

"What's the matter, honey?" she asked. "Don't you feel well?"

Sarah turned and buried her face in Grace's neck. She smelled faintly of flowers, probably from one of the cakes of fancy soap her grandmother had given her.

"I'm tired, Mommy," she said.

"Didn't you sleep well last night?" Grace asked, stroking the long, auburn hair that rippled over her slight shoulders. A mother-alarm sounded within her, reminding her that Sarah *never* had trouble sleeping.

"They woke me up," Sarah said.

"Who?"

"I dunno," Sarah said, pulling away. "Can I have some orange juice?"

Immediately, a maid who had been standing near a buffet came to fulfill the request. Like someone serving a princess, Grace thought.

"Sarah, who woke you up?" Grace asked again.

"I don't remember," Sarah said. "But they took me to this room and put me on a cold, cold bed. And they stuck me with a sharp thing!"

A chill tiptoed up Grace's spine. What a bizarre thing for a child to say!

"Sarah, I think you had a terrible nightmare," Grace insisted, more for herself than for the child. She hated to think of her precious baby being hurt while she slept soundly!

Sarah shook her head. "Nope. It was real. They stuck me and took blood."

Grace pulled out the child's arms, telling herself all the while she was being ridiculous. Maybe Sarah was thinking of her last doctor's visit, when they'd drawn a blood sample as part of her school-year checkup. Even though that was last summer, something might have made it creep to the surface of Sarah's mind.

Still, she checked over her daughter's arms. Not a mark on

them, she realized as her shoulders dropped a half inch with relief.

And what had she expected to find, she asked herself?

"I heard a—" Trevor started to say, then cut himself off.

"Heard what, Trevor?" Grace encouraged.

Trevor looked down at the scrambled eggs in his plate. "Uhm . . . I heard Sarah crying. I guess she did have a nightmare."

"I didn't hear anything at all," Seth said around a mouthful of bacon.

"You wouldn't hear a bomb drop next to your head," Trevor insisted.

Grace gazed at her older son for a few moments. She had distinctly heard him say "*I heard a*" before. A what? What had he stopped himself from revealing?

Any chance to pursue the matter was cut off as Veronica floated into the room, her multicolored chiffon dress like a palette of watercolors around her. Her eyes were bright, her hair perfectly coiffed. She looked even more beautiful today than ever before, Grace noted with a fond smile. Younger, somehow . . .

Veronica set four bright red boxes on the table. Two were rather large, and two were thick. Grace recognized them as boot boxes, and furrowed her brows with curiosity.

"What's all this?" she said with a laugh.

"I had ordered these before your arrival," Veronica said. "And I've been aching for the right moment to give them to you. Since you plan to go riding today, I decided that now was the time."

She handed each of the larger boxes to the twins, and the boot boxes went to Grace and Trevor. Seth ripped his box open and frowned as he pulled clothes out. It was clear he'd expected some kind of toy. But Sarah squealed with delight, popping a little cap onto her head.

"A riding habit!" she cried. "Just like a rich kid! Wow!"

"What's a riding habit?" Seth wanted to know.

"Something you wear especially when you're on a horse,"

Veronica said. "Why don't you take those upstairs and try them on?"

Grace turned and watched the twins carry the boxes from the room. Sarah was suddenly so bright-eyed and enthusiastic that she allowed herself to dismiss her worries. It had only been a bad dream last night, not some horrible torture session. She was a little annoyed with herself for even thinking such a thing. Who around here would want to hurt her child?

"Grace?"

Grace started at the sound of her name. She smiled at her mother and opened her box to reveal an exquisite pair of boots. Their soft black leather, intricately embossed with an equestrian design, told her they were expensive long before she saw the designer name stamped into a metal plate that curled around the heel.

"Oh, Mom," she whispered. "I've never seen anything so beautiful."

"I would have bought you a habit too," Veronica said, "but I thought you'd want to pick one out for yourself. I don't know your tastes very well."

She turned. "And as for you, Trevor dear, I thought you'd feel more comfortable riding in your own jeans."

Trevor had put on his own boots, plainer than Grace's but no less expensive-looking. He was tromping around the floor, staring down at them.

"Cool," he said.

"I think that's a thank-you," Grace offered.

Veronica laughed. "Well, I'll tell David, our stable manager, to expect you in about an hour."

Moments later, the twins tumbled into the room adorable in matching black-and-white outfits. Sarah's had a ruffled collar, which she stood tugging at until her mother called her over to adjust it.

"Aren't you two a darling pair?" Veronica said. "I knew the moment I saw these that you'd look wonderful in them."

"Do I get one of those stick things?" Seth asked.

"A riding crop?" Veronica asked, smoothing back a wayward lock of his auburn hair. "Maybe later. My horses are very gentle, and you won't really need one."

Grace realized she was glad to hear that. She'd never been on a horse, and as the new boots brought the reality of this new venture to mind, she knew she'd been a little nervous. She didn't really like the idea of sitting on the back of a huge beast that could easily throw her, kick her, bite her at the slightest whim.

Still, when the children eagerly called her to come with them to the stables an hour later, she gamely went along. It would be nice to do something interesting for a little while instead of dwelling on weird teenage girls and little boys who seemed to have secrets. And since they only had another day or two to stay here, why not enjoy it like a rich person would? What could be more genteel than equestrian pursuits?

Grace was surprised to see the young man who approached her. If she was twenty-nine, he was barely out of his teens. His hair was almost the same golden-brown as the dirt in the paddock, an unruly mop of waves tousled by the summer wind. He was wearing a green, short-sleeved Henley shirt, one corner escaping from the tight waistline of his jeans. His long, thin legs carried him swiftly to the group. When he got closer, Grace saw that his eyes were large and brown, almost as soulful as a horse's eyes. His freckled cheeks, round and soft as if holding on to the last remains of boyhood, pushed up into little mounds as his smile spread them apart.

"Hi, I'm David," he said. "Mrs. Chadman told me you'd be coming today."

Grace noted he didn't mention a last name, but she supposed he thought it was unnecessary. Andros had never given his surname either. Maybe it was just a habit of this estate's servants.

She shook David's hand. His grip was firm, the grip of someone used to having control over reins. A little bit of her nervousness was assuaged as she felt his confidence.

"I'm Grace Matheson," she introduced herself, and then thought it was probably unnecessary. David had said her mother had mentioned them. "These are my children, Trevor, Seth, and Sarah."

Seth got right to the point, saying, "Where are the horses?"

"Right this way," David said with a laugh.

He led them around the back of the stable, where a half-dozen beautiful animals stood with their tails flicking lazily at flies. One of them trotted over to the fence, curious. Grace's mouth dropped open at the size of the beast, and she took a step back. David reached for the horse's forelock and rubbed it hard.

"This is Magellan," he said. "He's always looking for food, which might explain why he's grown so big."

Grace swallowed, hard. "Uhm . . . you don't expect any of us to get on him, do you?"

"Oh no," David said, his golden-brown hair whipping back and forth as he shook his head. "Mag won't let anyone but me ride him."

"I think he's great," Trevor said.

Sarah was crouching down to peer between the rails of the fence. She pointed.

"Those two horses look exactly alike," she said. "They both have a white spot on their sides."

"They're sisters," David said. He called to them, and the twin horses came to him. "This is Sunshine, and this is Starbeam. They're a pair of Morgans. I've picked them out for you little kids to use."

"I have to ride a girl horse?" Seth asked, wrinkling his nose.

"Sunshine's the best of all my horses," David told him.

Grace guessed he was just saying that to appease the little boy. She was beginning to like him, especially his obvious rapport with children.

"Okay," Seth relented.

"What about me?" Trevor asked.

"Come on inside," David said, opening the paddock gate.

The twins ran in without hesitation, each going to a Morgan to make a fuss over it. David led Trevor to another horse, a spotted one that Grace recognized as an Appaloosa. She stayed behind with the twins, still fearful one of the horses might hurt them. They seemed playful enough, indulging the children's pats and pets, but Grace didn't want to take any chances.

"Mom, look at me!" Trevor called.

Grace turned from the twins and couldn't help a smile of surprise when she saw that Trevor had already mounted the horse.

"David helped me up," he said. "My horse's name is Caesar. Isn't he the best?"

"The best," Grace repeated doubtfully. Caesar looked awfully big.

"He sits like a born rider," David said. "Did he ever have lessons?"

At forty dollars per half hour? Grace thought. Aloud, she said, "No, never."

"Well, he's a natural," David said. "Now, for your horse."

Grace was somewhat relieved to see that she'd been given a Morgan herself, a horse with patches of gray that said it was probably the oldest of the group. Old and slow, she hoped.

"Champagne is a sweetheart," David said. "She's the most tame of our horses. Mrs. Chadman rides her, so she likes to have a woman on her back. I never mount her myself, and she probably wouldn't tolerate the kids. But she'll definitely like you."

Grace tilted her head, eyeing the horse doubtfully. It snuffled and moved closer to her, poking at her hand as if in search of something.

"Oh, Mommy," Sarah said, "we should have brought some carrots or sugar."

"Champagne likes peppermint drops," David said.

The children laughed at the idea of a horse that ate candy.

"Let's get you up now," David said. "It's time to begin our lesson."

In spite of herself, Grace found that sitting on a horse was enjoyable. As David had promised, Champagne was sweet. In fact, she was so easygoing that Grace found herself having to encourage her to move much. The twins squealed with delight as David led them. Trevor, after only a few instructions, was already trotting around the rim of the paddock. Grace, although concentrating on her own horse, was glad to see he'd found something to make him happy. Maybe her thoughts that he'd had something to hide were unfounded.

They took a break to have a picnic lunch on the grass. Mrs. Treetorn had brought out a basket of fried chicken, devilled eggs, sliced tomatoes, and lemonade. Grace spread the provided blue-and-white check blanket on the lawn, and the children sat with her to eat. She'd invited David, but he told her he'had some chores to catch up with.

"David's nice," Sarah said.

Everyone agreed. He was certainly the most personable of the servants Grace had met. The others either ignored her or only spoke when necessary. Andros was unfriendly, even a little creepy, while Mrs. Treetorn seemed to be a bit vague in the head. Of all the servants, David seemed to be the only one she'd want to befriend. Maybe it was because he was young?

It occurred to her that all the other servants were pushing their late forties or better. Why had her mother hired such a young man to take care of her horses?

There were so many things to learn about this estate, to learn about her family. But they'd have to wait until later, she decided as the children left the picnic to return to the paddock. They begged David for a ride, but Grace intervened.

"Not right after you ate," she said. "Why don't you go inside and use the game room? You need to get out of the heat."

"Oh, Mom," Trevor moaned.

"No, she's right," David said. "The horses can bounce you up and down pretty good. I wouldn't want any of you to lose your lunch."

"Gross," Seth said.

"Can we ride a little later?" Sarah asked.

"Sure," David promised. "Come back in half an hour."

The children ran back to the house, Seth trying to challenge Trevor to a game of Parcheesi. Grace was about to follow him, but David called her back.

"Yes?" she asked.

David shifted from one Etonic sneaker to the other, biting his lip. The confident horseman was gone now, replaced by a very young, very unsure person.

"I . . . uh . . . just wanted to welcome you," he said finally. "We were all pretty excited to hear that Mrs. Chadman had another daughter. I mean . . . well, Amanda hasn't been much . . ."

He cut himself off as if embarrassed by his insinuations.

"I know," Grace said gently. "Did you know Amanda? Was she here when you came to work for my mother?"

"I hardly ever saw her," David said. "But sometimes, she'd sit under that big sycamore over there and watch me work with the horses. I tried to invite her over, but she never came."

He paused. Grace thought he might be wanting to tell her something, but was unsure if he should.

"David, was my sister always . . . different?"

"As long as I knew her," David said. "I've been working here for two years. Mrs. Treetorn said she was pretty much okay until she lost her baby, but everyone else says she was disturbed from the time she was little. There was a story that she fell down the cellar stairs and smashed her head."

Grace brought a hand to her mouth to hold back a cry of dismay. "Oh dear Lord. What a horrible thing to happen!"

David gazed across the meadow. "She told me something after she found you, Grace. She said she was afraid, and that she wanted you to go away."

"Just her disturbed mind talking," Grace replied. Memories of Amanda's strange phone call came back to her: *She'll kill you all!*

"I hope so," David said.

"What's that supposed to mean?"

"Nothing!" David cried. "Look, I've got a million things to do. You'll bring the kids back later, won't you? We can go on a ride through the woods."

Grace nodded without speaking, and stood watching as David hurried back to the stable. Did he put any store in Amanda's strange warning? If so, why?

She thought of the doll Amanda had left on her bedroom chair. Maybe Amanda was jealous of her. Maybe she wanted to frighten her away. Grace found herself clenching and unclenching her fists as she headed back inside the house. Amanda wasn't here now, but even if she was, she'd never come between Grace and her newly discovered mother!

Grace was sitting at the desk in her room, sketching faces in her drawing pad, when the children came to announce it was time to go riding. She wasn't sure she wanted to get on a horse this soon, but decided that Champagne had been gentle enough and gave in. She closed the drawing pad, put her pencil into one of the cubbies in the desk, and followed them downstairs.

David was waiting with the horses, his smile as broad as it had been earlier that day. There were no signs of the wary young man Grace had seen after the morning's lesson. If he were worried about anything, he certainly wasn't showing it. She decided that she wouldn't dwell on his strange words either. It was just too beautiful a day, and the children were too happy for anything to bring Grace down.

"I thought we'd head into the woods," David said. "There's a clear path that cuts through the trees and comes out at a small lake on the other side."

"It sounds beautiful," Grace said.

David helped the twins mount their horses, then turned to give Grace a hand. She felt a little silly, considering how easily Trevor leaped onto his horse's back. It was the natural athlete in him, she thought. He took after his father. Grace herself had never been very good at sports.

"Can I go first?" Seth asked. "I wanna go first!"

"All right," David said. "But you keep a slow pace, just like I showed you this morning."

"Aww, I wanted to race Trevor," Seth drawled.

"No way," Trevor said. "Caesar and I are gonna take our time, aren't we, fella?"

He patted the horse's neck affectionately. Grace smiled, surprised how easily Trevor took to the animal. They'd never been allowed to have pets in their Tulip Tree apartment, but maybe she could get him something when they moved . . .

Seth started down the path, with Sarah following. David was third, to keep an eye on the younger children. Grace almost considered letting Trevor follow behind her, since he seemed so much more comfortable. But then she thought she ought to be watching him anyway, as a mother should, and took the rear.

The children were so delighted at the idea of riding horses that none of them spoke. Grace found herself turning her face up to the warm sun, breathing deeply to take in the smells of grass and flowers. That odd combination of roses, mint, and vinegar hit her, but the wind changed direction almost immediately. She was glad of that—the vinegar smell ruined the otherwise glorious summer aroma.

And there were gentle noises, the breeze carrying the melodies of birds and insects. Grace thought of a trick she'd learned once, that you could guess the temperature by counting a cricket's chirps. But the chirps were so fast and incessant that she could only think it was very, very hot. The idea of sticking her feet in a cool lake seemed very inviting.

They reached the woods. Almost at once, the temperature seemed to drop ten degrees. The trees offered a natural canopy against the sun, and the waving branches stirred the breeze like Mother Nature's own fans. She could still hear the crickets and birds, but now there was another noise. She tilted her head to hear it more clearly. It sounded like someone crying . . .

"David, do you hear that?"

But she realized that, somehow, the others had gotten ahead of her. She flicked her horse's reins a little, but Champagne was as caught up in the lazy July heat as she had been, and quickened her pace only marginally. Grace rolled her eyes towards the treetops and snapped the reins a little harder. She didn't know what she'd been so worried about—Champagne was actually *too* easygoing.

The horse moved just a little faster. Grace looked at the group gaining distance ahead of her, then glanced into the trees. A flash of white caught her vision, only to disappear into the deeper foliage. Then she heard a sound that she recognized as the last, shuddering gasp of someone who's been crying a long time.

"Who's in there?" she called.

A squirrel chittered at her and scampered up a nearby tree, but no one else responded.

And then she heard the awful sound of a child's scream. She turned at the last moment to see Sarah's horse buck up. Her own cry of horror mixed with Sarah's scream as the little girl was thrown from the horse. Wanting to waste no time in getting to her, Grace dismounted, awkwardly, and ran to her daughter. David was already off his own horse and at Sarah's side when she knelt down beside her daughter.

Sarah lay staring up at the trees, wailing.

"What happened?" Grace demanded.

"I don't know," David said. "It was as if something . . . as if something spooked her horse. Starbeam just reared up." He shook his head in wonder. "She's never done that before."

Grace was hardly hearing him. She was checking every inch of her daughter, grateful the little girl's fall had been broken by a cluster of bushes. She found a nasty cut on Sarah's arm. David, seeing it himself, immediately pulled a handkerchief from his pocket and wrapped the wound.

"Is Sarah gonna be all right?" Seth asked.

"Of course," Grace said breathlessly. "Sarah, can you move that arm?"

Sarah obliged, then wailed. "It stings!"

"It's the cut," David guessed. "Can you stand up, sweetie pie?"

Slowly, as if afraid to move, Sarah let the grownups help her to her feet.

"Well, she seems okay," David said. "But I'll take her back to the house on my horse."

Grace glanced at Starbeam, who was gnawing the bark of a tree as if nothing at all had happened. Then she looked back at Champagne, still a few dozen paces behind them.

"I think I'll run back," she said.

"What're we supposed to do?" Trevor asked.

Grace saw that he'd twined his thick fingers in his hair, and seemed ready to pull out a chunk of the chestnut locks. She braved a smile for him.

"You make sure Seth gets back okay, Trevor."

"I can get back okay!" Seth insisted.

"Not on that horse," Grace said, fearful the other child would be thrown.

"Sunshine didn't do anything," Seth replied. "She's a good horse."

David was looking perplexed as he helped Sarah into his own saddle.

"All my horses are good," he said. "I just don't understand what happened."

"Perhaps it was a wasp," Veronica suggested awhile later, as she stood with Grace in one of the downstairs bathrooms.

Sarah was sitting up on the counter, admiring the bandage on her arm and sucking a grape lollipop. She didn't seem any worse for the wear, Grace was glad to see. There were certainly no breaks or sprains, because Sarah had run into the house on her own power when David helped her off the horse.

"Could have been," Grace replied, recalling the strange crying she'd heard. She wondered if it had only been a bird of some kind, one that flew near the horse and scared it. Or spooked it, as David said. Funny choice of words, Grace thought. The flash of white she'd seen in the trees came to mind, like a brief vision of a ghost.

She shook the thought away and lifted Sarah from the counter.

"Can I go back outside?" Sarah asked as they walked out of the room.

Seth and Trevor were waiting there, and both looked relieved to see their sister was fine. Seth moved closer and put his arm around her shoulder, a gesture of twinly support.

"Don't you think you should take it easy, Sarah dear?" Veronica suggested, smiling fondly at the little girl.

"Nana's right," Grace said. "You had the wind knocked out of you pretty badly."

"I got all my wind back," Sarah replied.

"Still," Grace said, "I want you to take it easy. Maybe you could have a snack and watch a video."

Trevor stepped forward a little. "I'll put it in the VCR for them," he offered.

"Well, okay," Sarah relented. "But only if it isn't a movie with blood and guts."

"I saw that one about the pig," Seth said, leading his sister away.

The grownups watched the three children disappear down the hall. Seth was asking Sarah how it felt to fly through the air, and Sarah was milking the story for all it was worth.

"We should all bounce back so quickly," Veronica said.

"Tell me about it," Grace replied. "I'm still shaking inside, even though I know she's okay."

She turned to face her mother. "I think I'll go back into the woods, just to make sure nothing's there."

"What would be there?" Veronica asked with a frown that deepened the channels between her nose and the corners of her lips.

Grace paused. What was she going to say, that she'd seen a glimpse of white that looked like a ghost?

"I don't know," she admitted. "But it's for my own peace of mind. I'll be back in a little while."

Veronica followed her as far as the doorway. Standing on the front steps, she called after her daughter, "I could have Andros look!"

"It's okay," Grace said with a wave behind her.

By the time she got to the woods, she was telling herself she was being silly. What did she really expect to find? Maybe it had been a wasp that scared the horse, and maybe that white was only a bird of some kind. She wasn't at all surprised to find nothing but a broken bush when she reached the area where Sarah had been thrown. She finally chalked it up to a freak accident and turned to head for home.

Something caught her eye just then, a blob of peach and white that was inconsistent with the somber colors of the woodland floor. She moved closer to it and was surprised to find a filthy, old-fashioned baby doll half-hidden beneath a pile of damp leaves. She extricated the toy and stared at it in wonder.

Someone had put bandages all over it, leaving only the face and hands free. It was thickly wrapped like a mummy, some of the gauze rotting and old, some looking as if it had only been recently applied.

"I had to stop the bleeding," someone said. "I had to stop it before she took it all!"

Grace spun around and saw the young girl who had been on the roadway when she mailed her letter to Kitty. She was still wearing a nightgown, still stained bright red with blood.

"What do you mean?" she asked, moving towards her.

The girl looked terribly sad. "Get away from this place. Get away before she takes your children!"

She turned and bolted into the trees. Grace, still holding the doll, ran after her. But it was as if she'd vanished into thin air.

"Like a ghost," Grace whispered, her heart pounding.

Get out!

She heard the voice again, but it took her a moment to realize it was inside her own head. She couldn't move though, frozen in wonder at what she'd just seen. What could she make of a girl who seemed to appear and disappear at will, who always wore the same bloody nightgown? And the blood never turned brown with age, as if it was always fresh.

"Impossible," Grace told herself firmly.

And then, not wanting to be in the woods any longer, she turned and ran to the house.

NINE

▼

The children decided they weren't in the mood for a video. The ride had left them energized, and they looked for something active to do.

"We haven't tried the bowling game yet," Sarah suggested.

Trevor went to the miniature alley and flicked the switch. Tiny lights chased each other down the lanes, and the pinsetter whirred into action.

"Me first!" Seth cried.

"Sarah should go first," Trevor said. "It was her idea."

"No, Seth can go," Sarah relented, stepping aside to let her twin have the first ball.

They bowled a few frames, Seth accusing Trevor of cheating, Trevor insisting Seth was crazy. Why would he bother cheating at a baby game like this one?

"I can bowl a hundred game in a real lane," Trevor said with a touch of pride, "and besides, I don't cheat."

Sarah picked up the ball and rolled it towards the waiting pins. When she bowled a strike, she clapped her hands.

"All right, Sarah!" Trevor cried.

Seth, not to be outdone, picked up his ball and danced back and forth a little as he waited for the pinsetter to come down.

Nothing happened.

"It's jammed," Trevor said. "Wait a second."

He tried the switch, but the game remained frozen.

"Did I do that?" Sarah asked, worry rounding her blue eyes.

"No," Trevor said. He sighed. "I guess I'll have to find someone to fix it. You guys wait here, okay?"

He left the room to find of one of the servants. A maid was dusting book jackets in the library. When Trevor told her what he needed, she admitted she didn't know the first thing about bowling. Trevor couldn't find anyone else and decided to try Felix. He was pretty sure the chef would be in the kitchen.

As he passed one of the rooms, he heard voices behind the door. It sounded like Andros. Trevor paused, considering. Andros was weird, but he did seem to run things around here. If anyone would know how to make the pinsetter work, it would be the butler.

With his thoughts on his goal, and not on his manners, Trevor barged into the room without knocking.

And stopped short with a gasp.

Nana was standing with Andros, one hand on his shoulder, the other at his waist. It was obvious they'd been kissing and had broken apart when the door opened. Trevor was disgusted to see that Andros was holding the washcloth his mother had used to clean Sarah's wound. He had it pressed to his lips. Mixed with the water from the cloth, it seemed to the ten-year-old that a lot of blood was dripping down the tall man's chin.

"Oh gross!" Trevor cried. "What the hell are you guys doing?"

"Don't say 'hell,' Trevor dear," Veronica said, smiling sweetly. "We aren't doing anything at all."

"I'm telling my mother!" Trevor said, and turned to run.

He saw Andros lunge at him from the corner of his eye, but he dodged the man's grasp and bolted from the room. His stomach was in knots, and he felt shaky all over. They were drinking Sarah's blood! Why would they do that?

He reached the foyer just as his mother came in, carrying something that looked like a baby mummy. But Trevor hardly gave it a glance. He tugged at his mother's blouse sleeve and tried to tell her what he'd seen.

"Mom! Andros was drinking Sarah's blood!" he cried, agitated.

"Huh?" His mother blinked as if she was coming out of a trance.

"I said, Andros was drinking Sarah's blood," Trevor repeated.

"Trevor, that's ridiculous," Grace replied.

"I saw him!" Trevor insisted. "I mean, he was sucking the blood from that washcloth you used. And he was kissing Nana! It was disgusting!"

"Oh, Trevor . . ."

"Is something wrong?"

Both mother and son turned to see Veronica coming down the hall. Her arms were laden with flowers, which she laid down on the foyer table and began to arrange, in a Waterford crystal vase. She smiled at them.

"What's going on?"

Trevor squinted his eyes. "You know what. I saw you with Andros. You were kissing, and then Andros was sucking that bloody washcloth."

"Me and Andros?" Veronica laughed out loud. "Whatever you think you saw, the sun must have gotten in your eyes and made them play tricks on you. I've been out in the garden."

She showed him a daisy as if to confirm this.

"No, you weren't," Trevor said softly, defiantly.

"Trevor, please," Grace said, sounding impatient. "Mom, I need to talk to you."

Trevor combed his fingers through his hair. "And I need to talk to you!"

The sound of pounding feet filled the front hall, and Seth came to pull on Trevor's arm.

"Come on back, Trev," he urged. "Andros fixed the pinsetter for us, and it works real good!"

Trevor looked at him as if he was crazy. How could this be? Andros was on the other side of the house, and there was no way he couldn't have gone past without being seen. But then, the tall servant came from the hall leading to the game room, barely giving Trevor a second glance.

Then what, Trevor wondered with bewilderment, had he seen in that room near the kitchen?

He turned to talk to his mother, to make her help him understand, but she was already walking away with his grandmother. He sighed. He knew he wasn't imagining things, but he couldn't explain what had just happened.

"Trev-*or*!" Seth whined.

"Okay, okay," Trevor said, following his little brother. Silently, he decided there was something weird about his grandmother. And he wouldn't let himself trust her again.

In the parlor, Grace held the bandaged doll out for her mother to see. A look of sadness came over Veronica's face, and she sank wearily into the pale yellow damask cushions of the couch. She brought one of the throw pillows into her lap and absently fingered the embroidery.

"Do you remember how I told you Amanda lost a baby years ago?"

Grace nodded. "To a blood disease. Did she do this?"

"She saw the doll as her baby," Veronica explained. "She thought that, by bandaging it that way, she could stop the bleeding. But when the reality of her loss finally hit her, she buried the doll in the woods."

Veronica glanced over at the toy, still in Grace's hands. "I suppose, after all these years, animals and the weather helped bring it up again."

Grace looked down at the doll, trying to form her next words. She wanted to ask about the girl she'd seen. She was convinced now that the young girl she'd seen was a spirit. There was no other explanation. She thought the girl was trying to tell her something, but what?

She wanted to ask her mother if there were any family legends, any stories of revenants haunting the estate. But what was she going to do? Say, "Mom, I wonder if this house is haunted"? She'd only been here a few days, and Veronica hardly knew her, really. She didn't want to give her the wrong impression.

But she wouldn't have the chance to ask her strange question that afternoon. She realized suddenly that Veronica was crying. Great tears coursed down from her beautiful lapis eyes, one of them dripping onto the powder blue charmeuse pillow.

"Mom?" she said softly.

"I had such hopes for Amanda," Veronica choked. "She was such a pretty little girl, so darling. But she started changing when she was about eleven, when the first signs of her mental illness began to surface."

"Oh dear," Grace breathed. What kind of nightmare had her mother lived, to see her sister descend into madness?

She reached out and took the woman's hand. It felt small, almost birdlike, in hers.

Veronica smiled at her, her eyes shining. "What a miracle I found you, Grace!"

Grace, sensing how very sad Veronica's life had been, hugged her mother and vowed to be the daughter that Amanda could never be. No one would tear her away from this dear, loving woman!

After bowling a few half-hearted frames, Trevor left the game to the twins and went upstairs to his room. He intended to write down everything that had happened in the past few days, hoping the list might help him understand. When he got into his room, he saw his playclothes, freshly washed, folded neatly on top of his dresser. Immediately, he recalled the letter.

He was relieved, and a little bit surprised, to see it sitting on top of the clothes pile. Whoever had done the wash hadn't turned it over to Nana. Well, he thought, maybe they didn't think it was important. There was no name on the yellowed paper, no indication it belonged to this household.

Trevor picked it up and carried it to his bed, where he flung himself stomach-down on the thick comforter. He tore open the envelope and pulled out a letter that had been written al-most sixty years earlier.

"My mother and father have changed so much since their trip to the South Seas. Mother seems impatient with me, and I see disappointment in her eyes. I know she's ashamed of me, all weak and sick that I am. I'm growing more afraid of her."

The name was smudged, perhaps from a tear dropped there long ago, but Trevor could just make it out: *"Jeffrey."* Who was he, Trevor wondered. who was meant to read the letter, but never received it? And what kind of mother made her own son afraid of her? She must have been a monster!

"Like Veronica," Trevor mumbled darkly.

He heard knocking at the door, and his mother poked her head inside.

"Trevor, didn't you hear me calling you?" she asked. "It's time for dinner."

Trevor picked up the Star Trek novel that was lying open on his bed and tucked the letter between its pages. If his mother had seen him, she gave no indication. He gazed at her as he rolled off the bed, expecting her to say something about the things he'd said that afternoon. But she was blinking, star-ing down the hallway as if she had something on her mind.

"Are you okay, Mom?" Trevor asked.

"Fine," Grace insisted, a little abruptly. She smiled at him. "I don't know about you, but I'm starved."

Trevor was pretty certain things were not fine, but he knew his mother wouldn't talk to him if she had any problems. Why would she? He was only ten. If she really wanted someone to talk to, she could call Dad.

An idea came to him.

"Mom, when are we going home?"

Grace gave her head a little shake, like a person coming out of a dream.

"I don't really know, Trevor," she said. "I'm expecting a call from your father tonight."

"I hope it's soon," Trevor said, meaning it. "I miss Tulip Tree."

"So do I," Grace admitted. "But we haven't been here very

long. I'd like to stay for a few more days, if we can."

Trevor was about to say he wished they wouldn't stay, but held it to himself. Just a few more days—what could possibly go wrong in that time?

As promised, Craig called around eight P.M. Grace was sitting in the parlor perusing a doll magazine she'd brought with her on the trip. The children were in their rooms, enjoying quiet time. Veronica had said good night early, complaining of a headache. It was so quiet that Grace started when the phone rang. Expecting it to be Craig, she didn't wait for one of the servants to answer an extension. Instead, she picked up and said, "Hello."

"Don't they have people there to do that?" Craig asked.

Grace smiled broadly, her magazine falling to the floor as she sat up. "Hi, honey!"

"You sound great," Craig said, his loving tones evident even over the phone lines.

"I'm happy to hear your voice," Grace said. She thought about telling him what had happened that day, but held it back for the moment. There was no point in worrying him, especially since things seemed to be okay now. And what would he think, if she mentioned that she'd seen a ghost?

"Grace?"

She realized her thoughts had taken up her attention for a long time. "Sorry, just distracted. I'm a little tired. We went horseback riding today."

She could hear his snicker.

"You? On a horse?"

"More like the old gray mare," Grace said. "She was as docile as a kitten, hardly moved."

"How did the kids do?"

"Oh, the twins were adorable," Grace said. "Mom bought them matching riding habits. She gave boots to Trevor and me."

"Yeah?"

There was a hesitation in Craig's voice, and Grace sensed at once he felt uncomfortable hearing that a virtual stranger had showered his family with gifts he probably couldn't afford.

"Well, you should have seen Trevor ride," Grace said quickly, giving him something else to think about. "David—that's the stable manager—says he's a natural."

"So maybe we should buy him a horse."

Now Grace laughed, appreciating Craig's sarcasm.

"He can borrow this one any time," she said. She took a breath and got to more serious matters. "Craig, have you found a new place for us yet?"

"I'm in touch with a real estate agent," he said. "There are a few things. When I narrow them down to a handful, I'll call you here to see them."

Grace frowned. "Call me there? I thought I'd see you in a day or two. It sounds as if it's going to be longer."

"I'm afraid so," Craig said with a sigh. "Grace, they've asked me to go through a training program, effective immediately. They've even set me up in a paid apartment. It's too small for me, let alone five of us."

"Oh, Craig," Grace said, disappointed to know they wouldn't be together soon.

"I know, Gracie," Craig said gently. "I miss you so much. But this is part of the deal, and we can't look a gift horse in the mouth. You know how long I've been looking for steady work."

Grace closed her eyes and nodded in agreement, as if he could see her.

"They say it'll only be a few days," Craig promised. "But there's a seminar on Saturday, so that throws off the weekend."

"The kids'll be disappointed," Grace said.

"Tell them I'll drive down the very moment I can," Craig said. "And tell them how much I miss them and love them."

"They love you right back," Grace said. "Just like me."

They talked for a while longer, and when she hung up Grace was feeling a little melancholy. She didn't really understand it. She'd been away from Craig for longer periods than this when she went to her doll shows. But somehow, she missed him now more than ever.

When she went upstairs to say good night to the children, she told them what their father had said. The twins were so tired after such a long day that they hardly responded. Sarah was sound asleep even before Grace finished tucking her in, and Seth was nearly off himself.

But Trevor was sitting up in bed, reading his book by the bedside lamp. He frowned at her.

"I heard," he said. "What's a training program?"

"Sort of like school," Grace explained, opening his drawer and putting his clothes away. "You know, you could do this yourself, just like home."

"Okay, next time," Trevor said. "Mom, who goes to school on Saturday?"

Grace shrugged. "It's just the way they want to do it. Maybe they want to get him started as soon as possible and hope to gain a day by using the weekend."

"I get it," Trevor said with a nod. "Well, I sure hope he comes back soon. I really want to go home."

Grace sat on the edge of the bed. "Aren't you happy here? You seemed to like it at first, but . . ."

Trevor looked down at his lap, silent.

"Oh, I see," Grace said, nodding. "You've still got that strange incident in your mind. I know what happened now."

Trevor's head came up, his eyes wide with interest.

"Nana would have told you at dinner, if she'd been able to join us," Grace said. "But she told me what she'd learned a little while ago. That wasn't her in the room at all, or Andros. It was two of the servants. One had cut his lip, and the other was helping him."

"But it was Sarah's washcloth," Trevor said.

"Trevor, a rich house like this would have dozens of matching washcloths," Grace insisted.

Trevor opened his mouth. Grace could tell he wanted to say something, perhaps argue with her, but he clamped it shut again and said nothing. She decided there was no point in pursuing the matter. The idea of her mother with that old man was ludicrous, and the idea that Andros was drinking Sarah's blood even more so!

She got up and said, "You can read for another half hour, and then lights out."

She turned to walk from the room, not kissing him good night. He'd made it clear months earlier that he thought this was baby stuff, and she was used to it. But when she reached the door, he called softly, "Mom?"

Grace turned and saw Trevor's arms opened wide. She went to him with a smile and hugged him.

"Good night, sweetheart."

"Night, Mom."

Grace left the room.

Trevor had trouble concentrating on the adventures of Captain Picard and his crew, and he put the book aside after only a few paragraphs. So, Veronica had convinced his mother nothing happened. Another lie! He had no doubt who he'd seen in that room, but how to convince his mother?

He fell asleep promising himself he'd look for evidence that Nana and Andros had something evil on their minds.

He was dreaming about Romulans when someone shook him awake. Groggily, he turned to see the ghost boy, Jeffrey. All remains of the dream faded, and he sat up abruptly.

"Hi," he said. "Are you Jeffrey?"

The boy nodded. "I came to warn you. Don't let your mother believe in Veronica."

"Why?" Trevor asked.

"She kills people," Jeffrey said simply.

"Is she a kind of vampire?" Trevor asked. "Is that why she sucks blood? And is Andros a vampire too?"

Jeffrey shook his head. "I don't know what she is. But she kills. That's how she'll stay alive forever. She kills."

He vanished without another word, leaving an invisible, cold mist behind. Trevor tucked himself deeper into the covers, staring at the empty space beside his bed, where the boy had been only moments before. He was shaking all over, wishing he knew what to do.

Grace was awake deep into the night, worrying about Trevor, worrying about her mother, worrying that Craig would find a suitable place to live. She tossed and turned in the big bed wishing Craig was there to hold her and reassure her, maybe even to joke with her about everything.

Sleep claimed her at last. She floated into a dream, where she stood on the banks of a river watching the twins drifting away in a little rowboat. Someone dressed in a black, hooded robe was rowing it.

Don't go with him. Don't go with him.

She called to the children, but they didn't hear her. Sarah turned and waved, giggling.

It'll sink! The boat will sink, and you'll all drown in blood. She was sucking blood from that washcloth, Mom . . . That's how they get blood from babys . . .

SARAH? SETH?

"Mommy?"

The tiny, frightened voice didn't come from the dream Sarah's mouth, but from somewhere behind Grace. She turned to see Trevor, running bloody fingers through his hair, an expression of disappointment on his face.

Trevor, you're getting all messy . . .

"MOMMY!"

Grace's eyes snapped open, the dream abruptly ended. She saw the silhouette of a child at her bedside and reached to turn on her light.

"Sarah? What're you doing up, sweetie?"

Sarah's eyes were misted over, her lower lip jutted in a pout. The light reflected off the tears on her flushed cheeks.

"They took me to that room, Mommy," Sarah said in a tiny voice. "They made me lie in that cold bed."

"Oh, baby," Grace said, and folded a triangle into the corner of her blanket. "You climb right in here."

Sarah scrambled up into the big bed and pressed herself

close to her mother. Grace was surprised at how cold she felt, but reasoned it was because she'd walked across the hall without her robe or slippers.

"They stuck my arm, Mommy," Sarah went on. "It hurt."

"Who did that?" Grace asked, wondering what Sarah had been dreaming about. She was almost tempted to check the little girl's arm, but finally decided she'd find nothing. Hadn't she looked carefully the other morning after Sarah had described her dream? Still, it was the second time she'd mentioned a cold room and someone sticking her with a needle. Was there some significance to this nightmare, something she should be aware of?

But Sarah had snuggled deep into the fluffy down pillow and was already sound asleep. Grace reached and snapped off the light. Then she drew the covers protectively over her daughter, and, with her arm curved around the child's small frame, she fell asleep herself.

TEN

▼

A soft breeze tickled Grace awake the next morning, and she opened her eyes to see Mrs. Treetorn tying back her curtains. The plump housekeeper gave her a smile.

"Thought you might like to have your windows open, Mrs. Matheson," she said as she hooked the chiffon drapes with ornate gold-and-ivory tiebacks. "There's a wonderful breeze this morning. The weather seems so much nicer than the past few days."

Grace looked past her to the cloudless blue sky. Then she turned to find Sarah and saw she was gone. Mrs. Treetorn seemed to understand, because she said:

"Oh, the little girl went down to breakfast already. I'm afraid I woke her up when I brought your linens in this morning."

"I didn't hear you at all," Grace said. She yawned. "I must have been sound asleep."

"And no wonder, after such a busy day yesterday," the housekeeper said. She frowned. "I must say, though, that

Sarah didn't seem quite her cheerful self this morning. I hope she isn't sick.''

Grace thought back to the previous night and Sarah's strange dream. She shook her head.

"Just a nightmare," she replied, although part of her worried too. Then again, if Sarah had been ill she would have stayed here, Grace was certain.

"Poor dear."

Mrs. Treetorn gazed at her for a moment, her slight smile giving only a little substance to the vapid expression on her face. Grace looked back at her, wondering if she wanted to say something. But after a moment, the housekeeper's expression brightened to its normal cheerfulness. Without speaking, she only nodded once and left.

"I wonder if 'airhead' applies to someone that age," Grace whispered, folding back her covers and getting up.

She berated herself for the unkind remark. Mrs. Treetorn seemed nice enough, even if she was a little vague in the head.

"Mrs. Treetorn is the least of my concerns," she said, opening her drawer to pull out her day's outfit.

She chose a pair of white shorts, a yellow-and-white striped polo shirt and a bright yellow vinyl belt. Something about the day's cheery weather made her go a step further, and she took the time to twist her hair into a chignon. Later, she thought she might pick some small flowers in the field outside and lace them through her hair. She looked at her image in the mirror and was pleased.

Then she started laughing.

"Flowers in my hair," she said out loud. "Is this the way rich women behave?"

Shaking her head at herself, vowing she'd never become a snob, she went downstairs to find the children, hoping they hadn't finished breakfast yet.

The aroma of cinnamon and apples, toast and coffee were so enticing that she could have found the dining room blindfolded. She was pleased to see the children were still eating. Sarah had dressed herself in a pretty pink romper, and Grace

noted she'd made an attempt to comb her hair back into a
ponytail. She looked a little pale, Grace thought, but seemed
to be eating heartily. Grace was satisfied to see it was oatmeal.
If Sarah were coming down with anything, it would do her
good to be filled with something healthy.

Seth, who had his shirt on inside-out, looked up from his
yellow Fiestaware bowl and waved his spoon.

"Felix makes the best hot cereal," he said. "It's got raisins
and nuts and all sorts of good stuff."

"I like the maple syrup best," Trevor put in. "It's real,
Mom, not that fake stuff from the grocery store."

"Good morning, guys," Grace said. "Breakfast sounds delicious. Seth, you have to turn your shirt around."

Seth looked down, then behind himself, as if he didn't understand. Grace laughed as Trevor rolled his eyes.

Her mother sat with her back to the French doors, sunlight
creating an aura around her meticulous hair like a halo. It was
nice to see Veronica had joined them. She wondered what the
children had been talking about with their Nana while she was
still sleeping.

"Hi, Mom," she said.

"Good morning, Grace dear," Veronica said with a smile.
She was wearing a green-and-white plaid, sleeveless dress. A
choker of huge, clear beads, like giant glass marbles, circled
her neck. Grace thought she looked like a fashion model,
glamorous and pulled-together as usual. She wondered if she'd
ever gain her mother's fashion finesse. Maybe flowers in her
hair wasn't such a silly idea, after all.

"Aren't you going to sit down?" Veronica asked.

"Not yet," Grace said, and thoughts of fashion flew away.
She went to Sarah and knelt down beside her. "How do you
feel today, honey?"

"I'm tired," Sarah pouted.

Grace reached up and felt the child's forehead. It was cool.
"Do you hurt anywhere?"

Sarah shook her head. Grace smiled softly, standing. She
fingered the auburn ponytail that curled down Sarah's back.

"I guess you'll be okay," she said. "You just had a bad night."

"Oh?" Veronica asked as Grace took her seat.

"Sarah had a nightmare," Grace said, as a maid came and served her coffee. "She came into my room."

"Well, I suppose the house is still a little unfamiliar," Veronica said, "especially at night."

Grace reached for the large tureen in the center of the table and spooned oatmeal into the gilt-edged bowl at her place.

"It's creepy at night," Seth said. "I keep hearing noises behind the walls, like ghosts or something."

Trevor gasped, almost inaudibly, but since she was sitting next to him, it was loud enough for Grace to hear. She looked at her son, who was attacking his cereal with more gusto than he usually showed when eating. She wondered if he knew something, if he'd seen the girl who had appeared to her. She'd have to ask him about it later.

Veronica was handing her the syrup.

"Try this, Grace," she said. "I have it flown in from Vermont."

Grace poured the syrup on her oatmeal, watching the golden-brown liquid make a swirling pattern. The oatmeal was delicious, far better than the instant kind she used at home. When they returned—or, rather, when they moved into their new place in Bryce City—she'd have to make it a point to make something homemade like this once in a while. It would be a nice way for her kids to know she loved them, to know there was someone there to care for them.

Unlike the little girl who'd been named Debbie, who'd lived in foster home after foster home and was lucky when she got any hot cereal. Who bought candy bars and chips and ice cream with the little spending money she had and ate until she was so fat the other children shunned her . . .

"Mom, what's the matter?"

Trevor was whispering close to her ear. Grace blinked and turned, letting the memory of her childhood slip away. She smiled.

"Nothing," she insisted. She turned to the twins and said, "What do you want to do today?"

"Can we ride horses again?" Sarah asked.

"David said there's a lake," Seth put in. "I want to go there!"

"I'm gonna shoot some baskets this morning," Trevor said.

Grace and Veronica laughed. It seemed the children had everything planned.

"Well, we'll talk to David about the horses a little later," Veronica promised. "But he does his stable work in the morning. If you want to go swimming, I'll sit by the poolside with you a little later, after my work."

"Okay!" the twins agreed in unison.

Seth pushed his seat back, the legs scraping over the hardwood floor.

"Come on, Sarah," he said, "let's play hide-and-seek outside in the gardens!"

Sarah ran after him. Trevor finished the last of his orange juice and went outside also, leaving his mother and grandmother alone.

Grace's shoulders heaved up and down as she sighed.

"I wish I had that energy," she said.

"They're remarkable children, Grace."

She looked at her mother. "I think Sarah's okay, don't you?"

"Oh, I'm certain," Veronica reassured her. She looked wistful. "Oh, Grace. When I see how loving you are to those little ones, I feel so guilty to think I wasn't with you when you were growing up."

Grace put her napkin on the table and stood up. "Then we'll have to make up for lost time. And you've reminded me: have you had a chance to get my birth records?"

Veronica got up and the two women left the dining room.

"I've had the hardest time with that!" Veronica said. "My parents did their best to keep you a secret from their friends and business associates. To tell you the truth, I'm not even sure where they registered the birth. I tried the town where I had stayed with my aunt, but there's nothing there. It's a mystery, Grace.''

Grace sighed. Was this a part of her life that would be kept from her forever?

''Well, I'd appreciate it if you kept trying, Mom,'' she said.

''Of course, Grace,'' Veronica said. ''I'll keep looking, if it makes you happy.''

They shared idle chatter as they walked down the hall together, parting company at the door to Veronica's office. Grace stood outside for a few moments, thinking. Her childhood had been dreary and loveless. But just how much love had Veronica received, being made to feel ashamed because of a baby? How much had her parents resented the birth that they did their best to lock evidence of Grace's existence away forever?

Once more, she was confronted with questions about her family's past. She started walking, stopping at the door to the library. Pushing it open, she faced a painting of a Union soldier, who glared at her from beneath the fringe of chestnut hair that escaped his blue cap. She thought he looked a little bit like Trevor, or as Trevor would look in a few years. The soldier couldn't be more than a teenager.

''I wonder why there aren't more pictures,'' Grace said out loud. She went farther into the room, hoping to find some photo albums.

After fifteen minutes of perusing the shelves, however, she realized there were none here. She made a mental note to ask her mother later. It would be fun to see photographs of her relatives and ancestors, people she'd never met. Her curiosity was piqued even more than before now, and as she left the room Paula's idea came back to her. If there was nothing in this home library, could she find something in the public library? After all, her mother was CEO of a big company, and her parents were rich, society people. Surely, there had been articles written about the family.

She went upstairs to her room and found her handbag and keys. Then, calling the children, she announced they were going for a drive into downtown Careyton.

"What's there?" Trevor asked.

"Can we go to the big city too?" Seth requested.

"Will we be back in time to ride?" Sarah asked.

Grace laughed as she backed the car out of its parking space in a gravel clearing alongside the house.

"What's there is the library," she said, answering the first question. "I have no plans to see Indianpolis today, but maybe we can go there with Nana another time. And I don't know if we'll be back in time to ride the horses today, Sarah."

A collective moan sounded behind her.

"Oh stop," Grace admonished gently. "I just want to look up a few things. I'm sure you can sit and read while I work."

As it happened, there was a park right next door to the library. The children begged Grace to use it, and Trevor promised to keep an eye on the twins. Grace relented but made them promise to behave. Then she went inside and asked for the reference desk. Once in the large, main room of the library, she sat at a computer and typed in her request for articles. She typed in the Chadman name, as well as her mother's maiden name, Winston. Then she put in for articles on Windsborough Botanicals.

Milliseconds later, the small printer hummed out a list of titles. Grace was interested to see the earliest article dated back to the 1930s. She brought her list to the microfilm file and located the date. Loading the film into a machine, she turned the dial until she found the society section. Scanning over the pictures that filled the pages, she came across one captioned: DR. AND MRS. JORDAN WINSTON, LATE OF AN EXPEDITION TO THE SOUTH SEAS, AT THE GOOD SAMARITAN HOSPITAL BENEFIT. Grace studied the black-and-white photograph. The handsome couple, dressed in evening finery, smiled off at something that seemed to be over the photographer's left shoulder. Grace shook her head in wonder. Mrs. Winston was the very image of her mother. Could this be her grandmother?

She turned her attention to Dr. Winston, and an unexpected chill washed over her. There was something strangely familiar about his smile. It wasn't that he resembled her family; she would have accepted such a thing easily. There was something

else about him, something that made her think she'd seen him
before. She and Trevor resembled her mother, and the twins
took after Craig. None of them looked remotely like this man.

No, she took that back. She had inherited his chestnut hair.
But that wasn't enough to explain the subconcious effect the
photograph had had on her.

Well, she thought with a sigh, maybe she was only reacting
to the sight of family ghosts.

She glanced over the article, learning that Mrs. Winston's
first name was Helene, but it was only so much fluff and told
her nothing important. Thoughts of ghosts made her think of
the young girl, and as she loaded film after film and read
repeated articles, she hoped to find a picture of her. There were
none. Who could she have been, Grace wondered?

In 1951, the Winstons announced the birth of a baby daughter, Amanda. Grace thought her sister might have been named
for this woman, who would be her aunt. Would she meet her?
Why hadn't Veronica mentioned her?

After forwarding the tape, she had her answer. Baby
Amanda had died when only a few weeks old. Grace felt unexpected tears heating up her eyes. There was so much tragedy
in this family. Her grandmother had lost a child; so had her
own sister.

The twins were suddenly at either side of her, their whining
complaints bringing her research to an abrupt end.

"I'm hot!" Sarah said.

"And I'm thirsty!" Seth put in.

Normally, Grace would have scolded them for interrupting
her so rudely. But she was suddenly beset with the memory
of her pregnancy and how close she'd come to miscarrying
the twins. She put her arms around them and hugged them,
turning from one to the other to smother each with kisses.

"Let's get some ice cream," she said. "I've done enough
research for one day."

She left the library with only a little more knowledge than
before. If Veronica seemed willing, she'd ask about her Aunt
Amanda, and she'd request a few photo albums to glance over.

The idea of tracing her lost geneology fired her, and she couldn't wait to get back to the estate to continue her research.

At home, the children went to ask David if they could ride again, leaving Grace to continue her pursuit of her family history alone. She went to Veronica's office, where she planned to talk to her mother about the things she'd learned. About to knock at the door, she became aware of an argument that was taking place. She recognized her mother's voice, but who was the man she was with?

"You know we haven't had enough time to get what we need," he was saying, his tone urgent. "We've got to keep them longer! We haven't had a chance to test the boys!"

"Then do something about it," Veronica said. "The burden shouldn't always be mine."

"Nor should all the benefits," came the reply.

There was a moment of silence. Grace raised her fist to knock again, but the conversation went on:

"That wasn't fair," Veronica said. "We agreed that I'd be the one to use our limited supply. And now, with these new sources, we can both gain! Oh, darling, I know if things don't change you'll be lost to me forever. And I couldn't bear that!"

"How do you think it's been for me these past few years, seeing you change and being unable to keep up? Being so close to you, yet unable to have you!"

Grace was embarrassed to realize she was eavesdropping on a conversation between her mother and the man Veronica seemed to love. In her eagerness to learn more about her family, the idea that Veronica would have other important people in her life had slipped Grace's mind. Of course a woman as beautiful as that had a man who cared deeply for her!

Part of Grace knew she should walk away and leave the two to their privacy. She tried to do so, but there was an inquisitive part of her that was stronger, and she found herself hiding around a corner. What did this man look like, she wondered? What was his name?

When she heard the office door open, she came out of her hiding place and walked down the hall as if for the first time.

But she saw only her mother, alone, walking away from her. Grace thought to call her, but hesitated. Instead, she entered the office.

It was empty.

She turned a complete circle. There was no one behind the desk, no one sitting on the chintz couch or the green leather chair. She shook her head in bewilderment.

"Where did he go?" she asked herself in a whisper. "How could he get out without me seeing him?"

Maybe there was another door to this room, one that wasn't as obvious. It was a curious possibility in such a big house. But that idea was crowded out immediately by a new one: why hadn't her mother mentioned anyone special? Wouldn't she want to show off her newfound daughter?

"Just give her time, Grace," she told herself.

She walked from the room, heading in the direction Veronica had taken. She still wanted to ask about photo albums. But halfway down the hall, she stopped again as yet another idea occurred to her. Was it possible this man was jealous, afraid Grace would usurp his position as an important person in Veronica's life? For the first time, she really considered the implications of being the daughter of a millionairess. It would mean great changes in her life and the lives of her children. There might be connections to Windsborough Botanicals, a huge company. The children could be heirs to a fortune, something that would completely change their futures.

And maybe the man she'd heard wasn't happy with the idea. She thought about the rat she'd found in her bed. Was it a sign, a warning? She shuddered to think there might be other things left for her to find.

She couldn't very well confront her mother with the idea. Veronica would know then that she'd been eavesdropping. So she decided to pursue her original plan of action and hoped she'd soon learn more about this man. She finally located her mother outside in the field, where she stood talking to an almond-skinned man who seemed to be the foreman. Grace waited on the sidewalk that bisected the field, the warm breeze carrying the mixed scents of the growing herbs. No strange smell of vinegar, mint, and roses today, she noted. She wondered what part of the field held that unusual herb.

When Veronica turned and saw her, her face lit up with a smile.

"You're back!" she cried, walking over to her. She was wearing a large-brimmed hat with a circle of pink silk roses. They perfectly matched the rose print of her sleeveless dress. "Did you enjoy the library?"

"It was interesting," Grace said. "I found some articles about Jordan and Helene Winston. Were they my grandparents?"

"That's right," Veronica said. She hooked her arm through her daughter's, and steered her towards the shade of a wrought-iron bench that circled a nearby oak tree.

"Helene looks exactly like you," Grace said as she sat down. The back of the bench felt hard and bumpy through her shirt.

Veronica laughed. "People often compared me to Mama. I'm flattered to think I look like her. She was considered a very beautiful woman."

Grace shifted, a little uncomfortable. "Mom, I read about your sister, Amanda. What happened to her?"

"She died a few years before I was born," Veronica sighed. A few leaves, disturbed by a rushing squirrel, fell down around them. One landed in Veronica's lap. She picked it up and turned it over in her small, spotted hands. The hands of a grandmother. Grace wondered what she'd looked like ten years ago.

"It was a congenital problem," Veronica said. "Mama told me her heart just wasn't strong enough. They were afraid to try for another child, but God chose to give me to them."

"I didn't see any articles about your birth," Grace said.

Veronica looked at her. "After Amanda died, they stopped attending all social functions. It was just too hard for them to answer all those questions. I led a very quiet, very secluded childhood. Much of it was spent in boarding schools."

Grace shivered despite the cold. She'd had no idea her mother had grown up in an institutional setting much like her own.

"But it wasn't so bad," Veronica said, patting Grace's hand. With astuteness that almost seemed psychic, she added, "At least I knew I had parents to go home to. Not like you, stuck in an orphanage."

Grace was thoughtful for a moment. Then she said, "You told me they sent you away when you became pregnant because they were ashamed. If they didn't socialize, what difference did it make?"

"Oh, by then they'd returned to the party scene," Veronica said. "It had been twenty years since they'd lost Amanda. You understand I named your sister for mine?"

Grace nodded. "Mom, I was wondering if there were any photo albums?"

"I'm sorry, Grace, but there aren't," Veronica said. "You see, we had a terrible flood a few winters back. I had the albums stored in the cellar, and they were destroyed."

"How awful!"

"It was devestating," Veronica said, sadly. "A terrible loss. And even more so now that I have new family to share pictures with!"

Abruptly, she stood up, smiling. "But maybe it's time to start making new memories. I heard the children were riding today. I have a camera in my office. Do you want to take pictures of them? I think the twins are adorable in their riding habits."

"Great idea," Grace said, standing herself. It would be nice to think of something different for a while.

"I'll get the camera," Veronica said, and walked away. "Meet me on the path leading from the stables."

As it happened, it was a maid who brought Grace the 35mm Nikon. She explained that Veornica had received an urgent call from the office and had gone into the city with Andros. She left a message that Grace could take as many pictures as she wanted.

The children weren't in the paddock, so she guessed they'd headed towards the lake. She felt a little wary about that, but David had seemed trustworthy enough. She couldn't let herself become an overprotective mother just because of a few strange incidents. There would only be a few more days here for them to enjoy their grandmother. She didn't want to spoil it by worrying them.

As she headed towards the woods, she saw the group coming out. She stopped halfway, raising the camera to snap a picture as Trevor, first in line, headed for her. But she saw something else through the lens. Someone was sharing Trevor's horse.

She pulled the camera away. Trevor was alone now. Blinking, she decided it had only been a trick of the sun and the lens.

But when she put the camera to her eye again, she saw the boy. He had sandy-colored hair, and he seemed to be a little younger than Trevor. He was holding him around the waist, whispering something in his ear.

So that was why Trevor had been acting strangely. He had found a ghost of his own.

Grace snapped the picture, hoping to capture evidence of the child.

By the time the group reached her, she had managed to collect herself. She gave no outward indication of what she'd seen.

"We went to the lake, Mom!" Seth cried.

"Just there and back, Mrs. Matheson," David reassured her. "I thought we could return another day with you."

"It's pretty," Sarah said. "There were two swans!"

Grace smiled at her little girl. Sarah's braids had come undone, and her face was dusty. All the children were dirty from the ride.

"It sounds wonderful," she said, "but the three of you look like you need a bathtub, not a lake, right now."

Seth groaned.

"We have to help put the horses away," Trevor said.

"Of course," Grace said. "But come right inside when you're done."

She stepped aside, and they continued towards the barn. Grace lifted the camera again. This time, Trevor was alone on the horse.

Awhile later she met the children in the hall outside their rooms. Opening the bedroom door, she ushered Sarah towards a waiting tub of bubbles. She knew Sarah would be quick in cleaning herself up. Despite his protests that he hated baths, Seth would languish under the bubbles so long that Sarah would have to wait forever if he went first.

"You get out of that dirty habit," Grace said, "and put your robe on. I'll make a fresh bath for you as soon as Sarah's done."

"A bath in the middle of the day," Seth mumbled.

"You aren't going to sit at Nana's table smelling like a horse," Grace told him.

She turned to Trevor. He had been thoughtful enough to remove his boots downstairs, and now he stood barefoot next to his bed.

"Come on down to my room," Grace said. "You can use my shower."

When she got him there, away from the big ears of the twins, she asked, "Trevor, have you noticed anything strange about this place?"

Trevor frowned. "I already told you about Nana and Andros."

"That's not what I mean," Grace said. "Have you . . . met anyone new? Another child?"

"No," Trevor said, but Grace noted his voice was a little breathless, his eyes a little wider.

He was lying.

She decided to get to the point. Trevor was a smart child. He could accept her words, especially if he'd had experiences similar to her own. He needed to know she was there for him.

"Trevor, I saw something through my camera lens today," she said. "There was another boy on your horse. He was sitting behind you, and he was whispering in your ear. I think he was a spirit. I think there might be a few ghosts in this big, old house."

"I was all by myself," Trevor said. "You were seeing things."

"I know what I—"

Trevor's head swung up, his eyes flashing. "And I knew what I saw, but you won't believe me. Nana was with Andros. They've got something going on, and I'm afraid! They're going to kill us if we don't leave this place!"

"Oh, Trevor . . ."

"It's true," Trevor said. "Jeffrey told me—"

He cut himself off.

"Jeffrey?" Grace said, gently urging him. "Is that the ghost I saw?"

Trevor ran his fingers through his hair, staring down at his bare feet. Grace could sense he wanted to tell her something, but couldn't.

"You don't have to be afraid," she said softly. "The dead will never harm you."

"I know that," Trevor said. "I'm not afraid of ghosts. I'm afraid of Nana."

He looked towards her bathroom door. "Can I take my shower now?"

"Trevor, I think we need to talk."

"I feel skutchy," Trevor said, scratching a mosquito bite on his arm.

Grace realized her son wouldn't talk to her now. With a sigh, she got him a towel and directed him to the shower. Then she left him alone, hoping the warm flow of the water would help ease his fears. She knew that Trevor would talk to her when he was ready, and there was no point forcing anything out of him.

She decided to pursue her own search into her family history. It was tragic that so many old photographs had been lost in that flood. She thought it was kind of strange that her mother had stored the albums in a basement, a place where the damp might cause mildew damage as it was. Grace's own precious albums were on the top shelf of her small bedroom closet, competing for space with sweaters, shoe boxes, and an ugly vase someone had given her as a wedding gift.

"Maybe Craig will find a place where I can have a big bookshelf," she said out loud. "With walk-in closets and an attic . . ."

She shook her head at herself. Dreaming of a big place was silly. Even with a steady job, it would be a long time before they had enough money for a down payment.

But an attic would still be nice, her dreamier side interrupted her practical side.

She paused with her hand on the top of the banister and looked back down the hall. An attic . . .

Could there be something upstairs here? Surely there was more to this family's mementos than albums stored in the basement. With a new sense of purpose, Grace turned from the stairs and went in search of the attic. She recalled seeing a second staircase curving away from the narrow one that led up from the kitchen. Retracing the steps she'd taken with her mother, the night they'd found Trevor in here, she located the second-story landing.

The stairs that twisted up to the third floor were even narrower than those below, and Grace's shoulders bumped the wall at least twice each. She wondered who would use stairs like these. No strong, burly servant could make it. Certainly a pumpkin of a housekeeper like Mrs. Treetorn would find herself stuck!

She giggled at the thought, her laughter bouncing away from her like woodland sprites as she came to the top. Even though she knew the echoes were from her own voice, she still felt uneasy. She didn't really belong up here, all alone, snooping around in a house that wasn't her home.

But it should have been, she told herself. She should have been brought up in this beautiful place! And she had a right to know all about her family. If she'd never been given up for adoption, she'd know many of the Winston/Chadman secrets.

More determined than ever, she went to the first door and twisted it open. It was a small room, the large window at the back looking down on the road leading to the house. Obviously unused for years, its cracked windowpane provided just enough space for a sparrow's nest. Grace went closer and examined it. Broken shells lay forgotten, the last remains of babies that had learned to fly and were gone now. She made a note to come back and get it. Seth and Sarah would enjoy the nest, she thought.

The second room was locked. Though she was curious about it, she left it to check out the third door. This one opened on a room filled with boxes and trunks and a few pieces of furniture covered in cloth that must have been white when first draped. Now it was dusty, even moldy in places. There was a musty smell about the room, the strange odor peculiar to old papers and forgotten clothing. Grace switched on the light, and was delighted to see it still worked. Perhaps it hadn't been long since someone was up here, but they certainly did nothing to clean the place!

She moved farther inside and opened the nearest box. It was filled with books pertaining to various scientific fields, especially chemistry, human anatomy, and botany. Each bore a date, going as far back as the 1930s. Grace was surprised to see the authors' names: "JORDAN WINSTON," "HELENE WINSTON." Her excitement grew. It would be fun to peruse some of these volumes and maybe learn a thing or two about her ancestors.

She noticed the corner of a large frame peeking out from behind a covered dresser. Curious, she went to it and eased it out from the place where it had been left, forgotten for possibly years. Dust and mold came off on her hand as she gripped the gilded frame, but she wasn't repelled. She was too delighted with her find.

It was an oil portrait of a couple. Grace, an expert on costuming after years of dressing dolls, recognized the clothes as turn-of-the-century. She immediately saw the family resemblance. The man had her chestnut hair, while the woman had her full lips and high cheekbones. However, neither one had the strange lapis lazuli eyes that Veronica, her daughters, and Grace's children had inherited.

"Recessive genes," Grace said out loud.

She looked on the back of the painting, but the couple who had sat for it were not identified. Well, she'd have to ask her mother.

Gently, with great respect, she leaned the picture against the

wall. It was then that she noticed a small corner of paper
peeking out from behind an old bookshelf. Grace got down
on her knees and tried to pluck it out with her thumb and
forefinger, but her nails weren't long enough to get hold. She
stood up and grabbed the top and front of the bookshelf. She
pulled with all her might—the wooden piece was amazingly
heavy—and managed to free the paper just enough to make it
easier to grab.

"Well," she said as she picked it up. "Here's one photograph that survived that flood."

It was a black-and-white print of a couple holding a baby.
She recognized Jordan and Helene at once, although they were
much younger in this picture than in the one she'd found at
the library. Once again, she had the strange feeling she'd seen
Jordan before. Why did his face look so familiar, especially
those piercing eyes and that stern expression?

"I'm sure it will come to me," she said, and turned her
attention to the baby in the picture. It seemed to be about six
months old.

She turned the photograph over and read the date printed
on the back: 1938. Grace frowned. The baby Helene had lost,
Amanda, was born in 1951. Had Helene had babies thirteen
years apart? It wasn't unheard of, but it seemed strange this
first child was never mentioned in the articles she'd found. Its
bonnet and gown belied its sex; Grace knew baby boys wore
long dresses in those days.

"What happened to you, little one?" she asked the picture.

The baby only stared at her, a pout on its thin face.

"He died," came a voice so suddenly that Grace dropped
the picture with a scream.

She swung around. The teenager was there, still wearing the
nightgown with its bright red bloodstain. Grace put a hand
over her mouth and took a deep breath to calm herself. She
didn't want to scare the girl away this time.

"What . . . what happened to him?"

The girl only shrugged. She stared at Grace with a wistful
expression. Almost the way Helene had been gazing at the

baby in the photograph, Grace thought. Why was the girl so fascinated by her?

"What's your name?" she asked gently.

The girl didn't answer, but she slowly held out her hand. When Grace moved forward to take it, however, she snatched it away.

"Where's Amanda?"

"Maybe I can take you to her," Grace offered, hoping to gain the spirit's trust. "I can tell Veronica I want to see Amanda at the hospital, and . . ."

The girl's pretty face seemed to film over with a mask of pure trepidation.

"No!" she screamed, and turned to run from the room.

At that same moment, one of the journals came flying towards Grace. She ducked out of its way just in time. It sailed out the door, crashing to the hall floor.

Grace sped after the girl, nearly tripping over a small crate. By the time she reached the hall, the girl was gone. Grace knew there was no chance of finding her.

"Who are you?" Grace whispered. "And what are you afraid of?"

She picked up the journal, believing the girl had thrown it in her panic. It was dated 1938, and was written by Helene. Grace turned to January 1.

Fabulous New Year's Party last night at Cortland Manor, but all I could think of was the expedition Jordan and I are planning for June. Could this be the year we succeed? The year we finally discover the Fountain of Youth? I only pray the boy is all right. It would infuriate Jordan to think we'd be delayed because of his illness.

"What boy?" Grace wondered aloud.

She knew the journal would make fascinating reading. Tucking it under her arm, she carried it downstairs to her room.

ELEVEN

▼

More than anything, Trevor had wanted to tell his mother what he knew. He wanted to hand her Jeffrey's letter and let her figure it all out. He wanted to tell her how Jeffrey had appeared on his horse, so suddenly that Trevor had nearly taken a fall just the way Sarah had. Jeffrey had leaned close to him, his whisper a stinging cold blade that sliced through the thick summer air.

"Ride away from here," he'd said. "Ride away while you can! She's taking blood from your sister, and soon she'll have yours!"

Trevor thought his mother had looked as if she'd wanted him to talk to her, even if what he was going to say seemed crazy. She'd had a funny look in her eyes. Kind of the way grown-ups look when they're trying to get you to pull something out of your brain, their eyes widening the closer you get to the answer.

But Trevor didn't have any answers. Even if his mother were to believe he'd seen a ghost, she wouldn't understand Jeffrey's message. Trevor knew that, somehow, Veronica and

Andros had played a trick on him. He had to prove to his mother they were liars. Somehow, he had to get his mother to be there the next time Veronica and Andros pulled one of their tricks.

"But if I'm lucky," he said, "Dad'll bring us home before anything else happens!"

He put a few finishing touches on the model space shuttle he'd been building and set it to dry on the top of his dresser. Then he left the room and went downstairs, in the mood to shoot some baskets outside. When he approached the court, he was disappointed to see it was occupied—until David turned around and waved to him.

"Hey, Trev," he said. "One-on-one?"

"You got it," Trevor said, and immediately claimed the ball.

They skipped around the court for a while, not talking, all concentration on the ball and the hoop. Even though he was at least a foot shorter than David, Trevor was a worthy opponent and managed to score more baskets than the stable manager. Finally, David let the ball bounce away. He gave a deep sigh of defeat as he leaned over with his hands pressed to his knees, looking up at Trevor through his sweat-soaked bangs.

"Where did you learn to play like that?" he asked, his smile part grin, part grimace.

"I started when I was seven," Trevor said. "It's my favorite game, but I play hockey too."

"Keep it up," David replied, "and you'll be an all-star in the NBA."

This brought a smile to Trevor's face. "Yeah?"

"Yeah," David said. "Come on, you want a soda?"

"Well, I don't want to go inside," Trevor said, although a cold drink sounded good to him.

David beckoned him off the court. "Don't have to. I have a little refrigerator in my room."

They walked to the stables together. The horses were grazing now, and the paddock gate was open. Trevor followed David into the barn, then up a staircase.

"Wow!" he cried as he entered a small room. "You live up here?"

The walls were a continuation of the wooden planks that made up the barn below, but whitewashed and covered with posters of various sporting events. One large one over the bed depicted the Indy 500, a well-known baseball player was sliding into home on another, and a third honored Olympic games that had taken place before Trevor was born.

"This is my home," David said, a touch of pride in his voice. "It was all set up with heat and electricity when I came. Mrs. Chadman gave me the chance to live here or in the house. I like it here."

"So do I," Trevor said, walking to the desk. He picked up a science fiction book. "You like sci-fi too?"

"Only stuff I read," David said. He gave a little shrug. "I mean, except for stuff about horses. Anyway, let me get that drink."

He opened a small refrigerator and produced two Mountain Dews. Trevor popped his open and sat on the desk chair. David settled on the edge of his bed.

"So, do you like it here?"

"I don't know," Trevor said, looking down at the top of his can. "There's a lot to do, but it's strange too."

"How so?"

"Things happen," Trevor replied. "Things I can't explain."

"Maybe I can help you figure them out," David encouraged him.

"Well . . ."

Suddenly, Trevor found himself opening up. Maybe it was because David wasn't his mother, and he didn't have to prove anything to him. Maybe it was that the stable manager was young or that he was simply listening. But Trevor told him everything that had happened, right up to the moment when he had insisted to his mother that he hadn't met anyone unusual.

"Jeffrey," David said.

Trevor's mouth dropped open. "How . . . ?"

"I met him once myself," David said with a smile. "He told me to read some sort of letter, but I never found it, and he never appeared again. That must have been the letter you found in that box."

"Do you know who Jeffrey was?" Trevor asked. "How did he die?"

"Sorry," David said. "I tried asking about him, but no one seems to know about him. I figured there was some strange reason why he was kept a secret. I even asked the people in town, but they didn't have much to say. They don't talk much at all about this house, I found out."

Trevor leaned forward. "Really? How come?"

"Beats me," David said. "I get the impression some bad stuff happened here, but no one says a word. People in small towns like Careyton are pretty tight-lipped."

Trevor got up and put his empty soda can in the trash. He noticed a small hotplate and smelled the last traces of tomato sauce. While he was eating big, fancy dinners, David was cooking spaghetti all by himself.

"David, do you ever come into the house?"

"Only when I have to," David said. He held up his feet to show his muddy boots and indicated the dirt on his jeans. "I'd feel pretty out of place."

Trevor nodded, understanding. "That's what my dad said. David, do you think I could sleep here some night?"

"I don't think . . ."

"I wouldn't be a pest, really," Trevor promised. "I could sleep on the floor."

David peered at the younger boy for a long time. Then, quietly, he asked, "Are you afraid of something in that house?"

"Nana," Trevor admitted. "And Andros."

David threw his own can at the trash, hitting it squarely. He stood up and put a hand on Trevor's shoulder.

"Mrs. Chadman won't hurt you," he insisted. "I'm sure of that."

"What about Andros?"

David's lower lip disappeared into his mouth as he thought for a few moments.

"I'm not crazy about him," he admitted. "But I think he's okay. He just looks creepy. None of the other servants say anything bad about him."

"None of them say much of anything," Trevor pointed out.

David laughed. "I guess. Come on, let's go back downstairs. I've got stalls to clean, and your mother is probably looking for you."

They were halfway to the door of the barn when Trevor thought of another question.

"David, did you always live here?"

"Of course not," David said. "I used to live in Michigan. Why?"

"Was there someone here before you?"

"Yes," David said. He stopped, his frown deep and troubled. "Mrs. Chadman said he died. They found him near one of the basement windows. I guess he had a heart attack, because Felix told me there was a very strange look on his face. The kind of look you get when you're in pain or really scared, he said."

"Wow," Trevor whispered.

David reached out to ruffle his hair, brightening the mood. "Forget about that. And don't worry about Jeffrey. If he was going to hurt anyone, I think it would have happened already. I'll bet he's just glad to have another kid around."

"Well, I don't want to be around much longer," Trevor said. "Thanks for the soda, David."

"Anytime," the stable manager said, and turned to his chores.

Trevor was full of thought as he walked away. The other stable manager had collapsed near a basement window. Did he see something that scared him so much that he keeled over from fright? Maybe he was able to see into that hidden room. And if he could do it, Trevor reasoned he could too. But he wouldn't be scared. No way! He'd get a camera, take a picture, and show whatever he'd found to his mother. No, better yet, to his father when he came back from Bryce City. And then Dad would get them all out of there.

"But which window?" he whispered. There were dozens around the lower perimeter of the big Georgian house. "Which one leads to the hidden room?"

With determination quickening his stride, he went to the nearest one and tried to peer inside. The darkness below and the bright sunshine behind him created a mirror effect, and he saw only his own reflection in window after window. When another figure appeared after a while, he jumped up with a cry.

Andros was standing there, frowning. "You're being called to dinner."

"Okay," Trevor said.

He ran off before the old man could question what he was doing.

Dinner tonight, served on floral china, was a turkey dinner as elaborate as anything his mother ever made on Thanksgiving. He recalled her explaining that she never cooked turkey in the summer because it made the apartment too hot. But this mansion was so big that the heat from the kitchen never made it as far as the dining room. He wondered how he could find his way to that secret basement room in a house this large.

But the turkey was delicious, the mashed potatoes creamy, and the corn was crisp. He soon found himself lost in the meal, enjoying every bite as he listened to his mother and grandmother talking.

"I hope you don't mind that I was up on the third floor," Grace said.

"Not at all," Veronica insisted. She waved a hand at Seth. "Let the maid pour that gravy, Seth dear. I don't want it to spill on this antique tablecloth."

She smiled at Grace. "My mother left it to me, and her mother left it to her. It's very old. I inherited it when they died a few years ago while visiting the Middle East. They were caught up in a terrorist attack."

"Oh, that's awful," Grace said. She changed the subject quickly. "I found a picture upstairs of Helene . . . of my grandparents. Helene was holding a baby, and the picture was dated 1938. I know it wasn't your sister Amanda, since she died in 1951. Do you know who that baby might have been?''

Veronica frowned, the lines from her nose to her lips deepening. She cut a piece of turkey and ate it before speaking.

"I'm sure I don't know," she said. I'm sure my mother never had another baby. It must have been a relative's child.''

"Mo-om!" Sarah cried suddenly, giving the word extra syllables. "Seth's showing me his chewed-up mashed potatoes!''

When Grace looked at her son, he was all innocence, but he was chewing his food more vigorously than necessary. "Seth, that's no way to behave at the table.''

"We're probably boring him with our grownup talk," Veronica said, smiling indulgently at the little boy. "Seth, tell me about your day.''

As Seth began to speak, Grace pulled into her own thoughts, hardly tasting her dinner. She could tell her mother wasn't really willing to talk about the family.

Grace decided then and there, while sipping white wine that probably cost the total of a day's food budget at her own home, that she wouldn't be lost to her own sister, Amanda. She would visit her as soon as possible. Maybe, if she was lucky, Amanda might be able to fill in a few gaps about her family history.

After putting the children to bed later that evening, Grace went to her room. She picked up the cordless phone on her nightstand and carried it to the wingbacked chair where she sat comfortably and dialed Craig's hotel room. After ten rings, she decided he was probably out with his new boss or perhaps he'd met up with those old school buddies he'd mentioned to her. She was disappointed that she couldn't get through to him, and not just because she wanted to get his input on all the strange things that she'd learned since her arrival. With the day's activities long done and the house so quiet all she could hear was the hum of the air conditioner in her window, she felt very lonely. She missed Craig more now than on any trip she'd ever taken, even ones that were twice as long as this!

Sighing, she went to her bed and turned it down. A chilly breeze made her shudder, and she went to the air conditioner to turn it down. Movement in the yard below caught her eye. She squinted her eyes and realized it was the teenager, running across the lawn, her white gown billowing out like a cloud. Grace moved quickly to the other window and raised it. Like all the windows on this floor, it opened up onto a small balcony. The low sill made it easy to climb out, and Grace did so.

"Hello?" she called. "Please, come back!"

The girl, who seemed to be little more than a wisp of white fabric, didn't respond, but kept running across the grass.

"Hey!" Grace yelled.

The girl stopped abruptly, then turned to stare up at her. In the lights surrounding the exterior of the house, her face was almost luminous. She shook her head and held a finger to her lips. Then she turned and ran away, disappearing into the shadows.

Grace stared out at the yard for a while. When she turned around, the bed she'd turned down was completely made up again. She shivered violently, and as she rubbed her arms she knew it had nothing to do with the air-conditioning.

"Are you here?" she whispered.

The room was silent. Thinking of that horrible rat she'd found, Grace approached the bed cautiously. Grimacing with disgust, turning her head away so she wouldn't have to look at some monstrosity directly, she yanked at the covers.

The bed was empty.

Grace laughed a little at herself. It had been a busy day, and she probably only *thought* she'd turned down the bed. She was becoming paranoid!

She fluffed up her pillow and crawled under the covers, then opened the nightstand drawer. The journal she'd found in the attic was there, and she brought it into the bed to read. It wasn't about botany or anatomy, as the other books had seemed to be, but a day-to-day account of Helene's life. Grace thought the woman's social calendar must have been right up there with the Astors and Vanderbilts. She certainly seemed to be their equivalent here in Careyton.

Grace read for about half an hour, fascinated with Helene's mix of scientific speculation and social interests. For every line posing possible ideas for new inventions, there were two filled with opinions about this one's new hairdo or that one's servants or another's new beau. It was almost as if the journal had been written by two people!

She had reached March 14 and Helene's notes about a St. Patrick's Day benefit, when she suddenly realized something was missing. Except for the brief mention on January 1, nothing more was said about the sick boy.

"Well, I guess he wasn't her son," she said. "Surely a concerned mother would pour her heart out in a diary if her child was ill. But who could he have been? Is he Trevor's ghost?"

Grace let the question slide, suddenly too tired to wonder about it. She got out of bed to wash up for the night. When she walked into the bathroom, she gasped with surprise. Somehow, steam had settled on the mirror. But she hadn't taken a shower yet! And there was a message:

TALK TO AMANDA. SHE KNOWS.

Grace reached towards the message. As she did so, she realized the distorted reflection she was seeing was not just of her face, but of another woman's too. Grace spun around.

The bathroom was empty. She looked at the mirror again. It was crystal-clear, perfectly reflecting her wide-eyed stare. She snapped off the light and went to sit on the edge of her bed, cupping her hands around her face. She stayed like that for a long time, absorbing everything, gathering strength. Finally, she looked up, fixing her gaze on the dresser across the room.

"All right, then," she said. "I'll do what you want. I'll talk to Amanda. But I only hope she'll have some answers for me!"

Too agitated to sleep, she went to the desk and pulled out her drawing pad and pencils. She sketched faces deep into the night. They were the faces of her children, of her newfound mother, of Craig. And another face, a haunted young face, filled one of the pad's pages. It was the teenage girl, whom

Grace had drawn with a pleading expression. It was as if she'd
rendered her own questions and emotions onto the spirit's.

She drew almost feverishly, letting her art help her forget
her fears, until at last sleep claimed her and her head fell
forward onto the sketch pad.

Grace was dreaming that a woodpecker had landed on her
back and was pounding a hole into the nape of her neck. She
swatted at it, her real self imitating her dream self and waking
her up. The smell of furniture polish and paper greeted her,
along with a terrible stiff neck and aching back. She'd fallen
asleep at the desk.

She heard the tap-tapping, like a woodpecker, again and
realized it was the door. Moaning, a grimace on her face, she
rose from the chair and limped over to answer it. A maid was
standing there with the telephone. Without a word, she handed
it to Grace and walked away. Grace mumbled a greeting into
the line.

"You sound terrible," Craig said. "Are you okay, Gracie?"

"I feel worse," Grace replied. "I fell asleep in a chair."

"Doing what?"

"Oh . . . stuff," Grace said nonchalantly. "I found an old
diary my grandmother wrote. It's been a lot of fun reading
it."

She heard Craig sigh. "And I'll bet you were up all night
reading it."

"No," Grace told him. "I was sketching when I fell
asleep."

She wouldn't let him know that she'd been working *very*
hard to know her family history and that she'd been drawing
a picture of a ghost when she fell asleep. Craig had enough
on his mind with his new job, and she knew if she told him
any of that he'd worry too much.

"So what's up?" she asked, then yawned.

"Just calling to say hi before I take off," Craig said.
"We're having breakfast out, then I've got some lectures to
go to."

Grace wondered how many lectures there could be about

advertising but didn't say anything. If Craig knew how much she missed him, even after only a few days, it would give him yet another thing to be concerned about.

"I tried to call you last night," she said.

"Oh, my new boss took me to dinner," Craig said. "He seems like a nice guy. I think I'll like working for him. Well . . . I'd like working for anyone at this point. Listen, Grace, I've found a few possibilities for homes. I'll show you the write-ups when I see you."

"When will that be?" Grace asked. She hooked the phone between her chin and shoulder and started to undress.

"I'm not sure," Craig said. "I suppose it depends on how well things go today."

"Can you come down tomorrow?"

"Well . . ."

Grace threw yesterday's shorts across the room. They landed near the door, where she'd pick them up for the laundry chute.

"Craig, don't tell me they expect you to work on Sunday!"

She realized she sounded nearly hysterical, and cringed.

"Of course not, Gracie," Craig said. "But I'm not sure I could rush down there, then be back in time to start work on Monday. It's about eight hours round-trip."

Grace sighed. "I understand, honey. It's just that I miss you so much."

All right, she thought, *I said it.*

She waited for Craig to interpret the tone of her voice, to tell her that she sounded tired and maybe a little overwhelmed.

Instead, he said, "I miss you too." That was all. No warnings to be careful, to go slowly. Did this mean he had come to accept Veronica totally? She hoped so; she needed his support now more than ever.

"Are the kids up yet?"

Grace glanced at her watch, still on her wrist from yesterday. "It's early, Craig. But I'll tell them you called."

They spoke for a while longer, Craig ending the conversation by promising he'd come down to Careyton as soon as possible. Grace hung up wishing she had him there to give her an encouraging hug. Instead, she settled for the caresses of a hot shower. Her back and shoulders didn't ache quite so much when she got out, and when she got dressed she was feeling much better. The curtains were pulled aside now—Mrs. Treetorn must have come in while she was in the bathroom. It was a bright blue day, a day that encouraged her to do whatever she wanted.

Today, she vowed, she would go to the hospital and visit her sister.

As she was putting on her sandals, she realized that Mrs. Treetorn had come into her room to open the curtains only once during her visit. That seemed strange.

Grace gave her head a shake. "Don't start creating more mysteries in this house!"

By the time she got down to breakfast, the children were up. They enjoyed the meal together, then the children ran off to play. Grace was happy to see that Sarah was fine this morning. Maybe the nightmares had only been caused by unfamiliar surroundings. Now that she was beginning to know this place, Grace was certain they'd go away.

Mrs. Treetorn came into the dining room as Grace was finishing her last drop of coffee.

"I'm going into town today," Grace said. "Do you think you'd mind keeping an eye on the kids for a while?"

"Those darlings?" Mrs. Treetorn said. "I wouldn't mind at all. But Mrs. Chadman is in today. I'm sure she'll be the one to watch the children."

"Mrs. Chadman?" Grace echoed. "I didn't know my mother was home."

She hadn't seen her at all that morning.

"Mrs. Chadman always stays home on Saturday," said Mrs. Treetorn. She smiled at Grace, her cheeks like two blush-ripe peaches. "You go on to town and enjoy yourself. Don't worry about the children."

A short while later, Veronica saw her walking to the front door with her keys and purse, and stopped her.

"Where are you headed, Grace?"

"Into town to get some art supplies," Grace lied. She didn't know why she kept her destination a secret. It just seemed important to do so. "I did a lot of drawing last night and I'm running low on paper."

"I wish I could join you," Veronica said, "but I've simply got too much to do."

Grace managed a smile of her own. She'd never considered that her mother might want to come along.

"Another day," she said.

"We'll have many days together," Veronica replied. "Enjoy yourself!"

Grace said good-bye and left. As she was getting into her car, she noticed Trevor following David around the paddock. He was holding a rake—David must have given him something to do. Grace closed her door and started the engine. She was glad to see Trevor turning his mind elsewhere. She wondered if she should talk to David to see if Trevor had told him anything he wouldn't tell her.

"Then again," she said, flipping on the radio, "he seems like the kind of guy who'd keep a secret, especially one a kid told him."

The radio station was playing one of her favorite rock songs, and she hummed it all the way to the main road.

She didn't really know where to find St. Charles Psychiatric Hospital, where her mother had said Amanda was staying, but since the library was close by she stopped there first to look up the address. It would have made her uneasy to ask for directions face-to-face with a stranger, who might wonder what lunatic she was visiting. Grace had a feeling, one she admitted might be unjustified, that a lot of people still felt strange associating with anyone who knew the mentally challenged. As if they could catch something.

She found the address quickly and went back out to her car. St. Charles was only a mile from the library, and she found it quickly enough. The hospital consisted of three buildings: one small ranch-type house and two three-story brick structures, all standing on a vast, neatly trimmed lawn. Grace glanced up at the barred windows, and a small chill shook her in the summer heat. She couldn't help wondering if those bars were to keep the patients safe from the outside world, or (she recalled her fall down the escalator steps) to protect the outside world.

She followed a path to the house, guessing it was the administration building. It could just as easily have been someone's home, with neatly trimmed bushes flanking the front stoop and a floral wreath hanging on the front door. Grace read the small metallic sign that had been screwed into the frame:

VISITING HOURS: 1–3:30 P.M., 7–9 P.M.

She was several hours early, but she had no intention of waiting until this afternoon to see Amanda. It would be a lot easier for her to talk to the woman if there weren't a lot of other people milling about, paying visits to their own family members. Grace quickly thought up a speech to excuse her early arrival and opened the door.

The reception area was a well-lit, carpeted room decorated with Impressionist prints. A coffee table laden with magazines sat amidst a couch and several chairs. At first, Grace thought there was no one in the room. Then she noticed a man wearing a gray jumpsuit crouching down behind a television set. He gave her a quick frown, then returned to his work.

Grace went up to the window that separated the room from the reception desk. The woman behind it was busy filing something, so Grace waited patiently until she turned around. When she did, she jumped a little in surprise and brought a hand up to her chest.

She came to the window and slid it open.

"Yes, what can I do for you?"

Grace told her. The woman shook her head and pointed at a sign, a copy of the one on the front door.

"We can't disturb our patients' routine," she said firmly. "I'm sure you understand."

"Of course I do," Grace said, then launched into the speech she'd prepared on the steps. "But I'm going home to Tulip

Tree this afternoon, and this is the last chance I'll have to see her for a long time.''

A man wearing a white doctor's coat came into the room just then and put a file on the receptionist's desk. The woman turned and spoke to him, telling him who Grace was and her situation. Grace watched as his eyebrows went up in surprise, then turned as the door between the rooms opened and he came out with his hand extended.

"I'm Dr. Grant," he said. "Mrs. Chadman was right—you *are* the image of your sister."

He smiled, and added, "Or should I say, Amanda resembles you, since you're the older of the two."

"Dr. Grant, I know this is unexpected," Grace said, "but I really do want a chance to speak with my sister before I go home this afternoon. It's a four-hour drive from Tulip Tree, and I won't be able to get down here again soon."

It was a lie, since she had no idea when she'd be returning home, but she wanted to stress the urgency of her situation.

Dr. Grant, a handsome man who seemed to be in his forties, looked past her. Grace turned around, wondering what he'd seen. She noticed the repairman was gone.

"I'm surprised Veronica didn't come with you," the doctor said. "She gave me specific instructions that no one is to see Amanda unless she's present."

"My mother was unable to come with me this morning," Grace said. "But she knows I'm here."

"Maybe I can give her a quick call, to confirm her wishes," Grant said.

"No!"

Grace could have bit her tongue. She had wanted to sound assertive, not desperate. But Grant, whose profession had probably taught him to listen to the nuance of speech in his patients, must have understood the implication of that one exclamation. Grace realized he knew she hadn't told her mother about this impromptu visit. He took on a cool, professional demeanor.

"I'm sorry, Mrs. Matheson," he said. "But Mrs. Chadman was more than implicit about her wishes. No one is to see

Amanda. If you want to visit her, you can come back with your mother . . .''

"She's my sister," Grace said in weak defense.

"I know, and I don't understand Veronica's motivations," Grant said with a shake of his head.

Grace noticed the use of her mother's first name. How well did Veronica know this man?

The idea that this could be the man she'd heard in the office passed briefly through her mind. But she dismissed it. The idea of her mother and this much younger man was ridiculous, as ridiculous as Trevor's idea her mother was kissing Andros.

She sighed. "All right, I'll talk to her. But I hope she doesn't become upset with you that you denied me access to my own sister."

"I'll be all right," Dr. Grant insisted. If he'd taken up on the veiled threat Grace had made, he was showing no sign of it.

Grace turned and left. As she was walking down the path, something occurred to her. Why had she referred to Dr. Grant as a "much-younger man"? If he seemed to be in his forties, the abundance of gray at his temples giving away his age, then he'd be perfect for her mother, who would also be in her forties. Why had she considered him too young?

"Because my mother looks older than her age," Grace told herself aloud, startling a bird that was searching for insects in a nearby bush. It flew in front of her, shooting up to the sky with an angry chirping. Grace followed its path and noticed the repairman was now outside, raking leaves. He wasn't a repairman at all but a janitor. Grace realized he was staring at her. A small shudder ran through her, and she quickened her stride.

She was nearly to the end of the path when she heard a whispered voice say, "Amanda isn't here."

Grace stopped short.

"Don't turn around, just listen," said the voice. Grace thought it must be the janitor. She crouched down and pretended to be busy tying her shoe.

"They took her away a coupla weeks ago," the man said. "Screaming and yelling that someone was gonna kill her and take all her blood."

Grace stiffened. Hadn't the ethereal teenager said something about blood?

She started to turn, unable to help herself. "Did she say who?"

"Don't turn!" the man snapped. "No, but she was also yelling that some woman was a murderer, that Mrs. Chadman wasn't her mother, that she'd killed Amanda's sister."

"That's crazy talk," Grace said, wondering why Amanda would think Veronica had killed her. "Crazy talk from a disturbed woman."

"Maybe so," the janitor replied, "but it seems to me you ought to think twice about whatever it is you're messing with."

"Did they say where they were taking her?"

There was no reply. After a few moments, Grace stood up and turned. The janitor was some distance away from her, raking as if he hadn't been near her at all. She glanced at the administration building and saw Dr. Grant looking out one of the windows. The janitor must have known they were being watched.

Grace was unaware she was shaking until she tried, three times, to get her keys into the ignition. Why hadn't her mother told her Amanda had been moved?

And why would Amanda say that Veronica wasn't her mother?

TWELVE
▼

W eren't you able to find the art store, Grace?''

Veronica was kneeling on a small mat near a patch of flowers, wearing a broad-brimmed straw hat to protect her from the glaring sun overhead. She held a pair of clippers in one gloved hand, and a pile of cut flowers lay to her side. Grace blinked at her, like a person who had just awakened.

"Art store?"

"You were going to get some supplies," Veronica said.

Grace realized, too late, that she had never bought anything to cover her story. She'd been so stunned by what she'd learned that her original alibi, that she was going into town to get art supplies, was completely forgotten. She looked down at her mother, wishing she could see through her sunglasses, seeing only her own distorted reflection.

"I . . . uhm . . . I wasn't feeling well suddenly," she said.

Now Veronica got to her feet. She tore off the garden gloves and let them fall on the grass, then came closer to her daughter. Taking off her glasses, she peered at Grace as if studying her. Grace had hoped some truth might be revealed in her eyes, but all she saw was the concern of a devoted mother.

"What's wrong, Grace dear?" Veronica asked. "Do you need a doctor?"

Grace smiled a little, pretending to be weary. She hated the lie, but was it any worse than the lie she'd been told?

"I'm just tired," she said. "I didn't sleep well last night. I think I'll go up and take a quick nap."

"You do that," Veronica agreed.

Grace walked up to the front door, then turned.

"Where are the kids?"

"David's got them," Veronica said. "I tell you, I've never seen him so happy. He really likes children."

Grace nodded. She wasn't sure if being with David was a good thing for the kids. She wasn't sure who she could trust here.

She pushed into the house and lumbered upstairs to her room. She realized her story about being tired was only half a lie. She *was* tired, tired of being confused, tired of blank pages in her life. At last she'd had the opportunity to fill those pages, but instead of gaining a family, she'd taken on a whole new series of questions.

Grace caught her reflection in the mirror over her vanity. She sighed deeply and tucked in a wayward strand of hair. Then she leaned closer and spoke to herself.

"What did you expect?" she asked. "That you'd know your entire family history in less than a week's time? These things come gradually, don't they?"

She chewed her lip and waited, but her reflection had no advice.

"And why is it my business what my mother does with Amanda?" she said. "I can't expect to barge into their lives and act as if I've always been here, can I? If my mother wants to tell me about Amanda, she will. And maybe that old janitor was only repeating hearsay. Maybe Amanda didn't say those things at all."

But it bothered her. It bothered her enough that she knew she'd never be able to sleep that night until she confronted her mother and told her what she'd really been doing. She tried to push her worries aside, to accept things as they were. By the time late afternoon rolled around she was so agitated she found herself snapping at the children. They'd been swimming, and they were running through the house with dripping-wet bathing suits.

"Look what you're doing!" she cried angrily. "You'll ruin the carpets!"

The twins stopped short and stared at her in wonder. Trevor raked his fingers through his wet locks.

"Gee, Mom," was all he said, but his voice was full of disappointment. She'd never yelled like that before.

Grace took in a deep breath. "I'm sorry. I just have a lot on my mind. But you should have dried off near the pool."

"Sorry," Seth and Sarah said together.

"Me too," Trevor said.

They went upstairs. Grace watched them, and gave Trevor a reassuring smile when he turned to look back at her. The poor kid. He seemed to be having a mystery of his own in this house, but she was almost too preoccupied to help him.

When the children disappeared from view, she walked down the hall to her mother's office. She hesitated before knocking, expecting to hear the voice of that strange man again. But there was nothing. Veronica called her inside.

"What do you think of this?" she asked, holding out a small vial.

Grace breathed in a strong, fruity aroma.

"It's beautiful," she said.

"A new fragrance line we're considering," Veronica told her, capping the vial. She set it down in a small, velvet-lined box and closed the lid. When she looked at Grace again, she was smiling.

She's so beautiful, and there's so much love in her eyes. How could I doubt her?

"You're looking much better, Grace dear," Veronica said.

Grace, who hadn't rested a moment since arriving home, hardly believed that.

"Mom, I have to talk to you," she said. "I've learned some things, and I'm very confused."

"I'll see if I can help you," Veronica said. "But let's do it in the parlor. I was about to sit down to some tea."

Grace thought if she didn't say anything right away, she'd lose her nerve. But Veronica led her from the room and chattered on about trivial things, leaving her no room to talk. In the parlor, she tugged on a bellpull, then sat down on the couch. Grace took a seat in a chair.

"I have a confession to make," she blurted out. "I wasn't on my way to the art store this morning."

"You went to see Amanda."

Grace felt her heart skip a beat. She realized a look of total shock must have come across her face, because Veronica leaned forward and patted her hand reassuringly.

"Dr. Grant called me after you left," she said. "I do wish you'd told me about it. I would have gotten you in to see your sister."

"But she's not there," Grace said.

Now it was Veronica's turn to look surprised.

"Not there? What do you mean?"

Grace told her about the janitor. Halfway through the story, a maid came in with the tea tray. She set it down, then turned to leave. As Veronica poured, Grace finished her story.

"Nonsense," Veronica said with a wave of her hand. "Of course Amanda is there. Where else would she be?"

Here? Grace was going to ask, but didn't.

"But the janitor said . . ."

"I'll tell you what," Veronica said. She took a sip of tea before continuing. "Let's go back there right now. It'll only take a minute, and you'll be reassured that Amanda is getting the best of care."

Grace nodded. It would help ease her mind to see her sister.

"I'll call Dr. Grant right now," Veronica said. "You inform Mrs. Treetorn that she'll be watching the children for a few hours. We don't want to bring them with us."

"All right," Grace said, and stood up. An hour later, Grace was sitting in Dr. Grant's office. She had noticed the receptionist didn't hesitate to let them in when she saw Veronica

Chadman. Grace thought her mother might have some pull here—perhaps she was a benefactor?

Grant's office was a study of earth tones, as soothing as a view of the Grand Canyon. In fact, a poster depicting the canyon at sunset hung over a terra cotta leather couch. The rug was a rich rust and the chairs were the color of deer. The corners of the big desk were rounded, the windows draped with billowing curtains. The whole effect seemed to be to relax anyone who was there, but Grace felt anything but relaxed. Had the janitor made a fool of her?

Dr. Grant came in moments later and greeted them.

"Hello, Mark," Veronica said.

Grace noticed the fondness in her tone and wondered again if this was the mysterious man in the office.

"Hi, Veronica," he replied. He looked from mother to daughter. "Now it's even more clear that you're related. Those eyes . . ."

Veronica interrupted him. "Grace is upset about something your janitor told her. Do you think you can clear things up?"

"I'll try," Mark said, looking at Grace. "Tell me what he said."

Grace related her story, watching as Mark frowned and shook his head. Finally, he replied, "Todd Nolan isn't outside help. He's one of our patients, allowed to earn some pocket money doing repairs and helping on the grounds. No one can fix a TV like Todd."

"I saw him working on the one in the waiting area," Grace recalled.

"Did a good job on it too," Mark said. "Probably saved us a hundred bucks. But Todd has a problem in that he fantasizes a lot, makes up wild stories. It got so his family couldn't keep him."

"He's detached from reality?"

"In layman's terms, yes," Grant replied. "In reality, he has had very little contact with your sister. You needn't worry. She's safe and sound, and she was certainly never dragged off kicking and screaming."

Grace sighed. So she had been fooled. Was she becoming

paranoid, believing the warnings of a mentally ill old man?

"Can I see her?" she ventured.

"Sure," Mark said, standing. "Come with me."

The two women were led up a flight of stairs, then down a short hall. They passed a security guard and waited as Grant swiped his card through a lock. Veronica took Grace's hand and squeezed it, keeping it in her own as they followed the doctor. She didn't say a word, but Grace knew she was warning her to brace herself. What would Amanda be like? She'd seemed so fragile, so scared at the mall. What would she find?

She had her answer a few minutes later when Mark knocked at a door; then unlocked and opened it.

"Hello, Amanda," he said gently. "Look who's come to visit you."

Amanda was huddled on a cot in a small, neatly furnished room. The sunken eyes that looked up at the trio went wide at the sight of Grace, like a startled animal. Her lips, dry and peeling, worked silently. Grace thought she was trying to say something. But, for some reason, she was too terrified to speak.

"Can I have a few minutes alone with her?" she requested.

"I'm sorry, I don't think that's a good idea," Mark said.

"I agree," Veronica put in. "You know what she did to you at that mall, Grace. No telling what she'd try now."

Grace had a feeling Amanda wouldn't try anything at all, that her sister wanted to speak to her but was afraid. Was she afraid of Veronica? Or of the doctor?

Or was she just too far gone to know anything at all, even fear?

No, there was no denying those eyes. And Grace had another feeling, that the doctor was leaving something out. She needed to talk to someone else, someone not connected to this case.

"All right," she said at last. "Maybe another day, when she's had time to get used to me."

She smiled at Amanda, hoping the expression would encourage her sister to be brave.

"I'll come back," she promised.

Amanda only stared at her, her mouth still working.

They turned and left the room. Just before the doctor closed the door, Grace heard her sister utter one word: "Blood."

"What did that mean?"

"Oh, she says incoherent things like that all the time," Dr. Grant answered, locking the door behind them. "She might be recalling a blood test she had this morning."

"A blood test?" Veronica asked.

"Routine," Mark said. "One of the other patients on the wing came down with chicken pox. We wanted to see if she'd had them."

Grace hardly heard any of this. She was busy coming up with a plan. Finally, when they reached Grant's office, she had her idea.

"Excuse me, where can I find a rest room?"

Mark pointed towards a small hall that jutted out from this one.

"I'll be right back," Grace said, and left.

Instead of using the rest room, however, she began to search the building. She hoped to find the janitor, Todd Nolan. Fortune was in her favor, because he came out of a supply closet carrying a mop, just as she turned a corner. He had his back to her; his head was ducked down.

"Mr. Nolan?"

The man who turned was dark-skinned, and much younger than Todd Nolan had been.

"Can I help you, miss?"

"I was looking for Todd Nolan," Grace said. "Do you know where he is?"

"Sorry, but he's gone," the young man said. He shook his head. "It was a terrible thing that happened to him."

"What kind of thing?"

"Found him late this morning, in the supply closet. He cut his wrists."

Grace felt a chill rush through her. Nolan had committed suicide shortly after she'd left? But why?

"Was he a patient here?"

The black man shook his head. "No way. Todd was as sane as you or me."

He peered at her, his eyes thinning. "Who are you? Why are you asking all these questions about Todd?"

"I . . . I have to go," Grace stammered, and hurried back to the office.

Veronica and Mark were laughing about something when she entered the room. Grace did her best to hide the shock in her face, putting on a fake smile and expressing thanks to the doctor for letting her see Amanda. But the façade was a difficult one, and she had to keep her face turned away from her mother as they were chauffeured home.

She felt sick, a sickness brought on by feelings of confusion and betrayal. So many lies! So many questions!

"Grace dear?"

She shuddered involuntarily.

"Grace, are you ill again?"

God, yes . . . in ways you wouldn't understand, I think.

Why had Todd Nolan cut his own wrists?

"Put your head between your knees, dear."

"I'm all right," Grace said, not recognizing the husky tone of her voice.

She said nothing more during the drive home, closing her eyes and trying to absorb all she'd learned that day. It was hard to make anything of it, and the effort gave her a pounding headache. She excused herself to her room when they got home, crawling under the blankets because, despite the heat, she felt icy cold.

She fell asleep almost at once.

She dreamed once again that she was on the banks of a lake, and the children were sitting in a small rowboat. The oars were controlled by a figure in a dark cloak, but although he was rowing, the boat seemed to stay in one place.

Don't go with him. Don't go with him.

"*Blood!*"

It was her sister Amanda's voice, right behind her. She swung around, but saw only the vast panorama of the Grand Canyon. When she turned back to the lake, she was facing Dr.

Grant's office, instead. Trevor was sitting on the couch, David at his side.

"He was sucking blood from a washcloth, Mom."

"She wants your children," David said. *"She wants their blood."*

"No, the teenager told me that. You aren't supposed to say that."

"Mommy, Daddy's here!"

In the dream, Grace swung around. The office was gone, the Grand Canyon and the lake were gone. She was alone in a desert.

"Mommy! It's Daddy!"

But Seth was here. She could hear his voice on the wind. She could feel his hand on her arm . . .

"Mommy?"

Grace snapped awake, and saw the six-year-old staring at her with confusion in his eyes. She smiled weakly at him, pulling herself up.

"What's up?"

"Daddy's here," Seth told her. "He just drove up to the house and he's parking his car!"

Grace was fully awake now. A new wave of hope washed over her. With Craig here to help her, to give his input, she might be able to find some answers.

THIRTEEN

▼

Grace could hardly hug and kiss Craig enough when she found him waiting in the parlor. He laughed and said, "That's about the nicest greeting I've ever gotten."

"I just missed you so much," Grace said, resting her head against his shoulder. He felt so reassuringly strong.

"We missed you too," Sarah told her father. "Are you gonna stay here with us, Daddy?"

"Just until tomorrow night," Craig said. He looked at Grace, and added, "Classes got out a little early. I was invited to have dinner with the others, but I said I wanted to see my family. So I hopped in the car, and here I am."

"I'm so glad," Grace said, and hugged him again.

"Are you hungry, Dad?" Seth asked. "Nana has the best cook. His name is Felix, like Felix the cat."

Craig laughed. "I could use a cold drink. Wanna fetch one for me, Seth?"

Seth ran from the room without another word. Seeing the disappointed look on Sarah's face, Craig said, "You don't suppose Felix the cat has any snacks in his magic bag, do you?''

Sarah grinned and ran to find out. Now Craig looked around.

''Where's Trevor?''

''I don't know,'' Grace said, surprised her older son hadn't come to greet his father. ''I suppose he's outside somewhere, maybe shooting baskets or horseback riding. He's taken to the stable manager.''

''Well, I'm glad he's not inside on such a nice day, with his nose in a video game or one of those models,'' Craig said. ''I'll catch him a little later after I've rested up. Traffic around Indianapolis was pretty tough this time of day.''

The twins came in with a polished wood tray that held a tall glass of iced tea and a china plate with two brownies smothered in fudge sauce.

''This is great,'' Craig said, and sat down on the couch.

Grace saw how carefully he put the tray on the coffee table, as if the glass surface made him a little nervous. She recalled how awkward he'd felt around these fine pieces the first time he'd been here.

He picked up his glass and took a drink, gazing at Sarah over the rim. When he put it down, he called the little girl to him. She moved closer and smiled as he reached out to twirl a lock of hair that had come loose from her ponytail.

''How're you doing, sweetheart?'' he asked in a gentle tone.

''I'm fine, Daddy.''

''Are you used to sleeping in a different bed now?''

Sarah nodded. Seth moved in closer and said, ''Sometimes weird noises wake me up, Dad, but they never wake up Sarah.''

''Weird noises?''

Grace sat down beside her husband. ''Seth thinks there're people walking behind the walls.''

''That's pretty silly, kid,'' Craig said with a laugh.

''I heard it too,'' Grace said. ''But it's only mice, of course.''

Or rats, she thought, and shuddered.

Craig noticed the involuntary motion. Growing serious suddenly, he asked to children to leave. They went reluctantly, only after Craig had promised to play with them later.

"Grace, is something wrong?" he asked when they were alone. The joyful husband and father, happy to see his family, was gone. "Sarah doesn't look right at all. I noticed it the moment she ran up to my car. Has she been sick?"

"She's had a little trouble sleeping," Grace said. "The poor little thing has had a recurring nightmare. But she didn't wake up last night, and I think she looks better today."

Craig moved closer to her and kissed her. "Grace, you don't look like yourself either. I don't think that greeting I got was just because I've been gone for five days."

Grace sighed. Absently, she reached for his glass and took a sip of the tea. Then she set it down again and said, "Craig, strange things have been happening here. I've learned some things about my family, and I'm very confused."

When she looked at him, her eyes were full of pleading. "You don't know how happy I am to see you. Maybe you can help me straighten things out in my head."

"Tell me everything," Craig urged.

"I don't know where to begin," Grace admitted. She took a deep breath. "Okay, I guess I'll start with my sister Amanda. Do you know that baby doll I'd been working on?"

She told him how she'd found the doll with a needle stuck to its head, and how Veronica admitted Amanda was responsible.

"Do you think it's safe for you to be here?" Craig asked worriedly. "She sounds violent."

"She's back in the hospital," Grace said. "But there's something more interesting that's happened, Craig. I learned that my sister had a baby she lost years ago."

She continued her story, focusing on her sister. There would be time enough to tell about the rat in her bed, the spirit girl, and the journal later. By the time Craig finished his second brownie, she'd told him of her visit to the hospital.

"Why did you think you had to sneak there?" Craig asked, referring to the hospital.

Grace shrugged. "I don't know. It isn't that I don't trust my mother, but . . ."

"Well, it isn't as if she didn't keep things from you," Craig said. "Veronica might have let you know your sister was in the house that first night."

"Did someone mention my name?"

They both looked up to see that Veronica had come into the room, almost as silently as a ghost. Her shift, in multicolored layers of chiffon, floated around her like a spirit's raiments. Grace thought of her spirit girl and wondered how she could tell Craig she'd seen a ghost. She looked at her husband. His eyes were wide, his head tilted quizzically. Grace realized at once what put him off. When he'd seen Veronica, her hair was white, and her face more wrinkled. With her dyed hair and the facial treatments Grace guessed she'd been receiving, she looked much younger.

"Hello, Craig," Veronica said as she came closer. "What a nice surprise."

Slowly, Craig stood up. "Hello, Mrs. Chadman."

He looked at Grace, who could only shrug an explanation.

"I see that Felix has set you up with a snack," Veronica said. "I'm sorry I wasn't here to greet you. Too many things to do downtown. Has Grace been telling you about her visit?"

Grace reached over and gave her husband's big hand as hard a squeeze as she could with her small one. He seemed to get the message.

"Sounds like she's really enjoying herself," he lied.

There was a moment of awkward silence. Grace started to say something mundane to fill it, but Craig beat her to it: "So, how are mother and daughter getting along?"

"Oh, wonderfully!" Veronica said with great enthusiasm. "Grace is everything I ever dreamed a daughter could be."

"Not like Amanda, huh?" Craig mumbled under his breath. Grace cringed.

Veronica said, "I beg your pardon?"

Craig went to the French doors. "Nothing, nothing. Say, the roses look beautiful. Mind if I take a look?"

Veronica came up to him and hooked her arm through his.

Grace thought she saw Craig's shoulders go up a notch, as if he didn't like the older woman's touch. She took his other arm for support, and they went out into the garden.

"Let me tell you about the roses," Veronica said. "My grandmother started this garden at the turn of the century . . .''

Trevor, unaware of his father's surprise arrival, had accepted David's challenge to another one-on-one. Once more, he was beating the stable manager. He didn't think David was letting him win, the way his father sometimes did, because he was puffing and groaning with his efforts. Basketball came naturally to Trevor, who managed to sink one shot after another while his mind was on other things.

"Can I ask you something, David?" he said while lining up a shot.

"Shoot."

Trevor made the basket easily.

"No, I meant, 'Tell me,' " David explained.

"I know what 'shoot' means," Trevor said. He let the ball bounce away. "That other stable manager, the one who died. Do you know what window he fell near?"

David shook his head. "I didn't ask. But that's a strange question for a kid, Trevor. What's on your mind?"

"I'm trying to find a way into the basement," Trevor admitted, feeling he could trust this grownup. "I thought if I knew what window it was, that would be the one I wanted."

David furrowed his brows, then cocked his head towards one of the dark green benches that flanked the court. When they sat down together, he said, "First of all, what do you want in the basement? And second of all, what does that man's death have to do with it?"

"I think Nana and Andros have something hidden downstairs," Trevor reported. "The twins and I found a hidden door the first day we were here, behind a big, old dresser. Andros said there were electrical things in the room, but I think he was lying. Anyway, when I went back to check it out again, there was a padlock on the cellar door!"

"Maybe it's Andros's way of saying the cellar is none of

your business,'' David said with a laugh. ''If he locked the cellar, then it must be something dangerous. I'd forget about it, if I were you.''

''No way,'' Trevor said. ''One night, I heard someone crying down there. Like she got locked in. Andros showed up and he told me someone must have locked the door by mistake. But I think they did it on purpose!''

''So who do you think was down there?''

''How should I know?'' Trevor admitted. ''Anyway, I want to see that room. And I want to find a way inside through a window. But there are so many! We'll be gone before I can get to them all.''

''Would that upset you?'' David asked. ''To leave this place before solving your mystery?''

Trevor's face grew dark. ''I'd leave this place in a minute, if I could. But then we'd come back again and again. And I think it might be dangerous.''

''Trevor, I'm sure you're just imagining things,'' David said. ''In a way, I'm sorry I told you about the last stable manager. But that reminds me that you didn't answer my other question. What does he have to do with this secret room of yours?''

Trevor looked around to be sure no one was listening. He saw a gardener mowing the lawn in the distance and a maid was hanging sheets. They were alone.

''You said they found him dead,'' Trevor said, his voice quiet despite the privacy of the area. ''I think he might have looked through a window, into that secret room, and saw something horrible!''

Now David laughed out loud. He stood up and ruffled Trevor's hair. Frowning, Trevor smoothed it down again.

''What's so funny?''

''You,'' David said, simply. ''You have some imagination, kid. What do you think the guy saw, evil spirits?''

''No, I think he saw Nana and Andros,'' Trevor said. ''And what's the big idea, anyway, making fun of me? You saw a spirit too. You saw Jeffrey.''

David paused, his smile fading. He stared at Trevor for a few minutes.

"Yes, I did," he admitted. "I shouldn't tease you. There are some mysterious things here, but I think, in the long run, you'll find there's nothing evil going on. I'll say it again: Mrs. Chadman is one of the nicest people I've ever met. You just stay out of Andros's way, and I think you'll be fine. And forget about that room."

"No," Trevor said, standing. "I'm going to find it, and then you'll feel stupid."

He ran off the court, leaving the stable manager shaking his head. Trevor, more determined than ever to find a way to that secret room, returned to exploring the perimeter of the house. He'd been looking every opportunity he'd had, although there had been few. Either his mother or grandmother was around, or the twins were pestering him to play.

He'd developed a system to mark off the last window explored, setting a rock in the center of the dirt in front of it. He found this now, and moved on to the next one. And, to his excitement, he found it was unlocked! Carefully, after looking back over his shoulder to be certain he was well hidden by the bushes, he started to open it.

As if it had been trapped there for a thousand years, a horrible stench poured from the small opening. Trevor gagged, turning his face away and covering his mouth. He knew that smell. He'd had a hamster that had escaped a few years back and had died in the wall behind the kitchen. It was a hot summer, and his father had had to knock out a piece of the wall to remove the rotting body. This was kind of like that.

Something wet and cold dropped onto his hand. He shook it off, thinking nothing of it. Then, holding his breath against the smell, he went back to work. A few minutes later, the window was halfway open. The ancient paint made the job difficult, and the late-afternoon sun was no help. Trevor began to sweat.

Something else dropped on his arm. It was shadowy in here, hard to see. Trevor wasn't afraid of bugs, so he simply slapped the slimy sensation away. The window was almost open.

Then, suddenly, he felt something cold slither down his shirt collar.

"Gross!" he cried, jumping out of the bushes. He pulled his shirt open, and a worm dropped to the ground.

No, not a worm. A maggot, fat and wiggly. With a cry of disgust, he moved back from the window. Maggots were eating something that had died in there! He felt something tickle him inside his shirt.

Then two slimy things.

Three: one on his back and two on his chest.

Dozens, countless . . .

Trevor screamed, ripping off his shirt. There were maggots all over him, stuck to his skin, wriggling, disgusting.

"GET OFF! GET OFF! GET OFF!!!"

He slapped at himself, knocking the creatures to the ground. The sight of them all made him feel a little queasy, and he began to shake.

They crawled into the mud, one by one, and disappeared.

Trevor slapped one off his neck before it could get into his hair.

"I am not afraid, I am not afraid . . ."

He repeated this over and over, until the last of the worms had gone. Then he stood staring at the ground, wondering how they had disappeared so fast.

Wondering where they had all come from in the first place.

"Master Trevor?"

Andros's voice was like an arctic wind, grabbing hold of him and shaking him. He swung around to see the tall old servant staring down at him. How long had he been there?

"Your mother is looking for you," Andros said. He glanced down at Trevor's white shirt, all mussed-up now on the grass. "Your father has come, and dinner is ready."

"Dad? Dad's here?"

Pushing away thoughts of the maggots, Trevor grabbed his shirt and ran as fast as he could. It wasn't until he was near the door that he realized he'd left the window open. He considered going back to close it for just a second. But then he decided that it was hidden well enough. It was more important to see Dad, to tell him what had been happening here.

Dad would find out if Andros had anything to do with those worms, and he'd make that jerk pay!

He flew through the house until he found his family seated around the dining room table.

"Dad!" he cried, running to give him a hug.

"Whoa, I must rate pretty high for that," Craig said with a laugh. He held Trevor at arm's length. "Don't you have a shirt?"

"It got dirty," Trevor said, holding it up. "When did you get here? How come no one told me?"

Before his father could answer, Veronica interrupted, "Trevor dear, no one comes to my table without a shirt."

Trevor glared at her. How dare she interrupt him when he was talking to his dad, whom he hadn't seen in almost a week?

"Yes, Trevor," his mother put in gently. "Go on up and get a new shirt if that one is dirty. Then find the twins and bring them to dinner."

Trevor obeyed, deciding he couldn't talk to his father now anyway. A short time later, he returned with Seth and Sarah. They'd been running through the fields and had picked a bouquet of wildflowers. Nana made a big fuss and asked a maid to set them in a Limoges vase on the sideboard.

Dinner was pleasant, the conversation turned to trivial matters. But Trevor knew something was wrong. He could see the way his mother kept staring at his father, as if she had something to tell him. And he thought the twins sensed something too, because they were quieter than usual.

"How long are you staying with us, Craig?" Veronica was asking.

"Only until tomorrow evening," Craig said. "I have to be at work early Monday morning for my first day."

Monday morning, Trevor thought. He only had a short time to get to his father in private. Only a short time to make his father understand that there was something weird, something bad, in this house.

FOURTEEN
▼

I thought we'd never be alone," Craig said. He was lying in the bed with his arms crossed behind his head, the white comforter folded halfway down his chest.

Grace came out of the bathroom dressed in an oversized T-shirt, her chestnut hair hanging loose over her shoulders. She padded barefoot to the air conditioner and turned it down.

"Chilly in here," she said. "I think one of the maids turns up the AC about an hour before bedtime each night, to cool off the rooms. Most of the time, it's too cold."

Craig grinned mischievously at her. "So come here and I'll warm you up."

"Sounds nice," Grace said, and crawled under the covers. She snuggled up close to him, and he began to play with her hair.

"You smell good," he said.

"One of Mom's products," Grace replied.

"I noticed that vinegary smell when I got out of the car," Craig said.

"Really? I don't notice it at all any more. I suppose I've gotten used to it."

Craig sighed and pulled her even closer to him.

"I don't think I could ever become so used to a place like this that I wouldn't notice things around me," he said. "This isn't the same room we slept in when we were first here, is it?"

Grace looked around at the muted shades of coral and mint, with dark gray accents. Their first room had been a study of beige tones.

"I asked to be moved," she said. "I had a sort of . . . incident."

"What happened?"

She told him about the rat. He pulled away now, turning on his side with his head on his hand. His eyes were full of concern.

"My God, Grace," he said. "That could have been dangerous. Those things carry rabies!"

Grace shivered. She hadn't thought of that.

"Who would do such a thing?" Craig demanded. "Have there been other . . . incidents, as you called it?"

"Oh no," Grace said quickly, trying to reassure him. "Everyone's been very nice, or at least polite. But I've been trying to figure out what happened. Craig, I heard my mother talking to a man yesterday. I have no doubt from their conversation that he's someone special in her life."

"Her lover?"

"I think so," Grace said. "I tried to get a glimpse of him, but he seemed to vanish. There must have been another exit from the room, because I never saw him come out. It was as if he was a spirit."

"Strange," Craig said.

Grace wriggled herself around until her back was pressed against her husband's chest, spoon-fashion. He kissed her hair.

"If he makes any threat to you," he said darkly, "any threat at all, you tell me. I'll deal with it."

"I'll be okay," Grace said. "I don't suppose we'll be staying here very long anyway. As soon as you find a place for us . . .''

"You have to come to Bryce City and take a look," Craig said, brightening. Grace could tell he felt comfortable talking about their new home. "I have a few places in mind. When I get back Monday, I'll make an appointment with the real estate agent. She can take us around on . . . when?"

"As soon as possible," Grace said.

"I'll make it Tuesday," Craig suggested. "Can your mother babysit?"

"I'll ask her," Grace said, "but I'm sure she won't mind. She's very fond of the kids now, especially the twins."

"What about Trevor?" Craig asked. "I noticed a little tension there when he came into the dining room."

"I'm afraid Trevor's developing some strange ideas about his grandmother," Grace replied, "and this house. He seems to think we're in some kind of danger."

She thought of her conversation with David a few days earlier, when he had told her Amanda also feared they were in danger. She would have to tell Craig about that sometime, but there was just so much she could say in one night.

"What would make him think that?" Craig asked. "It isn't like Trevor to jump to wild conclusions. Did something happen to him?"

"Well, he thinks he saw something," Grace said, and proceeded to tell how Trevor had mistaken two servants for Veronica and Andros. When she finished, Craig had to agree the idea was ridiculous.

"But I'll talk to him," he said. "I'll see if I can figure out what's on his mind."

He kissed her again, this time moving from her hair to her ear to her neck. Grace turned herself around to kiss him back.

"Can we forget all these things for a while?" she asked softly. "I've only got you for a short time, after all."

"My feelings exactly," Craig said, and pulled her close for a kiss that was deeper, warmer, and more passionate than before . . .

*　　*　　*

Deep in the night, Grace felt someone shaking her. She opened her eyes, and came awake immediately to see the spirit girl at her side. Her eyes were wide, her grip on Grace's arm firm and icy.

"Did you see her? Did you see Amanda?"

Slowly, Grace sat up.

"I tried," she said. "But she didn't say anything."

"She was afraid," the girl said, frowning. "They make her afraid."

"A man named Nolan said she was taken away," Grace said. "But when I went back with Veronica, she was there."

Now the girl looked frightened. She finally let go of Grace's arm and took a step back.

"Don't go with her!" she cried. "Amanda won't talk if she's there!"

"Why?" Grace asked. "Why is Amanda afraid of our mother?"

There was a moan and a ruffling noise. The spirit girl looked over Grace's shoulder with wide eyes and vanished.

"What was that?" Craig demanded, sitting up. "I thought I saw—"

"You were just dreaming, Craig," Grace said.

He turned on the bedside lamp and peered at her.

"No, no I wasn't," he insisted. "You saw her too. You were talking to her, Grace. Will you tell me what the hell is going on?"

Grace took in a deep breath, steeling herself for her husband's skepticism.

"That," she said, "was a ghost."

Craig's mouth dropped open. He looked past his wife's shoulder, then turned his gaze to lock eyes with hers.

"A ghost," he said simply.

Grace nodded. "I know it's incredible. But this house is haunted, Craig. I didn't want to tell you before because it's so hard to believe."

"Of course it is," Craig said, although his expression was doubtful. "There are no such things as ghosts."

But he was blinking, as if trying to focus on the area where the girl had just been standing, as if trying to bring her back again.

"You know what you saw, Craig."

"People don't just . . . vanish," he said slowly.

"She does," Grace said.

Craig gave his head a rough shake and pushed the covers aside. He shuffled to the bathroom, mumbling to himself. Grace sat up and waited for him to return. Would he believe what he had seen with his own eyes? She needed him to believe in the spirit girl. Grace wanted to share the entire puzzle of her new family with her husband, and the girl was just too big a part of it to be ignored.

When Craig came out of the bathroom, the tips of the bangs that had fallen across his forehead were wet, his eyes bright. He'd splashed water on his face to wake himself up.

"Maybe you'd better tell me the whole story, Grace," he said.

Grace opened her arms to him, and he came back to bed.

"I saw her for the first time that day we came to meet my mother," Grace began.

Some time later, she drew the story to an end. She wasn't sure if Craig believed her completely, but he seemed willing to humor her. That was good enough for Grace, for now.

"If she wants to warn you about something," he asked, "then why doesn't she come right out and say what it is?"

"I don't know," Grace admitted. "But there's something else, Craig. Something that worries me. She isn't the only ghost."

"It's a big house," Craig said.

"Don't joke," Grace said, annoyed. "This one's a young boy, and he's after Trevor."

Craig pulled away a little.

"Trevor didn't say anything about that."

"He hasn't had two minutes alone with you," Grace pointed out. "And besides, he won't even talk to *me* about it. Trevor seems to have his own agenda regarding this situation. But I'll tell you something. Remember when I told you on the phone that I'd found my grandmother's journal?"

Craig grunted a positive reply.

Grace continued, "She mentions a sick child on the first page but never again. I wonder if the boy following Trevor could be the same one? Could he have died back then?"

Craig laid back, pulling Grace with him. She rested her head on his chest, listening to his heartbeat. For a long time, it was the only sound she heard. Finally, his chest rose and fell in a sigh.

"So, what do you want to do?"

"I was hoping you could give me some ideas," Grace said.

"Well, walking away from all this comes to mind," Craig said.

Grace shook her head, her long hair making soft noises against Craig's chest.

"No," she said. "I've found my mother at last, and no matter what, I'm not going to lose her."

"But it seems she's deceived you in several ways," Craig said.

"Maybe it's only my perception," Grace said. "Maybe she has her reasons, which she'll reveal to me when she feels the time is right."

"So you want to tough it out until you get some answers?"

"Or until you find us a new place to live."

Craig gave her a tight squeeze. "Then I'll have to work twice as hard to do that."

No more words were exchanged. Grace fell asleep in Craig's arms, feeling safer and more secure than she had in days.

Neither of them were aware that Trevor had been listening outside the door. A short time earlier, Jeffrey had appeared to him, just as the teenager had come to Grace. He'd shaken Trevor roughly until he was awake.

"What do you want?" Trevor asked softly, so he wouldn't wake up the twins. The door between their rooms was open.

"You found the way in," Jeffrey said. "Don't let it go. If you wait until tomorrow to climb in the window, you'll never get in."

"But it's the middle of the night," Trevor complained. He was tired, and it was starting to rain outside. He could hear the soft tapping of drops on his window, the scratching of a sycamore blowing in the wind.

"If you don't go in now," Jeffrey insisted, "it will be too late. And then you may never save your family."

Trevor's eyes thinned as he considered this. Finally, he rolled out of bed. He pulled his sneakers on over his bare feet and shrugged into his robe. It wouldn't be much protection if the rain grew stronger, but he might call attention to himself if he tried to rummage through the coat closet in the foyer in search of his jacket.

"All right," he said. "But it's dark, and I can't get a flashlight. You'll have to show me the way."

Jeffrey led him from the room. As they passed Trevor's parents' room, the young boy noticed a light was shining beneath the door. It was nearly three A.M. What were they doing up?

Then he heard his name.

"This one's a young boy, and he's after Trevor."

Trevor turned to look at his spiritual friend. He was alone in the hall.

"Jeffrey?" he whispered.

There was no answer. He shivered a little. Was Jeffrey right there, watching him? But if he was, why had he vanished?

"I found my mother at last . . ."

". . . she deceived you . . ."

He was only picking up bits of the conversation, muffled as it was by the heavy oak door. Nodding his head vigorously, he cheered his father on. Yes, Veronica had deceived his mother. She'd deceive them all until she got what she wanted, whatever that was. Dad had to talk Mom into leaving this place!

There was silence now. The light under the door went out. Trevor took a deep breath and moved on down the hallway. All he could do was hope. Maybe, at breakfast, he'd learn that Mom and Dad had decided it was time to leave. There was nothing he'd rather hear more.

Downstairs, he made his way to the parlor. He'd decided the French doors were the easiest way to get out.

The moon was hidden behind clouds now, and the night was so dark he could hardly make his way across the room. When he bumped into a chair, making it scrape along the floor, he froze. Had someone heard that? He waited for a long time, but nothing happened. No one came running downstairs; no one switched on the light to catch him in the act.

"I'm okay," he whispered.

He looked around in the dark, barely making out the shapes of the furniture.

"I could really use you now, Jeffrey," he said, but the boy didn't appear.

At last, he unlocked the door and walked out into the night. It was warm, despite the rainfall. The chirping of crickets mixed with the gentle patter of the rain on the wooden deck. Moving as quietly as he could, afraid his sneakers would make loud thumping noises that would bring everyone in the house outside, Trevor went to the stairs and down into the garden.

In the dark in the rain, it wasn't so easy to find the window he'd left that afternoon. He had to use the basketball court as a reference point, retracing the moves he'd made after his time with David. Finally, he came to the row of bushes he was certain hid the window he wanted.

But he couldn't move any farther. He could only think of those disgusting worms, crawling inside his shirt, trying to get into his hair. Worms that had appeared and disappeared as easily as ghosts.

This one's a young boy, and he's after Trevor.

"No," Trevor said firmly. "Andros did that to me, not Jeffrey! Andros made those worms happen!"

And if he could do something like that, there was no telling what else he could do. After all, hadn't he moved from one side of the house to the other in a matter of minutes, making Trevor's mother believe he'd never been with Veronica. What kind of powers did that man have?

The answer, he was certain, lay in the dark, secret room in the cellar. He crouched down, pushed branches aside, and moved in to open the window once again. It wouldn't budge. Trevor tried with all his might, but he couldn't open it. He guessed, to his dismay, that it had been locked from the inside.

"Jeffrey?" he whisper-called. "I need you! You can open this, can't you?"

Jeffrey didn't reply. If he was there at all, and Trevor couldn't be sure either way, he wasn't saying a word. Trevor knew he couldn't open the window without tools. But this proved something to him. It proved that he'd found a way inside, or else why would anyone have bothered to lock it up again?

He crawled backwards, out of the bushes. Sheltered by their branches, he hadn't realized the rain had grown stronger. A near-deafening crash of thunder made him jump to his feet with a cry. He half-expected Andros's big hand to fall on his shoulder.

But nothing happened.

Trevor knew there was no more he could do tonight. In spite of Jeffrey's warnings, he had to wait until he had the tools to open the window. Besides, if it was so important to the ghost, why hadn't he stayed to help. Trevor felt himself growing annoyed. More than that, he was getting wetter by the moment. He broke into a run, cutting across the grass to the deck. His sneakers squished loudly as he walked over the wooden planks to the parlor doors. Now, someone was certain to hear him. But he was too wet and tired to really care.

He went to the door and turned the handle.

Nothing happened. The handle moved just a fraction, then stuck.

"Oh no," he mumbled.

It was the other door he'd unlocked, of course. He tried that, without luck.

Someone had locked the door again! Did someone know he was out here?

Had Andros seen him and locked him out of the house?

A shiver racked his stocky frame, in spite of the warm night. He was locked out! What was he going to do now?

"Well, I'm not gonna cry," he said with determination,

running from the deck. He didn't care what noise he made now.

He thought he remembered which tree led up to Seth and Sarah's bedroom window. It was at the corner of the house nearest the stables. For a moment, he considered going there, to spend the night in David's apartment. But he thought that might get the stable manager in trouble, maybe even cost him his job. In spite of the way he'd doubted Trevor's worries, he'd been the closest thing Trevor had to a friend here. He didn't want to hurt David, so he banished that idea from his mind.

Instead, he found hand-and footholds in the aging tree and began shimmying up to his window.

He would knock until Seth came to investigate, he decided, and then his little brother would let him in. It would take a big bribe to keep the little kid's mouth shut, but it would be worth it just to be in his own dry, warm bed.

The branches were slippery in the rain, and he lost his footing a few times. Only his strong grip kept him from falling to the ground below. Just a few more feet to go . . .

He reached the window just as a crack of lightning brightened the sky. It turned the glass into a mirror—

—and Trevor was barely able to make out the form of someone on the branch behind him.

Before he could scream, a hand clamped over his mouth, and strong arms pulled him far back into unconsciousness.

Eyes were staring down at him. Voices spoke, sounding farther away than the mouths hidden behind surgical masks.

"We weren't going to do anything while the father was here."

"What choice do we have? He was snooping around."

"But he's already suspicious about the little girl. If another child seems ill . . ."

"We won't do much," said the first voice. Trevor couldn't turn his head, couldn't tell who was speaking. It was a man, but he couldn't place the voice. "Just enough to make him forget."

A sensation of something cold and hard against his back came to him.

Sarah's cold, hard bed.

He opened his mouth to scream but couldn't. Now he realized there was something around his head, strapping his mouth closed. He could only watch in mute, paralyzed horror as the white-coated figure at his side held up a hypodermic needle. Liquid shot into the air, liquid that Trevor was certain meant his death.

He struggled in vain, but only a muffled cry of terror came out as the needle was plunged into his hip.

"Trevor? Trevor honey, wake up!"

It was his mother. Trevor tried to open his eyes and call out to her but only succeeded in throwing up.

All over his own pillow.

Groggily, he pulled himself up onto his elbow.

"Mo . . . o-om?"

"Oh, Trevor," she said. "Come on, honey, let me help you out of bed."

"I'll get one of the maids to bring in new sheets," his father said.

Trevor turned to watch him leave the room, but his head hurt so much he could only close his eyes and lean against his mother.

"Gross," Seth said, standing in the doorway.

"Get back in bed, Seth," Grace ordered.

Trevor let himself be led into the bathroom. He didn't protest as his mother helped him out of his pajamas, then washed him down. The warm cloth felt soothing, reviving. He was already feeling better, although he was still shaking all over. He felt his mother's cool hand against his forehead.

"You don't seem to have a fever," she said.

"I'm okay," Trevor said.

But he wasn't so sure about that. What had happened? Vague thoughts of leaving his room came to him, thoughts of struggling with a locked door. They meant nothing.

He turned to the sink and brushed away the sour taste in

his mouth. His mother watched him with concern in her eyes, her arms wrapped around the pink seersucker bathrobe she was wearing. He heard activity in the bedroom and guessed a maid was fixing the bed.

"I heard you screaming, Trevor," his mother said. "Were you having a nightmare?"

I was in Sarah's cold, hard bed.

But he couldn't have been. Sarah had only dreamed about that bed.

"I . . . don't remember," he admitted.

He shuffled back into the bedroom. His father was gazing at him, as if waiting for him to explain something. He had a strange feeling of being in some kind of trouble, that he'd done something wrong. But he couldn't explain it.

"The bed is ready," the maid said.

"Thank you," Grace replied, dismissing her.

The maid gathered up the dirty sheets and left. Grace helped her son into bed, tucking him in as if he were a small child. He didn't protest that he was ten, too big to be babied. It felt good to have someone take care of him right now.

"How do you feel now?" Craig asked.

"Okay, I guess," Trevor lied. How could he explain that he felt as if something was missing, as if something important had just happened to him and he couldn't remember it?

His mother bent down and kissed his forehead. "Then try to sleep. We're right down the hall if you need us."

Trevor settled into his pillows and closed his eyes. Visions of people in white doctors' coats and masks came to him, but he forced them away. They made him feel sick again, and he thought it would be dumb to throw up after he'd just gotten new sheets.

"Good night, then," his father said, patting his arm.

"Sleep well, Trevor," his mother said.

After the grownups left, Seth called out from the other room, "Trevor?"

"What?"

"How come you went outside tonight?"

Trevor's eyes snapped open. Outside? The vision of him

struggling with a locked door came back, stronger than before. He was standing on the deck, in the rain, trying to get back into the house . . .

"I . . . uh . . ." again, he was at a loss for words, so he snapped, "None of your business, okay?"

"You don't hafta get so mad," Seth pouted. "I wasn't the one who was dumb enough to go outside in a rainstorm. And I wasn't dumb enough to climb a tree and try to get in a window."

Now Trevor sat up straight. It was coming back to him. Jeffrey had been here, had led him out of the room. Then he'd disappeared. Somehow, Trevor had made his way outside, but why?

The window. He must have been looking for the window. And, somehow, he'd gotten locked out of the house. The tree would have been the logical way to get back inside. "Why . . . why didn't you open it?"

" 'Cause you left," Seth said. "You didn't knock or anything. That was weird, Trevor."

Trevor nodded in the dark. Weird, yeah. But it was even more weird that he couldn't remember any of this clearly, including how he'd gotten back in the house.

A wave of nausea came over him again, and he curled himself up in a ball to fight it, pulling his covers around him like a protective shell.

As they walked down the hall together, Craig put his arm around his wife's small shoulders and held her tightly.

"Did you see his shoes?"

"Trevor's shoes? No."

"They were wet," Craig said, "as if they'd gotten muddy, and Trevor had washed them off."

"How could that be?" Grace asked. "It didn't start raining until late in the night, and he was sound asleep."

Craig opened the door, and they walked to the bed together. Outside the window, the sun was just beginning to rise, and the howling winds of the storm had become gentle breezes again.

"I think he went outside," Craig said.

"Why?"

They climbed into bed together. Grace snuggled up against her husband.

"Maybe he's looking for something," Craig suggested. "The same way you're looking."

"In the middle of the night?" Grace asked. "Outside?"

"I think you'd better have a long talk with our son," Craig said. "I don't like him sneaking around this place in the dark. It's dangerous."

Grace nodded in response. She closed her eyes, trying to fall asleep again.

There was nothing she could do about Trevor until morning. But the birds were starting to sing, and she knew she'd never be able to sleep.

"Something else bothers me," Craig said after a few moments. "Why wasn't your mother there? Her room is just around the corner from the children's. Surely she would have heard him screaming like that."

Grace started to speak, to defend her mother, but there was nothing she could say. She wondered about that herself. Didn't Veronica care about the child? Or had Trevor been so cold and rude to her lately that she felt unwelcome?

She clung to her husband, thinking he was leaving the next night, thinking she only had him to help her solve her mysteries for a few more hours.

FIFTEEN

▼

Trevor sat at the breakfast table with his chin resting on his hand, staring listlessly at the eggs Benedict he pushed around on a gold-rimmed china plate. Toast grew cold on a matching dish. His orange juice, usually gone in a gulp or two, sat untouched.

"Still feeling bad?" his father asked from the other end of the table.

"I dunno," Trevor said dully. He was too tired to know just how he felt.

His mother, sitting next to him, pressed a hand to his forehead. Trevor grimaced. He didn't want anyone making a fuss over him. He just wanted to *remember* what had happened last night to make him feel this way.

"I hate to say it, Trevor," his mother said, "but this is what happens when you wander out of the house at night, in the rain. What were you thinking about?"

"Is that what happened?" Veronica asked.

Her voice was pitched higher than usual, innocent-sounding. It made Trevor cringe. Somehow, he was certain she knew what had happened. Maybe she'd even done something to make him sick.

A vision of faces covered with white masks came and went.

"One of the maids found muddy footprints near the parlor doors," Veronica said, "and the deck had been cleaned before everyone went to bed last night."

She turned to her grandson, but Trevor looked down at his cold eggs.

"Why did you do that, Trevor dear?" she asked. "What were you looking for?"

"I don't remember," Trevor said, and that was partly true. He was looking for a window. He'd found it, and he hoped to get to it again. But he didn't remember anything else.

He heard the sound of pouring liquid and looked up to see a maid filling Sarah's glass. Sarah's cheeks were pink this morning, not grayish like they'd been before. He wondered if his sister had felt like this the mornings after she'd had those nightmares.

"Maybe he was sleepwalking," Craig suggested now, making small circles with a wedge of toast.

"Sleepwalking in a tree?" Seth asked. "Cool! I never knew you could climb a tree when you slept!"

If he'd been close enough to his little brother, Trevor would have kicked him. He vowed he'd do something just as bad to the twerp later.

"Seth, what are you talking about?"

Seth, not realizing he was digging a deep hole for his brother, told how he'd seen him in the tree outside his window.

"I saw him when the lightning flashed," Seth said. "But when it flashed again, he was gone."

Trevor tried to make himself disappear.

"Trevor Matheson," Grace said. "You locked yourself out of the house, and then you tried to climb a tree to get back in your room?"

"Bad move, Trev," Craig said. "With that lightning . . ."

Now Trevor felt even worse than before. He hadn't even considered the possibility of the tree being struck by lightning.

He heard his mother sigh deeply, a sound he hated. It had been a long time since she'd been really, really ticked off at him.

He braced himself for the worse.

"Trevor, I don't know what I'd do if anything happened to you," she said. "You might have been killed in that storm! I don't know what's on your mind, because you refuse to tell me. I don't know what you could have been looking for outside. But I do know that the little boy I love so much could have been killed last night."

"We're going to have to punish you, Trev," Craig said quietly.

The young boy nodded slowly. He felt tears rising, not out of fear of what his parents would do, but out of frustration. How could he explain his fears when he didn't understand them himself? How could they help him when they had their own problems?

"You'll be confined to your bedroom for the duration of this visit," his mother said. "No more going outside, day or night."

"Oh, Grace," Veronica put in. "I'm sure he didn't mean to act foolishly. Trevor knows he made a mistake."

Hearing her hated voice made Trevor's anger rise again. He pushed his chair back.

"I don't need you to stick up for me!" he shouted, and ran from the room. His voice echoed down the hall as he ran for the stairs. "JUST LEAVE ME ALONE!"

Grace buried her face in her hands. Had she handled that wrong? Trevor had to know his behavior was dangerous and unacceptable. But he was so sensitive and such a smart child. Maybe she should have had a reasonable talk with him.

"What's wrong, Mommy?" Sarah asked.

Grace looked up. The twins had come to stand on either side of her, matching expressions of concern on their little faces. She managed a smile for them.

"I'm just worried about Trevor," she said.

"He's a bad kid," Seth growled. "He made you cry."

"Oh no!" Grace said. "It isn't that at all. Listen, you don't need to worry about Trevor. We'll work this out. It looks like a beautiful day today. Maybe we can all go swimming later."

"Except Trevor," Sarah pouted.

Grace sighed wearily. "Except Trevor. Go on now, go outside and play."

The twins ran off. Grace stood up, and Craig followed her. Veronica remained seated, sipping delicately at a teacup.

"Well, what now?" Grace asked.

Craig turned to his mother-in-law.

"We were wondering about something," he said. "Didn't you hear Trevor screaming last night?"

Grace stared at her husband with wide eyes. She would never have asked that question, putting her mother on the defensive.

But Veronica's expression was guileless.

"No, I didn't hear him at all," she said. "Poor darling. He's had a rough night, hasn't he? If only we knew what made him wander off in the dark . . ."

She turned to stare out the window, pensive.

"It was pretty loud," Craig pressed. "I can't believe you didn't hear it."

"Oh, I was listening to music through a personal CD player," Veronica said with a dismissive toss of her hand.

"At four-thirty in the morning?"

"Craig . . ."

Veronica smiled at him. "I couldn't sleep. Too many business matters on my mind. It often happens. I doze off for a short period, then I'm wide awake again. I find that Mozart helps me relax."

To Grace's relief, Craig seemed to buy this idea.

Now Veronica stood up. "Grace, so much has happened these past few days. I know it seems I'm keeping things from you—"

"I don't think that at all," Grace blurted, and could tell instantly by her mother's expression that Veronica knew it was a lie.

"No, no, you have found some information on your own,"

Veronica said. "And I promise I'll fill you in as much as I can. But there's only so much I can tell you about the past twenty-nine years in only a few days."

She looked at Craig. "How much longer will Grace and the children be able to stay?"

"Grace is meeting me in Bryce City Tuesday to look at a new home," Craig said.

"I was going to ask if you'd babysit," Grace put in quickly.

"No need to ask," Veronica told them. "I'd be delighted. The twins are darling, no trouble at all."

Both Grace and Craig noticed she didn't mention Trevor, but they let the matter slide for the moment.

"Anyway, it will take some time to get things going," Craig went on now. "We have to move our things from the apartment in Tulip Tree, have to sign the necessary papers . . ."

"You know you're welcome to stay as long as you like," Veronica said. She smiled at Grace. "As a matter of fact, I'm glad the visit will be extended. I've got something to show you, Grace. Will you come upstairs with me?"

They followed her up two flights of stairs. Veronica fielded their questions, insisting what she had to show Grace was a big surprise. She stopped at one of the three doors; Grace remembered it had been locked when she was exploring.

"I wanted to wait until everything was done in here," Veronica said as she turned a key in the lock, "but I think you need to see this now. I hope it cheers you up."

She opened the door to reveal a large, sunny room. Grace's mouth dropped open, her worries forgotten for the moment.

Veronica had had the attic room turned into a studio for Grace's dollmaking business. Grace stood in frozen wonder, taking in the big worktable, the kiln, the supplies she would never have been able to afford on her own. She squeezed Craig's arm and gave him a look of surprise.

"This is . . . amazing," Craig said.

Grace said nothing. She moved farther into the room and ran her hand over the highly polished wooden shelves that went from floor to ceiling between two tall windows.

"We'll fill those with art books, paper, and fabric," Veronica said, "as soon as you let me know what you need."

"It's wonderful," Grace said at last. "Oh, Mom!"

She ran to her mother and hugged her. Then she broke away and went to look at the kiln.

"This is great," she said. "Better than anything I could buy."

Craig opened the doors of an armoire and traced his fingers along the wood inside.

"Is this an antique?" he asked.

"Passed down from my grandmother," Veronica said. "I wanted Grace to have it, as a link to her past."

Grace smiled at her from across the room. "I like that idea."

"I thought it would be a good place to store finished dolls and clothes," Veronica said.

"It's perfect," Grace replied. She came over and studied the armoire herself. "But how did you know what to buy for me?"

"I had one of my secretaries do some research," Veronica said. "I explained that I wanted everything needed to make porcelain dolls and the names of the best equipment brands. I had planned to have you use this during your visits here. It isn't quite finished, but I thought you needed something to cheer you up."

"Oh, it does, it does," Grace said. "I need to get back to my work full-time, especially with that show coming up next month. Sculpting has always helped me focus. Maybe if I'm working on a new doll, I'll be able to think clearly and answer some of my own questions."

Veronica smiled fondly at her. "Grace, if I can do it at all, I'll answer your questions."

Grace looked at her husband and noticed he was gazing at Veronica with a strange expression on his face. Before she could ask what was on his mind, Veronica said, "The closet is filled with supplies—buckets, paint, that substance you call porcelain slip. And I bought an array of paints."

She looked at her watch. "The time! I have to run to headquarters for a few hours. You enjoy yourself here, Grace. If there's anything missing, please tell Andros and he'll have it purchased for you immediately.''

Grace, still a little overwhelmed, could only nod and smile. She gave her mother another hug, and the woman left.

''Wow,'' Grace said, turning to her husband.

''Nice to have money,'' Craig said.

Grace furrowed her brows at him. ''You aren't jealous, are you? Because my mother can buy me all these things—''

''—and I can't,'' Craig said. He shrugged. ''A little, I suppose. But that's not what's bothering me.''

''What, then?''

''I can't help wondering if this is meant to be a diversion,'' Craig said. ''Something to keep you too busy to do any more research on your family.''

Grace went to the worktable, its polished surface pale yellow and completely free of scratches. It was twice the size of the table she'd used in their apartment kitchen.

''I don't think so,'' she said. ''They must have been working on it for a long time, and Mom couldn't have known I'd start looking up family history this soon after meeting her. Besides, she promised me she'd answer my questions, didn't she?''

Craig came to her side, leaning against the table with his arms folded.

''In her own sweet time,'' he said. ''And I'm curious to hear what she has to say about ghosts.''

''I wasn't going to mention that,'' Grace said. ''You were skeptical, and you've known me for years. I don't want my mother, who doesn't know me well, to think I'm crazy.''

''Maybe she's seen them herself.''

''She never mentioned them,'' Grace said. She grinned at her husband. ''But then again, maybe she doesn't want me to think *she's* crazy.''

She went to the closet now and found a package of clay. Bringing it to the table, she threw it down and began to knead it into pliability. Craig found a pair of three-legged stools and brought them around to her side of the table. Grace smiled a thanks at him and sat, and he took the other one.

"Anything in mind?" he asked, indicating the clay.

"I think so," Grace said. "I've been doing a lot of sketches lately."

She didn't mention that, one night, she'd drawn dozens of pictures of the spirit girl.

"I want to do a tribute to my mother," she said. "A two-doll set, one mother, one little girl. Maybe in period costumes."

"Sounds beautiful," Craig said. "I can't wait to see what you do with it."

He kissed her on the cheek. She laughed a little and held up her clay-covered hands.

"Wish I could hug you," she said.

"Never stopped you before."

She tilted her head. "Well . . . this isn't our own apartment."

"You can say that again," Craig said, looking around at the vast, sunny, well-equipped studio. He patted her shoulder. "Listen, I want to spend some time with the kids before I have to leave this afternoon. You'll be okay up here alone, won't you?"

"Why wouldn't I be?"

Grace knew what Craig was insinuating. He thought the spirit girl might return, and he wasn't sure what to make of her.

"She won't hurt me, Craig," Grace told him.

Craig seemed to understand what she was thinking, because he shook his head.

"I'm not talking about your ghost," he said. "This room is far from the rest of the house. Someone left a rat in your bed, Grace. What if . . . ?"

"Oh, Craig," Grace said with eternal patience, yanking off a piece of clay and kneading it into the shape of a head, about the size of her palm. "I'll be fine. You run off and take the twins into the pool, like we promised."

She wanted to tell him to look in on Trevor but decided

Craig could make that decision for himself. He gave her a kiss, promised he'd be back shortly, and left.

Craig had also thought of Trevor. He sort of felt sorry for the kid, even though he'd done a stupid thing that could have killed him. It was an incredible summer day, sunny but not too hot. It was a shame for a ten-year-old to be stuck in a dark room.

He sighed. Trevor needed to learn a lesson, didn't he?

But then, he was so much like Grace, so full of curiosity. He seemed to be searching for something on his own, the way Grace had been. Craig paused at his door. The least he could do was offer his help to the kid. Maybe Trevor would open up to him in a way he wouldn't with his mother.

Craig knocked. A sullen voice invited him inside. He found Trevor sitting on the floor with his back against his bed, his stocking feet dug into the plush carpet. Soft pings and faint, explosive noises emanated from the video game propped against his knees. Craig crouched down near him, folding his hands together.

"Hey, Trev."

"Hi."

"What're you playing there?"

"Crystock's Adventure," Trevor said.

"Is it hard?"

Trevor shrugged and switched off the game. He put it on the bed.

"I already beat it twice," he said. "But . . ."

Craig finished for him, "But there's nothing much to do in here."

Trevor seemed to find something interesting in the white-and-blue threads that made up his jeans, because he stared at his knees without answering. Craig, feeling uncomfortable in that position, got up and sat on the edge of the bed.

"I'm sorry this happened," he said. "But your mother is right. Going outside at night, in a bad storm, and climbing a tree—"

"I know," Trevor grumbled, in a tone that indicated he

didn't want to hear it again. He got up and went to his dresser, where he started to rearrange things.

Craig resisted an urge to go to his son and put his arms around him. That would make Trevor uncomfortable, he knew.

"Trev," he said carefully, "you know we're only concerned about you."

Trevor's head bobbed up and down, but he didn't turn.

"Maybe, if you told me what you were looking for last night," Craig suggested, "I could convince your mother to turn your sentence around."

Trevor picked up a model spaceship and turned it over in his hands. Craig had a feeling he wasn't really seeing it.

"Mom doesn't care what I think," Trevor said. "She only cares about finding out all she can about this family. She only cares about Nana and Am . . . Aunt Amanda."

"So? They're her family. She's bound to be excited."

Craig paused. Was jealousy the answer here? Veronica and Amanda had taken over Grace's life these days. Even though he knew it was only temporary, and that things would get back to normal as soon as he settled everyone into a new home, how did all this seem to a boy who was only ten?

"Trevor? Are you mad that your mother found a new family?"

"I dunno."

"Do you remember when the twins came?" Craig asked. "You told Mom to take them back to the hospital. You were mad because they took up so much of her time . . ."

Trevor swung around with such force that Craig instinctively pulled back, even though the boy was a head shorter than he was and halfway across the room.

"That's not it at all!" Trevor insisted. "If Nana was a regular person, I'd be happy Mom found her! It's all she ever dreamed about, isn't it? She's talked about it so much. But I'm afraid, Dad. Something bad is going to happen to Mom, to all of us!"

Craig stood up but still didn't approach his son.

"Trevor, Mom and I would never let—"

"She's going to kill us," Trevor said, tears gleaming in his lapis eyes. "Jeffrey says she's going to kill us all, because that's how she stays young forever!"

"Jeffrey?"

A strange look came over Trevor's face. What was it, Craig wondered? Shock? Embarrassment? Was Jeffrey supposed to be a secret?

"Trevor, who's Jeffrey?"

Without a word, Trevor turned back to the dresser. He opened a drawer, dug under some clothes, and pulled out a yellowed sheet of paper. He handed it to his father. Craig read the letter, but it meant nothing to him.

"This looks like it was written a long time ago," he said. "Where did you get it?"

"I . . . I found it in Jeffrey's old room," Trevor said.

"Does Jeffrey still live here?" Craig asked. The idea that an adult had terrorized his son, filling his head with crazy ideas that his Nana was a murderess made Craig's blood boil.

"No!" Trevor cried. "You don't understand! Daddy, Jeffrey is a kid like me!"

Craig felt something tighten inside of him, the instinctive need to protect his child, brought on by Trevor's babyish use of the word "Daddy."

"How could he be a kid?" he asked softly, but somehow he knew the answer.

Grace had her teenager, and Trevor had a young boy named Jeffrey . . .

"He died that way, Dad," Trevor said. "And now he's come back to help us. He told me we have to get away from here before something bad happens! He says she'll kill us all, so she can stay young forever!"

Now he burst into tears. Craig moved quickly, taking the boy in his arms.

"I don't want to die," Trevor wailed. "I don't want to die!"

SIXTEEN

▼

The sounds of raucous laughter and splashing water were carried through the open attic window. Grace looked up from her worktable, although she couldn't see the swimming pool from this point of view. She smiled. It sounded as if Craig and the twins were enjoying themselves outside.

She thought of Trevor and felt a moment of sadness. But she shook it away. Trevor had to learn.

Grace took in a deep breath, her slight shoulders rising and falling. She reached for her art pad and pulled it closer. A short time earlier, she'd gone downstairs to retrieve it, and now she was working the clay into a sculpture to match the series of sketches she'd made. She already had a name for this two-doll set: ''The Adoption.'' Funny how the girl in the picture looked very much as she had as a child: a little overweight, a little awkward. Standing with her hands clasped in front of a simple cotton dress, as if to shield herself from another rejection. These dolls would be a tribute to all homely children who had been passed over for prettier ones and to all adoptive parents who saw beyond looks into the heart of a child.

In the sketches, the woman resembled Mrs. Lynch. The time she'd lived with that family had been the happiest of her childhood. If only Mr. Lynch hadn't taken ill suddenly, leaving his wife with no time to care for a child, no matter how much she was wanted. If Grace had been able to grow up in that stable, loving home . . .

"I wouldn't have met my mother," she said out loud. Her voice seemed to echo in the spacious room.

She worked the clay, adding and subtracting to find the right proportion for the woman's face. Grace had decided to do the mother first. In a way, it was as if she was making sure there would be an adult there waiting for the little girl.

Even if they were only dolls.

Grace's lips spread in a smile. Even though she'd been here for nearly a week and she'd known about her mother for a while now, it was still hard to get used to the idea that she'd found her. And once more, she marveled at the woman's generosity. Imagine, remodeling an entire room just to make her daughter happy! Grace felt a little ashamed that she'd had doubts earlier. Veronica Chadman was more generous, more kind-hearted, more loving than any fairy tale mother Grace had ever created in her dreams.

And what had happened these past few days, really? The damaged doll she'd found in her room that first morning? The act of a disturbed woman. Poor Veronica, who had been forced to deal with Amanda's problems alone since the death of her husband, Cole. Sarah's accident on the horse? Just an accident and no more, Grace told herself firmly. There were gaps in her family history, but Veronica herself had said it would be impossible to tell her everything in just a few days. The only really hideous thing was that rat she'd found in her bed, but since nothing had happened since then she had to believe she was safe from whoever had felt the need to terrorize her. If someone was jealous of her new position in this family, that someone would have to come forward eventually. Then she would deal with him, or her.

She noticed that she was crushing the glob of clay in her hand rather than rolling it into a long, delicate woman's arm. Grace redirected her attention to her work, but her thoughts went on.

There was the spirit girl, of course. She seemed to be trying to warn Grace about something, but was too afraid to be clear about it. Then again, maybe she was as disturbed as Amanda. Maybe this type of mental illness ran in the family.

Grace shuddered. Veronica had said Amanda seemed okay until she was about eleven. David had said she fell down the cellar stairs, hitting her head.

Thinking of David made her think of Trevor. What secret was her son hiding? Was it only pre-adolescent surliness or was he really bothered about something? Grace decided she'd have to have a long talk with him to try to clear things up.

Almost as if he'd heard her thoughts, Trevor's voice came through the window.

"Over here, Dad! Throw it to me!"

Grace felt herself stiffen. What was Trevor doing out of his room? Putting her clay down, she went to the window to look out. The Olympic-sized pool stretched away from the house, a rectangle of brilliant blue cut into the emerald green of the surrounding grass. Craig and the children—all three of them— were throwing a beach ball back and forth. Mrs. Treetorn was standing on the patio, a tray of snacks and drink, in her chubby arms.

"I can't believe it," Grace whispered.

Why had Craig undermined her authority? By letting Trevor out after only a short time, he turned her into the heavy and became the good guy. She wouldn't have made Trevor stay in more than an afternoon! Didn't Craig know that? Her threat to keep him there until they left was only that—a threat. She wasn't cruel! Being locked in a room for days was something that had happened to her more than once. She'd never do that to her own child.

But she'd been so very angry at him. She shivered, despite the glaring heat of the sun that poured through the window. If Trevor had fallen from that tree . . .

A short time later, when Craig came into the room with his hair plastered to his head and his eyes shining from chlorine, she confronted him.

"Why did you let Trevor out?" she asked.

"Oh, I think the kid suffered enough," Craig said easily.

"Suffered?" Grace asked. "After barely two hours? He spends more time than that in his room reading! Craig, he was supposed to learn a lesson. He was being punished . . ."

Craig held up his hands. "Grace, I think we should go easier on him. He's going through a hard time. Adjusting to a new family isn't easy when you're ten—"

"I did it more than once," Grace mumbled, "and I didn't try to kill myself in the process."

Craig laughed. "Grace, he didn't try to kill himself. He was just locked out, and the tree seemed a logical way to get back in. Didn't you ever climb a tree as a child?"

"No."

"Well, I guess not," Craig said. "You're a girl, after all."

Grace's eyes thinned. "What does that have to do with it?"

"Nothing!" Craig said quickly. He hadn't meant to sound chauvinistic. "Anyway, I had a talk with him."

Grace felt her shoulders droop. Craig had beaten her to it.

"He really doesn't remember why he went outside," Craig went on. "But he's scared, Grace. You were right when you guessed that Trevor has a ghost of his own. His name is Jeffrey—"

"Jeffrey?" Grace repeated. Her own ghost hadn't yet revealed her name.

"He's been filling Trevor's head with crazy ideas," Craig said. "Something about Veronica taking blood and killing everyone to stay young. He . . ."

Craig paused, and the distant look on his face told Grace he had hit on an idea. He finally turned to her, his eyes solemn.

"You know something?" he asked. "That first day when we came here, I couldn't help wondering why Veronica looked so old. I mean, she could only be in her mid-forties if she was sixteen when you were born. But she looked sixty."

"So?" Grace said. "She's had a hard life. Running a company can age anyone, but to have a daughter like Amanda as well, with all her problems . . .''

"But she looks great now," Craig said. "Almost as if she's found the Fountain of Youth."

Grace rolled her eyes. "Oh, Craig! What did Trevor say, that she's some kind of vampire? That drinking blood brings her eternal youth, rather than eternal life?"

Craig stared at her for a few minutes, then grinned. "That is pretty far-fetched, isn't it?"

"It's ludicrous."

He went to the worktable and studied the miniature body parts scattered over its surface. The smooth pine, so bright a few hours ago, had grown filmy from bits of discarded clay.

"Think you'll have the doll done in time for your next show?" he asked, changing the subject.

"I hope so," Grace said. She knew she'd finish it. She'd never been more certain about a design in her life. Not only that, but she thought she might get a nomination for an award too. If not the grand prize in her category—

She started as Craig planted an unexpected kiss on her cheek.

"I love it when you get that dreamy look in your eyes," he said.

She turned around to face him, locking her arms around his waist.

"Just thinking about the doll show," she said. "I really believe I've got a winner going here."

"That's the kind of talk I like to hear," Craig said. "Not worries about a family you hardly know."

Grace didn't let him finish. She pulled herself taller and kissed him, savoring their moment together, refusing to let her worries get in the way of their love.

The twins were playing with the bowling alley and Trevor was working on a model when their parents came into the game room that evening. Craig was wearing a suit, and Grace had on the best dress she'd brought with her. It was a red crepe shift that came just to her knees, with white piping at the neck and along the pocket flaps. She'd pulled her chestnut hair back in a French braid, set off by a white bow. Red-and-white button earrings finished the look.

"Wow, Mommy," Sarah said. "You look pretty."

"Are you going out?" Trevor asked, worry in his voice. He screwed the cap on his tube of glue and stood up.

Grace smiled at him, her earlier anger forgotten. "We're all going out. Daddy's treating us to La Biblioteque."

Seth wrinkled his nose. "La . . . ?"

"It means 'library,' " Craig explained. "It's French."

"We're going to the library?" Seth asked, sounding disappointed.

Craig laughed, and Grace said, "You'll see. Run upstairs and put on your nicest clothes. Sarah, I've asked Mrs. Treetorn to do your hair for you."

"I want a French braid like yours, Mommy!"

"Then tell her that," Grace said.

With their arms around each other, the parents smiled as their children scampered upstairs. Going out as a family, especially when you had to dress up, was a special occasion.

"Are you sure you don't want to invite your mother?" Craig asked, tightening his arm around Grace's shoulders.

"I haven't seen her," Grace said. "She must have gone to the office."

"On a Sunday?"

Grace shrugged. "An executive's work is never done."

She smiled up at her husband and added, "Besides, I want this to be the five of us alone. We haven't seen each other in nearly a week, and when things start rolling with the new apartment, who knows when we'll be free again?"

Craig gave her a kiss, then pulled her closer for a longer, deeper one.

The children returned a short time later.

"Ready, guys?" Craig asked.

Seth and Trevor were wearing blue, short-sleeved polo shirts and dark blue twill pants. Sarah wore a sunflower-print jumper over a white blouse. Her hair was braided just like her mother's, with a white bow of her own. Grace guessed Mrs.

Treetorn had gotten hold of Seth, because his usually unruly auburn hair was slicked back neatly with a straight part. Trevor, on the other hand, seemed to have simply raked a comb through his thick locks.

"We ought to have our picture taken," Craig said as they passed a mirror in the hall. "What a handsome family!"

"I'm not handsome, Daddy," Sarah claimed. "I'm pretty."

They piled into the car Craig had rented for the trip. Trevor marvelled at the dashboard and asked a dozen questions before they had even rolled off the property. Finally, he settled into his seat and turned to gaze back at the house. He saw someone on the front steps.

"Andros is watching us," he said.

Grace turned around and saw the servant herself.

"Creep," she mumbled.

Craig laughed. "Forget him, okay? This is our night. I have to leave right after dinner, and I don't want it spoiled with talk of weird servants or . . . whatever."

"Agreed," Grace said.

La Biblioteque, as it happened, was housed in an old building that had once been a library. The card catalogues still lined one wall, and several old bookshelves remained standing. Now, however, they were decorated with antiques and objets d'art. The maitre d' didn't seem to know why the restaurant had been given a French name, but all the Mathesons had to agree it was some of the best food they'd ever eaten. After a dessert of crepes with strawberries—the adults' version laced with cognac—they headed home again. The twins were sound asleep when they arrived, and each parent took a child up to the bedroom. Trevor followed close behind, yawning.

"Do you really have to go tonight, Dad?" he asked.

"Yes, Craig," Grace put in. "It's so late. Won't you be tired on the road?"

"I have to be at work at eight-thirty tomorrow," Craig said. "It's my first day, and I can't be late. I had wanted to leave this afternoon, but it seemed important to be with my family instead."

He ruffled Trevor's hair, forgetting the boy didn't like to be touched.

"Just another day or two, I promise," he said. "I'll leave my office number with your mom. You can call me if you need to."

"Okay," Trevor said, realizing it was the best he was going to get. "G'night. Dinner was great."

He went into the bathroom to get ready for bed.

After tucking in the little ones, the adults left the room.

"I wish we had more time," Grace said.

"We will, once we settle in our new home," Craig told her. He put his arms around her. "Like I said to Trevor, it's only a few more days. And you have a lot to keep you busy here. When I see you Tuesday, maybe you'll have some more information."

They walked to the bedroom together. Grace ached to pull her husband onto the soft down spread, but she knew he had to be on the road soon, before he was too tired to go. She had to placate herself with the fact that she'd see him in only two days.

She helped him check his suitcase, then walked downstairs with him. The house was quiet as a tomb and as dimly lit.

"Where is everybody?" Craig asked softly. The solitude seemed to demand whispers.

"I guess the servants have gone to their quarters," Grace said. "I don't know what happened to my mother."

"Say good-bye to her for me," Craig requested.

Their good-bye kiss was long and warm, and Grace felt a tingle on her lips long after the taillights of Craig's rental car disappeared onto the distant highway. Sighing, Grace turned and went up to her room. She changed from her dress into a more comfortable jogging outfit, then padded upstairs to her studio in her slippers. Although she worked on her new dolls long into the night, she never saw her mother. She went to bed assuming the woman was simply caught up in her work.

Grace picked up the journal and tried to read, but her eyes were so tired that the words were simply blurs of blue ink. She put it aside and turned off the light, settling down. It was a cool night, and she kept her windows open rather than using the air conditioner. The sound of wind blowing through the sycamores was soothing, and soon Grace was lulled to sleep. Memories came to her in the guise of dreams, mind-videos of her early days with Craig. They were sharing popcorn at the movies. They were at the Indy 500 with Craig's family. They were in Grace's apartment, sharing the love that would bring Trevor, and marriage.

Then someone was screaming. In the dream Grace sat up and looked at Craig.

"Don't let her come between us," she said.

Craig shook his head with a frown and vanished.

Someone kept screaming.

And then Grace was awake. It took her a few seconds to realize the screams were *real*, coming from somewhere downstairs. Curious, her dreams forgotten at once, she got up and put on her robe. She hurried down the hall to investigate, grabbing the banister when she reached it and holding tightly as she descended into the dark cavern of the foyer.

Things might be hiding down there, she thought with a mind that had fully awakened. She tried to tell herself this was silly, but like a child afraid of the dark she sought the comfort of the light switch as soon as she reached the bottom of the stairs. The foyer was quickly bathed in the glow from the chandelier.

Something *had* been hiding in the shadows, something that cast its long, tall shadow on the wall in front of her. Her breath caught as she watched the dark silhouette sliding up towards the ceiling, growing bigger and bigger . . .

Grace snatched up an empty crystal candy dish and spun around on her slippered feet.

She was alone in the foyer, holding her makeshift weapon in defense against nothing. When she looked at the wall again, she saw only the pictures of painted trees. She told herself she was too old to be imagining things like this. There was a woman somewhere who needed help.

The reminder of her purpose made her realize how empty the house was, just as it had been when Craig left earlier.

"Where is everyone?" she asked out loud, her voice fading as it was carried up to the high ceiling.

Hadn't anyone else heard the screams? Or were they only part of her dream after all?

But then she heard them again, more bone-chilling than before. She determined they were coming from down the hall leading to the kitchen. It was dark down there, the foyer light illuminating only part of it. Fighting back her own fears, she strode purposefully towards the cries. She turned on another switch, illuminating the rest of the hall as she turned its bend. She saw the young girl, standing near the cellar door. She had her face buried in her hands, her long hair flowing around her like a shroud. It took Grace a moment to realize the mouselike squeaks coming from her were sobs.

"What's happening?" she asked gently.

"Amanda," was all the spirit would say.

Then she opened the cellar door and disappeared into the stairwell. Grace ran after her. To her dismay, she found the door was padlocked, as it had been before!

But, of course, ghosts could do anything.

She reached towards her hair for a bobby pin, planning to pick the lock if she could. But she had brushed it out before going to bed, and it hung free around her shoulders.

"Damn," she said.

She stepped back to assess the situation. Down below, the screams had stopped abruptly. Grace did the most logical thing she could think of at the moment. She reached up and knocked.

And then something cold pressed over her mouth and nose, and she felt herself being squeezed by the vise of a strong arm.

She fainted.

Trevor had also been awakened by the screams. He went on his own investigation, hating the dark loneliness of the house. It was even worse now than in the daytime. He walked slowly down the stairs, half-expecting a monster to jump out at him.

"Don't be an idiot," he whispered as a step creaked under his bare foot.

But when the screams sounded again, he jumped and grabbed the railing with both hands.

"I'll help you," a childish voice said from behind him.

He looked back to see Jeffrey on the stairs.

"What's going on?" he asked in a whisper. "It sounds like they're killing someone."

"Not killing her," Jeffrey replied. "Not yet. But she'll be okay. Your mother is the one who needs you now."

"My mother?" Trevor cried. Was someone hurting his mother? The thought made him quicken his pace, and he jumped over the last four steps.

Jeffrey led him down a hall. Near the cellar door, Andros was holding his mother in his big arms. Her head was tossed back, her hair flowing away from her pale, expressionless face. Trevor felt his joints turn at once to ice and fire. Tears sprung from his eyes, and with the wails of a feral child, he lunged at the old man.

"YOU KILLED MY MOTHER! YOU BASTARD JERK! YOU KILLED MY MOOOOTHERRRR!!!!"

SEVENTEEN

▼

Trevor's cries brought out numerous servants, tying bathrobes and pushing hair behind ears. They followed the group upstairs: Andros carrying Mrs. Matheson, whose arm swung loosely, with Trevor close at his heels. He was crying, yelling accusations, but the big servant ignored him. His only reaction was to turn slightly to the side when Trevor tried to grab at his mother.

"Give her to me!" Trevor shouted.

Behind him, unheard, the servants whispered among themselves in wonder.

His grandmother appeared in the upstairs hall, dressed in a pink silk robe, her hair falling in curls over her shoulders. To Trevor, it was like seeing the ghost of his mother. Veronica looked so much like her right then it was scary.

But the shock passed quickly, and he frowned.

"He hurt her!" the boy accused. "He killed my mother!"

"I found her unconscious near the cellar door," Andros said. He turned and gazed pointedly at Trevor. "Unconscious, not dead."

Then he pushed backward into Grace's room. Trevor rushed after him, waves of relief flooding him. His mother wasn't dead, after all! But she looked so pale . . .

"I heard screams," he said.

"Screams?" Veronica echoed. She gave Andros a questioning look, but he only shook his head. Then she turned to the servants who were milling about the door. She directed her question to the housekeeper. "Mrs. Treetorn, did you hear my daughter screaming?"

"No, Mrs. Chadman," Mrs. Treetorn said. "I didn't hear anything at all. It was the boy's screams that woke me up."

She was dressed in a cotton nightgown that made her look like a short, white barrel. A loose curler hung like a condemned man at the side of her pudding face. Trevor thought she looked bizarre, like everything and everyone in this house. Why hadn't they heard his mother screaming?

Unless they were ignoring her.

He shuddered.

"Trevor, maybe you should get a robe," Veronica suggested in a gentle, grandmotherly tone.

He glared at her. He wouldn't leave his mother's side as long as these people were with her. Maybe Andros had meant to kill her, but his plans were ruined when Trevor showed up.

"Mrs. Treetorn, please call Dr. Barham," Veronica was saying.

"Call my father too," Trevor insisted.

"Trevor dear, it's two o'clock in the morning," Veronica reminded him.

Trevor's expression was hard beyond his years. "Call my father, please."

Veronica sighed. "Very well. Mrs. Treetorn, the number is on my desk. Be sure Mr. Matheson knows what happened to his wife."

"Yes, ma'am," Mrs. Treetorn said, and left.

Veronica waved her hand like a queen, dismissing the small crowd of servants. Then she sat by the bedside and took her daughter's hand. Not to be outdone, Trevor climbed on the other side of the bed and held his mother's other hand.

"You can go now, Andros," Veronica said. "Bring Dr. Barham up when he arrives."

Andros left without a word. For a long time, grandmother and grandson were as silent as the unconscious woman in the bed, both staring intently at her for any sign of revival. Trevor found himself being lulled by the hums of the dark mansion, the far-off refrigerator and ticking clocks, the air conditioning. He began to nod off and was nearly asleep when Veronica's "Trevor dear?" startled him awake again.

She was smiling at him. He hated that phoney smile. Why did she bother, now that there was no one here to see her true self?

"I want you to know something," she went on. "I would never hurt your mother or any of you children. And I wouldn't allow my servants to do it either."

"I heard screams," Trevor said, "and I saw—"

"Enough of that," Veronica said sternly. "I won't have you making accusations."

The smile returned almost immediately. "But you must understand something. All my life, I dreamed of finding the little girl who'd been taken from me."

Trevor felt strange inside. How many times had his mother said almost the same words, substituting "mother" for "little girl?"

"Now that she's come back to me," Veronica said, "I only want the best for her. And you too. Haven't I given you wonderful playthings? Hasn't your stay here been like a vacation?"

Trevor didn't know what to say. The basketball court was great, so were the horses and game room. But, except for David, he didn't like any of the people here. And there was that hidden room . . .

"What's down in the cellar?" he demanded.

"Nothing at all," Veronica said. "Only storage, and the furnace."

"So why is it locked?"

"We keep some valuable things, down there," Veronica

said. "Andros suggested we should keep them locked away while you children were running about."

Trevor frowned at her. "Then how come there's expensive stuff all over the house, and no one tells us to keep away?"

He wanted her to mention the secret room. He wanted her to tell him all about it. But at that moment, his mother moaned softly and began to stir.

"Mom?"

"Grace dear," Veronica said.

She started to reach for her daughter's face, but Trevor moved quickly and cupped his mother's head between his hands.

"Wake up, Mom," he begged.

"Amanda . . ." Grace said. "Help Amanda . . ."

"Yes, we will," Veronica promised. "But first you have to get better."

"Help Amanda," Grace said again, and returned to her deep sleep.

"What's that supposed to mean?" Trevor asked, confused. His aunt wasn't here!

Before his grandmother could reply, there was a knock at the door, and Mrs. Treetorn led the doctor into the room. He was an old man with a horseshoe of white hair around his head, thin lips, and a pug nose. But his eyes were warm and understanding, and he went to shake Trevor's hand before turning to his grandmother. Trevor was impressed.

"Would you mind leaving for a moment while I examine your mother, young man?" he asked.

He was so polite that Trevor gave in. But he shot his grand-mother a warning look before leaving the room.

"Would you like a snack, dear?" Mrs. Treetorn asked, out in the hall.

Trevor shook his head. Somehow, he thought it might be dangerous to eat anything right now. They'd probably sneak something into it. Instead, he faked a yawn and headed back to his room. He was surprised to find both the twins sound asleep in Sarah's bed. Seth hardly ever crawled in with his sister. Trevor guessed one of them had had a nightmare.

Maybe Sarah, who had creepy dreams about cold beds and needles.

He stopped short, standing in the middle of the dimly lit room as a memory fought to surface in his brain. A needle. Why did he think he'd gotten a shot lately?

He needed to talk to Jeffrey.

Trevor pulled a candle down from his dresser top, where it had been left as a decoration. It was short and stubby, the dark blue wax decorated with moons and stars. Trevor opened the top drawer and pulled out a battered shaving kit his father had given him to hold his small treasures. Among the marbles, penknife, flashlight, and other toys, he found a half-used book of matches. He hadn't burned them himself—it was the picture of Saturn on the jacket that had intrigued him—but he knew he'd catch hell if he was caught with them. Fortunately, his parents trusted him enough not to be nosy, and never looked in the case. Tonight would be the first time he'd ever lit one.

He set the glowing candle in the middle of the floor and folded his legs into a pretzel, his hands on his knees. Staring at the flame, he whispered Jeffrey's name over and over.

The boy appeared almost at once.

"Why did you leave me?" Trevor asked.

"I only wanted to bring you to your mother."

"Was Andros trying to kill her?"

Jeffrey shook his head. "That's not what they want right now."

"Who was screaming?" Trevor asked. "Was it my mother?"

"No," Jeffrey said. "It was the woman in the cellar."

Trevor asked if she was in the secret room, and Jeffrey nodded. Smoke from the candle circled around him like an ethereal being, more ghostly than the boy Trevor was seeing.

"Tell me about the secret room," he asked.

"It's a laboratory," Jeffrey replied. "They do experiments down there."

Trevor's heart was beating like a triphammer.

"What kind of experiments?" he urged.

"They mix strange plants with blood," Jeffrey said.

"They've been taking blood from you and your sister and your brother. Tonight, they were using the woman in the cellar. She didn't like it."

Trevor rubbed his arm as if to alleviate the phantom pain of a needle prick.

"Who're they?" he asked. "Is it Veronica and Andros?"

But Jeffrey was on his feet now, backing away, until his figure became grossly shadowed and elongated by the candle on the floor.

"You have to get away from here," he warned, "before she finishes you all!"

He was gone.

"*Jeffrey?*"

A second later, Sarah started to cry and was quickly joined by her brother. Trevor cringed, realizing he'd spoken too loud. He blew out the candle and set it on the dresser, then hurried into the twins' room.

"Take it easy, guys!"

The twins were sitting up in bed, hugging each other. They looked strangely pale, their eyes darkly rimmed as if they hadn't slept in days.

"Don't let them hurt us," Seth begged.

Sarah turned and buried her face in her twin's shoulder. Trevor sat on the bed and tried to comfort them.

"Who?" he asked, hoping to gain a clue. "Who hurt you?"

"The people behind the walls," Seth said.

"What are you talking about?" Trevor demanded. "Did someone take you to the secret room? Did someone stick a needle in you?"

Sarah began to scream in terror. Trevor tried to hush her, sorry he'd made the suggestion, but it was too late. His grandmother strode into the room a few moments later.

"What's going on here?" she asked.

"They had a nightmare," Trevor said, glaring at the woman as if to say he knew it wasn't a nightmare at all.

"Both of them?" Veronica said, incredulous. "You poor darlings. Would you like to come downstairs and have some hot chocolate?"

Sarah pulled away from Seth and put her arms around her grandmother's neck.

"Don't let them hurt me, Nana," she whimpered.

"There, there," Veronica soothed. "It was only a dream, dear."

She held out her hand to Seth, who crawled from the bed and took it. Trevor wanted to shout, to tell them they shouldn't trust the woman. But they were finally calming down, and he didn't want to scare them any worse than they'd already been.

"Where's Mommy?" Seth asked as Veronica led him, barefoot and robeless, from the room.

"Mommy's sick," Veronica said. "She needs to stay in bed."

She looked at Trevor. "Dr. Barham says it's a virus. He gave her medicine, and she should be up by tomorrow."

Trevor nodded, relieved. Only a virus . . .

He saw his grandmother's eyes shift, and realized he hadn't put the matches away.

"We'll talk about that tomorrow, young man," she said darkly.

"What're you going to do about it?" he sneered in a low voice after she'd closed the door. "Spank me? Or maybe cut my throat and take all my blood?"

He listened for the sound of footsteps on the stairs, then jerked open his door and ran to check on his mother. Her room smelled like that strange plant: roses, mint, and vinegar. Jeffrey had said "they" used strange plants to mix with blood. Had the doctor given his mother one of Veronica's poisons?

He rushed to her side, pressing his head against her chest. Her heartbeat sounded okay, her breathing was steady. Jeffrey had said they weren't going to kill her tonight. If Trevor had his way, they would never get near her again.

Suddenly exhausted, feeling very alone, he stretched out on top of his mother's thick down comforter and closed his eyes.

"Hurry and come back, Dad," he whispered, just before sleep caught him up in its deep folds.

* * *

Trevor was still in his mother's room when he woke up the next morning, dawn light coloring the blankets rosy pink. He reached out his arm, aching from an uncomfortable sleep position, and pressed his hand against his mother's forehead. It was cool and dry. She sighed deeply and shifted in the bed but didn't wake up. Carefully, not wanting to disturb her, Trevor got out of the bed. Whatever had happened last night, it seemed his mother was okay now. He would let her rest, and later, when she woke up, he'd ask her what had happened.

He walked quietly back to his own bedroom. Next door the twins were still asleep, cuddled together in one bed. Trevor stepped on a squeaky stuffed animal and cringed, but the noise didn't wake his siblings. He was about to turn to his dresser when a thought occurred to him, sending ice through his veins.

Why hadn't they heard the noise?

Trevor hurried into their room. Nana had taken them down for hot chocolate last night . . .

"Seth?" he whispered frantically. What if there was something in that drink? "Sarah?"

Seth moaned, and Sarah wiggled with an annoyed look on her face. Trevor leaned his head back and breathed in a deep sigh of relief. They were just tired, that was all. He went back to his room and pulled out a pair of denim shorts and an Indy 500 T-shirt from his dresser. After he dressed, he went downstairs and outside. He didn't pass a soul on the way, but he knew that David would be up. Dew spattered on his legs as he cut across the field to the barn, and an occasional cricket jumped out of his path. The crickets were already in symphony this morning, promising a scorcher of a day.

David was filling the water trough when he approached, and looked up to say, "Hi, Trevor. Why are you up so early?"

Trevor shrugged and pulled himself up to sit on the fence. "I need to ask you a question," he said.

"Shoot."

"Have you ever been down in the cellar?"

"That again?" David asked, walking to the spigot to turn off the hose. He gestured towards the barn, and Trevor jumped from the fence to follow him. David opened Magellan's stall and led the horse out to the paddock. "You got up this early to ask me about the cellar again?"

"Not just that," Trevor said. He told him what had happened the previous night. "And Jeffrey told me there's a laboratory in the cellar. He says they mix blood with some strange plant."

"That's ridiculous," David said, returning to let Sunshine out of her stall.

"Seeing ghosts is nuts too," Trevor pointed out, following close behind. "But we both saw Jeffrey!"

"He never spoke to me," David said. "Maybe he was only a trick of my mind." He picked up a rock and threw it out of the way. "Trevor, maybe it's best that you don't let your imagination get away with you. Sometimes, there are things little boys shouldn't know about.

"I'm not little," Trevor protested. "I'm ten. And I need your help. I found a way into the cellar, but you know what? There were hundreds of worms there! They were crawling all over me! And when I looked, Andros was there. I think he did that. I think he made my mother sick too. They fed her that funny-smelling plant."

David, who had been busy working with Starbeam, stopped short.

"What?" Trevor asked, reading the disturbed expression on the stable manager's face.

"You said Mrs. Chadman was going to call your father?" he asked.

"Yeah," Trevor said. "Why, what's wrong? David, why do you look so scared?"

David let Starbeam go and turned to put his hands on Trevor's shoulders. His grip was so fierce it almost hurt, but Trevor didn't try to wiggle away from him. It was as if David's green eyes were a magnet locking to his own blue ones.

"When your dad comes," David said, "tell him you want to leave. Scream, yell, throw a fit, but make him say yes. You have to get out of here, Trevor."

Trevor felt like crying with relief. At last there was an adult who believed something was wrong here.

"Then . . . then my grandmother really is a bad person?"

David shook his head, letting the boy go.

"I'll never believe that about Mrs. Chadman," he said firmly. "But I don't trust Andros, and I know something strange has been going on here ever since I came. If I tell you something, do you promise to keep it between us?"

"Swear to God," Trevor promised solemnly.

"One day, I went into the house to collect my pay, and I took a wrong turn. I passed that cellar door, and I heard horrible screams down there myself. I asked Mrs. Chadman about it, and she said Amanda had probably locked herself in the storeroom down there."

Trevor made a face. "Storeroom? Andros said it was for electricity."

"You know something?" David said. "I don't think it was for either. And I don't think Amanda locked herself in that room by accident. She sounded terrified. I've never heard screams like that."

Trevor nodded in agreement, recalling the chilling cries he'd heard the night before.

"What do I do now, David?" he asked. "Dad won't be here until late, I'm sure. He just started a new job and I know he can't just leave. How do I keep my mother and the twins safe?"

"I think you'll be okay today," David said. "If Andros did do something to your mother last night, he's drawn too much attention to himself to try anything new today. Mrs. Chadman would have him out on his ear if he did."

Trevor wanted to say that he thought his grandmother would help Andros finish the job, but he kept quiet. He didn't understand why David trusted her but realized she could be very persuasive with her phoney smiles.

"Just do whatever you usually do," David said. "You can come out for a ride after breakfast or swim in the pool. I know—we'll go one-on-one again. Maybe this time I'll beat you."

He was smiling, and Trevor couldn't help returning the smile. With David at his side, he'd be okay for a few hours.

And then tonight, he'd beg his father to take them away.

"Just don't be by yourself," David said now.

The warning was enough to chill the young boy, despite the heat.

EIGHTEEN

▼

T revor kept a close watch on his mother that afternoon, declining David's offer for a basketball game. He only left her a few times to check on the twins, and he even ate his meals there. His grandmother tried to tell him this wasn't necessary, but he simply glared at her and turned away. Until his father arrived, he wouldn't leave her alone.

But dinnertime came, and still there was no word from him. Trevor was certain he would have at least called. When Mrs. Treetorn brought his dinner up on a tray, he asked, but the housekeeper simply shook her head. Seth and Sarah were behind her with trays of their own.

"We want to eat in Mommy's room too," Sarah said. She leaned close to her mother's face and stared at her eyes. "Why isn't she waking up, Trevor? Why is she so sick?"

"I don't know," Trevor admitted.

"I wish Daddy would call," Seth said.

Mrs. Treetorn patted his head, and Seth cringed. Trevor wanted to tell her he hated that but said nothing.

"Don't worry," she said. "He'll call as soon as he can.

Didn't your mother say he just started a new job? The poor man is probably busy."

"Yeah, probably," Seth agreed.

When Mrs. Treetorn left the room, Trevor leaned closer to the twins.

"You know what I think? I don't think Andros called Dad at all. That's why he hasn't called."

Sarah took a bite of a drumstick and chewed thoughtfully.

"What should we do, Trevor?" she asked.

"I'm going to call him myself, right after dinner," Trevor said. "When he hears what's going on, he'll come right away and get us out of here."

"I want to go back to Tulip Tree," Seth said.

"Me too," Sarah agreed. "I don't like this place any more."

They ate silently for a while, each deep in thought. Sarah was thinking they might take Nana away from here too. It would be nice if Nana could live with them. Seth was staring at the walls and listening for any strange sounds. Everyone thought he was silly, but he knew the sounds were real. But who were the people he heard walking back there? Why did they want to hurt his family?

Trevor was wishing his father would call, wishing his mother would wake up. Almost as if by a miracle, she began to stir in the bed. Trevor put his glass of milk down and stood up to go to her. She had her eyes open, and she was smiling weakly.

"Trevor?" she asked in a quiet voice. "What happened?"

"Don't you remember?" Trevor asked. If she didn't remember, how could he prove his story to his father?

Slowly, Grace sat up in bed. She closed her eyes tightly, rubbing them with her thumb and forefinger. Then she opened them and looked from her oldest son to the twins and back.

"I heard someone screaming."

Trevor breathed a sigh of relief.

"So did I," he said. "Mom, something weird happened. You were out cold, and Andros was carrying you."

Grace made a face as if the thought of being in that strange man's arms repulsed her.

"I thought he'd killed you," Trevor said. "But this guy named Dr. Barham came and said you were sick. They gave you that funny-smelling plant for medicine."

"Really?" Grace asked, her eyes wide with interest. She looked out the window. "What time is it? How long have I been out?"

"It's dinnertime, Mommy," Sarah said. "Are you hungry? Do you want my green beans? I hate green beans."

Grace laughed. "I could eat a horse."

Almost as if on cue, one of the horses in the barn whinnied loudly. All four Mathesons laughed. Trevor felt himself relaxing, glad to see his mother could be happy despite their situation. But his smile soon faded. He had to tell her there was danger here.

"Nana told Andros to call Daddy," he said.

"Oh, I don't think he needed to bother," Grace said. "I feel much better now."

Trevor noticed a fleeting expression of confusion on her face and guessed she was trying to remember everything.

"But I don't think he did it," he went on, " 'cause Dad never called you. I was going to do it myself."

Grace patted his arm. "You're such a good boy. So brave. But I can call Daddy myself."

She swung herself out of bed, cringed with the effort, and got to her feet. Trevor let her lean on him as she walked to her chair and picked up the robe lying across its back.

"First, though," she said, "I need something to eat. My blood sugar is low, and I can't think straight."

Trevor knew she meant she couldn't remember much of last night. Leaving the twins to gather up the dinner dishes from her floor, he walked out into the hall with her.

"We both heard screams coming from downstairs," he said to help refresh her memory. "You were by the cellar door . . ."

Grace stopped at the top of the stairs. "I had just seen . . ." She shook her head.

"What did you see?" Trevor urged.

"Never mind," she said. "I heard screams from down in

the cellar. The door was locked. I felt someone behind me . . . She frowned. "The rest of it is gone."

"Ask Nana to let you into the cellar," Trevor suggested. "Ask her about the secret room. Whoever was screaming might have been trapped in there."

Grace looked at him with worry in her eyes. After a few moments, she nodded, then led him downstairs. They found Veronica working in her office, Andros at her side. Trevor swore she was buttoning her blouse when they walked in and wrinkled his nose.

Nana and that creep, what a gross idea.

"Oh, Grace, how wonderful!" Veronica said brightly, coming around the desk. "I'm so glad you're up!"

Andros left the room without a backward glance.

"Are you okay? Should I call the doctor again?"

"I'm fine, Mother," Grace said. "Just a little disturbed."

Veronica's bright expression fell. "What can I do to help?"

"Show me the cellar," Grace said.

"What a strange request," Veronica said.

Trevor stepped forward. "She's going to try to talk you out of it, Mom."

Grace hushed him.

"No, I won't," Veronica said. "You're welcome to go downstairs, although I can't imagine what you think you'll see there."

She pulled a key from her desk and led the way. Trevor's heart was beating with excitement. At last, they'd see the hidden room. His mother would believe him, and they'd leave right away. Maybe they wouldn't even take the time to pack.

The cellar stairs creaked beneath his feet, and he remembered being nervous on them the first day. Everything seemed the same down here, same boxes, same stretch of vast, empty space. Trevor cut around the women and ran to the tall, antique dresser at the back of the room.

"Move it," he said.

"Why?" Veronica asked. "There's nothing back there."

"There's a door," Trevor said. "A door to a secret laboratory. I know what you're up to, Nana. I know you're making strange things in there, using our blood.''

"Trevor . . .'' his mother said, but there was a weakness in her voice he'd never noticed before.

Veronica's sigh was loud against the cinder block walls. "Very well. But I'm certainly not going to move it myself.''

She went upstairs. Trevor froze, thinking he and his mother were about to be locked in. But she simply called to someone, then came back downstairs again. A few moments later, Andros appeared.

"You'll see how silly you are," she told Trevor. "Once and for all, we'll put this idea of a secret room to rest.''

The dresser was a big, heavy piece with six drawers and dull brass fixtures. Trevor thought it must weigh a ton, but Andros moved it as if it were a pillow.

And there was nothing behind it. Nothing but cinderblocks.

"There was a door here!" Trevor cried. "I saw it! The twins saw it too! Just ask them!''

"Trevor, calm down," Grace said.

Trevor moved along the wall, patting it wildly. "No, no, wait! They blocked it off! They filled the space with new blocks!''

But he realized even as he spoke that the blocks looked as old as the surrounding ones. His shoulders slumped, and he hung his head abjectly. They'd played a trick on him. His mother would never believe in him again, and it was all Nana's fault. Now he'd never save his family.

"I know I heard screams down here," he heard his mother saying.

He looked up to see her staring at his grandmother. "That wasn't my imagination, and I don't think Trevor imagined hearing them either. Mother, I want to know: is Amanda in this house?''

"Amanda is in the hospital," Veronica told her.

"What kind of medicine did Dr. Barham give me?''

Trevor began to smile. Silently, he rooted his mother on.

"I wouldn't know, Grace dear," Veronica said. "But we can certainly call and ask him.''

"I'd like to do that."

Veronica clapped her hands together. "Let's get out of this cold basement. Felix fixed fried chicken for dinner tonight with several wonderful side dishes. You must be starving, Grace."

"Famished," Grace admitted.

They went upstairs. Trevor felt strange knowing Andros was a few steps behind him. The hairs on the back of his neck prickled in anticipation of those big, cold hands.

Nothing happened, but Trevor didn't relax until the tall servant walked away from them. Trevor noticed he hadn't bothered to padlock the cellar again.

Although the food Felix had prepared was excellent, Grace hardly tasted it. The doubts that had been slowly creeping into her mind these past few days had grown stronger. She wanted more than anything to trust her mother, a woman who had shown her only love and kindness. But there were so many loose ends, so many questions Veronica always managed to evade. Grace *had* heard those screams last night. Trevor's story had proved it wasn't her imagination. If it hadn't been Amanda in that cellar, then who? And why wouldn't anyone talk about it?

She suddenly remembered when Trevor said Andros told him the blocked-off room was for electrical equipment. She'd agreed it was best to keep it away from the children. But there was no extra room at all downstairs. There was nothing but boxes and old pieces of furniture. Why padlock the cellar, then?

"Grace, you look disturbed," Veronica said. She had been sitting across the table, sipping coffee from a delicate Royal Doulton cup, watching Grace silently.

"I'm going to Bryce City, Mother," Grace said, making a sudden decision. "Even if Craig doesn't have a home for us, we need to get away from here."

"Why?" Veronica asked, her lapis eyes wide. "I've done all I can to make you happy here. Don't you like it?"

Grace's lips turned up in a very small smile. "It's wonderful. But you know we can't stay forever anyway. And things have been happening, disturbing things."

"But . . ."

"I know there must be a rational explanation for it all," Grace cut her off, "but I can't think clearly right now. The children and I need to get away from here."

"You make it sound as if there's danger here," Veronica said, frowning.

"Is there?"

Veronica's head snapped up. "No! Of course not! I wouldn't let anything happen to you. I don't understand why Trevor hates me so much. I'm so happy to have such a handsome little boy for a grandson, but he . . . he . . ."

She began to cry, her face contorting as she turned to stare at their reflection in the night-darkened French doors. This time, Grace didn't come around the table to comfort her. She knew it would make her feel bad and would influence her decision to leave. But she knew this was for the best. Tomorrow, they'd be out of here. With a few days and a few miles behind them, Grace might be able to understand what was happening. She prayed her mother was right, that she was mistaken.

But somehow, she didn't think this would be true.

She pushed her plate away and stood up.

"I'm . . . I'm sorry, Mother," she said. "But the sound of those screams grows louder and louder in my mind. I have to get away from here."

She turned and left the room, fighting tears of her own.

Trevor sat in the game room, his thumbs clicking over the video game controller. Flashes of color from the television painted his solemn face, but he hardly noticed the game. He was playing by instinct, as if his hands knew what to do without the help of his eyes. His brain was busy with other thoughts: how to find that secret room. He knew his mother wanted to leave tomorrow, but he knew if he didn't prove its existence once and for all, they'd come back eventually. He never wanted to set foot in this house again as long as he lived.

He was convinced the window he'd found that day the worms had appeared was the right one. Andros had caught him and had put a spell on him to stop him. And someone had been watching him the night he was locked out.

That wouldn't happen tonight. Tonight, he'd get out without being seen.

His mother came into the room, dressed in her robe and nightgown. Her face was pale and there was red along the edges of her eyes. Trevor knew she was feeling weird about this place. He put the controller down and went to her. At ten he was only an inch shy of her, and she felt surprisingly small in his arms. Moms were supposed to be strong, weren't they?

"I can't wait until we leave tomorrow," he said, pulling away.

"I called your father," his mother replied. "He's got a place for us to stay temporarily. But Trevor . . ."

He watched her turn to gaze out the window, and for a moment his heart rate quickened. Would she see how he'd unlatched it?

She turned back to him again. "I don't want you to hate your grandmother. Whatever family secret is going on here, she has her reasons for not telling me, I'm sure. After I've had time to be away for a while, I'll come back again—"

"No!"

"—and clear things up."

"I don't want to come back here."

"You don't have to," Grace said.

"Promise?"

"Promise."

She looked around. "Where are the twins?"

"I dunno," Trevor said. "I haven't seen them since just after dinner."

"Well, it's their bedtime," Grace said.

She gave her son a smile before leaving the room. Trevor came to the door just as the twins were approaching, their grinning faces blotched with chocolate.

"Felix made us a special dessert," Sarah said.

"For our last night here," Seth added. Trevor watched as his mother wiped a line of chocolate from Seth's cheek. A little part of him felt jealous. It was his last night too. Why hadn't Felix made anything for him?

He shook the thought away. He didn't need favors from anyone here! Pulling himself back into the room, he went to a jigsaw puzzle that was spread over a table and began to push pieces into it. Again, he worked without much thought. His own bedtime was an hour from now. Would his mother let him stay up? Would his plan work?

"If it doesn't," he whispered, "at least I'm out of here tomorrow."

Later, when his mother came back again, he asked permission to stay up and read.

"I can't sleep," he said, "and I don't want to disturb the twins."

His mother reached out to him, her fingers barely touching his face as she pushed a lock of hair away. Trevor thought it was funny that he didn't like being hugged or touched a week ago, but now he only wanted to be held and reassured like a little kid. He fought the urge to embrace her as he had today. If he did, she might sense something was up.

"All right," she said, to his relief. "But I'm turning in myself. I want to get an early start tomorrow, so your father can meet us on his lunch hour. Good night, Trevor."

"G'night, Mom," Trevor replied.

He went to the bookshelf and retrieved a book without even noticing the title. When his mother closed the playroom door, he was settled in a couch and pretending to read. She would go upstairs thinking he even knew what was on the pages. Afraid she might come back, he stayed that way for what seemed an eternity.

He first saw Jeffrey as a reflection in the window and gasped. He hadn't even been aware the kid was sitting next to him.

"Where'd you come from?" he asked.

"I've always been here," Jeffrey replied. He pointed upwards. "They've all gone to bed. Everyone. Now's the time."

Trevor squinted at him. "Time for what?"

Jeffrey turned to stare at the window. Trevor sighed. Of course, Jeffrey had probably been watching him. Somehow though, it didn't make him feel creepy. Not like knowing Andros watched him all the time.

"Are you sure Andros is asleep?"

"Andros is busy," was all Jeffrey would say. "So is Veronica. But you don't have a lot of time."

"Right," Trevor agreed, putting the book aside. Without thinking, he'd reached in Jeffrey's direction. The book went right through him and settled on the couch. Trevor gasped. Even knowing and accepting what Jeffrey was, it was still disconcerting to realize he wasn't solid flesh.

Trevor got up quickly. With a quick look back at the door to be certain it was still closed, he went to the window. But Jeffrey appeared in front of him suddenly, blocking his way.

"What's the matter?"

"The lights," Jeffrey said.

"Oh yeah, the lights."

Trevor went to the switch and doused them. He let his eyes adjust to the sudden darkness, then moved to the window. He was outside, the window closed again behind him, in less than a minute. But as soon as he started making his way around the perimeter of the house, hidden by junipers and azaleas and rhododendrons, some of his bravado began to fade. All these windows looked alike in the dark! How was he supposed to find that special one?

"I'll help you," Jeffrey said.

He led him directly to his goal. Trevor crouched down and found, to his surprise, that the window wasn't locked. Maybe Andros thought the worms were scary enough to keep him away.

Wrong, you jerk, he thought, not daring to speak aloud.

He turned to wave a thanks to Jeffrey, but the other boy was gone. With a deep breath, he pushed up the window. When he climbed through it and jumped, he found himself in a dark, narrow passageway. He had tucked a small flashlight into his pocket, and he pulled this out now to shine it in either direction. The light hit a nearby wall at one end, so he turned and walked in the other direction. It smelled funny in here, like wet, rotten wood. No, worse than that. Like something had crawled in here to die, forgotten in the darkness. Trevor shuddered. Dead things, darkness . . .

"Cut it out!" he told himself firmly.

Suddenly, he noticed horizontal threads of light along the wooden wall. He quickly turned off the flashlight and went to them. Peering through the cracks, he saw a table set up with beakers, test tubes, and a flaming Bunsen burner. Triumph quickened his heartbeat. He'd found the hidden room! And it was a laboratory, just as Jeffrey had said.

He turned his head another way and saw a hospital gurney. Memories of his "dream" flashed back to him. It wasn't a dream at all, was it? Somehow, they'd brought him in here that night. And they'd been doing it to Sarah too! Anger began to fill him. When he told his mother and father, they'd have these people thrown in jail forever!

The sound of a door opening startled him back away from the wall. Carefully, he moved closer again and was surprised to see Andros and his grandmother. No, not surprised. Confused. How had they gotten in there? Was there another secret passageway?

He realized he was shaking with the fear of being discovered and hugged himself tightly as he listened.

"She's getting too suspicious," Veronica was saying. "If she leaves tomorrow, we may never get her back again, and then we'll be ruined."

"Then we must work quickly," Andros said.

"We'll do both twins tonight," Veronica said. "Felix has them well prepared."

Trevor saw Andros shake his head. He realized his hair was even darker than it had been yesterday. Hadn't his mother said something about Andros dying it? What a weirdo.

"I would suggest the older boy," Andros said. "He's a troublemaker and it might be best to . . . put him out of the way."

Icy fingers grabbed at Trevor's chest as he realized they were talking about him. He knew exactly what "out of the way" meant.

"No," Veronica said firmly. "We may need him in the future. We need both boys. Who knows what their wives will produce?"

Andros pulled Veronica close to him and leaned down to kiss her. For a split second, Trevor forgot himself. Disgusted by this display of affection between two hated people, he gasped. The adults turned abruptly to the wall, looks of surprise on their faces.

In a flash, Trevor turned and ran for the window. He had to feel his way in the darkness, the walls cold and surprisingly dry to the touch. The narrowness of the passage made it hard to run, and he stumbled over an untied shoelace. When he came down his hand landed on a round, smooth rock. Trevor tried to push it out of his way.

There was something strange about its shape, jagged on the bottom, two holes at the front.

When he realized what he held in his hand, he gasped hard to keep back the scream that wanted to escape. It wasn't a rock at all. It was a small skull with a jagged hole at one temple. Someone had murdered a baby.

He didn't let himself think of that horror but shimmied up to the window and outside.

Andros was standing there.

"In trouble again, young man?"

Trevor screamed, wondering how Andros could have moved that fast. He dodged him, racing across the grass, shouting for help. He knew he couldn't get back into the house, to his mother, and headed for the stables instead.

"DAVID! DAVID, HELP ME!"

He saw a light come on in David's apartment, and just as he stumbled into the paddock David was running out the door, dressed only in his jeans.

"Trevor, what the hell?" David demanded.

Trevor saw him look over his shoulder, and turned to see Andros closing in.

"Let me inside! He's trying to kill me!"

"Andros, what are you doing?" David asked. He jerked his head to the door and Trevor moved around him, to the safety of the barn.

"Don't interfere," Andros said, trying to follow the boy.

David moved to block his way. "Hey, man, you can't—"

"I have no time for this!" Andros roared, the sound of his voice making Trevor stop and turn.

As he watched in sickened horror, the big man grabbed the stable manager by both sides of the head. As if he were cracking open a jar, he gave it a hard twist. Trevor screamed as David's body, the head lolling strangely to one side, fell to the ground. His flight response kicked in a split second later, and he turned to run up to the apartment. But Andros was quicker and grabbed him from behind. Trevor's last sensation before falling into darkness was a pressure against his mouth and nose and the strange combined smells of roses, mint, and vinegar.

NINETEEN

▼

The sounds of someone shouting in the yard below jerked Grace from a deep sleep to complete awareness. Curious, she went to the window to investigate but could see nothing across the vast expanse of lawn and garden behind the house. She reached for her robe, which lay across the suitcase she had packed and set up on her dresser. A few moments later, she was at her mother's door, knocking. This time, she wouldn't wander off in search of the screamer. This time, she'd take someone else with her.

"Screams, Grace dear?" Veronica asked. There was a look of skepticism in her eyes. "I heard nothing."

"No one ever does," Grace mumbled. Louder, she said, "It came from out by the stables. Will you come check with me?"

"All right," Veronica agreed.

As she passed the children's room, Grace held up a hand.

"I just want to check on the kids real quick."

The twins were sound asleep, Seth half out of the bed. Grace straightened him up and went to Trevor's room. His bed was empty.

A moment of panic engulfed her until she realized she'd given him permission to stay up late. He must have fallen asleep on the couch in the game room.

"I need to find Trevor," she told her mother, and explained the situation.

The front door was opening when they came down the stairs, and a field hand entered with Trevor cradled in his arms. The worker's tired face was wide-eyed with alarm, and he spoke to Veronica as Grace took the boy from him. It had been Trevor she'd heard screaming!

"I found him on the ground by the stables."

Grace knelt down to put her son on the parquetry tile of the floor. He was too heavy to carry.

"Trevor?" She spoke loudly, patting his cheek. "Trevor, wake up!"

"There's more, Mrs. Chadman," the worker said, and Grace heard a tremor in his voice. "David . . . he's dead."

Grace's head snapped up. "What?"

"What do you mean?" Veronica demanded.

The worker swallowed. "He's hanged himself."

Grace closed her eyes against the horror. She heard her mother order the field hand to get Andros. When she opened her eyes, she was relieved to see Trevor had come around. He blinked to focus on her, frowning.

"Mom . . ."

"Shh," Grace said. Had he seen what David did? "Let's get you upstairs."

She helped him to his feet, keeping her arm around him as she led him up the big staircase.

"Grace dear," Veronica called.

Grace paused to look back over her shoulder.

"I'm sorry."

Grace said nothing in reply. What could she say? Thanks? Apologies accepted? Nothing would make David's death all right or erase the horror her child had witnessed.

"I wanna go home now, Mom," Trevor said. "Please!"

"As soon as possible," Grace promised.

She took him to her own room and settled him in the bed.

His chestnut hair was flecked with detritus from the paddock. Gently, Grace began to work it out as she spoke to him.

"What were you doing outside, honey?"

"Looking for the room," Trevor admitted. His voice was distant, tired. "I thought there might be another way inside."

"Did you find it?"

Trevor was silent for a while. Grace could tell he was wrestling with his memory. Funny, it was the same way she'd felt after she'd come around herself. It was like trying to fit together pieces of a puzzle when most of them were missing.

"I don't know," Trevor whispered. He yawned. "I'm tired."

Grace patted him and stood up. "Go to sleep, then. Everything will be all right in the morning."

Even if I have to leave this place right now, she added in her mind.

She walked to the telephone on her dresser.

Because it was after midnight, she was surprised when Craig answered her call after only one ring. He explained quickly that he'd had a late dinner with his new colleagues, then asked with concern why she was calling. After she explained, he said, "I'll drive down. I can be in Careyton by morning, and I'll get you out of there."

"I was going to drive myself."

"Not alone, not with the kids," Craig said. "I knew something was going on at that place, and I don't want you to handle it by yourself."

Grace smiled fondly. Her knight in shining armor.

"I've been doing okay," she said. "But I really would like your help too. We'll be ready to go as soon as you arrive."

They exchanged a few more words, then Grace hung up. Leaving Trevor, she went to the twins' room to check on them again. They seemed fine. For a moment, she thought about bringing them into her own room. But they might be frightened, and she didn't need two hysterical six-year-olds on her hands. She returned to her room and sat in the chair beside her bed, remaining awake for the rest of the night. Faint voices, the words unintelligible, rose to her from the floor below. They were taking David's body away. She said a silent prayer for the young man who had been so kind to Trevor, then sat staring out at the stars until sleep claimed her just before dawn.

Then someone was shaking her awake, and she opened her eyes to see Craig looking at her with concern on his tired face. She cried out and threw her arms around him.

An hour later, without breakfast, they were pulling away from the house. Sarah twisted around in the backseat and watched the house retreating.

"Nana looks so sad," she said.

Grace looked back. Her mother was standing on the steps, wiping tears from her face. There hadn't been a scene, thank God, but she felt bad nonetheless. And she felt something more—guilt. Why? She was only trying to protect her family! Was it because she knew how much her mother had already suffered?

She reminded herself that Veronica seemed to be implicated in a series of lies too. Grace turned to stare stonily at the road ahead.

Craig was driving. He'd taken his rental to a station in Indianapolis and had been left off by a cab. Grace saw the dark circles under his eyes and knew the long trip from Bryce City had tired him out. He said his boss had given him permission to come in a few hours late. Would he be in any shape to work today at all? But she'd hardly slept a wink last night, and in her agitated state she didn't trust herself behind the wheel. She promised herself, though, that she'd take over the moment she thought he seemed distracted. And with that, she fell into an uncomfortable sleep.

Some time later, Seth's voice sliced through the blank, non-dreaming slate of her mind.

"I'm hungry," he announced, his voice sounding loud and far away at the same time.

Grace sat up, blinking away the sting in her eyes. The sun was fully up now, the road bright.

"How long have we been driving?" she asked.

"About an hour. We'll stop for breakfast in a little while,"

Craig said. "I remember seeing a diner along the road."

At breakfast, everyone ate in silence. Grace caught herself comparing the simple but delicious food to the feasts Felix had laid out. She shook it away with a vigorous snapping of her wrist as she prepared a sugar packet for her coffee.

"You okay, Grace?" Craig asked.

"I guess," she said. She tore the packet open and poured it out. "I was thinking how unfair it is. I find the mother I always dreamed about, and the dream turns into a nightmare."

"Maybe Veronica isn't involved at all," Craig offered. "Maybe you'll end up finding a rational explanation for all this."

Grace looked up at him, surprised, but she could tell at once by his expression he was only saying this to make her happy.

"She's a witch," Trevor said quietly.

He was struggling with his own thoughts, trying hard to remember exactly what he'd seen last night. They said David had hanged himself, but that didn't seem right. They said he'd passed out, that a field hand had found him. But he knew there was something more . . .

The Mathesons finished breakfast and got on the road again. Craig took them to the hotel where he'd been staying. It was a nice place, his room paid for by the company, but Grace thought sleeping five to a room would be a hard adjustment. They'd never even had to do that up in Tulip Tree!

With the estate far behind her, she began to realize she missed her friends. What was Paula Bishop doing now? She'd been forwarding the mail to the Chadman address. Grace made a mental note to call her and tell her to hold on to it from now on.

"Can we look around, Dad?" Seth asked.

"Sure," Craig said. "Why don't you find your bathing suits? There's a pool downstairs. And later, I can take you to the local video parlor. My boss's son tells me it's awesome."

"Nana had video games," Seth replied.

"Nana had a big pool," Sarah added.

Still, they got their swimsuits and headed downstairs. Grace looked at Trevor, who was staring at the television without seeing.

"Don't you want to go in to?" she asked.

Trevor shook his head.

"Well, that's probably for the best," Grace said. "But would you do me a favor? Would you keep an eye on the twins?"

"Sure," Trevor said, and followed his siblings without another word.

Grace caught the surprised look on Craig's face. "What?"

"That was easy," he said. "When was the last time he volunteered to take care of the twins?"

"Trevor's changed in the past week," Grace said. She sighed deeply. "I only hope this experience doesn't affect him in the long run."

"I doubt he'll become a murderer, Grace," Craig said. "He might write a horror novel or two, but he won't become a murderer."

His attempt at a joke, even a lame one, made her smile. She realized how much she'd missed seeing him every day. But that little kitchen in Tulip Tree, where he'd come up behind her and kiss her neck while she kneaded clay or perhaps stirred a pot of spaghetti sauce, seemed to belong to another world, another life.

He put his arms around her, and she snuggled close to him.

"I hardly had the time to say hello to you," she said.

"Hello," Craig said, and pulled her down on the bed.

At the poolside, Trevor sank into a chaise lounge and watched his brother and sister splashing in the water. Although his eyes were focused on them, his mind was elsewhere, still trying to put the pieces of last night together. Nana was very upset this morning, and those sure looked like real tears on her face when they left. But it was probably all an act. He knew what a phoney she was. The only good thing about it was that Andros wasn't around.

The thought of that name sent a shiver through him. Andros. Why did he think the man had done something last night?

"Trevor, look at me!" Seth shouted, then did a trick in the water.

"That's cool, Seth," Trevor said.

"I learned it practicing in Nana's pool," Seth said.

Sarah blew a string of wet hair away from her nose and mouth.

"I wish we were back there again."

"Not me," Trevor said. "I don't ever want to go back. I miss my friends—Billy, Andy . . ."

Sarah folded her arms over the edge of the pool and rested her chin on them, thoughtful.

"I guess I would like to go skating with Susan again," she said. "And Kathy still has one of my Barbie dolls."

The twins began to talk about their old friends and who they'd see again when they went home. Trevor didn't bother to tell them that they weren't going to be living in Tulip Tree any more. Bryce City was their home now. But anything was better than Careyton, than his grandmother's home.

A woman dressed in a pink uniform, with a hotel logo on the pocket, wheeled a noisy metal cart by him. Trevor watched her gather up wet towels.

And something snapped in him. It was as if the image in the shining metal was not of the poolside but of scenes he'd witnessed the previous night.

He remembered it all.

"Seth, Sarah!" he cried. "Come out! I've got to tell Mom something!"

Craig had a business meeting he couldn't cancel, being new man in town, and with great reluctance, he left Grace with the promise he'd be back as soon as possible. Alone in the room, Grace hoisted her suitcase up on the bed and finished unpacking. As the suitcase became empty, she noticed something small and rectangular in one of the pockets. She reached in, and, to her surprise, pulled out Helene Winston's 1938 journal.

"How did this get in here?" she wondered.

She knew she hadn't packed it herself. Had the spirit girl left it for her? She'd been the one to lead Grace to it in the

first place. Grace put the suitcase down on the floor and
climbed across the bed, lying face-down as she opened the
journal. If the ghost *had* packed this, then she was trying to
tell Grace something.

When she opened the bookmarked page, she realized at
once that it was much deeper into the book than where she'd
left off. Had the spirit girl moved it to force Grace to read this
section? The page was dated in the summer of '38.

*Jordan and I have always searched for new ways to incor-
porate Nature's bounty of medicinal plants into the chemistry
of the modern laboratory. With this in mind, we set sail for a
small, uncharted tropical island . . .*

Grace read on in fascination, hardly believing this had been
penned by her own grandmother, sixty years ago. Helene
wrote that a rumor had been circulating among their acquain-
tances that a Fountain of Youth really did exist, somewhere
in the South Pacific. Jordan took up the challenge to find this
miracle, and the two scientists left their comfortable American
surroundings for a long voyage.

Grace noticed that days, sometimes a full week, passed between Helene's writings. Nearly a month had gone by when
they finally reached their goal.

*Although I have seen voodoo and other magic in practice,
I never met a people like these natives. They practice a strange
ritual: drinking a potion of herbs mixed with the blood of
their offspring. They believe, I am told, that the innocence
of children, especially babies, will ensure eternal youth in
the adults.''*

Grace shifted herself around on the bed, sitting cross-
legged. She felt as if she was reading a weird sci-fi novel.
She'd heard of cannibals, but what people would endanger
their own progeny? It certainly went against procreation of the
species as the fundamental drive of all animals, including man.

She read on: *The natives keep few secrets, and they have
willingly told us about their herbs. My guess is that they don't
believe we can make the magic work for ourselves. But there
are other, more innocent, uses for these plants. Some are
mildly stimulating, some calm the nerves. Lotions concocted*

*with the herbs render the skin of the tribe's women smooth
and lovely, even the older women. The men are all strong and
virile. The eldest, what I imagine must be a chief of sorts,
although there are no royal trappings, claims to be eighty. Yet
he'd just fathered twin boys two weeks before our arrival!*

"Good for him," Grace mumbled. She felt cold, and not
from the room's air-conditioning. The story was becoming
more and more unnatural.

*We were very honored when we were asked to join the cel-
ebration. Little did we know that "celebration" meant sacrifice. One twin was killed, his blood drained into cups and
mixed with herbs. All family members drank the potion. I
should have been repelled by the murder of an infant, but I
could only feel exhilarated! To think that parents would give
up their own children for the good of others. Death for pro-
gress' sake.*

"Oh, that's disgusting," Grace said. Her back had become
uncomfortable, so she carried the book to a chair and settled
there.

Helene Winston, and perhaps her husband too, was insane.
How could she accept the death of an innocent baby so read-
ily? And the blood-drinking, was it somehow connected with
Veronica? Trevor had sworn they were sucking blood from a
washcloth that day . . .

Unable to resist, she turned back to the book again, even
though its macabre writings had raised gooseflesh over her
skin.

*Within a day, we saw marked changes in those who drank.
Wrinkles and gray hair were vanishing, eyes became brighter
. . . I should write about those eyes, the deepest, darkest blue
I'd ever seen.*

"Like lapis lazuli?" Grace wondered aloud, and didn't
know why she'd said it. Surely her unusual eye color, and that
of her mother and the children, had nothing to do with natives
on a remote island?

Just then, Trevor burst into the room, his face flushed with
excitement. Still dripping from the pool, the twins came in
close behind him.

"Mom! I know what happened! I remember!"

"Trevor, really?" Grace asked. She put the journal aside.

She saw the twins watching them, wide-eyed with curiosity. Would Trevor's information frighten them? They'd already been through enough, she thought. She held up a hand.

"Wait, Trevor," she said. She found her purse and dug out some money. "Seth, Sarah, why don't you treat yourself to an ice cream at the restaurant?"

Grace was uneasy about letting them go alone, but she was more worried about the effect Trevor's words would have on them. But she reasoned that the elevator opened up directly across from the restaurant downstairs, and it was unlikely the children would get lost.

"All by ourselves?" Sarah asked worriedly.

Grace managed a smile. "You're a big girl, aren't you?"

"I can do it," Seth said with confidence. "Let me hold the money."

"You can get anything you want," Grace said. "And I'll be down in a little while."

Sarah opened the door, and the twins walked uncertainly into the hall. Grace watched them until they reached the elevator bank.

"Don't talk to strangers, okay?"

Seth clicked his tongue. "Oh, Mom! We aren't that dumb!"

Grace wondered if she was right to let them go, but when she turned and saw the anxious look on Trevor's face she knew their conversation had to be private.

"Where's Dad?" Trevor asked.

"Gone to work," Grace said. "Trevor, please, what do you know?"

Trevor took a deep breath, and said, "I saw the towel cart, and it made me remember something. I did find the secret room! It's a kind of a laboratory, just like Jeffrey said."

He saw a momentary look of confusion cross his mother's face at the mention of Jeffrey's name. He knew she'd heard of the ghost before but didn't stop to elaborate on it.

"There are two of those beds like in hospitals, the ones with wheels?" he went on.

"Gurneys," Grace said, rubbing her arms. "Sarah's cold metal beds."

"There's lab equipment too" Trevor said. "Nana and Andros came in . . ."

"They didn't see you?" Grace asked.

"No, there's a kind of space between the outside and inside walls. I was hiding there."

"And you heard the things they said?"

"Everything," Trevor replied.

He related the entire incident, struggling with the words to describe the real reason for David's death. When he finished, he fell back on the bed and sighed with the deepest melancholy. It was an exhausting story.

Grace said nothing, not letting thoughts creep into her mind, not letting herself think or hope or despair. It had all been a nightmare.

Trevor sat up, worry darkening his eyes. "We don't have to go back there again, do we?"

"Not if I can help it," Grace said. "I'll certainly never bring you children."

"Really?" Trevor asked.

"My word of honor," Grace said. "Veronica has hurt you enough already."

She was surprised at the ease with which she called the woman by her first name. God, how could that monster be her *mother?* It was too much to consider right now, especially with Trevor staring at her like that. Was it accusation she saw in his eyes?

She tried to put on a brave front. "We've been through the worst of it, Trevor, and we're all safe. Why don't we wait until Daddy comes back to discuss this? Besides, I think the twins have been alone too long."

"Okay," Trevor said. "Dad will know how to keep them away from us, won't he?"

"Daddy and I will both figure it out," Grace promised. "You don't have to worry about this. Let's go to the restaurant now. I know a sundae isn't much after what you've been through, but . . ."

"It's okay, Mom," Trevor said.

As they walked from the room, Grace was surprised that Trevor took her by the hand. It was almost as if he wanted to hold on to her, to make sure nothing got her. Could something get them here? she wondered.

She shook the thought away. Grace was pretty certain they were safe for the time being especially with Craig nearby.

Still, as she shared ice cream sundaes with the children in the restaurant, she couldn't help glancing out the window at the parking lot below and wondering when the limousine would show up. What would she do if it did? Could she keep her composure, her brave facade, if Veronica got out and begged for understanding? In spite of everything, in spite of only knowing her for about a week, Grace still felt a warm spot in her heart for the woman she'd been calling "Mom." True, the spot was becoming smaller, darker, and colder, like a dying star. But it was still there, for now.

"Can we go to the pool again?" Seth asked.

Grace was pleased to see the twins weren't dwelling on their abrupt departure from the Chadman estate.

"Sounds like a good idea," she said. "I'll put my bathing suit on too."

Trying to cheer the kids up, and mostly to help Trevor deal with witnessing David's murder, Grace kept them busy all afternoon. She looked through the brochures in the hotel lobby rack and found a miniature golf course nearby. They ate lunch at a fast-food restaurant, then headed to a movie. Through it all, the twins giggled and joked with each other as if nothing at all was wrong. Grace kept a close watch on Trevor. He seemed all right, although once in a while he would sigh and rake his fingers through his hair. It seemed he would get through this just fine, so long as he never had to face his grandmother again. She knew he was dealing with the horror in his own way, and that he'd cry tears for David later in private.

Later, Craig met them at the hotel. He was carrying a packet, which he presented to Grace.

"I went to the real estate office today," he said, "and told them we're desperate to find a place. It seems our luck has turned around, because the woman showed me a great little Cape Cod. It doesn't have much property, but it's in our price range, and the sellers are willing to move quickly. Do you want to take a look at it, then head out to dinner?"

He looked around the room. The twins were sound asleep, exhausted after their long day. Trevor was staring at the television, a blank expression on his face. And Grace was hugging herself as if chilled. He knew at once something was wrong.

"What?"

Grace told him everything, starting with Helene's writings and ending with the story of Trevor witnessing David's murder.

"My God, I knew that woman was a monster," Craig said, exhaling the words on breath he'd been holding through Grace's story. "I don't know what an old journal has to do with this, but if someone was directing you to read it, it's significant."

"I agree," Grace said. "There are too many coincidences between Helene's writing and things that have happened lately. I wonder if she passed her knowledge down to my mother?"

"It would explain a lot," Craig said. "No matter what, we don't let the children out of our sight. And we're going to contact the Careyton police."

Grace held her hands up in defeat. "What do we tell them? We can't prove anything. Do you think that room exists even now?"

Craig sighed, sitting down on the bed. He turned to see Trevor looking at him, the blank expression replaced by one of interest.

"What do you think, Trev?" he asked.

"Maybe the police can see those bricks are new," Trevor suggested.

Craig nodded.

But Grace said, "It would take a search warrant to even get

into the basement, let alone start tearing the wall down. There isn't enough time for that."

"Then we just stay away from her," Craig decided. "And we keep her away from us. When she calls, ignore her. Don't answer her letters. In fact, we won't even tell her where we're living."

"She'll find out," Trevor said darkly.

He turned to the television to see an image of a hanged man, his head tied up in a sack. Grace went to the set and snapped off the story of a far-off war.

"Maybe she won't try," Grace said. "After all, she probably could have stopped us from leaving, but she didn't."

"I don't understand that," Craig said. "And I don't trust her."

"Me neither," Trevor agreed.

"Neither one of you ever did," Grace pointed out.

Now she turned to the packet Craig had given her. She'd put it on the dresser in order to tell her story. It seemed a good way to divert her thoughts, because she was certain too much more discussion about her mother would make her go crazy. And she didn't want to read more of the journal right now, not with its sick stories of infant sacrifice.

There was a photograph in the envelope of the house. It was so much like the one she'd dreamed of owning up in Tulip Tree that she knew Craig had picked it out on purpose.

"That picture was taken three months ago," Craig said, "so of course the azaleas aren't in bloom right now. Do you want to see it now?"

"Let's drive by it," Grace told him. "I'll want to see it tomorrow, in the brightest part of the day."

"Then wake up the twins," Craig said.

A short time later, he pulled into the driveway. No one was living in the house at the time, so it was easy to walk up to the windows and peek inside. Grace fought an urge to compare the tiny, quarter-acre plot of land with the Chadman estate. She didn't let herself imagine parquetry tile on the floors or chandeliers hanging from the low ceilings.

Craig put his arms around her. "It isn't a mansion, but we can make it our little castle."

Grace nodded, amazed at how he could read her mind.

"Do I get my own room?" Sarah asked. "I never had my own room before."

"I think we can arrange that," Craig said with a smile.

The twins began to make plans for their rooms, chattering all the way to the restaurant where they shared dinner. Trevor had seen a park with a basketball court nearby and decided he'd probably like Bryce City. Dinner had the strange spirit of cheer masking sorrow, hopes for the future pushing back fears of the past. And the present. No one mentioned Veronica, Andros, or the mansion even once.

Not until Grace was tucking the twins into one of the room's double beds.

"Can Andros get to us here, Mommy?" Sarah asked in a small voice.

"Not for a second," Grace insisted, although part of her thought otherwise. She wouldn't let that part get its say and forced herself to be positive. "And if he even tries, Daddy will knock him out the window."

"On his butt," Seth said with a giggle.

"Seth!"

"Daddy's or Andros's butt?" Sarah asked, guileless.

"Cut it out, you two," Grace said. "Settle in and go to sleep."

"I'm not tired," Seth insisted, but he was snoring softly less than two minutes later. Sarah's breathing was slow and steady too.

"It might be a hard night," she said, climbing in next to Craig. Although it was early, they were all exhausted.

"We'll be okay," Craig said. "And it'll be easier tomorrow."

Trevor, stretched out on a cot Craig had had brought into the room, clicked the channel changer until he found a movie he had wanted to see. It was a sci-fi epic that Grace had heard was terribly gory. She knew nothing would be cut from it—this was cable TV—but she didn't stop him. Right now, she'd let Trevor have everything the way he wanted it.

An alien with a shining black carapace and a head that seemed nothing but mouth and teeth was sucking human blood through its proboscis when she fell asleep.

She saw Veronica in her dreams, standing between two gurneys. The twins were lying in either one, and IV tubes ran from their necks directly into Veronica's mouth. She sucked hard at them, then pulled one out to offer it to Grace.

"Delicious," she said. "The Fountain of Youth, Grace dear."

Grace woke up abruptly. The room was pitch dark, the TV turned off. Her heart was pounding, and a fine sweat had broken out over her skin despite the hum of the air conditioner.

"Just a dream," she whispered to herself.

But she still felt something was wrong, something in reality. It wasn't the vestiges of her nightmare that made her feel this way. She accepted it for what it was: mother's intuition.

Something was wrong with the twins.

Grace jumped from the bed and hurried around to the other one. She reached out to find the children in the darkness, expecting her hand to land on Sarah's hip, expecting Seth to moan in his sleep.

She felt nothing at all.

Fighting down the wave of panic that threatened to knock her over, she reached for the light. Immediately, Craig and Trevor sat up.

"Mom?"

The twins' bed was empty. Craig got up himself, the scene registering on his tired brain at once and snapping him fully awake.

"They've gone to the bathroom together," he guessed, and checked.

His face was pale when he came out.

"It's empty," he said.

"They're gone," Grace whispered, pressing her stomach with her fist to fight the ball of ice that was forming there. "She's taken them!"

TWENTY

▼

Grace insisted on driving, needing something to divert her attention from her fears. If she let herself think the twins were lost to her, the feelings of despair would destroy her. She had to get to them before it was too late, even if it meant pushing beyond the speed limit.

"How could she do this to us?" She asked the question out loud, but it was more to herself than the others.

Craig shook his head, gazing at her in wonder. The way she clamped her hands around the steering wheel, staring at the road ahead with her jaw tight, made him think of old movies he'd seen of soldiers steering military Jeeps wildly through battlefields. She looked like a woman going to war. He felt the same fears as she did. He prayed the twins would be all right. But he could only imagine the sense of betrayal she must be enduring right now, the sense of loss.

"Dad?" Trevor asked quietly. "How did they get in the room?"

"I haven't been able to figure it out," Craig said. "The deadbolt was still on from the inside. We were three stories up—and the outside window doesn't open. There's no other way into that room.''

"She's a vampire," Trevor growled. "Maybe even a witch. She can do anything."

Craig didn't disparage his son's remark, not this time. The idea that Veronica was something strange, even something magical, didn't seem so far-fetched when you were riding along a dark highway in search of two children who seemed to have vanished into thin air.

They kept silent for the rest of the trip, but Grace was certain the sound of her heartbeat was filling the car with louder and louder thumps the closer they got to Careyton. It seemed it was pumping adrenaline through her whole body, because she felt herself growing stronger and stronger with each passing mile. How dare they hurt her babies?

At last they reached the town. It seemed everyone must be sleeping, because they didn't pass a soul on the road leading to the Chadman estate. Grace parked the car a distance away, angling into dark shadows cast by the forest of trees. She realized this was where she'd seen the spirit girl on the day Grace was out mailing a letter. A sense of dread washed over her, a feeling Andros would be waiting for them. But when they got out of the car, she saw they were alone. The only sounds were the soft crunching of their own footsteps and the symphony of crickets.

The fence somehow seemed higher and more forbidding than before. Grace thought of the first day they'd come here, when the gate had opened by itself. Craig had made a joke about Big Mama. Was someone watching them now, from a hidden camera? No, she was certain she would have seen a video setup in the house during her stay.

(Like you saw the hidden room, Grace?)

She wouldn't let paranoia sink in, afraid it would turn the righteous terror she felt into the wrong kind of fear, the kind that would make her go weak at the last minute. She needed the kind of fear that would make her fight like a mother tiger.

"Are we gonna jump the fence?" Trevor asked in a whisper.

"It might be wired," Craig said. "I can't imagine a rich woman like Veronica would live in a place without security."

"So how do we get in, Dad?"

Grace saw something move inside the gate. It opened slowly, as if under its own power, much like that first day.

"They know we're here," Craig said, disappointment in his voice.

Then Grace saw the familiar face of the spirit girl, strangely luminous in the dark night. She was beckoning them inside.

"It's all right," she said. "Follow me!"

"Grace?"

Grace hurried inside, following the road to the front door. The spirit girl had vanished again, but Grace sensed her presence nearby. She was grateful for this unusual ally, knowing it would be difficult to get around this place on their own. They walked silently down the road to the house, keeping under the shadows of the sycamores. Craig was at the front, Trevor next, and Grace took up the rear. In spite of the help she'd received from the spirit girl, she was terribly nervous. She thought she saw a movement on the lawn in the distance. It was only a statue. A creak of wood, probably only a rabbit jumping over a fallen branch, made her heart leap. There was no one watching her back. Any moment now, someone would come out of the darkness and grab her and maybe twist her neck the way Andros had killed David *My God,* she thought, *did Trevor really see that?* It would all be so silent Craig and Trevor would never know until they turned around and . . .

NO! she shouted in her mind, and forced the paranoia away again.

At last, they reached the house. Since Trevor was the one who knew how to find the secret room, Craig let him take the lead now. Trevor paused at a corner of the house, pressed hard against the quoins that decorated its brick facade. Carefully, he peeked around the bend. Then he nodded to his parents. They followed him around the perimeter, keeping low like burglars. Trevor went to a window and crouched down. But when he tried to open it, it remained shut tight. Craig moved in, but even with his strength he couldn't budge it.

"Are you sure it's the right one?" Craig whispered.

"Positive," Trevor replied.

"I bet they nailed it shut after they found Trevor down there," Grace said.

All three crouched to face each other. The only thing missing was a campfire; they were already living a horror story.

"Well," Craig said, "if we're going to get to that room, we have to find a way in fast. It's going to be daylight in an hour or so, and we won't be able to work in secret."

The word "secret" made something click in Grace's mind.

"Do you remember how Seth kept saying there were people behind the walls?"

Trevor nodded vigorously. "I thought he was nuts. But—"

"But he wasn't, was he?" Grace finished. "He was hearing footsteps through a secret passageway! It must run behind the children's rooms!"

Craig looked up at the darkened house. "But how do we get inside?"

"I . . ."

Grace was wishing the spirit girl would make another appearance when she felt a cold touch on her arm. With a gasp, she turned, expecting to face her mother or one of the servants. But they hadn't been discovered. The teenager was standing at her side again. She turned and walked away. Grace looked at her husband and son and guessed by their blank expressions that they didn't see anything. She had no time to explain things to them. She took to her feet and began to follow.

"Where are you going?" Craig called.

"Shh!" Grace hissed. "Just follow me!"

Father and son exchanged glances, then jumped to their feet. Craig was more than a little uneasy about all this, especially after the gate had opened by itself. To his surprise, Grace went boldly to the front door.

"What are you going to do?" Craig said, with only the slightest hint of sarcasm in his voice. "Ring the bell?"

But Grace, following the spirit girl's gestures, simply turned the knob and walked in. Craig steeled himself for a trap, but no one jumped out as Grace walked across the foyer to the main staircase. Pulling Trevor, he went inside too. Grace was moving silently, almost as if in a trance, but something about her look made Craig realize she knew exactly what she was doing. In a few moments, they were entering the rooms where the children had slept.

Although they'd only left a day earlier, the rooms had already been stripped down. Mattresses lay coiled and tied on boxsprings, furniture was covered with white sheets, the rugs had been rolled up and removed. It was as if the children hadn't been here at all.

Grace turned to ask the spirit if she knew the way into the secret passage, but the young girl was gone.

"Look for some kind of hidden panel," she said. "If they were taking Sarah out of here at night, it had to be someplace with easy access."

"The back of the closet?" Craig suggested.

Trevor shook his head. "Uh-uh. We kept a bunch of stuff in there. I would have heard it if anyone moved things."

"The bathroom," Grace thought. "It's separate from both rooms yet close enough."

But a quick scrutiny of the walls showed solid grout between all the tiles. They went back into the room. Trevor started pushing the wall in various places, Craig worked with fixtures, Grace stood gazing around.

Her eyes fell on the flat, recessed panels beside Sarah's bed. She had never noticed it before but saw now that picture hooks hung on all but one. She peered closer, expecting to find a hole that a picture had been hung there after all. There was none.

"Craig!" she called in a whisper.

She ran her fingers along the trim molding, finally locating a small, loose section. She pressed it. Although she'd been expecting to find this, she still caught her breath as the panel slid to the side. A wave of disgust suddenly passed through her.

"My God, she set the bed up right next to this! She was taking Sarah directly from her bed!"

Craig squeezed her shoulder. ''Save it for later, Gracie. We have to get moving.''

All three Mathesons entered the dark passageway. It took a moment to orient themselves to their place in the house, and when they guessed the location of the secret room, they walked that way. They moved silently, not daring to speak, every muscle and nerve on edge. When a crack of light filled the space from a room on the other side of the wall, they paused to listen. Craig peered into the crack. Grace could barely make out his face as he shook his head. The room, although lit, was empty.

Something scuttled across the floor, squealing in protest at these intruders. Grace's hand flew to her mouth to stifle a scream. She felt Trevor reach back and touch her arm reassuringly. He knew how she felt about rats.

The practical side of Grace knew it had only taken them about three minutes to reach the hidden staircase, but it seemed an eternity had gone by. Slowly, quietly, they descended to a large, closed door. Craig held up a hand, then pressed his ear against the cold, splintery wood. He gave Grace a thumbs-up and slowly opened it.

They walked into the lab Trevor had seen from the other secret passage. Grace took in the gurney and the medical equipment, all too real now. Up to this moment, there was still the possibility the whole thing was a mistake. But now she had to admit her mother was doing some kind of sick experiments.

''What is all this?'' Craig asked, his voice soft with horror.

He picked up a bottle and showed it to Grace. She shuddered, knowing at once that it was blood. Sarah's? Seth's? Or perhaps it had been taken from Trevor.

''Jeffrey said they use blood to stay alive,'' Trevor said.

''I don't understand at all,'' Grace admitted.

Craig put the bottle down. ''We don't have time to speculate. We've got to find the twins!''

All three Mathesons backed up a step as the door creaked open. Grace reached for a scalpel, planning to use it as a weapon. But Mrs. Treetorn came in with hands held up in a gesture of peace.

"I heard you come in," she said, "and I've been following you. Come with me, Mrs. Matheson. I know where the twins are being held."

She led them back into the passageway and up the hidden staircase.

Grace was bothered by the woman's attitude. She acted as if children disappearing in this place was a routine occurrence. And she didn't seem the least bit unnerved by her surroundings. How long had she known about the lab?

"Do you know what's going on here, Mrs. Treetorn?" Grace asked, keeping close at the plump woman's heels.

"I'm afraid not," the housekeeper admitted. "But I must admit things have been strange here lately, ever since we learned Amanda had found you."

Grace's mind was a flurry of activity as she followed the housekeeper. Why was the woman being so helpful? If she'd known something was strange here, why hadn't she warned the Mathesons of danger?

There was no time to demand answers, because Mrs. Treetorn had stopped and was pushing a panel out. Grace and the others followed her into a room that Grace was certain she'd never seen before. It was a child's bedroom, the walls decorated with little animal pictures, the matching twin beds made up with bright yellow spreads. There, sitting on a blue rug laden with uncountable toys, sat the twins.

"Seth! Sarah!" Grace cried, and started for them with open arms.

Something held her back. She looked over her shoulder to see that Craig had grabbed her arm. He was looking at the children with a strange, befuddled expression on his face.

"Grace, something's wrong," he said.

"What do you mean?" Grace asked, turning back to her children again. "Seth, Sarah, come . . ."

Her words were cut off when Sarah looked up at her. Her lapis blue eyes, usually shining, were so dull it seemed a light had gone out in them, and the darkness within spilled over into circles. Her hair was lackluster, her expression slack. Seth had the same haunted look about him.

"Mom, they look sick," Trevor said.

Grace nodded. It was as if they'd been ill for weeks, not just missing a few hours. She saw now that Sarah was holding a doll wrapped in a filthy blanket, and the truck Seth was rolling along the floor was rusted and missing a wheel. They both looked like refugees, and neither reacted to their parents.

"What the hell is this?" Craig demanded. "Mrs. Treetorn, what . . . ?"

"She's gone," Trevor said. "We should get out of here, shouldn't we?"

"Damn right," Grace replied, setting her teeth hard. "I'm going to kill Veronica for doing this!"

"First things first," Craig said. "You take Sarah; I'll get Seth."

The children were like limp rag dolls as their parents lifted them from the floor. The doll Sarah held fell from its filthy, torn blanket, thumping to the floor. Grace's mouth dropped open at the sight of it, but what she saw there on the blue rug shocked her beyond screaming.

It was the mummified remains of a baby.

"She . . . she murdered a baby," Grace managed to choke out.

"Ugh!" Trevor groaned. "Why does it look so weird?"

Craig, pressing Seth's head to his shoulder, took a quick glance at the hideous corpse. "It's tiny and badly formed. It looks like it was born too early."

"What the hell is Veronica doing with it?"

"Who cares?" Trevor said, jumping from one foot to the other with growing agitation. "We've got the twins. Let's get out of here!"

He pulled open the door to let his parents out of the room.

"I see you've found my little nursery," Veronica said. She was standing in the doorway, dressed in a frothy pink dress that billowed around her small frame like cotton candy. Her hair, as rich and dark as Grace's chestnut locks, hung in shining curls over her shoulder. Her makeup was flawless on a dewy complexion, but the smile on her carefully painted lips was humorless. Mrs. Treetorn stood next to her, her vapid expression replaced with a cold, hard glare.

"I did as you asked, Mrs. Chadman," she said.

Veronica nodded and waved her away. For a split second, Mrs. Treetorn's smile came back, but it faded quickly as she turned.

"Get out of our way," Craig said.

He moved toward the door, his face a mask of determination. Suddenly, a deafening *crack!* filled the room, and Craig let out a cry of pain. He stumbled, falling against a bureau and knocking a lamp on the floor. At almost the same time, a statue burst into a thousand pieces. Through it all, he held fast to Seth, even though a bright, red bloodstain was blossoming across his sleeve.

He'd been shot.

"CRAIG!"

"DAD!"

The shouts were simultaneous. Grace hurried to her husband. His face had gone completely pale. Unable to hold Seth any longer because of the burning pain in his arm, he let the boy down, but stood in front of him protectively.

"What did you do?" Grace screamed at her mother.

"Not me," Veronica said. She tilted her head.

Grace noticed the man at her side now. He was tall, one arm still held up with the a gun aimed at them. There was something familiar about him, perhaps in his cold gaze, but she couldn't place him. She was certain she hadn't seen him in the past week, but felt she should know him.

"You shot my husband," she accused in a mix of disbelief and anger.

"I barely scraped him," the man said. "If I'd intended, I could have burst his heart. The bullet skinned him and hit that statue."

Grace reached for Craig, but her fingers stopped just a fraction of an inch away from the bloody sleeve.

"I'll be okay, Grace," Craig gasped. "We've got to get out of here."

Grace saw the way he trembled as he bent down to pick up Seth again. She never felt more proud of, nor more in love with, her husband than at that moment. Through his horrible pain, he only thought of his child's safety. And this made her determined to find out what the truth was.

She looked at her mother, chilled so deeply by her grim stare that she drew Sarah closer in a subconscious effort to make her warm.

"I . . . I don't understand this," Grace said. "Why are you doing this to us? I'm your daughter! These are your grand-children! Why would you want to hurt them?"

Veronica's laugh was more youthful, more giggly than Grace had ever heard. She gazed up at the tall man at her side, her eyes adoring. Grace thought this must be the man she'd heard in the room that day she'd eavesdropped on her mother's conversation.

"Shall we tell them?"

"Might as well," the man said.

The two giggled again, like teenagers keeping a secret from an anxious friend.

"Mother?" Grace urged.

"Not exactly," Veronica said. "Your mother died twenty-nine years ago, a few months after giving birth to you. She tried to run away from us, tried to give you to strangers! But we found her and brought her back."

She looked away, her fists clenching and unclenching. In-stinctively, Grace moved closer to Craig.

"Wicked, useless thing!" Veronica went on. "She was un-natural, that one! No amount of threats, no tortures would make her reveal your whereabouts!"

"She committed suicide by stabbing herself in the stomach one night," the man put in. "It was a bloody mess, but the worst of it was thinking we'd never find you."

"But . . . but you . . ."

Grace looked at Craig, unable to find the words she wanted to say. The feelings of betrayal that had been rising in her were reaching a boiling point.

"If you aren't Grace's mother," Craig said, his words coming with difficulty as he fought the pain in his arm, "then how is . . . Amanda . . . related to her? Are they sisters?"

"Amanda is your aunt, Grace," Veronica said, refusing to acknowledge Craig's presence.

"How can that be?" Grace demanded. "She's younger than I am!"

"She's nearly twenty years your senior!"

Trevor listened to all this with a strange mix of understanding and disbelief. Jeffrey had said they used the blood to stay young . . .

He stepped forward, boldly. "Maybe they used the magic potion from that lab downstairs on Amanda! Maybe she's the one we heard screaming the other night!"

Grace thought of the spirit girl, standing outside the cellar door and commanding her to help Amanda.

"What have you been doing to her?" she asked, unable to fathom the idea that the other woman was so much older and her aunt.

"Nothing at all," the man at Veronica's side insisted. He leaned closer to Trevor and said, "Some little boys have overactive imaginations."

Trevor stumbled back. "You're Andros!"

"Trevor, it can't be ..." Grace cut herself off. She knew her mother had somehow grown younger in appearance over these past weeks. When she looked closely at his eyes, she realized this truly was the moribund servant. His creepy looks had been replaced by a strangely handsome visage, his white hair was a wavy cap of brown.

"What are you doing with my children?" she demanded, so shocked her voice was no more than a whisper. "What are you doing with their blood?"

TWENTY-ONE

▼

Andros was still holding the gun when Veronica led them downstairs and into the parlor. The Mathesons sat crowded on the small divan. Sarah was cradled asleep in Grace's lap. Trevor held Seth close to him, his younger brother's head flopped against his shoulder. Grace looked at her older son and gave him a smile of encouragement, then reached across the two boys to touch Craig. Her husband sat with his hand pressed against his wound. It looked as if he'd already stopped bleeding, although his face was still pale. He caught her gaze and turned to her.

"I'm okay," he whispered.

Grace knew this wasn't exactly true but had to accept it for the moment. Right now, as they sat here like hostages, she hoped to dig her way to the truth.

"Will you tell me what's going on?" she asked, looking up at Veronica.

The other woman tossed a hand. "Why not? You won't live long enough to reveal our secrets."

"Mom . . ."

Grace patted Trevor's leg. "It's just a threat."

"No threat," Veronica said. "But where do I begin? It's such a long story."

"Please tell me," Grace implored. "Did Helene and Jordan Winston tell you of the things they learned on that tropical island?"

"How did you know about that?" Veronica asked.

"I read some of Helene's 1938 journal," Grace said.

"How did you get it?" Andros demanded.

Grace shrugged and said, "I found it in the attic."

Andros looked upset, but Veronica seemed untroubled.

"Then you know what a remarkable discovery they made," she said. "A virtual Fountain of Youth."

Trevor wiggled in his seat. Seth was growing heavier by the moment.

"There's no such thing," he said, as Seth's head dropped onto his lap. He put his hand on his little brother's head, surprised at how sweaty he felt. He wished he and Sarah would wake up.

"What did they do about it?" Grace pressed. "I had only read as far as the . . . the sacrifice of the twin."

She'd been trying to keep her voice calm, to let Veronica think she wasn't afraid, but talking about that long-dead child made her voice crack. Had the twins been a beautiful babies like Seth and Sarah? Had the child's mother wept for them?

"A splendid moment, that ceremony," Andros said.

"How would you know?" Craig wondered. He noticed Andros pointed the gun at the floor now but still held his finger on the trigger. The big man was only a few feet away. Could he make a mad dash, grab for the weapon and rescue his family?

He rejected the idea. Andros had already shown he'd use the weapon, and Craig's bravery might get them all killed. These were crazy people he was dealing with. How could Andros know about some remote island ceremony? The man looked positively enraptured.

Veronica continued the story.

"Jordan and Helene brought some of the herbs home with

them and learned to cultivate them. This is how Windsborough Botanicals began.''

"Of course, we never put the extra, *secret* ingredient in our retail products," Andros said. "That was for our privilege alone."

"*Your* privilege?" Grace asked. "Then this *was* passed down to you?"

Veronica's smile was enigmatic. "In a manner of speaking."

This was all too incredible to Grace, but she ventured another question in the hopes it would lead her to the truth. All the answers, she knew, were like pieces to a giant puzzle.

"You said they used children's blood," Grace said, "but it had to be offspring. You didn't kill Amanda . . ."

She gasped as something occurred to her. "There was an obituary written in 1951, for another Amanda—your sister."

She was about to ask if there was a connection when Veronica snapped, "You're getting ahead of the story! Amanda wouldn't be born for years yet. But we already had Jeffrey. We tried to mix the herbs with his blood, but we both became terribly sick after injecting it. You see, Jeffrey had leukemia. He was of no use to us."

Trevor made a face. Veronica and Andros were Jeffrey's real parents? No way! He looked up at his mother and saw by the look on her face that she was as disgusted as he.

Grace was wondering how cold-hearted someone could be to talk so callously of a sick child, no matter how many years had passed since his death. But there was something wrong here, she realized. Whoever Jeffrey was, he seemed to have died in the late 1930s, over fifty years ago. Veronica was talking as if she were his mother!

"When he died," Veronica said, "I tried for another child. It was stillborn at seven months."

"But . . . Helene Winston was the one who . . ." Grace stammered.

"*I* am Helene Winston!" Veronica snapped. "I was born in 1915! Our formula worked!"

"If you were born in 1915, then you must be . . ." Grace

stopped to do the math. No, it was impossible to believe this youthful beauty sitting across from her was over eighty years old!

"It took us years to perfect it," Andros put in. "The first babies were too weak to withstand our experiments."

Grace made a sound of disgust and clutched at her stomach. What kind of monsters were these, who would experiment on their own babies?

"Wait a minute," Craig cut in. "Didn't anyone get suspicious of you when you suddenly started getting younger?"

"Of course," Veronica replied, although she kept her eyes on Grace. "But the Korean War was a convenient way to cover ourselves. We pretended that Jordan enlisted, and that I followed him over there as a Red Cross volunteer. We let everyone think Jordan had been shot down in battle, and that I'd committed suicide in my grief. In truth, we were hiding out in Europe, perfecting our formula. We were able to take a little blood from our daughter each week to maintain ourselves. It wasn't enough to hurt Amanda."

"But the child who died in 1951," Grace said, confused. "That would be at the time of the Korean War. There were two Amandas?"

"No, you little fool," Veronica said impatiently. "We only pretended Amanda was dead. That way, no one would ask about her. It was easy enough to keep her hidden. She wasn't the type of child who would try to run away. She wasn't mentally right even then. And everything she needed was here."

Everything but a loving mother, Grace thought.

"But we found that, the older she got, the less the formula worked," Andros said. "Somehow, the blood of very young children is best. But we knew we could bide our time, because one day Amanda would be old enough to bear a child."

"She was twelve when we came back to America," Veronica said. "We returned to this very estate, posing as relatives. We were no longer Helene and Jordan, but chose different names—they don't matter now, but of course we'd written our will to mention these newcomers as heirs, so no one questioned their appearance."

Grace pulled Sarah close to her. The little girl didn't wake up, and for a moment Grace had the sick feeling she had died in her arms. She pressed her hand against the small back and felt a strong heartbeat. She kissed the top of Sarah's hair, wet with perspiration and smelling strange.

"We arranged for someone to father her baby . . ." Andros said now.

"A twelve-year-old?" Craig asked, horrified.

"We needed the offspring!" Veronica snapped in a strange attempt at justification. "But we soon learned there would be no other child, at least not through Amanda. When she didn't become pregnant after several tries, we took her to a trusted doctor friend."

"Dr. Barham?"

Veronica tossed a hand. "Dr. Barham is new to this. It was his father. He told us that Amanda was born with a deformed uterus. Can you imagine? How could two brilliant, attractive people such as Jordan and myself give birth to such an aberration?"

Grace bit back the urge to comment.

"You said you take blood on a weekly basis," Craig commented now. "What happens if you don't? Are you like a vampire or an addict? Or do you go through cycles?"

"Cycles?" Andros asked. "You make us sound like insects."

"I wouldn't insult bugs that way," Trevor growled under his breath. No one paid attention to him.

"I like the analogy, Grace dear," Veronica said. She smiled to see Grace shudder at the endearment. "You know that some insects lay eggs to feed on the offspring of others. We, on the other hand, feed from our own offspring."

"You didn't answer my question," Craig said. "Is this an addiction?"

"We consider it a medication, of sorts," Veronica said. "Like a diabetic needing insulin, or even a hyperactive child on Ritalin."

Grace thought of another question. "If the blood of children is best, how have you managed to survive all these years?"

"Through Amanda," Andros replied. "The formula we make from her isn't ideal, but it's been enough to sustain us. And we help keep her young enough to provide for us by giving her small amounts of the formula."

"You made her drink her own blood?" Craig asked.

"Of course not," Veronica said. "An IV is more efficient."

The sound of a woman's screams replayed in Grace's mind.

"That night I heard someone in the basement," she said softly. "You had Amanda down there, didn't you?"

"We bring her back here once a week from the clinic," Veronica said. "But Amanda is growing weaker with time. The day came when we had to choose which one of us would benefit from her. We agreed it would be me."

She reached for Andros (for her husband, Grace told herself) with such a look of fondness in her eyes that it seemed the Veronica Grace had come to know was back again. But a soft moan from Trevor brought her back to reality, and she reminded herself that Veronica Chadman—Helene Winston—was nothing but a phoney.

"He's had to suffer so terribly," Veronica said, talking as if to a baby. "The tiny bits of formula we've been able to spare for him have kept him alive, but he'd aged terribly."

"Until we finally had the twins as long as we wanted them," Andros said, straightening himself to his full, almost monstrous height. "You did us a favor when you left. It was easy to get the twins and bring them back here, and we had hours to work rather than minutes."

Veronica reached up and stroked his cheek, free of the wrinkles that had been there just a day earlier.

"Now that we don't need her any longer," she said, "we might leave Amanda at the clinic."

As if that cold and clinical place had a far-reaching life of its own, Grace thought she felt icy fingers move along the back of her neck.

"Amanda deserves better than that hellhouse," she said.

"We can hardly put her in a better place," Andros said. "Someone might learn the truth and steal our secrets."

Grace's eyes thinned, and her jaw tightened. "Someone will

learn the truth, I promise you. As soon as we leave—''

Veronica's laugh reminded her of a vulture cawing over a dying man in the hot dessert.

"You'll never leave," she said. "We need you to replace your sister."

Craig leaned forward so abruptly that Andros lifted the gun. Pain shot through the wound in his arm, a cruel reminder of his vulnerable position. He sat back, gingerly touching the spot where blood had begun to coagulate.

"You aren't taking my children," Craig said evenly, although he gritted his teeth in pain, "and you aren't taking my wife. I'll kill you first."

Andros laughed and said, "But I'm the one who's armed. And who's to say whom I might decide to kill first?"

He shifted the gun abruptly, aiming it at Trevor. The boy gasped, pushing himself back. Craig wrapped his good arm protectively around his son.

"Leave him alone," he ordered.

Andros laughed, a weird sound from a man who had never smiled in all the time Grace knew him. He was more verbose than before too, and that in itself was unnerving. She saw that the direction of this conversation needed to be averted before Craig provoked this madman further.

"Wait," she said. "Tell us how you got into the hotel room."

"Some things are best left a mystery," Andros said, lowering the gun.

Trevor's heart was pounding as he glared at the man. Was that crazy guy really going to shoot him? No, he was sure his parents wouldn't let that happen. But still, he wanted Andros to admit there was something supernatural going on, that Andros had unusual powers. Hadn't he gone from one side of the house to the other the day Trevor had seen him sucking blood from that washcloth? Hadn't he gone from the lab to the outside only seconds after Trevor had found the secret room?

"Explain it to me, anyway," Grace insisted.

Trevor waited, but to his disappointment, Andros simply said, "The locks at the hotel were flimsy. I can move very quietly. I was out of the room, the two children in my arms, in a matter of moments."

There was a plethora of questions in Grace's mind, questions she needed answered if she was ever going to understand this. Another one popped up from the brew, one Craig himself had wondered about that first night they stayed in the house.

"You say this formula can keep you young," she said. "But you looked sixty when we first met you. Why?"

"As I said, Amanda is growing weaker by the day," Veronica replied. "It wasn't until you came here with the children that we were able to revive ourselves. Andros chose to keep his intake to a minimum, until the time was right."

"When would that have been?" Grace demanded.

"After the baby was born," Veronica said with a smile.

"What baby?" Craig asked. "Grace, my God, are you . . . ?"

"Definitely not," Grace said.

"But you will be soon," Veronica insisted. "You'll bear a child for us in the way Amanda never could."

The idea was so twisted, so sick, that Grace completely lost the façade of composure she'd put on for this confrontation. Anger erupted like lava, burning and furious. She put Sarah aside and jumped from the divan with a scream of rage, her fingers bent into talons.

"You bitch!" she cried.

"Grace, no!" Craig shouted, leaping to grab her just as Andros swung the gun in her direction. Before she could reach Veronica, Craig pulled her back. She started to gasp for breath, so shocked by what she was hearing that she thought she was going insane. She bent forward to put her head between her knees, fighting waves of nausea.

It was a tiny voice that brought her back.

"Mommy?"

Grace sat up slowly, wiping tears of rage from her eyes. Sarah, cuddled in Trevor's lap, stared at her with huge eyes. She was awake.

"Mommy, they hurt me," she said softly.

"Oh, Sarah," Grace said, opening her arms to let the little

girl crawl into them. She looked up. "What the hell have you done to my children?"

"We haven't harmed them, really," Veronica insisted. "Only sedated them with a perfectly acceptable soporific. It was hard enough getting blood samples from Sarah, let alone taking a pint from each of them. She fought like a tiger cub!"

"Good for you, Sarah," Craig said.

"I hope you bit her," Trevor put in.

"What about Seth?" Craig asked now. "Why isn't he waking up?"

"He will in time," Veronica said. "The children are of no use to us dead. That is, until a new one arrives."

"I will not be breeding stock," Grace said darkly. She rocked her daughter back and forth, trying to console her. What horrors had taken place in that lab downstairs? Sarah had talked as if they were nightmares, but it was all true. Everything Veronica said was true. In a house where she'd seen spirits, how could Grace believe otherwise?

But who was the spirit?

"I've been seeing a girl here," she said softly, staring at her reflection in the French doors. "She wears a long, white nightgown with a bloodstain on the front. Her hair is the same color as mine, but it's long and parted in the middle. Who was she?"

When Veronica didn't reply, Grace looked up. Her mother was staring at Andros with a look of surprise on her face.

"Maybe she saw a picture?" Veronica was asking her husband.

"We have no pictures of Margaret," Andros said. "We destroyed them after she died."

Veronica looked at Grace. "How do you know about her?"

"I've seen her, spoken with her," Grace said. "Didn't you know her spirit haunts this place?"

"We've never been aware of her," Veronica admitted, nonplused. Grace couldn't help a smile at this small victory. For once, there was something she knew that these monsters didn't.

"Tell us who she is," Craig pressed.

Veronica sighed. "Margaret was a blessing given to me when we learned Amanda was useless as a child-bearer. She was perfectly healthy, and her blood was so rich we could even spare some for her sister. Amanda was mentally unbalanced by then, but we still needed her blood. Keeping her youthful meant we'd have her longer. Oh, Margaret was a beautiful child! And so bright! She might have been a scientist, carrying on our work. But she wasn't so bright as to know when a boy was making a move on her. We had planned to have her give us the child we needed, but the little tramp got pregnant on her own."

"Pretty good trick," Craig growled with sarcasm.

Veronica ignored him. "Amanda knew what we wanted to do, so she helped Margaret run away. They managed to stay hidden long enough for Margaret to have the baby and put her up for adoption."

A cry escaped Grace's opened mouth as reality hit her, hard. The spirit girl, Margaret, was her real mother! That was why she'd been trying to help her!

"You lying witch!" she cried. "You made me think you were my real mother and that you loved me! But you killed my real mother, didn't you?"

The mother she'd dreamed about all her life . . .

The anger shot up from within her again, not just the anger of a mother defending her children, but of a little girl who'd been lied to and betrayed. Without another moment's thought, Grace reached for a heavy crystal vase at her side. Roses and water flew in an arc as the vase became a projectile from Grace's strong arm. She missed her target, knocking Andros off balance. Grace leaped at Veronica, clawing her face with cries of anger. Her ring caught the corner of the older woman's lip, tearing it. With unnatural strength, Veronica pushed her away. Grace turned briefly to see where Craig was, but there was a couch between them. He couldn't come to her defense.

Craig had seen that Andros had dropped the gun. Instantly, he was on his feet, diving for the weapon. The bigger man rolled towards it, but Craig grabbed it just as Andros's hands brushed the barrel. He aimed the gun.

"We don't want to hurt anyone," he said, keeping his voice calm even though his chest was heaving up and down. "We only want to take our children and get out of here."

Grace stood up on shaking legs. The word children made her turn to the divan. Seth had come around, and the twins were hugging each other. But Trevor was nowhere in sight!

"Craig, Trevor's gone!"

Somehow, the boy had managed to sneak from the room while the grownups were fighting.

"He must have gone to the lab," Veronica guessed.

"We have to stop him!" Andros shouted.

They ran from the room, leaving Grace, Craig, and the twins on their own. Craig had a nose bleed, but he merely wiped at it with the back of his fist and started for the door.

"Stay with the twins," he commanded.

"No!" Grace cried. "Trevor needs me!"

"But—"

"Craig, please," Grace begged. "This is my fight alone, and we can't drag the little ones with us!"

Craig realized there was no point in arguing with her and no time. It was a battle she had to fight herself or be forever haunted by this nightmare. He nodded quickly. Grace recalled that Veronica and Andros had led them out through a panel in Veronica's office, and she ran to find it again. For a moment, she nearly panicked to realize she didn't know exactly what part of the wall they'd exited. The room was large, and precious moments would be lost searching it.

"What now?" she asked, frustrated.

She felt a cold touch on her arm, and turned to see the spirit girl, Margaret. With all her concerns focused on finding Trevor, she didn't stop to wonder that this pretty teenager was her real mother. Instead, she begged her for her help.

"That one," Margaret said, pointing.

Grace entered it quickly, barely muttering a thanks to the ghost. She raced through the passage, praying all the way that she'd get to Trevor on time. What was he up to? If Veronica or Andros dared to hurt him . . .

Her muscles were tight and her fists clenched as she burst

through the panel leading to the lab. There, Trevor was throwing a kind of tantrum, knocking beakers and test tubes to the floor as he screamed in anger. She looked around in amazement, silently rooting her son on in his rampage. IV bags hung in shreds, blood spattered the walls.

"NO!" Andros roared from the other side of the room, leaping for the child.

With a cry of her own, Grace jumped to intervene, but suddenly Andros hung suspended in midair. A split second later, his large body slammed against the wall, hard enough to crack the plaster.

"Andros!" Veronica cried, running to his aid.

"Margaret, did you do that?" Grace called out in wonder.

The spirit girl didn't answer. No one saw that it was Jeffrey who was helping Trevor, his years of loneliness and pent-up anger giving him strength beyond that of even a revenant child. To Grace, it looked as if Trevor was somehow managing to push over a heavy table on his own. When at last the place was completely trashed, he ran to his mother. Grace hugged him protectively.

Veronica, still kneeling beside Andros, looked up at Grace with wild eyes. "You stupid fool! Do you think this will stop us? What next, burning the fields? We have plants overseas! We'll simply rebuild . . . Grace, what are you smiling at?"

Grace couldn't help herself. A delicious feeling of vengeance was overtaking her sense of anger and betrayal. Blood still dripped from the split lip and scratches she'd given Veronica. But there was something more: two lines ran from the corners of her lips to her nose, lines that hadn't been there a few minutes ago. Wrinkles wove across her forehead, gray hairs were appearing among the chestnut locks.

"You're losing the blood you took from the twins," she said, matter-of-factly.

Andros reached up and turned his wife's face to him.

"Helene! We must stop the bleeding! You're getting older!"

Veronica picked up a broken piece of mirror and examined

herself. A look of horror crossed her face as the glass verified her husband's words.

"Get the twins! Get them back in here!"

"Helene, we don't have . . ."

"I'll cut their wrists!" Veronica screamed in frustration. "We drain the blood into this jar and add the herbs . . ."

As if those hideous words tied together every strange and terrible thing she'd heard tonight, they brought Grace's anger to a dangerous peak. She no longer saw a loving mother in front of her but a monster who was planning to torture her babies. With a scream, Grace grabbed a shattered beaker from the floor and flew at the older woman. She raked it across her face, opening a gash that nearly took out the woman's eye. A great rush of blood flew out with Veronica's scream of rage, spattering Grace with prickles of ice.

But blood is warm, isn't it? Grace thought, amazed at what she'd done. She took a step back.

"Damn you!" Veronica roared, her hand flying to her face. Blood gushed through her fingers and stained her pink gown.

"Get away from her!" Andros cried, shoving Grace away.

He fell to his knees beside his wife, and desperately tried to hold the ragged flesh of her cheek together, as if his big hands could contain the flood of youth that poured from her.

Trevor rushed over and put his arms around his mother. Locked together, they watched in horror and amazement as the loss of blood had a terrifying effect. Little snakes of white slithered through Veronica's hair, so quickly that at first Grace didn't realize her hair was going shock-white. They seemed to move into her skin, because wrinkles were appearing at an incredible rate. The eyes that gazed at Andros, begging for help, grew paler and paler until they were only a shadow of the gorgeous lapis color they'd been.

"She's getting old, Mom," Trevor whispered. "Like she's supposed to be!"

"Jor . . . dan . . ."

The voice wasn't soft and refined as Grace remembered; rather it was like a crackling of dried leaves, a scratch of sandpaper.

"Helene, darling, no! Don't leave me!"

Grace thought she looked as if she'd even grown smaller, as bones dried and bent. Like a body that had grown too used to steroids, Veronica's couldn't take the loss of her drug. She didn't look like a woman in her eighties. She looked . . . ancient.

Trevor made a retching sound and turned away. When Grace looked, she saw bits of skull through the skin that was beginning to peel away from Veronica's face.

With a great shudder, Veronica went limp in Andros's arms. There was a moment of stunned silence.

Then, Andros's furious cry filled with small room. He let the twisted corpse fall to the floor and lunged at Grace and Trevor. Instinctively, she shoved the boy behind her.

But Andros never reached them. A pair of scissors suddenly appeared in midair, slashing the big man's throat. He collapsed at Grace's feet, one hand twisted in a claw. As Grace held Trevor, Andros's own body went through the same hideous metamorphosis as his wife's.

A slight giggle made Grace look up. The teenage girl—Grace knew it was Margaret, her mother—held up the scissors in triumph. She smiled at Grace as if to say the horror had ended. And then she vanished.

Grace burst into tears. She let go of Trevor and fell to the floor, shaking violently. She was Debbie again, for the moment, a fat little girl who had known only rejection and betrayal. Why, she asked herself, had she ever expected anything to be different for her?

Why had the dream of finding her mother turned into a nightmare?

TWENTY-TWO

▼

It was the cries of her children that made Grace look up a few moments later. Seth and Sarah ran up and threw their arms around her. Grace hugged them tightly and smothered them with kisses. Their faces were streaked with tears, and they looked tired, but they were no longer the limp rag dolls they'd been a few minutes ago. Holding them close, she looked up over their heads as Craig followed them into the lab.

He read the question in her eyes, and answered, "They suddenly came around, and they wouldn't wait for you to come upstairs. It was as if a spell was broken."

Grace nodded. "Maybe one was."

Trevor hurried to his father, his feet scrunching on broken glass. With an arm around his son's shoulder, Craig surveyed the damage in disbelief.

"Did you do this, Trev?"

"I had a little help," Trevor said, not bothering to elaborate.

"But Veronica, Andros . . ."

Craig didn't know what to make of the bodies lying on the floor. They looked like two ancient people, but he thought he recognized the pink dress Veronica had been wearing. Was that a bone showing on the woman's arm? He shook his head to clear it, unable to believe what he was seeing.

"Grace, what happened?"

Grace took a deep breath and told him.

"They had to keep the blood within them," she said in the end. "The few scratches I gave Veronica caused her to grow older. I grabbed a piece of glass and . . . and . . . oh dear Lord, Craig!"

She bit her lip hard to keep from crying again.

"It's okay, Mommy," Sarah insisted in her gentle, caring way.

Craig helped Grace to her feet.

"Nana was a bad person, wasn't she?" Seth asked.

"Very bad," Craig said.

"I killed her," Grace said softly, disbelieving. "She was so full of evil, but I'm the one who—"

Her words were cut off when Mrs. Treetorn burst into the room.

"What have you done?" she cried. "Murderer! I'm calling the police!"

Something snapped inside Grace. She wasn't the cause of all this! She hadn't killed babies or manipulated people's lives in a sick quest for eternal youth!

She straightened herself up and turned to the housekeeper, her eyes as hard as the lapis lazuli stones they resembled. Her fists clenched at her sides, as a new strength, the strength of a mother who has saved her children, filled her.

"You'll do no such thing," she said evenly. "Veronica and Andros are dead. Amanda is unable to do much, so I'm the head of the household now. You'll be taking orders from me now. First, you'll give me a list of all the people who know what my—"

She cut herself off before saying the word "mother." Feelings of betrayal began to cut chinks in the armor she was building around herself. She took a deep breath.

"I need a list of people who know what Veronica and Andros have been doing," she went on. "Then, every servant involved will pack his or her bags and get the hell out of my house."

"Andros and I were the only ones who knew the truth," Mrs. Treetorn said.

"Nevertheless, I want the staff dismissed," Grace insisted. "And don't think you can fool me again. I'll know."

"You're the bold one," Mrs. Treetorn said with disdain. The airheaded housekeeper seemed gone now. "What do you think the police will say when they see the bodies?"

A worried look began to melt Grace's cool exterior. Craig caught it. He'd been amazed at Grace's strength. Feeling great pride in her, he walked over to Andros's corpse. Even after death, the process of decay was accelerated. He gave what was left of the shoulder a slight kick.

The corpse disintegrated into a pile of dust, the clothes lying like forgotten laundry.

With a gasp, Mrs. Treetorn moved to Veronica's body. But Trevor was faster. There was a look of wicked satisfaction on his face as he kicked the remains, hard. Like a half-empty bag of flour, she collapsed in a cloud of dust.

"What bodies?" the young boy asked, turning to stare at the housekeeper.

Wide-eyed, Mrs. Treetorn opened her mouth to protest. But she seemed to realize she was defeated, because she mumbled a promise to obey Mrs. Matheson's orders. Then she turned and left.

"Wow, Mommy," Seth said, his voice cutting into the silence that filled the lab now.

Craig reached out to touch his wife. "Grace, are you all right?"

Grace nodded. She *was* all right.

"Let's get the children the hell out of this place," she said.

"They all slept with surprising soundness at a nearby motel that night, perhaps because of exhaustion and perhaps because it was a much-needed catharsis. But Grace woke up in the early hours of the morning and found she couldn't close her eyes again. A thousand thoughts and worries rushed through her mind. She had committed murder yesterday . . .

Murder.

She shivered so violently that Craig woke up. In the almost complete darkness of the room, he pulled her close to him. Grace tried to find comfort in his warmth, in the steady, strong beat of his heart. But her own heart was too sick.

"Can't sleep?" Craig whispered.

Grace shook her head, her hair making soft whispers on his chest.

"I'm feeling guilty," she admitted.

"About what?" Craig asked. "Defending your family? They would have killed us without a single thought. And can you imagine what kind of life they'd have given the children."

A sourness balled up in Grace's stomach as she thought of her sister. Her aunt, she corrected herself.

The thought of poor Amanda's tormented life, a life her children might have had to face, brought out the anger in her. Craig was right; she'd done what she had to do. But would others see it that way? She'd been defiant enough yesterday with Mrs. Treetorn, but someone was bound to wonder what had happened to Veronica and Andros.

"What if Mrs. Treetorn tries something?" she asked. "What if she gets back at us by filing a missing persons report?"

"Then the case will remain open indefinitely," Craig said.

"But the police will do an investigation," Grace said. "We'll be suspects, especially if the housekeeper tells them about the fight we had."

Craig tightened his grip around her.

"What will she say? That you hit Veronica across the head? You just counter with the truth: she was about to kill Trevor. And then all you have to do is show them the lab."

"They've probably destroyed it by now," Grace said.

"All right," Craig said. "But hitting someone doesn't mean killing them. And you had nothing to do with Andros's death. Grace, the corpus delecti are missing. No bodies, no murder case."

Grace sighed. "Still, I wish I could put this behind us completely. Even if Mrs. Treetorn doesn't report anything, someone at Windsborough is going to come looking for my—for Veronica. Somehow, we have to tie up all the loose ends so that no one bothers us.''

She felt Craig turn away from her. When he came back again, he said softly, "It's four in the morning. Something will come to you tomorrow. Try to sleep now, Gracie.''

"I don't think I can," Grace said.

But she did, holding him tightly.

She was awakened by a kiss on the cheek a few hours later. Sarah was gazing at her with wide eyes. They were still rimmed with dark circles, but Grace was pleased to see the color had come back to the child's cheeks.

"I had a bad dream, Mommy," she said.

Grace opened her blanket and the little girl climbed inside.

"Oh?" Grace asked.

"I dreamed Andros took me and Seth," Sarah went on in a small voice. "They stuck us with needles and made us stay in a scary room."

Grace realized Sarah had no conscious memory of the previous day. She thanked God for that, not wanting the twins to dwell on the horror they'd endured. Hopefully, Seth would be as vague about it as his sister.

"Well, you're safe now," she said. "Safe with Daddy and me. Sarah, do you feel okay this morning?"

"I'm hungry," Sarah said.

Grace couldn't help a small laugh.

"You kids can all go down to the breakfast buffet when the boys get up," she said.

She knew a good meal wasn't a panacea, but at least some healthy eating would help the twins get back their energy—a first step to recovery.

"Can I have pancakes?"

"You can have anything you want," Grace said.

Sarah rolled out from the covers and went to the room's second double bed. She jumped into it and shook Seth awake.

"*Sarah!*" he whined.

Trevor moaned, awakened by Seth's cry. Craig stirred and opened his eyes.

"Sarah thinks it was a bad dream," Grace whispered.

Craig nodded, his expression indicating that he, too was grateful for that.

"How you feeling, Seth?" he asked his younger son.

"Yucky," Seth said.

Both his parents stiffened. Would Seth have full memory of their ordeal?

"My stomach is growling," he added. "I'm starving."

The collective sigh that came from Grace and Craig was barely audible as they glanced at each other with relief.

"You can go downstairs to breakfast as soon as you get washed up and dressed," Grace said.

Trevor was out of his bed and heading towards the bathroom. "Me first. Those two take forever."

Later, Grace asked Trevor if he'd supervise the little ones at the buffet.

"I need to talk to Daddy privately," she said.

"Okay, Mom," Trevor said without argument.

Grace noted a maturity in him that hadn't been there a week earlier. She was proud of the way he was facing this. Then again, he was just a kid. She prayed the horror hadn't forced him to grow up too much.

"Maybe we can go to that new Robin Williams movie," she offered, smiling encouragement.

"Great," Trevor said, and managed a small smile of his own.

After they'd left, Grace went into the bathroom for a relaxing shower. As the water poured down on her head, she suddenly had an idea. She knew exactly what she would do about Veronica and Andros. Toweling off, she wrapped herself in her robe and went into the room, where Craig sat watching television and eating a donut brought up from room service.

"I'm going to call Ivy Haberman," Grace announced.

"Ivy Haberman?" Craig asked. "Can you trust her?"

"I don't know," Grace admitted. "But she's closer to this than anyone, so she'll be able to understand. If she was in on it, she'll have enough to hide that she'll be forced to cooperate with me. And if she isn't, I can at least get some advice from her. I'll feel her out, make her think my mother simply took off without notice, and that I want to ask her a few questions.''

"Why don't you go see her?" Craig asked. "I called in sick this morning, so I can watch the kids. Didn't you say something about taking them to a movie?''

"Yes, I did," Grace said. "Why don't you take them? They can use all the cheering up we can offer them.''

"I'll do that," Craig agreed.

A few hours later, Grace was walking into Ivy's office. She had put on her best outfit and had twisted her hair in a bun. The look gave her an air of confidence that she really didn't feel. What business did she have here, at a multimillion dollar company, acting as if she owned it now?

Did she own it, she wondered as she stepped off the elevator on the top floor of the Windsborough Building? Grace realized she'd never even seen the company's headquarters. It made her wonder again how much her mother would have revealed to her if she hadn't learned the truth for herself.

Ivy Haberman's office was large and comfortably furnished. The windows that wrapped around two corners offered a panoramic view of downtown Indianapolis. Ivy was sitting behind her desk, in a sleeveless shift of mauve linen. A cream-colored bolero jacket hung on a brass coatrack to her side. She looked up with surprise at the sound of Grace's voice.

"Mrs. Matheson!" Ivy cried out. "Mrs. Treetorn told me what happened to your mother . . .''

So Ivy knew Veronica was dead. Grace realized there was no point in lying to her.

"She wasn't my mother," Grace said evenly, taking an offered seat. Something made her decide to put the lawyer on the defense. "I think you know that.''

"I . . . I . . .'' The lawyer, once cool and poised, seemed completely nonplused now. She took a deep breath and calmed herself. "I knew something was going on there. I've been suspicious for some time.''

"How so?" Grace pressed, feeling the woman out. Just how much did she know?

"There were questions about her past that Veronica never answered," Ivy said. "You see, someone wanted to do a biography on her, as part of a series on women in business. She adamantly refused to be interviewed, even if it meant good publicity for the company. I was curious myself, so I checked the Hall of Records. I couldn't find anything about Veronica Winston—her maiden name, you know."

"She could have been born in another state," Grace suggested.

Ivy shook her head. "Veronica says she was born right here in Indianapolis. I finally decided she was hiding something from her past, something terribly shameful."

You don't know how right you are, Grace thought.

"And there was something more," Ivy went on. "One night, after I had stayed late at the mansion going over tax papers, I thought I heard someone screaming from down in the cellar."

Grace stiffened. That must have been another night when they'd brought Amanda back to the house for their evil procedures.

"Andros denied it, of course," Ivy said. "But I decided to watch and wait. I parked my car down the road a bit, hidden in the darkness. Not a few moments later, I saw Andros driving the limousine out the gate. Amanda was looking out the window. I realized then that the woman I'd heard screaming was that poor soul."

"Why didn't you say anything?"

"I don't know," Ivy said. "Selfishness, I guess. My position here means too much to me. It still does."

She looked pointedly at Grace when she made that last statement.

"All right," Grace said. "I'll accept your explanation for now. If you're willing to help me, your job will be secure."

"I understand," Ivy said. A small smile crept over her face. "You'll be happy to know I've spent the entire night thinking about a solution to all this. It's a way to keep the police away, and anyone else who might ask questions.''

Grace tilted her head. She felt wary that this woman, who had worked so closely with Veronica, wanted to help. But maybe the remark about being selfish wasn't made offhandedly. Maybe she was one of those corporate vipers who thought of herself first. If so, she'd be an asset to Grace—at least, for now.

''How?'' she asked.

''I've decided that Mrs. Chadman is going on an indefinite leave of absence.''

Ivy pulled open a drawer and took out a letter, which she handed to Grace. It stated that Grace Matheson was to be in charge of things until the woman's return. The signature matched her mother's perfectly.

''I'll let rumors fly that she's on a honeymoon,'' Ivy said, ''with her servant, Andros. Everyone will be so stunned they won't question this. In time, we'll receive a letter from overseas stating Veronica is happily married and doesn't intend to come back. I have a friend in Paris who can handle that. And I don't think anyone here will be suspicious. Veronica wasn't . . . popular with the employees.''

Grace suppressed an urge to laugh. Then she grew serious again.

''Why are you doing this?'' she asked cynically. ''It can't just be to save your job.''

Ivy sighed. ''You may not believe me, but we're both caught up in this web. I've been Ivy's lawyer for many years now. Do you think anyone would believe me if I said I knew almost nothing about what was going on? It's to my benefit as much as yours that I do everything I can to allay suspicions.''

''All right,'' Grace said. ''I don't have much choice but to go along with this. But if you ever try to implicate me or my family . . .''

Ivy held up both hands. ''Threats aren't necessary, Mrs. Matheson.''

They sat in silence for a few moments, staring at each other.

Grace wanted to believe Ivy, needed to believe her, but she'd been betrayed so many times in these past weeks that she didn't dare let her guard down completely. And she supposed that Ivy might have her doubts, too. After all, Grace did murder her long-time employer.

It was Ivy who spoke first.

"You know, you'll be new CEO here," she said. "What would you like to do first?"

Grace's answer was swift.

"Sell it all."

Ivy sat back. "Are you sure?"

"I don't want to have anything to do with this place," Grace said bitterly. "I wouldn't associate with a company born of an evil idea. And I want the estate sold, too."

She thought a moment, ideas forming in her head like bubbles at the top of a steaming pot.

"There was a stable manager named David," she said, realizing she didn't know his last name. "I want ten percent of the sale of the estate sent to his family."

"That will be a lot of money," Ivy pointed out.

"Not enough for the parents of a murdered child!" Grace snapped. She shuddered to think how close she'd come to losing her own.

She looked at Ivy again. "What about the murder? Have you spoken to the police?"

"Mrs. Chadman put me on the case right away," Ivy said. "They believe it was a suicide, and the parents haven't asked for an investigation."

"Good," Grace said. She didn't need the added problem of a murder investigation, especially now that the killer was dead and gone. "Now, how can I get in to see my sister?"

"I'll call Dr. Grant right now," Ivy said. "With Mrs. Chadman gone, I don't think he'd dare keep you away."

He didn't. Dr. Grant was very contrite and very quiet as he led Grace down the hall to her sister's room. Grace recalled Veronica saying she'd worked with his father. How much did this man know himself? Was he a big part of this nightmare or was he as much a victim as she and Ivy?

Amanda was sitting on a cot, her bare legs stretched out from under a cotton gown. She drew them up close to herself and threw her arms over her head, turning away with a cry.

"It's okay, Amanda," she said. "It's only me. It's Grace."

Amanda whimpered in terror. Grace looked back over her shoulder.

"She's afraid of you," she said to the doctor. "Please get out."

"But . . ."

"I know she won't hurt me," Grace insisted. "I want to talk to my sister alone."

With a look of resignation, Dr. Grant left the room. Grace heard the door lock behind her. Slowly, she went to Amanda's bed and crouched down. She reached to touch the woman but pulled her hand back.

"Amanda?" she said softly.

She knew that somehow, beyond logic and reason, this was her aunt. It was just easier to think of her as her sister as she had for these past weeks. Finding out her mother was her grandmother was hard enough to deal with, and Amanda really did look young enough to be her sister.

"It's me," she said. "It's your sister, Grace."

Now Amanda's head swung around, her eyes wide.

"My sister is dead," she said. "They killed Margaret a long time ago, because she wouldn't tell them where the baby was. I never knew either."

Something told Grace the truth was the best way to approach this disturbed woman.

"I'm that baby," she said.

Amanda's expression twisted into confusion.

"I grew up," Grace went on. "I've been living in foster homes all my life. Do you remember the day we met at the mall?"

Amanda's eyebrows knitted together.

"I was selling dolls," Grace said. "You came up to me, wearing a pink coat . . ."

Now Amanda grinned. "The dolls were so pretty. Like Margaret's baby. Do you know that Margaret had a sick baby first? It died."

Grace thought about the doll she'd found, covered with bandages. Was that Margaret's work, not Amanda's?

"But I lived, and I'm all grown up now," Grace said. Carefully, she pulled herself up to sit on the bed. "Amanda, will you tell me about Margaret?"

"I loved her," Amanda said. She stared at the blank wall in front of her. "I didn't want them to hurt her the way they hurt me. When she found out she was pregnant, I knew what they'd do with the baby. So I helped her run away. They caught us and tried to punish us."

She spoke in the monotone of a person under hypnosis, of someone who had pushed a horrible ordeal so far away that it seemed to belong to another person. Grace put a hand on Amanda's arm. The woman didn't react but continued her story.

"Margaret told me she was terrified she might slip and tell them where you were," she said. "So she killed herself to keep quiet."

Grace cringed.

"They buried her in the woods," Amanda continued. "They tried to make me talk, but I wouldn't. No, ma'am, I just wouldn't tell them where that little darling baby was hiding!"

She turned to Grace. "They would take her blood, you know. That's what they do to babies. Then they make them have new babies when they grow up."

"I know," Grace said softly. "Amanda, do you want to leave this place?"

A smile spread over the other woman's face, a paler, older version of Grace's own.

"When? When can I leave?"

"I'll make arrangements today," Grace said. "I'll find a nice place for you, with pictures on the walls and people to talk with. And there will be a big yard too. No one will lock you in a horrible room like this again!"

"And no more needles? Please, no more needles? I don't like it when they take blood from me."

"Not a drop more," Grace vowed.

Amanda threw her arms around Grace and hugged her so tightly Grace felt herself being asphyxiated. She laughed and pried herself loose.

"Everything's going to be okay now, Amanda," she said. "You're my family, and nothing is going to hurt you ever again."

TWENTY-THREE

▼

For the next few weeks, the children refused to leave Grace's side. Sarah still woke up from an occasional nightmare, and Trevor had become very protective. Once, when a stranger stopped to ask for directions, he glared at him in such a way that the man took off shaking his head in wonder. The children even accompanied her to the bank when she filed for a mortgage to buy the little house. When the banker learned she was the new CEO of Windsborough Botanicals, he approved the mortgage at once. Grace knew she could buy the little place outright, but somehow she thought that doing so would make it seem as if the house had come from Veronica. This was something she wanted to do with Craig and no one else.

Still, even the sale of Windsborough didn't give her the sense of closure she'd thought she'd feel. She'd started this with gaps missing in her life. Now she felt she hadn't closed them; she'd only added new ones. Even putting her sister in a nicer home couldn't help her feel complete.

She knew what she had to do. It was time to return to the estate, to find and keep whatever might connect her with her mother, Margaret, and her true family. Yes, Veronica and Andros were part of that, but they would remain forever a dark foil in her history, a history she now hoped to complete by searching everywhere for any information at all about her family.

Paula Bishop came down to visit, and when she heard what Grace had in mind she offered to babysit the children. The Mathesons had been living in their house for just a week, and some of their things still remained unpacked. Paula herself brought down some odds and ends she'd been keeping for Grace while she was away.

"Mostly art supplies," she said. "I sure hope you're going to start on a new doll soon, and put this nightmare behind you."

"I'm going to try," Grace said. "That show is coming up in a few weeks, and in spite of everything, I do want to go. But first I have to finish up a few things at the estate."

"Take your time there," Paula said. "The kids'll be fine with me."

"Thanks," Grace replied. "Unfortunately, Craig is busy on a project. I'll have to go alone."

Trevor, who had just walked through the front door with a bike helmet tucked under his arm, heard this.

"You don't have to go there alone, Mom," he said. "I want to go with you."

"Why?" Grace asked. "I thought you hated the place."

"I want to say good-bye to Jeffrey," Trevor replied.

Paula looked from mother to son. "A friend?"

"You could say so," Grace said. "All right, Trev. Get yourself ready. We'll leave in a little while."

She told the twins she was going shopping at an outlet center some distance from the house. There was no need to worry them about her real plans.

"Boring!" Seth drawled.

"I'd rather stay with Paula," Sarah said.

It was exactly the reaction Grace had hoped for. She knew the twins would never agree to come to her real destination. They were still traumatized by what had happened. In the past weeks, the color had come back to their cheeks, and the night-mares had begun to fade away. But she saw no point in bringing them to the source of those nightmares.

Grace called Craig and told him of her plans. He agreed it was the right thing to do, although he wished she would wait for the weekend when he could join her.

"I need to do this now," Grace said, "while I'm brave enough to face anything else I might find there."

"I think we've learned all the dark secrets of the Chadmans," Craig said. "Or maybe I should say the Winstons."

"Veronica and Andros were still Helene and Jordan Winston when they had my mother," Grace replied, twisting the phone cord between her fingers as she leaned against the kitchen counter. "My maiden name is Winston."

They exchanged good-byes. Then, Grace thanked Paula and left with Trevor. She didn't have to give her friend instructions. She knew the twins were in good hands and hardly thought of them during the drive south. Once in a while, she'd glance over at Trevor to see him staring out the window at the passing scenery.

"What's on your mind?" she asked.

"I wonder if Jeffrey's still there," Trevor said. He turned to her. "Y'know something? This is crazy, but isn't Jeffrey your uncle?"

Grace bit her lip as she stared at the highway. She hadn't yet figured out who was who on her newfound family tree. Her so-called mother was really her grandmother. A teenage spirit was her mother. Maybe, in the picture she'd found of Helene and Jordan, the baby was Amanda and Margaret's brother. She'd never seen the boy the way Trevor had, except from a distance through a camera lens, but it was possible he was the child named Jeffrey that Veronica and Andros spoke of with such disdain.

She shivered, imagining the cold life that child must have led. In a twisted way, his leukemia had saved him from the horrors his sisters faced.

"Are you cold, Mom?"

"I'm all right," Grace insisted. How many times had she

said that in the past weeks, when in truth, she would never be 100 percent all right?

There were no more words, not even when they pulled up to the estate. Grace got out of the car and opened the gate. There were no video cameras now, no one watching their approach. The gate wasn't even locked. Grace had trusted Ivy to put a caretaker on the place, but she hoped she wouldn't run into the man. She didn't feel like talking to anyone. The fields were empty of workers, making her wonder just how many were under Veronica's evil spell. Felix, the cook, was gone now. Ivy insisted he knew nothing of what had happened, but there was no point in staying in an empty house. A few of the maids, also innocent, had left for the same reason.

The mansion was cold and dark when they walked through the front door, despite the oppressive heat.

"I'm gonna look for Jeffrey," Trevor said, and ran up the big staircase.

Even though the house was still completely furnished, his footsteps seemed to echo in all directions. Grace went up more slowly, heading to the attic. She stopped first in the studio Veronica had had built for her. A half-finished doll still lay on the workbench. Grace picked it up, deciding to bring it home and finish it. She would take nothing else from here. These were things Veronica had used to try and buy her trust. The rundown kiln and other equipment she'd brought from Tulip Tree would do, as would the basement studio her husband had built in their new home. Grace would instruct Ivy to sell these items, as well as anything else she didn't take, and donate the money to charity.

Next, she went to the room where she'd found the old photograph. There was an empty box there, and she used this to collect a few things. Picking up the photograph from the turn of the century, she stared at the couple who might be her great-grandparents.

"Is there a reason neither of you have lapis lazuli eyes?" she asked. "Did the herb the Winstons brought back from that remote island alter us in some way?"

She set the oil painting down into the box.

"And did you know that your daughter was a monster?"

She glanced at the books she'd found just a few days earlier. Hoping she might find some more answers about her family's past, she packed several volumes, planning to read them later.

On the floor below her, Trevor walked through the dark and dusty hallway. There was no need for quiet now that the house was empty. He cupped his hands around his mouth and shouted out Jeffrey's name.

"JEFFREY? HEY, I'M BACK!"

There was no answer. Trevor made his way to the boy's room, hoping to meet up with him there. He wanted to make sure Jeffrey was all right, now that Veronica and Andros were gone. It was weird to think they were his mother and father. Even weirder to imagine Jeffrey was really his uncle!

"JEFFREY?" he tried again. His voice bounced off the walls, making the portraits of Trevor's ancestors seem to call out the boy's name. Still there was no answer.

"Where are you?" Trevor said, quieter now.

He pushed into the bedroom. The sun was shining through the window, dust particles dancing in the beam. Everything was just as Trevor had found it that first day, but there was no sign at all of Jeffrey. Trevor turned around.

There was a message on the wall, written in careful but childish handwriting:

THANK YOU, TREVOR.

Trevor stared at it for a long time. He realized now that he'd never see Jeffrey again. What was it grownups said about ghosts? That they haunted the earth because they weren't at peace. He couldn't help a smile. Now that those two monsters who were Jeffrey's parents were gone, the spirit boy *could* rest.

"You're welcome," he whispered.

He was about to leave the room when he thought of the box under the closet floor. He retrieved it, tucking it under his arm and heading down the hall to find his mother.

*   *   *

Grace was struggling to carry one of her boxes to the stairs when she became aware of another presence. Expecting to see the caretaker, she swung around. But it was the spirit girl who stood there. Slowly, Grace put the box down. She didn't want to scare her away.

Then she laughed at herself. Scare away a ghost, especially one who had saved her life?

Especially one who was her mother?

"Mom," Grace said, reaching out to her.

Margaret smiled wearily. "I tried to help you, I did. Amanda did too."

"I know," Grace said. "Amanda is all right now. I've taken care of her."

Margaret nodded, a look of satisfaction crossing her pretty face. Grace couldn't help wondering what she might have looked like if she had lived. As a matter of fact, Grace realized she looked much as Grace herself had as a teenager!

"Good-bye, Deborah Mary," Margaret said, using Grace's real name.

"Good-bye, Mom," Grace replied.

Margaret disappeared. A moment later, Grace felt a flutter across her cheek, like a kiss. She stood there in the hall for a long time after, touching the spot on her face in wonder.

Then she picked up her box and carried it downstairs. She found Trevor in the hall, a cigar box in his hands.

"What's that?" she asked.

"Just some stuff," Trevor said cryptically.

Grace nodded, understanding that Trevor had secrets to keep now.

"Gather up anything you want here quickly, Trevor," she said. "I want to go home to our family."